Maxim Jakubowski is a London-based novelist and editor. He was born in the UK and educated in France. Following a career in book publishing, he opened the world-famous Murder One bookshop in London. He now writes full-time. He has edited a series of fifteen bestselling erotic anthologies and two books of erotic photography, as well as many acclaimed crime collections. His novels include *It's You That I Want To Kiss, Because She Thought She Loved Me* and *On Tenderness Express*, all three recently collected and reprinted in the USA as *Skin In Darkness*. Other books include *Life In The World of Women, The State of Montana, Kiss Me Sadly* and *Confessions Of A Romantic Pornographer*. In 2006 he published *American Casanova*, a major erotic novel which he edited and on which fifteen of the top erotic writers in the world have collaborated, and his collected erotic short stories as *Fools For Lust*. He compiles two annual acclaimed series for the Mammoth list: *Best New Erotica* and *Best British Crime*. He is a winner of the Anthony and the Karel Awards, a frequent TV and radio broadcaster, a past crime columnist for the *Guardian* newspaper and Literary Director of London's Crime Scene Festival.

Also available

THE MAMMOTH BOOK OF

Best
New Erotica

Volume 9

Edited and with an Introduction
by Maxim Jakubowski

ROBINSON

RUNNING PRESS
PHILADELPHIA · LONDON

Constable & Robinson Ltd
3 The Lanchesters
162 Fulham Palace Road
London W6 9ER
www.constablerobinson.com

First published in the UK by Robinson, an imprint of Constable & Robinson, 2010

A copy of the British Library Cataloguing in Publication
Data is available from the British Library

UK ISBN 978-1-84901-008-5

1 3 5 7 9 10 8 6 4 2

First published in the United States in 2010 by Running Press Book Publishers
All rights reserved under the Pan-American and International Copyright Conventions

9   8   7   6   5   4   3   2   1
Digit on the right indicates the number of this printing

US Library of Congress number: 2009929918
US ISBN 978-0-7624-3828-0

Running Press Book Publishers
2300 Chestnut Street
Philadelphia, PA 19103-4371

Visit us on the web!

www.runningpress.com

Printed and bound in the EU

Contents

Acknowledgments

"Alert" © 2008 Laurence Klavan. First published in Sliptongue. com. Reprinted by permission of the author.

"Exam Room 3" © 2008 N. T. Morley. First published in ALT. com. Reprinted by permission of the author.

"Good Kitty" © 2008 Shanna Germain. First published in *K Is for Kinky*, edited by Alison Tyler. Reprinted by permission of the author.

"2.04 a.m., Our Hostess' Second-floor Walk-In" © 2008 Savannah Lee. First published in *Clean Sheets*. Reprinted by permission of the author.

"The Baptism" © 2008 Remittance Girl. First published in *Erotica Readers and Writers Association*. Reprinted by permission of the author.

"The Rise and Fall of the Burlesque Empire" © 2008 Maxim Jakubowski. First published in *Ultimate Burlesque*, edited by Emily Dubberley and Alyson Fixter. Reprinted by permission of the author.

"Sebastienne" © 2008 N. J. Streitberger. First published in *The Erotic Review*. Reprinted by permission of the author.

"The Painted Doll" © 2008 M. Christian. First published in *The Painted Doll*. Reprinted by permission of the author.

"Chocolate Girl" © 2008 Sam Jayne. First published in Sliptongue.com. Reprinted by permission of the author.

"Purple Tulip" © 2008 Tsaurah Litzky. First published in *Sex For America: Politically Inspired Erotica*, edited by Stephen Elliott. Reprinted by permission of the author.

"To Dance at the Fair" © 2008 Donna George Storey. First published in *Dirty Girls: Erotica for Women*, edited by Rachel Kramer Bussel. Reprinted by permission of the author.

"Meter Violator" © 2008 Kelly Jameson. First published in *Ruthie's Club*. Reprinted by permission of the author.

"A Secret Night in Grouse Woods" © 2008 Karen Sutow. First published in *Men In Shorts: An Erotic Anthology*, edited by Lori Perkins. Reprinted by permission of the author.

"The Gift of the Magic Lump of Coal" © 2008 EllaRegina. First published in *Literotica*. Reprinted by permission of the author.

"Iced" © 2008 Erin O'Riordan. First published in *Lucrezia* magazine. Reprinted by permission of the author.

"The Beloved of the Gigolem" © 2008 Ian Watson and Roberto Quaglia. First published in *The Beloved of My Beloved*. Reprinted by permission of the authors.

"Two Birds, One Bush" © 2008 Amanda Fox. First published in *Clean Sheets*. Reprinted by permission of the author.

"Ménage à Denim" © 2008 Jeremy Edwards. First published in *Ruthie's Club*. Reprinted by permission of the author.

"Maze" © 2008 Erin Cashier. First published in *Fishnet*. Reprinted by permission of the author.

"Measure A, B, or Me?" © 2008 Alison Tyler. First published in *Sex For America: Politically Inspired Erotica*, edited by Stephen Elliott. Reprinted by permission of the author.

"Just Another Girl on the Train" © 2008 Catherine Lundoff. First published in *Dirty Girls: Erotica for Women*, edited by

Rachel Kramer Bussel. Reprinted by permission of the author.

"A Different Kind of Reality Show" © 2008 D. L. King. First published in *Yes, Ma'am*, edited by Rachel Kramer Bussel. Reprinted by permission of the author.

"The Dress" © 2008 Kristina Wright. First published in *Rubber Sex*, edited by Rachel Kramer Bussel. Reprinted by permission of the author.

"The Bet" © 2008 Thom Gautier. First published in *Lucrezia* magazine. Reprinted by permission of the author.

"Such a Special Couple" © 2008 Kristina Lloyd. First published in *J Is for Jealousy*, edited by Alison Tyler. Reprinted by permission of the author.

"Georgie Cracks the Case" © 2008 Kathleen Bradean. First published by Torquere Press. Reprinted by permission of the author.

"The Depths of Despair" © 2008 Rachel Kramer Bussel. First published in *Spanked: Red-Cheeked Erotica*, edited by Rachel Kramer Bussel. Reprinted by permission of the author.

"Sex Scenes: Detention" © 2008 Polly Frost and Ray Sawhill. First appeared on the *Sex Scenes* CD. Reprinted by permission of the author.

"Fucking Ugly" © 2008 Mike Kimera. First published in *The Erotica Readers and Writers Association*. Reprinted by permission of the author.

"Sign Your Name" © 2008 Saskia Walker. First published in *K Is for Kinky*, edited by Alison Tyler. Reprinted by permission of the author.

"Improvisation" © 2008 Craig Sorensen. First published in *Lucrezia* magazine. Reprinted by permission of the author.

Introduction

Maxim Jakubowski

Welcome back to the realm of the senses.

It's been nearly fifteen years since I began compiling this anthology series (although this particular volume is advertised as the ninth in the series, there were five additional books before we began numbering the anthologies . . .) and I keep on being amazed and delighted that, year after year, erotic writers still manage to surprise, push the envelope, challenge my perception and that of the many readers who follow the Mammoth Erotica series every year.

When we began, erotica was still somewhat undercover, with the exception of canonical authors and books like Henry Miller's, Anaïs Nin's, Anne Rice's, *The Story of O*, etc. The art of the erotic short story was still to a large extent in its infancy. This was very much due to the fact there were so few outlets for it, either in magazines, anthologies or book format.

This has changed a lot since then. In parallel with this series the redoubtable Susie Bright launched her Best American Erotica annual volumes, which lasted well over a decade, and I think that our combined influence soon sparked a minor renaissance that continues to this day.

In order to uncover the forty-two stories in this book, all previously published in 2008, I had to read through over thirty other anthologies, countless print magazines, many of which published the occasional erotica, as well as a plethora of web magazines. The latter market is one that has exploded over the last ten years, and I must confess that I have been pleasantly surprised by the average level of quality found there (as well, naturally, as the worst too, in view of the generally poor levels of editing practised on the Internet . . .). But an increasing number of erotica writers are making their presence known first on the web, before graduating to print, and I am grateful for the Internet's role in fostering erotic short story writing. A more recent phenomenon is that of e-books. They also lend themselves particularly well to our medium, even if the general level of competence is still, in my personal opinion, rather low, not unlike the early years of Internet publishing. But it provides an invaluable literary laboratory, which encourages new writers and offers a training ground of sorts, for which we must be grateful.

Again, I am especially proud to be able to present many new names here for the first time: Laurence Klavan is no unknown, having won the prestigious Edgar award for his mystery fiction, but this is, to the best of my knowledge, his first foray into the waters of erotica; Larry Smith has already been published in the revered literary *McSweeney's* magazine; Carrie Williams is the author of several well-received erotic novels; while others like the mysterious Remittance Girl, Karen Sutow, Thom Gautier, Erin O'Riordan, Roger Bonner, Amanda Fox, Erin Cashier and Mark Farley are all newcomers to our series and may be big names for the future. Another first for this volume is the small audio play by Polly Frost and her husband Ray Sawhill, which has only appeared so far on CD.

In addition, there are several handfuls of repeat offenders, or should I describe them as the usual suspects; some have now clocked up regular contributions to the Mammoth Erotica series while others made their initial appearance only in the last year or two. It's great to have them all back.

Writing about sex, and emotions, is nowhere near as easy as many imagine. Just because it is a human activity that all of us think we know all about means that not only taboos must be broken when it comes to describing it with a modicum of authenticity and honesty, but the author must try to relate to the reader in a particularly naked way. Our sex lives are a secret that only our close ones actually perceive correctly, and when you put pen to paper (or in this day and age, finger to keyboard) you have to find a way that strangers can relate to your story, your complex relationships. If you cannot achieve this connection then the end result can prove either vulgar or clichéd or both. This, for me, is where the frontier lies between erotica and pornography. It's an eternal debate and will continue to rage forever, I have no doubt. But I strongly believe that the stories we offer you in this volume will both titillate you and make you think, will trigger your imagination, sometimes make you question your own acts or relationships or past experiences, and might also scare and/or amuse you. Or all of the above.

If they achieve any of these aims then I feel we have achieved the goal of our sensual mission.

So, enjoy another year in the daring and provocative world of the sexual imagination. Shudder, hold your breath, smile, allow your heart to beat just that touch faster, and give in to all your most secret senses. This is erotica at its best.

Maxim Jakubowski

Alert

Laurence Klavan

Hands, so many hands of other travelers were hanging beside her own, lined up like winter coats in a closet or fish in a school under the sea – or like trains themselves, waiting to take off, trains stopped in their tracks, that was it – except one hand, his hand, more disobedient than the rest, moving up her thigh, then gently beneath her skirt, the fingers cool and slightly chapped even though it was summer.

Allie was trembling but so was everyone else: trembling and rocking back and forth and sometimes lurching forward as if pushed from behind. Allie was aware that her reaction to riding the subway was like someone's in 1904 – the year the system started, an overhead sign informed her – but she was, after all, innocent of the experience, never having done it before.

And it was twice as terrifying today, she knew, despite the unclean conditions then, the – she could only guess – cholera and diphtheria and the TB, that was the other one, at the turn of the century. It was so much more treacherous today that she never would have agreed to come if not for – and now she thought of nothing other than his hand, because his fingers had found and were touching the little raised flower stitched on her underwear between her legs. His was like a blind man's hand and so she closed her eyes to be like him and only know what it was like to feel and never see, never in a crucial way to know anything but what you felt. Doing this, only feeling, in the dark, she went into a new tunnel, one that led back to the blackness of her sleep that morning, a tunnel she had exited by opening her eyes.

Allie had been angry those few hours earlier – she was a punitive girl, punishing, which was surprising, for she was short and blonde and pale and pretty, and others in their shallowness assumed that she was sweet – she'd been angry because she had not wanted to come, had spent eighteen perfectly pleasant years without going down to the city, which was ninety miles south of the town where she was and had been born. Why should she add to her "experience" in such an arbitrary way, like those people who fly private planes without expertise or jump into gorilla cages just for the "rush" and end up in frozen pieces on foggy mountaintops or as bloody stumps in fake zoo streams, their last startled sense being pain, their final feeling regret (or who were so drunk that they were dead already before being blown or torn to bits)? She had no sympathy for these people who asked for what they got – and since she was unlike them, was sensible and not stupid and heedless, she was angriest at herself for agreeing to go. She had been weak – being guilty was a way of being weak – and that especially irked her.

But Dan Stabler was an old family friend and had offered her a job in his store for the summer, right after she graduated from high school. Loafin' was the town's most popular bakery and café, and while Allie hated the store's stupid name and having to wear the apron with the smiling slice of bread on it – a logo other people liked, apparently, though how many over the age of four, Allie couldn't imagine – she had accepted. Allie hadn't gotten into Picard, the local college, and so would have to wait to apply again next year. She didn't want to go any farther from home – and why should she when there was a perfectly good school within driving distance, she could even keep her old room; it was pretentious and phony to want to "see the world," wasn't this the world right here? Of course it was.

Her parents hadn't been as happy as she thought they'd be when she said that she'd be staying put, had never really understood her only applying to one place, and had gone behind her back to ask Dan if he had something, anything, for her to do. When he came up with the job, invented it out of thin air, by adding another counterman, woman, or whatever, her parents made it plain there would be no saying no.

Allie thought they'd be glad to still have her around, but the job seemed like a punishment for what they felt was her bad idea. (Allie's scolding sensibility was a direct inheritance from them, but she didn't make the connection, for she always felt totally justified in her harsh and severe judgments of others.) So how could she refuse when Dan asked her to do more, to work the stand in the Farmer's Market down in the city that day, because someone else had gotten sick?

That meant getting up at five to take the trip, sitting beside Dan on the lumpy front seat of his bread truck, while he listened to the radio repeat the same exact weather report (sunny and hot, sunny and hot – what did he expect, it was summer?!), depressing news stories from overseas (we're here, aren't we? We're here, we're not there!) and songs from the seventies, a time when apparently all people had lank and dirty hair, took too many drugs, and sang songs that made absolutely no sense at all (well, why don't you give your horse a name? – then your horse would have a name!).

Dan, who still looked like someone from that era, actually remembered the words well enough to repeat them in a flat, horrible voice that sounded like the world's worst walrus singer. Allie had never had an opinion of Dan – he was like a hundred years old and so hardly even alive to her – but today she disliked how he dwelled on the radio's news reports about the city, the threats to the city, and actually turned it up to catch every last disgusting detail.

This was, of course, another reason Allie had not wanted to go and for her to condemn anyone reckless enough to live there. She had no doubt the threats were real and that the government people communicating them were sincere. This was just the sort of thing you'd expect to happen in such a place, and what was wrong with warning people? She herself would want to be warned (which wouldn't be necessary, because she wouldn't be living there) and she would heed those warnings. Even now, as Dan changed channels to hear the same information from a different source, she said, "Maybe we should just turn around and go back."

The remark unnerved Dan enough to make him snap off the radio altogether. He considered being concerned enough to lose a day's profit, and it was clear it was a new idea and not one he was at ease with.

"It'll be okay," was the best he could come up with; then, after additional thought, "Why let our enemies win? It's our country."

Stymied, Allie didn't say anything, just looked out the window at the highway, increasingly crowded and unclean as it approached New York. Roadkill was being replaced by potholes, as if nature itself had ceased to exist and great gaps were now appearing as evidence of a new nightmare world, and all would soon collapse as a result. She bet Dan thought that worry would protect him, when only turning back (or not even going) was the only action that made sense. But that would take guts, and Dan was too greedy.

"I had a piece of the walnut loaf this morning," she said, petulantly, to punish him. "I almost broke a tooth."

Dan didn't answer right away, then said, quietly, "Then you should talk to your parents about orthodontia."

Referring to her parents had the desired effect – she felt young and diminished and guilty again about her aimless summer, which she had been sure her mom and dad would want to share with her, and why hadn't they? – and took the focus off his bread, which truth to tell, wasn't bad, and she had never even tried the walnut. Dan seemed to be getting sneakier as they hit the bridge that brought them into town, as if he were absorbing a big city character through the automatic traffic pass Velcro-ed to his windshield that let him be billed later. (And that was another modern idea she couldn't abide: you ought to pay then and there.) Allie pulled over her the sweater her mother had insisted she bring, as if it were a lead apron to prevent her being filled with the same flaws now entering Dan. Then she saw him peel off the pass and place it in the glove compartment, which he locked; he never had to do those things at home.

Allie looked at the big buildings, the suffocating crowds, the water that surrounded it all – everything made vulnerable to attack because of its decadence, irresponsibility, and excess. She found herself getting angrier and angrier, the way she always did when – and her parents knew this even if she didn't and she absolutely did not – she was utterly, unbearably, and to her unforgivably afraid.

The Farmer's Market was held at Union Square, on what looked to Allie like a big concrete slab that probably used to be a parking lot. It scalded in the morning sun, and not even the stand's awning provided any relief. Allie started sweating the minute she left the truck, and large dark rings appeared on her white track team T-shirt that looked like those potholes in the road. Now she was marked, damaged, too, by "progress."

A never-ending parade of people filed by, some obviously on their way to work, looking self-important yet also stifled and suffering in overpriced suits, others obviously wasting their lives riding rollerblades on the way to nowhere. The people who bought bread from her were stingy young executives who forfeited fifty cents for tiny raisin buns not big enough to feed a baby or demanding yuppie mothers who acted entitled to stop traffic with their strollers and didn't say "thank you" when Allie handed them their loaves. She felt like a hick serving at the pleasure of sophisticates, and she bet she was better read than any of them. (Who had gotten through the whole "Dune" cycle last summer? Certainly not that young business boy whose hair goop couldn't hide his hair loss and who bought a tiny bun.)

Throughout the morning, Dan acted pleasant and didn't even seem to feel the heat. He told her, "acting surly never sold a scone," but she pretended not to hear and walked disgustedly back to the truck for more bread.

Dan had parked in an allotted area behind their stand, right near a rope that cordoned off the lot. She thought it looked like a carny van in a circus convoy she'd seen once in a movie; at day's end, they'd pull up stakes and go someplace else where people made fun of freaks. She was carrying out a new supply of *miche* – and leave it to New Yorkers to buy the bread with the phony Frenchiest name – when she was stopped by someone's voice.

"Hey."

Allie looked up and over the rope that separated the market from the rest of the metropolis, the only thing that lay between her and its awfulness, a protective ring she hadn't realized was a comfort until she looked up and over. A skinny boy her own age was resting on the rope, oblivious it appeared to cars flying by, hardly making the effort not to hit him.

His face was dark, darker than any in her own town – he was Spanish or Italian or Jewish, it was all the same to Allie – and his hair wasn't even brown but so black it seemed to have been colored, but it couldn't, could it, he was a boy. Still, it was a pleasant face, the face of an orphan in a bombed-out Italian town during World War Two she'd seen in a documentary once in school, and his voice had the innocence of a child when he asked, above the street sounds, "What's it, bread?"

Allie, of course, had been taught not to speak to strangers, so she didn't respond right away. But the question was so open, direct, and benign – and the questioner so seemingly guileless – that after a second she said, with much less hostility than she'd intended, which surprised her, "Well, what does it look like?"

The boy took the question as he heard it – not as rhetorical or sarcastic but as sincere – and answered, "Bread."

Was he kidding, this kid? He didn't seem to be – and he wasn't flirting, either, not in the usual way, which is what Allie had figured at first. A weak wind made her belly feel cool and she remembered that her shirt was sweated through, he could clearly see the flower pattern on her bra; but the boy didn't look there, didn't direct one guilty glance, engaged her eyes the whole time, which was a first since she was fifteen with men and boys of any age. (Allie wasn't a virgin but her experience was limited to one encounter with an ex-boyfriend which didn't even last as long as the commercial break on the TV not muted opposite them. Since then, she spoke in a worldly and dismissive way about men and love-making, unable to admit that hers was a subjective observation based on one unpleasant event and not an objective wisdom that put all others in the shade. In truth, she wished simply to put off doing it again for as long as possible.)

But that was not an issue here: the boy seemed as innocent as a sprite, like a spirit of the forest that had escaped to the city and gotten lost. Is that why he asked about bread? she wondered. Was he hungry?

"Here," she said, keeping her voice down, and then reached over the rope and handed him one and then two of the little raisin buns, let the yuppies buy something bigger.

Without looking again at him, she turned away with her bag of *miche* and started back to the stand. Behind her, she heard over car horns, sirens, and boring cell phone conversations, his small voice saying, "thanks," with a surprise that convinced her he had not been angling for it but had only asked her something to be friendly or maybe to make his own morning less monotonous or maybe even because he thought she looked miserable and wanted to help. All of these possibilities – but especially the last one – made Allie turn around suddenly and less subtly than she'd wished to smile at him or do something, she wasn't sure what. But the boy was gone, his place taken by the traffic of which he had been so unafraid.

Allie returned to the stand where Dan was, and where he was impatiently wondering why she'd been gone so long. Apparently, it was the height of over-consumption and time-wasting hour; after nine, they'd merely be selling food to people who were hungry.

"I got lost," Allie said, aware she was being slightly too snotty, but it was too late.

As the day wore on, and she waited on more jaded or entitled people, she thought that seeing and feeding the boy by the truck would be the highlight of the day; everyone else had much uglier motives than he. She found herself checking out the crowd, craning for any sight of him, but soon felt it was silly: he didn't seem to have the same empty purpose or worthless destination that might make him one of them. His ambling was honorable, like sidling by a stream or sauntering down a dirt road, inviting adventure in its natural state; it was not his fault that he had wandered onto an artificial world.

It was a world where, for instance, there was no shade. More fat gobs of sweat dripped down her back to her waist, making the other side of her shirt sheer as well. Allie thought she heard a sizzling sound behind her; with a smirk, she supposed that something had been set ablaze by the sun or was merely manifesting the burning hatred she was sending out. Then, slowly, she realized it was static from a transistor radio: Dan had been a few hours without upsetting updates, and that had been too long.

"Uh-oh," she heard him say, holding the radio close to his head. "Oh, no."

Allie was even more curious than annoyed, so she bent a little backwards to pick up what now worried him.

"Alert," was all she heard, because the radio was practically covered by Dan's hair. "Credible threat" and "subway."

For a second, sneering, Allie shook it off. How weird was Dan, cruising through stations until he found something to upset him – which he could then, what, disarm with his anxiety? What a nerd he was. But then she saw him spin the station again and then again, and each time the information was the same.

"Trusted source . . . Below ground . . . Possible bombs . . ."

Now the fact that every voice said the same thing seemed more disturbing than tedious; it was a bulletin their obligation to report, a repetition for everyone's own good. Allie slowly felt the awful heat around her head replaced by a kind of cold, as if someone had rubbed an ice cube on her, the way her mother would in the summer when she was small.

She missed her mother terribly now, and her father, too.

Ninety miles north seemed the space from where she stood to a star in the sky. It would take her a thousand years to get home, and a different species would have evolved there by the time she arrived. She was trapped.

When Allie looked at the faces flying or trudging past, she couldn't help but add another element to their expressions: an awareness in their eyes that something awful was around them, a threat that loomed above like a giant bird from a bad horror movie, its massive wings spreading and obscuring the sun. (It was just a coincidence but a convenient one that a cloud – the first of the day – had just passed over.) She refused to feel compassion for them; indeed her contempt grew – or did it drop? – to a new degree. What did you expect, living here? Don't come crying to me! In other words, she placed her own panic and her hatred of it in herself on them.

She soon realized that the imagery wasn't exact: the threat – credible, corroborated, or whatever the hell they said – was from below, not above, in the subway, or would be once the bad people completed their plotting and gave the signal to begin. So it was more like a giant burrowing worm was underneath them all, another idea from an awful movie, that soon would suck them under and obliterate them – and they would have gone down not by accident but of their own accord, entered by a simple staircase, even paid for the privilege of being killed.

She thought it only added to the anxiety they all must feel everyday, entering the tunnels of a transportation system Allie would never in a million years want to take. Just thinking of the subway made her start to sweat more, and it wasn't the sun, it was no longer that strong. The idea of being crammed next to all those people, nose to nose, nose to neck, zooming into oblivion, was bad enough on a normal day: now it seemed inconceivable.

Slowly, she started to see the people passing without pigment, as pale as ghosts – like zombies, that was it, their skin sallow, their eyes scooped out, their steps scary because they were so slow, dogged, and steady. Allie felt faint, or what she imagined was faintness because it was the first time she'd felt it, and she nearly fell into one of the cheap fold-out chairs Dan had set by the stand.

She thought she passed out for a while but she didn't, she just sat there with her eyes closed for a minute. When she opened them again, the crowd pushing past was bigger than before and going the other way: it was the evening journey home from work. This was the second "big sales" period; there were two more hours before they could leave. Allie glanced at Dan, but he was counting change for customers, the radio now barely audible. There would be no fleeing early while he could still earn.

Everyone was doomed, and Allie realized that she wasn't angry any more; for the first time, she could admit it, she was afraid. But since she had to be angry at someone, she decided to denounce those who would judge and condemn her fear: well, how else was she supposed to feel? What were they, crazy? This allowed her to cross over to this new emotion, as if using a rock in a river as her bridge to another bank.

When Allie focused on the crowd of the condemned again, to her surprise, she recognized a face.

She was sure that the boy from before was standing across the square. Was she imagining it or was he smiling at her and even coming closer? If she waved at him, would she be making a mortifying mistake and have to turn her wave into a hair comb, like a comic she'd seen on TV?

She wasn't wrong: immediately, as if moving on an imaginary escalator, the boy was at her booth, standing right before her, they were no longer separated by a bungee cord or whatever wrapped around the fair. Each was on the inside now, and Allie felt safer just seeing him.

"So," he said, "how's business?"

Allie couldn't answer: she had no idea, it seemed fine, busy, lots of bread had been sold, so she only shrugged and saw it was the right reply, he didn't care, either, was just making conversation, needed an excuse to come back, and that made her smile at him, with her biggest and maybe only real smile of the day.

"I'm Sonny," he said. Sorry? Ari? What had he said? It was obviously his name and she hadn't heard it and within a second it would be too late to ask again, and then she never could – and there it was, it was too late, she'd never know.

Resigned to it, "I'm Allie," she said, and at least the name she imagined he had sounded a little like hers, so that was something.

"You, do you work here or—"

"I come from a little upstate." A little upstate? What did that mean? She couldn't even speak English, how appealing was that?

"Look, uh – you going back right away, or—"

Was she? She had no idea, was not in control of her life – she turned to check with Dan, and he was at once selling a chocolate croissant to a lady too fat to be buying one and speaking on a cellphone crushed ridiculously between his shoulder and his tilted head, probably to his wife, who had gray hair Allie thought was way too long for her age.

When she turned back, she was aware that the boy could have seen again through her soaked shirt, her bra straps through the crude track team stick figures – she was completely exposed to him everywhere, and her mom's sweater had long since fallen to the ground – but again his eyes were on hers and seemed never to have moved.

"I don't know," she said, and thought she sounded stupid, without a thought in her head, his worst image of someone from "a little upstate."

"Well, maybe I could show you around – we could take a walk or something – see the city – I mean, if you feel like it."

There was something in the way he said it – it went beyond his tentative quality, which was courteous, by the way, not clueless – that didn't mean mere tourism; he was offering himself up as a companion in an unstable world currently under siege, at least that's how she heard his idea, as a form of – not presumptuous or pushy but protective – partnership. If he'd intuited earlier that she was unhappy, now he knew that she was nervous; he was her link to something essential and real, not tricked-up like the city she believed they both were lost in. This made her agree to go and made Dan immediately a minor detail she could handle without really caring how.

"Let me just deal with this," she said.

Dan was now off the phone and customer-free, so unfortunately he had a clear head with which to hear Allie's request and in which to find a new cause for concern.

"But we're going back soon," he said, and then added something about Allie's parents which this time she didn't let sway her, as if she were ignoring an insult, and then he even mentioned the "alert," which Allie couldn't say but sensed that she alone would now be safe from. Assuring him that she would soon return and knew his cell phone number – actually, just yelling this back to him as she ran away – Allie was gone, the boy behind and then right beside her, Sonny or Ari, or whoever he was.

Enormously relieved, Allie found herself jabbering on to him – about her family, the whole college thing, her job, Dan, the city, the country, what she wanted from life – an explosion of honesty that was a working definition of trust, at least to her, who was wary of almost everyone. The boy said nothing yet still seemed to hear – a plus given how other boys just listened long enough to learn when you'd stop and let them start talking – and the crowds, no longer of zombies or horror movie victims but merely hot and harried people, seemed to part for them and let them pass.

Allie was talking so much that she didn't notice where they were headed: across the pavement space of Union Square that led to, among other places, a park, a set of stores, and the wide thoroughfare of 14th Street.

None of them was where – with a brief but definitive touch of her arm – the boy signaled her to stop. When Allie looked up, people were no longer coming directly at them like rain on your windshield in a thunderstorm but were safely off to either side. She saw what they had reached: the entrance to the subway, the 4, 5, 6, N and R.

"What do you mean?" she asked, as if he had said something

instead of simply stopping, and then she even smiled a little at the absurdity of what she saw.

"What's the problem?" he said. "Haven't you ever been on it?"

"No," she said, inferring "of course not," and how had he if he was just as innocent as she?

"Well, this is the day to do it," he said, "with this phony alert – this is when it'll be the most fun."

Phony? It was as if his words were in a foreign tongue – or words you've repeated so many times they're incoherent – and it took a while before Allie could turn them into words she knew. Suddenly, she understood: he was not like her, an alien visitor, he was the opposite: a native so steeped in this environment he knew its every corner and so cynical he could distinguish a false alarm from a real emergency – and laugh about it – and then go right into the teeth of where it was supposedly least safe.

Allie instinctively felt the cell phone in the little fanny pack tied about her waist (which of course tagged her as from out of town), then turned back to see the stand where Dan was waiting. But it was lost behind New Yorkers, as if they had closed over and consumed it, an experienced army that kills with one shot an amateur naïve enough to intrude on its territory.

When she turned back, the boy was beckoning her, his face promising only pleasure – no, nothing that profound, just dumb fun, and amazed she wouldn't take the opportunity, how many would she ever have?

It was hard for Allie to go back to anger once she'd experienced fear – she'd left it on the other shore as it were, when she'd crossed over – and it was hard to feel fear once she'd experienced trust. She was young, younger than most people her age, and so insecure that she held onto every emotion fiercely until she could find a new reason all by herself to release it. With whom would she be safer, someone as ignorant as she or someone who knew the city better than anyone else? Of course – what were you, nuts?

So she let the boy guide her gently toward and down the stairs.

Immediately, it was like hell – so many steamy people on the narrow staircase you could take only tiny steps, orderly enough going up and down on either side, until someone decided to breach the boundary and cross over and then all became chaos. The boy preceded her and, in the crush, her hand slipped from his and she grabbed onto the back of his belt, a gesture more intimate than she'd intended and one that made her fingers touch for a second the bare small of his back before she could loop them on the leather again. His skin was cool and covered in a thin down of hair as dark as everything else about him – except for his eyes, which she had only now noticed were blue-green and shone as bright as an animal's from its den when they're the only things you see. Soon they reached the floor of the station and the last sight of any sun vanished; there was no reversing course, at least not without her clawing through that crowd again and alone, for he was obviously committed to continuing.

"Come on," he said. "This way."

Holding her hand again, he weaved expertly through an onslaught of other people as if he was a white water rafter and they the waves, or some other image from "a little upstate" she clutched to keep calm. In truth, there was nothing from the natural world about what he did: he was more like a video game player entering and ace-ing an invented environment, evading all enemies, and since she had never played before, what had been trust became total and utter dependence; she could not make a move without him.

They passed a table where police were opening and examining the bags of commuters, supposedly at random but really targeting young and attractive women. Allie heard her companion scoff, seeing this – saying "right" with a special spitting take on the "t" – before tugging her hand harder.

"Down here," he said, and they went – it was possible! – even lower.

Descending to the next level, Allie again held onto his belt, but this time she intentionally dipped her fingers over it and onto him, curling them so she'd rub against and feel his hair and scratching him a little when she did, in a way that could have been deliberate or not, he'd never know. How could she not want to become closer to him when he was all she had and without him she was literally lost?

Soon they had no choice but be inseparable, for there was no room at the base of the stairs to edge apart. So many people waited for a train to come down the track that they milled in a giant mass, stuck together with sweat and the stink of themselves. Her front pressed against the boy's back, and since he wore a white T-shirt, too, it was as if she had partly disappeared into him, like the invisible man does into things in other, older movies.

If something exploded now, there would be no saving anyone, each person would be propelled into and annihilate his neighbor. But Sari knew it was nonsense and there was nothing to worry about; he remained almost dry on the damp platform; she noticed it when, with absolute ease, he brought her arm around him onto his stomach and held her hand there; and her heart beat so powerfully she was sure he must feel it: they were so connected now her heart was pumping into his.

Then, from a distance, the track was illuminated. They all stirred, like refugees hit by a spotlight, their emotions ranging from anticipation to relief to fear. The ground started rumbling and Allie suddenly held the boy's hand tighter, her fingers wrapping around his palm.

"Here we go," he said.

The sound grew louder, the light became brighter, it seemed as if the station itself was about to erupt, no bombs were even needed. Then the rumble was joined by a shriek of gears that hurt her ears and what seemed a hysterical, high-pitched, mechanical scream from a new gizmo that could feel and express pain. Allie saw the "R" of the train cab come at and pass her, blowing up her hair, the letter seeming to stand for some place mysterious, a final destination far in the future where there were only letters and no names. The train lasted forever before it finally stopped, the doors opened, and there was no turning back.

Allie saw that inside there was already no room. Each seat was filled and riders jammed the aisles, pressed together in brightly colored summer clothes, like the roasted peppers in that unopened jar in her mother's kitchen. Allie imagined it was impossible each had enough air, but what was there was cool and that was something, a seductive reason to get on and stay.

And they did get on, all of them – even if someone had wanted to walk away, he couldn't, there was no way out. Allie felt the new people must make the train bulge out from its sides, as in a cartoon – but, amazingly, it maintained its shape as they added to what could not be increased.

She and the boy managed to make it to – or merely were rammed toward – a middle pole, which Allie grabbed onto as if it were a floating relic of a shipwreck that kept her from being swept away. She wrapped herself around it and, from behind, the boy wrapped around her, and Allie felt this was the last place they would ever be, they could never leave and would have to live there.

They waited for what seemed an unbearably long time, the cool air slowly being diluted and polluted by the hot air from the platform, which seeped in like poison and threatened their survival. Then, after an almost comical ding-dong of a make-believe bell, the doors coughed and stuttered and finally closed.

Their savage peeling into the dark of the tunnel made her cry out, once, weakly, not sure she made a sound; but since Sari had promised, she was certain it was no longer death they were racing to find, and her freedom from fear was like discovering a second, braver self, and it was thrilling in a new and startling way.

As they left any recognizable place and were imprisoned at high speed in a tube, Allie's cries grew louder, became a kind of moan, and she scanned the signs overhead that told her of the system's origins to center herself somewhere, anywhere, in space.

It was then that she became aware of the hands at her side and felt one hand, his hand, moving slowly and determinedly beneath her short denim skirt with the sparkly studs she thought so cute until it reached the rose (was that what it was?) that bridged her thighs.

"I want to hold all your flowers," he whispered, and then his other hand moved to encircle and squeeze her right breast, the cup of the bra covered by its own bud. (He had seen her! How had it happened without his even sneaking a peek? Was it a bizarre gift all boys had or had he merely looked so cleverly he hadn't been caught?) Then he kissed gently at her neck and said, almost with sorrow, "I wish I had a hundred hands to hold all your flowers," and his fingers moved under her panties, as if burrowing to the place from which the rose had grown.

He put one, then two, then three fingers inside her, and Allie was ashamed and grateful that she was growing wet, and she moaned more and, never having done this before, darkness all around her, her death no longer imminent, moved her hand down amid all the other hands to press him in deeper. Then she got so wet his fingers fell in to their knuckles, and he caught her nipple between the first and second fingers of his other hand, as if he were using a soft scissors to snip it or something. She couldn't think straight, it was all connected – the flower – like she and the boy were connected, and she leaned her head back so her cheek was on his, and she came, which only ever happened to her when she was alone, using that old embroidered pillow her parents had given her as a tenth birthday gift.

"This stop is Times Square," someone who wasn't real announced.

It was every man for himself now – no more of one mind, some in the car struck out on their own, showing little concern for those who stayed behind, indeed using their arms and legs as springboards or stepladders to get out the door. Disentangling from each other, Allie and Sari were soon among this exiting and unsentimental group, though Allie whispered "excuse me" to a woman she practically jabbed unconscious with her elbow, a courtesy attributable to a country upbringing not yet as far behind her as Union Square.

"Let's go uptown," the boy said.

Soon there was a new platform and more new people – would she ever see the same face twice in New York? Allie wondered. (In her own town, even the guy at the gas station remembered she'd been a colicky child.) Well, of course you would: she had seen the boy again, as clear as if she'd conjured him; if she'd hadn't so desired, he would have disappeared. This was another truth about the city: you could work your will on it just as it did a job on you. If it called an alert, you could become awake in your own way; it was a contest of wills that anyone could enter, even Allie.

Now it was as if the boy and she were starting something over – was it their lives? as big as that? – because the new train they fought to board was numbered 1, the first of its kind. It was just as jammed, and they quickly laid claim to the same center pole, the way an old couple always had the same seats in the movie theater back home and resented you irrationally if you had the temerity to sit there.

This time, from behind, he hung his hands off the belt of her skirt, the sides of his thin arms brushing her breasts and even flexing a little, so she'd feel it. This time, as they took off, she felt the erection in his jeans up against her behind, half-exposed in her tilted and distorted panties, still not fully fixed from the last time. He used it to push open her cheeks the way he'd barreled by people in the crowd, and it felt fatter than the only other one she'd felt, the one of her ex-boyfriend, what was his name, and she tensed her ass around it, something she'd never done before and yet knew immediately how to do. He moved slowly up and down against her opening, and then suddenly he stopped moving and his arm rang tightly around her waist and he kissed into her hair and whispered, "Oh, no, not here," and Allie felt sorry she had forced something from him, a promise or a story from his past, except she suspected he really was going to share it with her, anyway, and only wanted her to think she'd convinced him to, she was that sophisticated now.

After standing there utterly unconscious, Allie looked up. For the first time, she was aware of someone watching her, from only inches away. It was a middle-aged man in a business suit with a ferrety face and a five o'clock shadow Allie was immediately prepared for his disapproval – and weirdly she couldn't look away, as if not allowed not to wait for it – but instead he stared back with a mixture of desire and disgust so strong that it startled her. She had never been aware of provoking such intense feelings in someone (though she had, in the very guy from the gas station who'd seen her grow up, though he never stood so close, that was another difference in the city). Allie stared back to confirm and then truly understand what she had inspired. But her comprehension was cut short by their arrival in a station she had not even known they were approaching.

"Seventy-second street," an unseen robot woman said.

They raced across the platform to the 2 train – child of the first, look what they had created! – and, as far as they were concerned now, the more crowded the better. For a change, they sat down, covered by a curtain of people, and he had one hand under her and the other around her and his feeling and fingering of her was so intense she felt it caused the train to blast by stations, as if the thing itself was staring at them and lost its place, as Allie herself had, so far from home. Then she noticed the word "Express" where the train's number was and knew that meant they had been matching its momentum and not it their own. To muffle her moans, she pushed her tongue into the boy's ear, another new experience, and it tasted nasty like everything adult did, she figured, before you learned to like it.

They got off at 125th Street, a stop actually and improbably outside. The crowds were sparser, and the boy seemed in no more hurry to catch another ride. Instead, holding her hand as gently as a child, he guided her slowly to an escalator so long it looked like something out of that song "Stairway to Heaven"

Dan had droned along with, except this one led oddly up to Earth, which turned out to be a street hiding shyly beneath an elevated track.

The boy brought her to a brownstone, the bottom floor of which held a Spanish restaurant, and the tasty smell of cooked bananas followed them up the stairs until they climbed so high they lost it and stopped at the top.

His apartment had two or three rooms and, though they were alone in it, Allie could tell there were other inhabitants, that maybe he still lived with his family, too; she hoped so, for this would link them more.

In the kitchen, which had a bathtub, he gave her a glass of water but he was kissing her before she could finish it. His own room had just a bed and TV and a few self-help books on shelves. He mumbled something about his mother having gone to work; it was around five and, if she had just gone and was not now coming home . . . but before she could ask or he offer anything else, he was on his knees, raising her skirt, kissing lightly between her legs, then licking at the rose itself before, nearly begging her, he took off her underwear altogether.

It was different from how it had been on the trains – they were alone, obviously, and less hot because a breeze blew in from the window – yet she still had a sense of their subverting other people's desires, maybe just his mother's now and not the whole city's. And it was different from the other time for her – there were no TV ads in the background, no sounds at all except an occasional car horn passing or a car radio playing salsa – and it was not as fast as the first time: as he completely undressed and touched and kissed her all over, she felt everything he intended her to feel, and when she reciprocated it was not out of resentful obligation as before but with a sense that getting and giving were now the same thing, a new idea she could not completely explain, even to herself.

She whispered "wow" when she finally found him in her hand, almost unnerved by how much there was and how complicated it seemed. There were so many lines and streams and little dots like stars upon him, as if he had his own transportation system and was so big the map of it was magnified, she could find her way around it easily: she was surprised by how much more excited she was about this penis than the last one.

He fought a condom onto himself and she helped him do it, gingerly, not wanting to hurt him, but she did, anyway, when the rubber got caught in the hairs at the base, and he had to pull each one out individually, wincing the whole way.

Then, it was funny, both were wearing nothing but gold chains. Allie's said "Allie" and his said "Tony" – it was his real name at last; she read it the instant he entered her, as if she really only knew him then, and she said his name and kept saying it each time he pushed inside, expanding her knowledge of the world. He came a second after she did, he actually had that ability, it was incredible, and Allie thought (typically for her, for she was still the same girl) he was one of the very few and maybe the only person on Earth who did.

Then he turned her over on her belly and straddled her and whispered, as an apology, "I have to do this," as if it was a secret no one else could ever know, and he didn't enter but only adorned her, and his sweat and other body liquids lacquered her, and she felt enjoyed to the last drop like that turkey on Thanksgiving everybody liked so much; so little had been left of it, and that's what she wanted, too, to disappear for his pleasure, leaving only bits of skin behind; he'd need a new one of her next year.

Afterwards, he considerately cleaned her off with a Kleenex, then kissed her gently from her neck to her knees before she saw his pretty face again.

She slept for an unknown amount of time, anywhere from two minutes to twenty-four hours. When she woke up, not knowing where she was, she saw the boy too close to be in focus, stretched alongside her, staring right into her eyes and smiling, like a child waiting for a parent to get up.

They took a shower together, and they would have started up again – there was something about his being so wet and scrawny except for, well, you know where; and ready to go again, he was like the New York City subway, available at any hour – but, through the tiny bathroom window, she saw that the sun had set, and she realized what time it must be and what trouble she was in.

Allie was surprised how different the kinds of disobedience could make you feel. This kind immediately eliminated any interest she had in more love-making and made dread an almost physical feeling, a form of nausea.

She quickly put her clammy clothes back on, which were soaked by shower water she had hardly wiped away, and her hair was so wet it dripped even more on her shirt and skirt and onto the floor, where it made an amazingly big puddle for someone with such a small head, and it was helpful to concentrate on that and not on the dialing of Dan's cellphone on Tony's home phone, which was just about to end, oh, why weren't there more (a never-ending amount of) numbers to it?

To her relief, Dan was more frantic than furious, and his cellphone had such bad reception she only caught every other excoriation. His main points, however, were clear: he had trusted her and she had betrayed him, he hated but would have to tell her parents, this was no day to be running around wild in the city, he didn't know who this boy was, anyway, and they had to leave now, not in half an hour but now.

Allie noticed that Dan could give full flower to his fears now that the day was over and there could be no more selling of *miche*. Nonetheless, she would have been mortified by his admonishments if Tony had not been standing beside her in his underwear, dripping wet as well, making screamingly funny faces to mock what he was sure Dan was saying. When he put his hands on his narrow hips and strutted around like a stupid idiot, then moved his lips as if Dan were a pissed-off pigeon or something, Allie had to lightly bite her cheeks not to laugh when she said, "I'll be there as fast as I can."

When Tony heard that, he got strangely serious. He pulled over a piece of old newspaper, then swiftly scribbled on its side margin, then raised for her to read: "Take the train. I want to see you off."

The certainty of the words impressed Allie, more than Dan was impressing her – after all, what had he done for her today? Tony knew where it all stood in the city – the truth about the threat – he was the wisest person she had ever met, and she felt closer to him than to anyone in the world. Egged on by Tony nodding over and over, pointing to his penciled message – not aware he looked kind of funny now, because he was the one so serious – Allie obediently blurted out, "I'll take the train," then pressed the button and deserted Dan, a gesture nowhere near as satisfying as slamming down the phone but the best she could do and actually not so bad.

They took the subway back downtown. By now, there were only a few passengers scattered through the cars, those who chose not those who needed. The tension – the terror – of commuting during a catastrophe had eased, and the people who remained were either resigned or indifferent to it, and too few for it to be fun or feasible to fool around in their midst. Besides, the urge had passed.

When they reached Penn Station, it seemed massive and clogged but not in a good way. Allie felt small and lost in its frankly grubby expanse – so many people were pushing valises on wheels with the sad faces of those traveling to funerals of friends – and she held onto Tony's arm tightly now, not wanting him to drift away an inch.

She noticed that he seemed impatient, glancing around, as if anticipating something. "All's clear here," he said, and sounded disappointed.

Then the two of them stopped, because they were forced to.

Three policemen in the near-distance were waving at them and everyone else. Not wasting time with courtesy, they yelled to "go back" and "get out." Soon other officers of all sizes and both sexes were crudely herding then virtually pushing them back the way they came.

Dozens of them were deposited outside, many obviously late for trips they had planned much longer than Allie had her own.

Those who joined them were offended, annoyed, or – quietly but it was clear – made uneasy by having this happen. Allie heard someone say, "They found something," and someone else, "a suitcase," and finally, in a New York-accented voice trying hard to sound more inconvenienced than afraid, "Jesus Cwist." Then there was the approaching sound of sirens and car after car after car of cops pulled up.

When Allie looked to Tony for an explanation, she saw he was smirking in his by now signature style.

"Idiots," he said, with certainty. "All of them."

Allie was comforted by his typical tone of voice which seemed to restore and bring about calm. Yet she couldn't help recalling that he had said he'd see her off, yet had never mentioned seeing her again. And that he breathed a bit easier – and spoke with satisfied bitterness – now that the cops had found a bag.

"It's nothing," he said. "A fake. And they fell for it. They always will."

He lit a cigarette, something she had never seen him do, and exhaled smoke with indifference into the surrounding crowd. He appeared to enjoy the discomfort it caused and replied with a smiling obscenity when someone asked him to stop.

Allie couldn't help it, she saw more images from awful movies: Tony dissolving into a wolf or whatever villain the actor really was. Was there not a second he could be serious about such a thing? Was that how deep his disgust with the world went? And what did that say about how he felt about her? She was afraid to ask.

Slowly, she felt an alteration in herself, as well. She felt her judgment of others returning; from fear of being tossed away by him, she was morphing like people in movies, too, back into a moralist.

"Well," she said. "I think it's awful."

"What?"

"That someone would do such a thing. Plant a bag."

They certainly would never have done it back home – a phony phone call was the worst kind of prank they pulled.

"Don't get on your high horse," he said.

"I'm not."

"You're going to buy into this now?"

"Well, why not? What would officials get out of faking it?"

"Lots of things. Keeping us controlled. Making us behave. And what do you mean, 'get out of it'? It's not like you did so badly by it."

The remark shook Allie like seeing a death notice in a newspaper of someone she knew. She imagined ringing in her ears like a kind of cash register, the daily exchange of services that went on where they were, that you would always hear as long as the city existed, no matter how many silent computers took their place to do the tally: the way of a world in which people lived too close to do anything decent with each other. Even in this new era – even if it was the end of the world – there were opportunities to make a deal, and she'd been smack in the middle of one and was mortified by it.

"Please get away from me," she said.

Allie fought through the new crowd – after those which had been so secret and stimulating, this one felt fit to suffocate her. Her need to escape was greater than the crowd's to gather and so soon she was free of it and him, the boy she hated now because she was vulnerable and he had made her ashamed.

"Help me, help me," she said to a female cop whom she crashed into and who – not very kindly – told her to please clear the area.

Allie hid a few blocks away in a chain coffee store, one not yet transplanted to her town. She checked out the window with false casualness, but she never saw Tony approaching. Did she want him to pursue her? Definitely not, which meant yes, though Allie was so rattled it was hard to imagine what he could have said to mollify her, and besides, he didn't come or couldn't find her.

Soon some of the people chased from the station had drifted as far as she had fled and were standing outside and smoking, philosophically. A few even joined her in the shop, shaking their heads at the modern world, and that's how she heard that the station was open again, the emergency was over, and the bag had been a bad joke.

She walked back in the dark, asking strangers for directions when she only had to retrace her steps, not wanting to know, to be at ease any longer in this environment. When she reached the station, she saw no one she recognized – he was not there waiting, in other words. She paced outside, ostensibly to catch her breath but really to see if he'd show up; but she was soon shooed inside by overeager cab drivers who could tell she was a tourist (the fanny pack was just the beginning) and wished to take her anywhere on Earth for way too much.

On the escalator going down and in, Allie called Dan's cell and told him she was on her way, her parents shouldn't worry, let him break it to them that she'd be late. Maybe – she thought with hope that was really fear that was really disillusionment – they might not mind so very much.

Dan was still on the road, alone in his truck without even bread along for the ride, and was relieved and conciliatory. He told her what train to take, something she could have learned for herself, if she hadn't again made herself helpless.

After she boarded, Allie watched out the window to see if Tony would come running in, last-minute, like someone from another movie, a romantic one this time, and maybe he'd get stuck on the train because he'd taken so long to say he loved her, and he'd have to actually go upstate with her, and that would be the end. But he didn't come or had gone to the wrong car.

The train pulled out – it was a commuter model, with cushioned seats unlike the subway and still sort of crowded, for there'd been back-ups due to the disruptive bag. Allie stared at the receding platform and thought about the boy. She cried in great choking, child-like sobs, hoping the humiliating sound would be smothered by the train's exhaust. Then she dried her face on her bare forearms, for she had no tissue or even sleeves.

By going to her home the train seemed to be taking her back in time. Yet – like everything else on Earth – Allie was actually going forward. Slowly, she felt even angrier now than before she'd come, more prone to punish, and this was a mere glimpse of how she'd be later in her life.

On her cellphone, she dialed 911 and spoke loudly enough to be heard by the operator but low enough not to disturb her seatmate, a man dozing fitfully. She didn't know the boy's last name or actual address, but she knew his first name and the number on his family's phone, and she thought someone could use the information.

"He was dark, probably foreign. Maybe he had something to do with planting that bag."

Even though he was innocent, he might be taught a lesson and given a good talking to. She didn't say her own name and hung up when they asked.

Then the train went into a new tunnel, one so dark she could no longer see herself. And in it, she fell asleep.

The alert, in which the boy had not believed, was about to become very real for him. For Allie, it would quickly become an edited, censored, self-aggrandizing anecdote she repeated to her family and friends back in town. And, inevitably, it would fade like a flower, until it was a memory as distant, foggy, and half-forgotten as a dream.

Exam Room 3

N. T. Morley

It had stopped raining and the sun was out by the time Jessie parked in the lot and entered the doctor's office, but she kept her raincoat buttoned. "I'm Jessie Adams, I've got a 5:30 with Dr. Hannah," Jessie told the receptionist. The receptionist was probably in her mid-twenties, with red hair, freckles and a slim, tautly athletic figure. She handed Jessie a clipboard, she asked, "Would you like to hang up your coat?"

Jessie blushed a little. "No, thanks, I'll keep it on," she told the girl, and sat down to fill out the paperwork.

She filled out the new patient form and handed over her insurance card, feeling the thrill of being about to commit what must surely be a Federal offence. The receptionist photocopied the card and gave it back to Jessie, looking suspiciously at her tightly buttoned double-breasted raincoat.

"You're sure you don't want me to take your coat?" the girl repeated. Jessie saw that her name tag said "Marie".

Jessie blushed deeper. "I'm sure, thank you."

"Please have a seat." Jessie did so. On the far side of the glass, Dr. Hannah walked up to the counter. Jessie recognized him from his photo; he was a very good-looking man in his mid-forties with a strong jaw and salt-and-pepper hair. Dr. Hannah looked Jessie over as he passed. She shivered under her bulky coat. He disappeared into the back. A few minutes later, Marie came around, opened the office door and said, "Jessie? Come on back."

Marie did not take Jessie's blood pressure or weigh her; instead, she led Jessie right to an exam room. She opened the door, emblazoned "#3." "Please undress from the waist down; you'll find a gown on the counter. You can leave your shoes on," Marie added, with a slightly disapproving glance at Jessie's high-heeled pumps, ". . . and get on the table. You know the drill." She pursed her lips.

"Thank you," said Jessie, and entered the room.

As soon as the receptionist was gone, Jessie unbuttoned her raincoat and took it off. She wore neither bra nor panties underneath, and she did not don the gown.

Instead, Jessie climbed mostly naked onto the exam table, which was tipped up in a sitting position, and obediently put her feet in the stirrups, spreading her legs wide. The cool air of the examination room brought out goosebumps on the smooth flesh of her freshly shaved sex. Her nipples stood hard, almost painfully so. She let her hands rest on her spread thighs, her fingers toying with the satin straps where her garters met the lace tops of her white stockings.

Jessie's heart pounded and her breath came short; she stared at the back of the door, feeling the fear and exhilaration from knowing it was open. Several long agonizing minutes passed; every time she heard footsteps going by in the hall outside, Jessie fought the urge to jump up and put on her coat.

She almost fainted with fear when the door finally opened. There was a split-second of utter terror until she saw that it was indeed Dr. Hannah, and that although she could see into the hallway over his shoulder, it was empty.

Then Dr. Hannah stood there with the door open, displaying shock, looking Jessie over with mingled surprise and pleasure. Jessie almost cried out to beg him to close the door, but he took his time. For a few moments Jessie thought he was going to leave it open through the exam. When she heard more footsteps – one of the nurses, probably – coming down the hallway outside, Jessie almost moved her hands to cover herself, only barely.

Dr. Hannah closed the door before the footsteps arrived. But he did not lock it behind him, a fact which made Jessie's heart pound harder as he looked over the documents on the clipboard.

"You're Jessie Adams," he said, and she nodded nervously. "I see you've made yourself comfortable."

"Yes, Doctor," she said breathlessly. "I'm hoping for a complete exam."

The doctor's eyes roved from top to bottom and back again over Jessie's mostly naked body, taking in her long dark hair, her full red-painted lips, her bare breasts tipped by nipples that were obviously hard, her naked belly bridged by a skimpy white garter belt, her lace-top white stockings and red stiletto-heeled shoes tucked into the stirrups. His dark eyes met her bright green ones and he smiled wickedly, then let his eyes take a slower circuit, approving of the curve of her breasts, the smoothness of her shaved pussy, apparently pleased that the photos she'd sent were, in fact, recent.

"Oh, I'll give you a complete exam," he said. "But what seems to be the problem?"

"Hypersexuality," she said breathlessly. "The desire to engage in human sexual behavior at a level high enough to be considered clinically significant."

Dr. Hannah pursed his lips disapprovingly. "I'll be the judge of that," he said. "A word to the wise, Miss – if there's one thing doctors hate, it's self-diagnosers. Sounds like you've been reading Wikipedia."

Jessie blushed. Dr. Hannah stepped up to the counter, his back to Jessie, and took out two disposable rubber gloves. He pulled them on with snaps, then reached out to the pump dispenser. Jessie never thought the gurgling sound of a pump could make her go all wet inside like that, but it did. When the doctor turned around with one gloved hand glistening, Jessie's eyes went wide.

"Aren't you going to lock the door, Doctor?"

His eyes looked deep into hers. "Why?" he asked. "Afraid somebody will see something?"

Jessie couldn't suppress it; as his slick, cold, gloved hand found her sex and slid in – two fingers, stiff and clinical – she let out a gasp and then a low moan. Her pussy had been moistening since she'd stepped out of the shower, all freshly smooth and ready for her date. As his fingers slid into her, the businesslike feel of them invading her wet and ready sex sent a shudder all over her body and she said, "Oh God, oh God, oh my fucking God." He began to finger her, feeling for the swell of her G-spot, testing the depth of her cunt, touching the firmness of her cervix deep inside. He probed firmly at first with two fingers, then three, filling her as his fingers worked in and out in as businesslike a fashion as a deep finger-fuck could offer. Jessie moaned softly. Her eyes blurred; she surged off the exam table and found herself bent forward, pressed against the doctor, her palms flat on his chest, his scent filling her nostrils, mingling with the smell of antiseptic and latex and medicine as he fucked her.

"Ms. Adams," growled the doctor, his fingers thrust deep inside her, the tips curved against her swollen G-spot, his thumb on her firm clit. "If you won't stay on the table, I'm going to restrain you. And if you moan one more time, I'm going to have to take care of that, too."

Jessie shivered all over as she relaxed back into the chair, struggling not to moan. She bit her lip as the doctor began to finger her again, thumbing her clit as he did so. His other hand found one firm C-cup breast and with latex-sheathed fingers he began to caress it, pinching her nipple lightly. When that made her open her mouth wide and fight to stifle a cry of pleasure, he moved to the other breast and teased her nipple till it was even harder, then pinched firmly while working her clit and her G-spot at the same time. Jessie could not hold back; she let out a strangled moan and lunged forward against the doctor, pressing her face into his neck and panting deep, smelling him as he fucked her.

The doctor's fingers came sliding out of her; he stepped back, tsk-ing. The wet glove came snapping off, and a panting Jessie relaxed back into the chair, feeling the horrible emptiness and desperate hunger of her cunt. She let her fingers rest on her splayed thighs and desperately panted, "I'm sorry. I'm sorry, Doctor."

"Not good enough," he growled, tossing the single wet glove into the trash bin. "We can't have you groping for me when I'm trying to diagnose you," he said, and went back to the counter, which stood atop a metal cabinet of supplies.

From his pocket he took a ring of keys. He stooped over and unlocked the bottom drawer, then fished around in it. Jessie heard the rattle of metal and the swish of straps, and she'd figured out what was coming just as he turned around.

Dr. Hannah came toward her holding two pairs of leather restraints, a black collar, a pair of nipple clamps and a ball gag. The ball gag had a fat leather strap and a padlock, and the collar had a chain attached.

Jessie's head spun; she couldn't believe she was going through with this. She tried to close her thighs as Dr. Hannah came to her, but he put his hand firmly on her knee, looked her in the eyes and said, "No." His firm gaze and that single word melted her and she spread her legs and opened her mouth. He pushed the ball gag between her red-painted lips; she left a smear of lipstick on his gloved fingers. With his other hand he positioned the strap and clicked the padlock; when she looked frightened he said, "No use resisting, you'll have your exam, Miss Adams," and Jessie's cunt tightened against the hungry emptiness he'd left when he withdrew his fingers. She looked down submissively and nodded, and did not look up to meet Dr. Hannah's eyes as he circled the black leather collar around her neck and padlocked it. He tested the collar's chain – a leash, really – and attached it to a ring at the back of the exam table, ensuring that there was just enough play for Jessie's minimal comfort, but that she could not sit forward even if she tried.

There was a click as Dr. Hannah padlocked Jessie's leash to the chair; then he went to work strapping her down.

First he secured her wrists with the padded restraints; these attached with locks to the table near her waist. She felt a pounding surge of panic but did not resist as Dr. Hannah buckled and then padlocked the restraints around her ankles.

Once he had her bound, Dr. Hannah stepped back to admire his handiwork. Jessie was secured to the table at ankles and wrists, collared and ball-gagged, and while the ball gag effectively reduced her desperate moans to tiny, faint whimpers, her instinctive struggles against the leather straps made the table creak a little bit, and she was flexible enough to successfully press her knees together.

Dr. Hannah shook his head disapprovingly, went to the drawer, and came back with two thick leather straps. Jessie wriggled in her bonds as he slid one strap around one of her knees and secured it to the side of the table, then cinched it tight. She let out a stifled yelp behind the ball gag as her knee was forced wide. He repeated the procedure with her other knee, leaving Jessie forcibly spread and helpless.

Dr. Hannah took a moment to look her over, then went to the counter and got another glove.

Before he could snap it on, the intercom crackled.

"Doctor, I'm finished for the day. Everyone else is gone. May I lock up and go home?" It was Marie's voice.

Struggling against the restraints, feeling her lips tight against the gag, Jessie tried to cry out as the intercom went quiet, just to see if she could. All that came out was a muffled moan, halfway between fear and pleasure, but the sound of it excited her. The doctor shot her a disapproving look and showed his contempt for her attempts at escape by leaning over and hitting the intercom button.

Though she hungered to struggle, Jessie remained quiet; she didn't really want the receptionist to know what was going on in here. In fact, the knowledge that she was about to be left alone in the office with this semi-stranger made Jessie's whole body ache with sensation. She looked him over hungrily, knowing that once they were alone he would use her – lube her up and use her, fucking her as she lay helpless strapped to the table, fighting fruitlessly against the tight restraints. She arched her back and pushed her pelvis into the air, clenching the muscles of her sex tightly as she fought. She was helpless. There was no escape. It was about to happen. She'd be left alone with the doctor, and he'd fuck her. With a whimper behind the ball gag, she let the fight go out of her muscles, and relaxed all over with a shudder.

"Not just yet," said Dr. Hannah. "I have an exam I need help with. Come into Number 3."

Jessie's muscles went taut against the bonds. Her eyes went wide. She had not expected this; bound, exposed, fingered, even fucked in front of another woman? Had she even checked that box on her fetish form?

Dr. Hannah looked at her with a cruel grin. He looked from one of her hands to the other; she had only to cross her index and middle fingers of both hands and he'd release her, she knew. Staring at him, she saw the fire in his eyes, felt the hunger in her pussy. She spread her fingers very wide apart, saw him smile, chuckle with satisfaction.

Dr. Hannah smiled and said, "I guess the gag's no longer necessary – but I like you better with it." He snapped the glove on and lubed up his fingers, taking his place between Jessie's strapped-open legs. He slid his slick fingers deep into her, not pausing for two but forcing three right into her, finding her G-spot easily, using his thumb on her clit while he caressed her sensitive nipples. She could feel his cock swelling hard against her leg as he leaned forward to finger her deeper. Jessie's eyes rolled back in her head as he finger-fucked her. God, she was going to fucking come. She was going to come so hard she was going to scream behind the gag. She was so close.

Jessie heard footsteps in the hall outside. Marie entered the exam room. She looked over Jessie's bound and mostly nude body, writhing on the doctor's hand, and said, "I see you do indeed know the drill, Ms. Adams."

Jessie could only respond with a muffled groan from behind the gag. Dr. Hannah took his fingers out of her.

"How can I help, Doctor?" asked Marie.

"She's diagnosed herself," he said darkly. "With hypersexuality. What do you think?"

Marie approached Jessie and leaned down to peer at her cunt. The receptionist's fingers slid up Jessie's inner thighs and began to caress Jessie's smooth, dripping sex. Jessie squirmed in her bonds.

"It's possible," said Marie. "There's a lot of it going around."

Dr. Hannah snapped off his gloves and discarded them, then held out a fresh pair for Marie. "She checked heterosexual on her intake form," said the doctor. "But she also checked 'Anything goes'. Let's find out which impulse is stronger. No need for lube."

"Yes, Doctor," said Marie obediently. Jessie breathed hard behind the gag as the receptionist put her gloves on and slid her fingers deep into Jessie's sex. Jessie's eyes rolled back. She shivered all over as Marie's slender fingers, two of them, began to caress her clit, her vulva, her cunt. The doctor came around behind Jessie and reached over her shoulders, caressing her tits as Marie fingered her deeply. Jessie writhed.

"What do you think?" asked Dr. Hannah.

"She's definitely going to come," said Marie.

"Then let's make it more interesting," said Dr. Hannah. "If she's hypersexual, no reason not to use her good. If she ever gets cured, we'll wish we had."

Jessie was so close to coming she barely understood what was about to happen to her; she just wanted more, harder, deeper. Marie continued to finger her – but went slower and slower with each stroke, and Jessie realized Marie intended to make her wait. Then Jessie felt Marie's fingers coming out of her, going down further, finding the tight hole against the edge of the exam table, teasing its opening while her other hand went deep inside Jessie's cunt again. "Anal play" – she'd checked it, all right, which was another case of her adventurous libido being greater than her experience level. A thousand horny fantasies of being fucked in the ass so hard she begged for more didn't mean she'd ever actually done it yet – she was a virgin there.

But there was no backing out now, not without interrupting her exam, and that was the last thing Jessie wanted to do. Still, the tautness in Jessie's fingers as she felt Marie caressing her ass derived from the comforting knowledge she could cross her fingers and call a halt to the scene if she decided she could not lose her anal virginity here, with strangers, in an exam room. But as she felt the slick fingertips caressing her rear hole, it became clear there was no reason for Jessie to be reluctant; the skill in Marie's fingers was obvious. How many anal virgins had she deflowered right here on this very exam table? Nervous but eager, Jessie surrendered her ass to Marie's control.

Marie expertly teased open Jessie's ass, relaxing it more with each caress. Lube dribbled out of Jessie's slicked-up pussy and eased the surrender of her unopened back door. Finally the receptionist slid two fingers into the virgin entrance, and Jessie felt it opening up as she surrendered. Unexpected pleasure made her shiver all over as she was penetrated in both holes.

Marie continued to finger Jessie in ass and pussy both as Jessie felt the doctor's arm steadying her. He pulled the pin from the exam table and tipped her back, stretching her out on her back. Marie's fingers disappeared from her pussy, and Jessie whimpered. Before Jessie knew what was happening, the doctor had tightened her leash to tip her head back and unfastened his own pants. He slipped his cock out and rubbed over her drool-moistened lips, forced wide around the ball gag. The scent of his cock intoxicated her; Jessie felt his cockhead leaking pre-come as he rubbed it on her face. He deftly unlocked the ball gag and pulled it out of her mouth.

She gasped for air as he steadied her head with her neck stretched easily back. He guided his cockhead to her lips and began to penetrate her mouth.

"Deep-throating" – yes, she suddenly realized, she'd checked it. She felt Marie's fingers opening her ass wider – three fingers, now, as she relaxed. Her clit and G-spot ached against the skilled fingers, new pleasures surging deep in Jessie's body as she got ready to be entered as she'd never been entered before. She'd wrestled over whether to check it or not and, as she felt his glorious cock sliding rhythmically into her mouth, deeper with each thrust, Jessie racked her brains to remember if she'd also checked "face-fucking" or not. She'd gone wet to the knees when she read it, and she was pretty sure she'd checked yes. "Oh God," she thought, "I'm going to be face-fucked," and that worked for her so well that she spread her fingers and flexed them just to make sure she didn't accidentally cross a couple of them.

Jessie felt Marie's fingers coming out of her ass and pussy; she was so close to coming, and Marie knew it. Jessie could feel the empty hunger as her cunt and ass quivered with the sudden vacancy; she would have begged for more, but her mouth was full, and she was about to be fucked in an entirely different way.

Suspended between fear and eagerness, Jessie took a deep breath around Dr. Hannah's cock and let his cockhead find the entrance to her throat. She obediently tried to take it as he slid into her. She felt her throat contracting at the first pressure, then again at the second; he let her breathe and held her head more firmly, looking at her hands and seeing the fingers spread, tight with hunger. She inhaled deeply; he slid firmly into her throat and she took him, her whole body surging with pleasure as she felt herself fucked till she was filled.

Relaxing and opening wide around Dr. Hannah's cock, Jessie surrendered to him, letting him guide her. She remained still as he used her throat, letting her get a breath after every few thrusts; after long minutes of being fucked that way her throat felt open, eager, used. He pulled back and laid his wet cockhead against her lips, and Jessie obediently began to make love to it. She extended her tongue and slurped eagerly from the head to the shaft to the balls, and Dr. Hannah guided his cock from her lips to her cheeks to her throat to her hair to her breasts, letting Jessie follow it with her hungrily lapping tongue. Then he held her firmly and slid back into her, letting her breathe deep before he entered her throat and began to fuck her rhythmically.

Jessie surrendered to the deep fucking of her face, her whole body relaxing in her bonds. That's when she felt the pressure of Marie's body between her forced-open thighs; Marie was no longer wearing her lab coat, but was wearing something else entirely, and the feel of it at Jessie's entrance made the helpless girl gasp and cough around Dr. Hannah's cock.

Dr. Hannah pulled out of Jessie's mouth, leaving a glistening string of drool between his cockhead and her wet, lipstick-smeared lips. He let Jessie look down to see herself about to be penetrated, her legs strapped open and spread wide, Marie now stripped nude except for a black collar and a black leather harness and the glistening black dildo jutting out of it. Her teacup breasts were freckled and perfect, capped by pale pink nipples. On the redhead's girl-next-door face was a savage look of pleasure as she prepared to fuck Jessie.

Panting, her face wet with spittle and the doctor's sweat and pre-come, Jessie stared at Marie and moaned.

The dildo's thick head was big enough that even after the long wet finger-fucking Jessie's ready cunt and ass had received, Marie needed to part Jessie's lips with her fingers in order to get it properly into her. Jessie's eyes went wide and she uttered a gasping, "Oh fuck! Jesus . . ." as she was penetrated. The thick lubed head popped into her and slid easily against her G-spot as Marie's body tipped forward to press against Jessie's. Marie was just tall enough to lean forward and give Dr. Hannah's cock a wet slurp above Jessie's face as she penetrated Jessie to maximum depth, coaxing another expletive from the patient. Then, hand wrapping around the swollen organ, Marie bent down and kissed Jessie open-mouthed, the first time Jessie had ever really kissed a girl. The feeling of the deep feminine kiss, so different from a man's, made Jessie's body tingle all over; the fact that she was receiving it while Marie's strap-on was thrust up deep into her cunt was enough to make her head spin.

Marie withdrew her tongue from Jessie's mouth, still holding Dr. Hannah's cock. She guided it down to Jessie's mouth, and the patient opened wide to let Dr. Hannah face-fuck her as Marie took hold of Jessie's opened thighs and began to fuck her.

Jessie could feel every inch of the shaft sliding deep into her cunt as Dr. Hannah gripped her hair and slid, gently at first, deep into her throat. Jessie relaxed around his shaft and let him sink deep into her. He began to slide again and again down her throat, pulling out every few thrusts to let her catch her breath, and Jessie writhed pinned between the two as Marie rhythmically filled her cunt with the big dildo. As Dr. Hannah drew back further and more often, it was obvious that he was getting ready to come, and her throat was tight and receptive enough to get him off with only a few more thrusts. Hungry for it, she opened wide and let him take her mouth as he wanted it. Drool ran everywhere; her pussy, too, was running wet, and she was going to come so soon she could have beaten him to it.

But then Marie drew back, letting the head of her cock spread Jessie's entrance. Jessie let out a whimper, said desperately, "Please," but never stopped making love to Dr. Hannah's cock, which he guided all over her face to keep the job interesting for her. Then the big, fat head of Marie's cock stretched Jessie wide, wider, still wider, till her eyes rolled back – and it popped out. Jessie continued to eagerly suck the doctor's cock even as she heard the gurgling sound of the lube bottle. Had she been in her right mind, that sound would have told her exactly what was about to happen to her, but Jessie was so close to coming she was far from her right mind, and totally absorbed with the task of servicing Dr. Hannah's hard prick.

Her ass was already lubricated, relaxed and opened, but the size of the cock presented a challenge. Jessie whimpered as she struggled to relax around the pressure of the huge cockhead; her mouth working against the side of Dr. Hannah's cock, she looked up at Marie as if to beg her to be gentle. But Marie was already testing the tightness of Jessie's ass, and knew exactly how to tease her so she opened for it. Their eyes met as Marie began to finger Jessie's pussy, easing her toward orgasm. As she mounted closer, the pressure of the dildo increased and Jessie's ass felt hungry, wanting it more with every stroke of Marie's fingers into her cunt; when the firm thrust finally came, Jessie opened for her first anal fuck like she'd always dreamed she would. Her asshole stretched around the dildo's thick head and relaxed onto the shaft, as Marie slid her fingers out of Jessie's cunt and leaned forward to seize Dr. Hannah's cock and guide it back into Jessie's mouth.

Jessie mouth opened eagerly for the doctor's cock, but this time she was not going to be fucked there. Marie knew that the doctor was going to come, and she stroked his shaft as Jessie's lips circled the head. Marie leaned forward and kissed the doctor deeply, pumping his cock as her cock found its deepest point inside Jessie's virgin ass, fucking the patient to the hilt. The doctor's firm hand – there was no mistaking that sure touch – began to work Jessie's clit, then filled her pussy with two fingers, curved so his palm could press her swollen nub and bring her off. It worked like a charm – Jessie began to come uncontrollably, ass filled with cock, pussy stretched by two fingers, clit surging against the doctor's thumb. Pleasure exploded through her body as the warm slickness and sharp taste of Dr. Hannah's come flooded her mouth. She swallowed easily, hungry for more, taking every pulse of semen until the doctor's cock began to soften in her mouth and Marie's hand ceased its pumping.

Dr. Hannah withdrew; Jessie lay whimpering and moaning on the table as Marie drew back, too, that impossibly thick cockhead teasing open the tight entrance of Jessie's ass until finally, with a pop, it came free. Jessie looked into the pretty freckled face, and Marie stared ravenous at her; she pulled buckles quickly and the harness and heavy dildo hit the ground with a thump. Marie climbed onto her helpless patient and pressed her mouth hard to Jessie's, closing her thighs tight on Jessie's leg.

As Jessie accepted the kiss, she felt Marie savagely rubbing her wet sex on her leg. She struggled against her bonds, trying to press her knee against the receptionist's clit, but she was bound too well. Jessie heard the snap of a rubber glove, and saw Dr. Hannah taking his place behind Marie; his fingers went easily into her and Marie's mouth came off of Jessie's, the receptionist gasping, "Oh my fucking God," as she surged forward and then, moaning, pushed back onto the doctor's hand. He went deep and fucked her expertly, her naked body sliding against Jessie rhythmically until Marie let out a cry and came on his fingers. She trembled all over and relaxed against Jessie's body, kissing her again and then licking her way down to Jessie's breasts, suckling her sensitive nipples.

Jessie took a deep breath as she felt Dr. Hannah unlocking the padlocks, unfastening the straps. Marie remained against her, uttering a soft purring sound as she caressed Jessie's nipples with her tongue. When Jessie's limbs came free she put her arms around Marie and began caressing the receptionist's nude body; Marie moaned softly, but Dr. Hannah reached around and hooked his index finger through the thick ring of Marie's collar, pulling the naked receptionist away.

Marie obediently climbed off Jessie, and stood naked and panting beside the table.

Dr. Hannah tsk-ed, guiding Marie away. Marie dutifully picked up her lab coat and began to put it on, leaving the rest of her clothes on the exam room floor.

"If you want to make love to her," said Dr. Hannah as Marie buttoned her coat, "you'll have to make a follow-up visit."

Jessie stared after Marie as she left the room. She lay there, wet and sticky and panting, her wrists still feeling the straps even though they'd been removed.

Dr. Hannah fastened his pants, made a few notes on her chart. He looked Jessie up and down and smiled.

"See the receptionist on your way out," he said, and left the room.

Jessie decided not to put on her coat before doing so. She'd decided she wanted a follow-up visit after all, and it was definitely an emergency.

Good Kitty

Shanna Germain

Kicked to the curb. That's how I feel. I've been in my cage at the rescue center for what seems like forever. But I know it's just been a day. I can't see the clock on the wall from here, but I can hear it ticking. Tick-tick, counting the minutes off that I'm alone, unowned. Counting the time since my master dumped me here. Traded me out for another kitty.

My neck feels bare without its collar. My throat hurts. I tell myself it's just the air in here, all the fur flying, but I know that's not the truth. I gave him four years. I wore his collar and showed off for his friends and lapped his cream. I went on kitty play dates and never minded when he decided to pet another pussy. But I would not, could not, handle it when he brought another kitty home to live with us. I tried, I did. I kept to myself, I avoided her, I tried to pretend I was just fine with it. In the end, I turned into a prissy bitch. Every time he touched her, I'd sulk in the corner. His new girl and I fought, tooth and nail, as they say, and here I am.

The front door clicks open and we all sit at attention, dogs and cats alike, as best we can in our small cages. It's a girl in black spandex, her red hair bobbed at her neck. She looks only at the kitties, poking her red nails between the bars in front of a few. When she gets to my cage, she stops. Her eyes are intensely green, cat-like in their own way. I shrink to the back of my cage, feeling the wires pressed into my bare spine. She scares me, although I can't say why.

"Pretty kitty," she says, her voice a low purr. She dangles two red-tipped fingers inside the cage. "Come here, pretty kitty."

I don't want to obey – I've never had a girl master – but I don't want to be in this cage anymore either. Maybe she'll take me home, put a collar back on me. Maybe this hard-looking girl is better than another night in this cage. Better than another night alone.

I lean my head forward, just enough that she can stroke my hair. "Good girl," she says, pressing her thumb to my cheek. A shiver runs down my spine, and I feel a surprising surge of desire.

She takes her fingers out of my hair and flips up the tag on the front of my cage to read it.

"Callie, long-haired female," she reads. "Housebroken, that's good. Playful, loves lap time. Not good with dogs."

"Oh," she says. "It says you don't play well with other pussies either." Her eyes are back on me, that intense green, and I wonder if she's the other cat and not the master after all. "That's too bad . . ." She hesitates a second, as though I might correct her. But I don't. I can't. It's true. And besides, I may be a stray, I may be uncollared at the moment, but I'm not about to break rules and speak.

And then she's gone, down the row, to look at the other kitties, kitties who play well with others. I want to say something, to call her back to me, to rub up against her fingers and lick her palm. To let her know that maybe I could be okay with other pussies, to ask her to reconsider. But when I open my mouth, nothing comes out. Not even a kitten-squeak. Just silence, and the reminder that my throat aches with the kind of lonely pain that not even this green-eyed girl can fill.

I hear her talking down the row, but I can't see her from where I sit. And, before long, I have to watch while she leads another kitty, a short-haired blonde, down the aisle. They both turn to look at me, and I close my eyes.

I'm curled up on the shelter blanket, wrapped in dreams of my last master, when I hear the voices outside my cage.

"Came in last night," says a voice that I recognize. It's the woman who checked me into the shelter. "I'm surprised someone hasn't snapped her up." She lowers her voice until it's a whisper. "Someone just dumped her on our doorstep, this gorgeous girl. Can you believe it?"

"That is hard to believe," says a voice. Very male. Somehow very in control. The sound alone sends a shiver through me.

I crack one eye open, to see who's talking. All I can see are a broad pair of shoulders and a wide chest, wrapped up in a white button-down. His shirt sleeves are rolled up, showing off muscled forearms and wrists. No jewelry. He talks with his hands, fluid and confident dips and rolls.

"What's wrong with her?" the hands ask.

"Nothing as far as I can see," the woman says, her voice getting lower with each word until I can hardly hear her. "Her former master wanted another kitty in the house, it seems."

"Imagine that," he says. "I find a pussy does best if it's given undivided attention." My own pussy twitches when he says it. His fingers play along the bars of the cage, but don't enter.

I wonder if he can see me. I always thought I was pretty – my last master reassured me of that in so many ways – but now I'm not certain. Still, I want to show off my best parts, so I stretch out on the blanket, curve my hips and ass up and out. I rest my head on my hands and open my eyes, so he can see them if he looks in – I've got Siamese eyes, that blue-blue.

"Does she come when she's called?"

"Most kitties don't," she says.

"I knew there was a reason I preferred dogs." But his laugh says he doesn't mean it.

The man leans down to peer into my cage. I try to pretend I'm not looking, that I don't care, but I catch a glimpse of salt and pepper hair, dark brown eyes framed by tortoise-shell glasses. A little scruff around his face, but it's nice, and thin lips. He looks nothing like my last master, which makes me both excited and nervous.

His fingers come through the bars, wiggle in the air at me.

"Hey there, sweet girl," he says, like he's known me all his life. I sniff his fingers; they smell like cedar and sweet cream.

"Come here," he whispers. I think about his question of whether kitties come when they're called. I always do – did – for my last master. I like that feeling of doing what I'm told. So when he calls a second time, with "here, kittykittykitty," I move close enough so that he can reach me through the bars. When he buries his fingers in my hair, it's just hard enough. I rub myself against him, loving the pressure of his strong fingers against the back of my neck.

"Oh, yes, you're such a good girl," he says. "Aren't you?"

I'm getting wet just listening to him talk. When he stops moving his fingers, I butt up against him with my head until he starts again.

The woman clears her throat. "We do have private play rooms where kitties and their potential owners can get acquainted," she says. "Would you like to take her there and see if the two of you are a good fit?"

I hold my breath as he rubs my head with a little less pressure. Will he say yes? Or will he, too, decide he doesn't want me and move on to another kitty?

"What do you think, sweet girl?" he asks. I rub against his fingers, trying to convince him to say yes.

He pinches my earlobe between his fingernails and I let out a little yowl of surprise.

"Maybe later," he says. I look up at him, surprised and hurt, but he's already taken his fingers away and is moving down the row.

After that, I don't know what to do. No master's going to take me home. I'll be stuck here forever. I'll grow old watching other masters come and pick out cute kitties. I lie down on my blanket and close my eyes, trying not to cry. Every time I swallow, I feel exposed. I want to go home.

A couple of hours later, the nice woman who rescued me opens my cage.

"C'mon little one," she says. "Let's go." She holds out a collar that says AFRS on the side. That's where I am, the Rescue Shelter. If I put that collar on, does it mean the shelter owns me? Does it mean they've given up hope that I'll ever be rescued? I cower against back bars.

"It's OK," she says, her voice soothing me. "It's just temporary."

She clicks it around my neck. I'm ashamed to wear this collar and to be on the end of her leash – the AFRS printed on both basically tell the world, "dumped kitty walking here". But I follow her down the aisle.

Outside a door, she leans down to take the collar off.

"Go on in," she says, holding the door open for me.

I go through it, and it's him. The man from before. He's bigger than I thought, tall and his shoulders are wide. In front of him, he's laid out a blanket. I can tell it's his, because it doesn't say AFRS on it, and because when I step on it, it's way softer than the one in my cage. There are two bowls, empty, that look too clean to belong to the shelter. And on the table beside him, a black bag. But the thing that catches my eye is the leash and collar set in front of it. Dark purple. Brand new, and set with little silver slivers. I can already feel it against my skin. My throat has never felt so naked, so vulnerable. My heart too. Maybe he'll take me after all.

"Come here, sweet girl," he says. "Sorry to make you wait, but I needed to get a few things."

I crawl up to him and wonder what to do now. My old master always wanted me to rub my head against his shins, but I don't know if this is what he wants. So I wait to be told.

Without saying anything, he steps to the side of me. He just looks. Quiet, and for a long time. I arch my back for him, and drop down onto my forearms. And then he steps beside me and does the same thing. My pussy feels him watching and it wants to hide, but I force myself to stay still and let him look.

He runs a hand over my head and down my back. When he gets to my ass, he squeezes it and then gives it a little smack. It doesn't hurt, but it's loud. I don't even jump.

"I don't know," he says. "You seem awfully well-behaved. I wonder what you could have done to end up here?"

This is a trick, I know. To see if I'll act out, or give him an answer. I stay totally still, on my knees and forearms, waiting to see what he'll do.

He squats down behind me and runs his fingers down my thighs on the outside. Just his fingertips, with enough pressure that I wonder if my skin turns even whiter beneath his touch. He strokes the back of my thighs, moving closer and closer to my center.

"Pretty pussy," he says and I think he means me, but also he means the part of me that he's almost touching. That I so badly want him to touch. He's so close I can feel his breath against my skin.

I lean back into his fingers, asking for it. Please.

"Oh no," he says. His fingers go away, and he stands. I can't hear anything from behind me, and I don't dare look. I worry that I've ruined it, that he's going to take me back to that cage.

Footsteps, and then he's in front of me. Without looking at me, he picks the black bag off the table, and disappears again. I hear the clasp of the bag, the paper and something soft all rubbing together. The sounds excite me, even though I don't know what they are.

He touches his fingers to the bottom of my pussy, not on my clit, but close. And then he shows me how wet I am by sliding two fingers inside me. I clench around his fingers, to try and keep them there, but he just laughs and pulls them out.

"My, you are a greedy girl," he says. "If I didn't know better, I'd think you'd been a stray for a long time."

I smell the lube before I feel it, and my body responds. My nipples tighten against the blanket, and my pussy starts a slow pound that I wonder if he can see.

Then I feel it – he's lubed a dildo, and he's twisting it into me like a corkscrew. I'm so wet that I doubt he needed lube, but I like the sound it makes, the kind of slow squish as it enters me. When the dildo is all the way in, he taps the end of it. I'm so full I feel that little tap all the way down inside me.

He presses something small and hard against my ass, and I raise my head in surprise. I nearly look back at him over my shoulder, but I stop myself.

Still, he sees.

"You can look," he says. "All good kitties need a tail, don't you think?"

I look over my shoulder. He holds a small black butt plug with a long kitty tail attached. The color matches my hair. I'd never had one before, and I can't wait to see how it looks. I arch my butt in the air, to tell him that it's perfect.

I watch him as he slides it inside me. Even lubed up, it's big, bigger than I'm used to, and he goes slow, letting my body open up to the pressure. I feel it filling me up, until I'm not sure I can take anymore. And then it's all the way in. It gives me a perfect tail, long and sleek. I twitch my ass, which makes the tail bat back and forth and wiggles the butt plug and the dildo inside me.

He laughs. "I'm glad you like it." With both hands, he strokes my tail. The butt plug hits all my pressure points, and I'm afraid I'm going to come. I make a long, low sound, half squeak, half meow, and turn back to the front. I can't watch anymore.

He walks around to the front of me, his hand trailing over my ass and up my back as he goes. He unzips his jeans so slowly I can hear each of the teeth as they come apart.

"Most kitties I know love cream," he says. I try not to feel my heart stutter when he says that. Does he know a lot of kitties? I don't want the answer.

He slides his jeans and underwear down. God, he's gorgeous there too. Slim hips and muscular thighs. And then his cock. It sticks out from under his button-down, long and wide, and I want to lick it. I want to see what he tastes like, to know what it would be like to have him fill my mouth the way I'm filled everywhere else.

He puts his hands in my hair again, that just-right pressure until I'm practically purring against him.

"How about you, sweet girl?" he asks. He makes a ring around his cock with his fingers, offers it to me.

I touch my tongue to my top lip. Yes please.

"Go ahead," he says. I lean forward and touch my tongue to the base of his cock. He tastes of clean salt and wood, something fragrant. Pine or cedar. I lap at it while he holds himself out to me, following the veins that snake just beneath the skin. It's so hard I can feel the skin stretching around it.

I take just the tip between my lips and run my tongue over the smooth bulb there. He moans, and the sound makes me clench around all the things he's put inside me.

He pushes all the way into my mouth, and I take as much of him as I can. It feels so good to feel him pulsing on my tongue. I suck him, hard and then soft, taking little nibbles sometimes, until his breath gets harsh and ragged. Pre-cum coats my tongue and I lap it up, playing the tip of my tongue around his hole. I suck on the shirttails that hang on either side of his cock, letting my tongue feel the rough fabric. With the fabric on my tongue, I lick him again, just to see if he likes the way it feels, like a wet kitty tongue. He hisses between his teeth and his cock jumps.

When I take all of him inside my mouth again, he puts his hands around my throat. Not hard, but like a temporary collar. Like a way to claim me for now. The thought makes me so wet I can feel the dildo start to slide out of me.

"Don't let it," he says. And I clench my pussy hard to keep it in. I know it won't stay for long, so I'm grateful when he moans and arches against me. "Don't stop," he says. "I want to give you my cream. I want you to lick it all up."

His cock pulses in my mouth and then he floods me. He tastes salty, but sweet, and I wonder if he ate something just for me, to make it taste like that. I swallow it all, and then lick every drop from him. I nestle my tongue in his balls, and lick him until he's clean.

He pulls up his pants, and sits in the chair in front of me. "You're such a good, good pussy," he says. "Do you want to come home with me?"

Before I can answer, he dangles the collar in the air, and I swipe at it, but miss, which makes him laugh.

"Do you think you want this?" he asks.

He holds it out in front of me, a hand on each end, so it's flat. All I'd have to do is put my neck on that strip of leather and I would be his.

"Don't say yes unless you're sure," he says. "I don't have any other pussies. You'll be my only one, but I'm not always as nice a master as I was today."

I'm counting on that. I stretch my neck out until I can feel the leather collar against the bottom of my neck. He wraps the leather around my skin. The buckle makes a small metallic sound as he fastens it. When I swallow, I feel the smooth weight of the leather against my throat.

"Now you're mine for a long time, sweet girl," he says.

I sure hope so.

2.04 a.m., Our Hostess' Second-Floor Walk-In

Savannah Lee

I had certainly never looked into a man's eyes before when we were both stuffed with cock.

Jeff and I had just blundered into our hostess's second-floor walk-in closet, and Jeff had just slid it in me from behind, when I got the dread/thrill pinprick on my flesh that told me we were not alone. Yikes, maybe that was why the light was already on. I pushed aside a well-cut D&G jacket on my left to discover – him: startled, amused and, I couldn't help but notice, fuck-eyed.

Just like me.

Besides his eyes, I put together a jumbled impression. He leaned, like I did, on the waist-high skirt bar for his man to have him from behind. I saw tousled hair, a soft mouth, an incongruous 'beater, and a very strained white thong.

Ordinarily I'd have checked out the thong. This time, the eyes won. I'd seen bulges before. I hadn't ever seen eyes quite like that. The eyes of a doe – a male doe. Deep and hurt, proud and fucked. In fact, it was too much. I glanced away.

"Hello," he nonetheless offered, rather sweetly.

Jeff, behind me and still clueless, jumped eight feet. "Ohmigod!"

The stranger's lover reached out and thumped Jeff on the back. I felt the shock waves. "No problem, man. Great party, huh? You do your bitch, I'll do mine."

What did he call me? I whipped my head around to try to see this guy, but got that pushed-aside jacket in the face. Nonetheless I snapped, "Hey, let's have some respect for the receptives here."

Jeff gave a stoned, dudely laugh and pulled me back on him harder. "I'll respect you when I'm not, like, reaming you."

The hidden man gave a laugh that didn't sound nearly as all-in-good-fun as Jeff's had. He made a similar move on my counterpart, who took it with a soft groan and a whitening of his knuckles on our hostess's skirt bar. I actually felt kind of worried and wanted to ask intrusive questions about lube sufficiency. But I became fatally entranced by the look of mingled transport and suffering on his face.

He must have felt this, because he met my eyes.

"I'm sorry," I said, "I didn't mean to stare."

"Oh, go ahead," he told me with a sad smile.

So I did. Oh yes, I feasted my gaze on his tender mouth and taken eyes.

"Wow, Meg," said Jeff cluelessly, "you just got a lot wetter."

He would, of course, not just say that, but say that while this guy and I were still in eye contact. I wanted to sink through the floor.

But the guy didn't laugh or gloat. Instead, those starkly cock-fucked eyes shared only vulnerability to exactly that kind of embarrassment. My heart fluttered at his kindness.

So did the rest of me.

"Wow!" cried Jeff. "Now you're dripping down your—"

"Shut," I said warningly, "up, and fuck me."

My buddy's partner shifted next to Jeff. His voice was a rude intrusion, like tires over gravel. "I wouldn't let my bitch talk that way to me."

Now it was my buddy's turn to wither in mortification. I tried to offer him the same safety with my eyes that he'd offered me.

Jeff meanwhile explained, "I don't really have rules about how Meg can talk to me. You know? We're not D/S or anything."

A sandpapery chuckle. "Neither are we!"

"Ohhhhkay," said Jeff.

I stared in horror at my beautiful friend, who was now officially martyring himself to that creep.

He leaned closer and murmured, "It's all right, he . . . he gets this way."

"What do you mean?"

Even softer and closer. "Shhhh. He's right there."

I leaned closer too. "You're not helping him."

"Yeah . . . you're right. Meg." He tried out my name.

I asked him his.

Before he could answer, the creep cut us off. "Your name is BITCH," he yelled, then decided to prove it by ramming my friend into the bar so hard the whole closet nearly came down. The jolt caused Jeff to knock an ovary and I buckled with a yell.

"Are you okay?" Jeff and my unknown friend chorused. Two hands went to my back.

Jeff's hand was concerned and reassuring. The stranger's hand . . . the stranger's hand knew. Infinite in its delicacy and tenderness, it knew what I felt.

We met eyes again, and we did not look away.

Until there was another jolt and the enraged creep began piling it on. He started fucking my still nameless friend cruelly, fucking him to hurt him. My friend dropped his gaze to save his pride and marshal his strength.

Well. I would not let him be alone.

"Jeff," I said. "Give it to me hard. Hard."

I took the stranger's hand.

He lifted it up and together we grasped the high bar. I can't tell you how much that meant to me – that he accepted me, that he offered himself in return, and that he took us up to higher ground. Though I don't suppose it looked like any kind of triumph. More like ocean passengers clinging to a wreck. I suppose in a way that's what we were. The storms that pounded us were inside us, but that didn't mean we weren't going to drown. The truth was, we were both of us struggling to hold on, both of us trembling, both of us reduced to fuckholes.

In his eyes I saw the pathos of it, indistinguishable from the beauty.

But in my own, despite it all, I felt the power. Even the pride. After all, if we were fuckholes, what were the men who were using us? They were fuckers. Fuckers. No one wins. No one gets out of here alive.

Jeff came with a smothered moan, a beautiful sound of surrender – the fucker fucked. The creep gave a yell like his load was a pistol shot, like he wished it would tear through his lover-victim and take his heart. "Fuck you," he prosaically added, with a shove. I caught sight of him then – shiny bald head, shiny testosterone-furied eyes, shiny livid face. He was wearing a cream-colored suit into which he zipped his shiny red cock and stalked out.

Jeff sounded exhausted. "Well thank god that's over. Let's go, Meg."

I said, "I . . . I'll be right there."

Jeff closed the door behind him.

Alone now, the stranger and I still held hands up on the bar. I looked at our fingers entwined, more than entwined, jammed in each other. Knuckles white. That was what it had taken to survive what we had desired.

That was how much we had given each other.

I pulled him to me and wrapped my arms around him, one survivor to another.

He was still half-hard against me.

At that moment I realized something. "You were grabbing the bar the whole time," I said. "Or my hand." He didn't understand what I meant.

I said, "You couldn't touch yourself. And no one else did. No one really gave you anything. Any pleasure. Any . . . love."

"Oh . . ."

I knelt down and took out his shaved, half-swollen cock. I opened my mouth.

He said, "No."

Well, of course, duh. Dejected and embarrassed, I bowed my head.

He bent and took my arms. "I don't want you down on your knees." He brought me to my feet and brushed some hair off my forehead.

The moment was too intimate to deny, but I didn't see where it could go.

"So what happens now?" I pleaded.

He went half-shy, half-wicked in the eyes.

"Oh . . . my," I said. "Are you going to fuck me?"

In answer, he went all the way down this time to his abandoned jeans and came up with a telltale little packet.

"That is," he amended, stopping himself before he opened it, "if you actually want another run. That guy really hammered you."

" 'That guy' who?" I said.

He looked me over with frank admiration.

"Respect the receptives." That seemed kind of clumsy to say out loud right now though. The moment called for something less formal than advocacy or analysis. So I popped a little fist in the air and said, "Bitch power!"

"Oh . . . let's not try to reclaim that one tonight. Let's let it go." He tore the condom packet open.

"What should we call ourselves? Sisters? Let me help." It was green; it turned his prong alien as I unrolled it.

It was easy for him to breach my wet and well-used hole. I just hiked my leg and he went all the way in.

And we looked at each other.

Now we were across the familiar divide. My eyes were still the eyes of the filled, the invaded, the taken, but his had changed. His were the eyes of the possessor.

I think he felt it even more keenly than my other lovers because he knew it from the other side. Jeff, when I looked in his eyes at these moments, had an innocence about him. But my still nameless friend *knew* what he was doing, oh, how he knew.

Then he proceeded to do it . . . differently.

He was soft. Not his dick, but how he used it, and held me, and gazed in my eyes, yes, my bitch eyes. Oh.

I never would have believed that that could do it for me. I was one of those girls that liked to be fucked. By men who saw it as their role in life to give a like-minded woman the slamming she deserved. They could be neo-hippies like Jeff, they could be go-getters like my last one, but when it came to fucking, they had to lay me down and mean it. This even influenced my taste in music. I never liked the sweet pop boys. I listened to the hard stuff. That's just how I was.

This man, though he was inside me, retained the gentle nature of the bottom that he was. But I loved it. I loved looking in his empathetic eyes, feeling his tender motion inside me. He aimed not to take me but to feel me, to live inside me, to ease our walls into a nice fit as if they were going to stay that way. To know me, really, in a way that I'd never thought of that word before.

Damned if it didn't make him the butchest thing in the world to me right then. Or maybe that was the only way, given my own desires, that I could explain it to myself. Whatever, it took my breath away. Looking in those eyes, so soft and male, I—

—turned to stone as our closet door tore open.

There stood the creep.

"I knew it!" he shouted. "I knew it! I knew it!"

My friend clutched me in simultaneous protection and appeal.

For a minute I felt like anything could happen, by which I meant that this guy was going to put us in the hospital. Then he let out a red-veined, anguished scream. He crumpled to the carpet.

"Paul!" he wept. "Paul! Paul!"

Now that he was on his knees, I got a view of the crowd he'd brought with him. Yes, we had an audience. Half of them looked shocked to see Paul with me (those would probably be the ones to whom he was out) and the other half looked shocked, and mortified, at The Creep. (Those would probably be the ones to whom Paul was . . . um . . . in.)

Okay, and then that lot started staring at us too, because after all, there we were in mid-fuck. And *now* they were shocked to see him with me.

I came to my senses and threw my arms around him, pushing his face down into my closet-side shoulder to give him what safety and protection I could. Inside me, he was ten times harder, reacting perversely to the humiliation and fear.

Which was about when Jeff arrived.

"Meg?" He blinked.

"Um, hi," I said.

The creep's loud sobs interrupted us. "Paul! I'm sorry! I was just so afraid of losing you! I thought if I was a real man you'd love me! Or at least be too scared to leave me. I didn't care which!"

At this alarming revelation, Jeff forgot all about me and crouched down in front of the distraught creep. Earnestly he said, "Dude, it's not okay to make your partner scared of you."

"Who asked you?" the creep shouted at him. "You're the one who couldn't hold on to your woman! Look at her, she's fucking my man!"

"Um, excuse me, your man is fucking her," Jeff pointed out.

"She came on to him!" argued the creep. "I saw her looking at him!"

"No fucking way!" Jeff fired right back. "He came on to her! He was all 'go ahead and look at me' and shit!"

This would have necessitated more or less immediate breakup if it had actually been as Neanderthal as it sounded, but I could tell he didn't mean it – he just didn't want to let this guy win.

Our adversary was equally determined. "Well, he only said that because she was coming on to him."

"She was not!" Jeff shouted, getting more rhetorically sophisticated by the minute.

"Yes she was!" bellowed the creep.

Was this rational? Was this anything? What the fuck. They were a pair of pre-schoolers with hormones.

Oh god, we all were. Blind and confused, puppets of drives and imperatives that were as far beyond us as the simplest self-understanding was beyond a child. With disbelief, I thought, We're going to get in cars and drive home after this.

And look at the mess we'd be leaving behind. No mommy or daddy to clean it up. No nice teacher to calm us down and talk us through it, or even to give us all a good swat and tell us to snap out of it. I wished there was. Authoritarian psychology made horrible sense to me right now.

I swung off of Paul so we could put ourselves back together and get out of here. For me, it was as easy as letting my dress fall back down. I stood in front of him to shelter him as he bent down for his jeans. It seemed like he was half-crying and trying to suppress it. His face was wet with sweat and tears.

"Are you going to be all right?" I asked him softly.

He didn't answer. He didn't even admit that he'd heard. Having shared too much tonight, he was now closing off completely. I couldn't say I didn't understand. My poor wild deer.

He and I weren't finished, but that obviously didn't matter now. Neither one of us was going to come tonight. I left the walk-in and took Jeff's arm.

As we turned away, I looked back at my fucked beauty. There was one last flash of the eyes.

I knew that would be all.

The Baptism

Remittance Girl

1870, Annam, French Indochina

The church of Dak Rede was a small wattle-and-plaster affair, perched inconveniently on the crest of a hill, just beyond the reach of the humid clutches of the jungle. Its placement, however, afforded the cool morning and evening breezes so dismally lacking down in the village below.

The young, recently ordained Jesuit priest surveyed his meagre and apathetic congregation with a sigh. Kissing the surplice in his hands, he draped it over his narrow shoulders. There were only five congregants: two he had bribed to attend with a promise of rice, and one was asleep and snoring, even before Father Jean-Michel had intoned the first few words of the Latin mass.

He'd been sent to the Kon Tum highlands of central Annam, to this poor, insignificant village, to bring the word of Christ to these wretched natives, to save their ignorant souls from eternal damnation. But as far as he could tell, they were all – and he included himself in this – already there.

No amount of coaxing would induce the attendees to participate in any of the proscribed responses; he'd given up trying to make them do it. So he simply said them himself. He quickly finished the reading of the gospel and skipped the sermon altogether. Father Jean-Michel didn't speak Vietnamese and the only person in the village who spoke French with any

real fluency was a Chinese apothecary who resolutely refused
to attend mass.

As he launched with as much vigour as he could muster into
the Credo, somewhere, close by, a late-sleeping cockerel woke
up and began screeching its existence to the whole village. As
the priest invited the worshippers to the table of Christ, in
Latin, the chicken was calling out, "Here I am, I'm dinner!
Come and get me," in a language much more familiar to the
souls he was attempting, and failing miserably, to save.

He turned, as prescribed, and opened the little doors of the
tabernacle, to retrieve the communion implements. He deftly
flicked a dead cockroach off the tarnished silver salver, before
turning back to place the things on the altar.

To his surprise, he realized that while his back had been
turned, his congregation had grown. Three young, almost
identical women had slipped into the back of the church
and seated themselves in the last pew. Pretty maids all in a
row, mused Father Jean-Michel vaguely, as he performed the
transubstantiation – changing the bread and wine into the
body and blood of Christ.

At the appropriate time, he perfunctorily invited his
congregation to take the host, assuming no one was listening,
and no one would come up to the altar to receive it. They never
did. But to his amazement, the three girls, for what else could
he call them, filed up to the front and presented themselves
in a line. It took Father Jean-Michel a moment to get over the
shock. He quickly took up the plate and went to the rail, unable
to take his eyes off the trio. Each wore the same dark silk tunic
over white silken pants, each wore their hair in identically long
and neatly plaited braids, each looked up at him from under
epicanthic-lidded, almond-shaped eyes.

"The body of Christ," he said, holding a small round wafer
out to the first one. She took it in the palm of her hand and
placed it on her tongue discreetly, giving him, he was almost
positive, a hint of a smile.

"Body of Christ," he repeated, stepping before the second
girl. No – not a girl – for at close range their superficial

samenesses evaporated. This one was a little shorter and more rounded of body. In fact, her breasts were remarkably large for a native of the Indochine, where most women possessed boyish, androgynous figures by European standards. Father Jean-Michel gave himself a mental chastisement and held out the host. This girl did not hold up her hands for it, but opened her mouth instead, offering the tip of an impossibly red, betel-stained tongue. Despite his best efforts, the priest's heart began to race as he placed the wafer on her tongue and watched it disappear into that dark, velvety interior. Her lips closed, shutting him out, and she whispered, "Amen." The priest shook himself out of his reverie and moved on.

The third was the tallest. He looked into her face, expecting the same lowered eyes as the other two, but this one's gaze did not waver from his – it pushed back as if having substance and power in its own right. He had the sensation of having something thick, black and viscous forced down his throat.

"Body of Christ," he managed, after freeing his gaze from her eyes. He stared at her mouth.

The woman's lips were almost obscenely plump. Like a ripe purple plum, squeezed and split in two along its cleft, they parted to reveal an almost serpentine tongue. It slithered out, curling at the tip like a whore beckoning a client. It required all the willpower the priest had to raise the host and lay it upon that profane altar. His fingers shook as he did and brushed against her open lips.

In that instant, he felt a needle-like sting that made him snatch his hand back. Glancing down, he noticed a small drop of blood had budded like a carnal pearl from a tiny wound at the tip of his index finger. Father Jean-Michel returned his gaze to the woman's mouth, confused. But it had already closed, her luxuriant lips curved into a smile.

Unable to quell a sudden and overpowering vertigo, the priest stepped back, jostling and almost upsetting the altar.

"Go . . . go in peace," he croaked, and stumbled towards the back door of the church.

★   ★   ★

Every muscle ached, as if he'd been caught like prey in the coils of a boa constrictor. Father Jean-Michel had, like everyone else in Indochina, suffered numerous bouts of fever, but this felt like none he'd ever had before. He groaned pitifully, pulling himself free of his miserable, sweat-soaked sheets. Lethargy dragged at his shoulders and it was only after what felt like a monstrous battle that he managed to sit up and hang his legs over the side of the cot.

It was late afternoon and the rains had started. The murky green light that always accompanied the monsoon storms gave his room and the view of the village beyond his window an underwater quality. Nothing could be done, nothing accomplished until the downpour was over, and Father Jean-Michel granted himself the refuge of curling back up on the mean pallet and retreating into fevered dreams.

He dreamed of dragons, huge and sinuous, moving through the ebony waters in a river gorge. There were three of them; iridescent scales breached the placid surface here and there, meeting to intertwine before dispersing to pursue their solitary frolics again. The dreams left uncomfortable erotic echoes that coiled like the dragons themselves in the pit of his stomach and groin. The priest rolled over, struggling to purge himself of the after-images, and stared at the wall beside the bed. The paint had peeled back and flaked away to reveal a conspiracy of black mould. In his fevered state, the stains on the wall took on ominous shapes. Someone – the last priest to be posted to the village, Jean-Michel assumed – had scratched the word "*merde*" into the soft, crumbling plaster with a fingernail.

Oh, God, what had he done to deserve this?

What had possessed him to say those things to the Bishop of Rouen? Why couldn't he have kept his mouth shut? This posting in the deepest of all hells had been his Dantean punishment for remarking that if the Church really cared about its flock, it might consider spending less money on itself and more on the poor. Two months after the quip had been made, he'd found himself struggling up the muddy hill track to the village with a coolie behind him carrying his few possessions. He had been assured that the priest he was replacing would be there to help him settle in, but the Church and the crumbling residence had been abandoned for more than a month.

"Père . . ."

Father Jean-Michel groaned again and rolled over.

"Père!"

He sat up, clutching the damp sheet around him, head spinning, nausea overwhelming him.

His servant, Hai, hovered at the threshold to the priest's room. "There is a woman asking for you."

"Really? Oh."

He felt so ill, the priest considered telling Hai to ask her to come back another time. But in nine months, no one had ever come to see him, no one had ever called him to perform last rites, or officiate at a wedding. How would it play out in the village if, the first time anyone bothered to ask for his help, he sent them away?

"Tell her I will come shortly. Just give me a moment to get dressed."

He waited until Hai retreated back into the shadow of the hallway, and forced himself to get up. At first his legs felt so weak, he was unsure he could keep himself upright, but he took a few deep breaths and blinked, and stumbled over to where his underclothes and his cassock lay, draped over the back of a chair.

Hai brought tea for the visitor, as Father Jean-Michel hobbled into the reception room. Like everywhere else in the house, it smelled of damp and rot. No matter how thoroughly he tried to air it out. The climate's corrupting influence was everywhere, and would not be defeated.

His visitor sat on the hard mahogany bench that served as a sofa. It was impossible to see her, for a heavy black veil almost entirely covered her head. She wore a loose, dusty black tunic that exposed only a pair of almost bone-white hands, as if two dead albino spiders had crawled up and died in her lap.

"Madam?" he said, cordially, wincing soundlessly when he lowered his aching bones into the chair opposite hers. The priest nodded his head at Hai, who hovered in the shadows of the room, waiting. "Will you take tea, Madam?"

"No . . . Father. I won't." The voice rustled and hissed like dry leaves on a stone path.

Although the rain was still pouring down in sheets, and the room was very dim, Father Jean-Michel looked into the tunnel of the woman's headscarf, and almost recoiled at the sight. His guest's face stared out from the surrounding layers. Two shiny black eyes set into a hideous face. Pale skin stretched tautly over her bones in such a way that it was impossible not to think he was looking into the eyes of a cadaver. But the oddest thing was that the woman had a dreadful skin complaint. The skin itself was seamed in such a way as to give her the appearance of having scales instead of human skin. A lipless slit of a mouth smiled at him, revealing a toothless black maw. "Today you met my daughters, I think."

The woman's French was accented, but understandable. It was the slurry, rasping sound that was disconcerting. "Ah," said the priest. "Yes, yes. They came to mass. Your daughters?" Impossible that three such exquisite creatures had come from the womb of this . . . atrocity.

"Indeed. And they have asked me to come to you, and make a petition on their behalf."

Father Jean-Michel nodded, still unable to stop himself from staring into the shadowed ruin of her face. "A petition? Of course, I would be happy to accommodate you in any way I can, Madam. If I can," he added, remembering when a parishioner had asked him to bless his pigs for luck. "What can I do for them?"

"They want to be baptized."

The priest was shocked into silence for some moments. My God, he thought, perhaps all my efforts to bring the Gospel to this place of spiritual emptiness had finally borne fruit. Then he remembered the morning's mass. "Baptized? But they took communion this morning. They acted as if

. . ." He hesitated a moment. "One is not supposed to take communion without first undergoing conversion, and being baptized," he said. The words came out quickly, like an outrage or an admonishment. This wasn't the way to attract people to the faith, he thought. "Well, it's not usual," he added, in a softer tone.

An uncanny, bubbling noise emerged from the old woman sitting opposite and her small, black frame twitched. It took Jean-Michel a moment to realize she was laughing. "Forgive them, Father. In everything my daughters are impulsive and over-eager. It was youthful exuberance, and not a lack of respect."

"And you, Madam, are you a Christian?"

"No."

"I would be honoured if you would allow me to perform the sacrament of baptism for you as well."

Again the little black form shook, and the bubbling returned. "No-no. I am far too old for all that."

"But for that very reason, Madam. Baptism would ensure your place in God's everlasting kingdom. It is never too late."

With the sound of clicking bones, the heavily covered woman got to her feet. "Oh, it is far too late for me, Priest. A different kingdom awaits me. "The finality in her words would tolerate no argument. She shuffled on small, hidden feet to the entrance, opened the door before Hai could reach it for her, and stepped out into the torrential rain.

"I do not like that lady, Father."

"A baptism," the priest said, clasping his hands together, his illness and fever forgotten. "Three baptisms in fact! This is wonderful. Wonderful!"

"Père?"

"I shall . . . I think . . ." Father Jean-Michel paced around the reception room in a high state of excitement. Suddenly he stopped and tilted his head towards the ceiling. "Oh, thank you. Thank you, Lord! You won't be sorry. I'll bring your Gospels to this wilderness yet!"

"Père!"

The priest glanced at Hai with annoyance. "What? What? Can't you see? This is the beginning of everything. And in this place . . . I shall honour the baptism of our Lord Jesus Christ. Not in a mean little font like they do in Rouen, but like St. John did, in the river. I will baptize these women in the river!"

Hai shrugged. "Take care, mon Père. I do not like that woman."

It brought the priest to a halt. "What do you mean you don't like her? How ridiculous! What's the matter with you?"

Shrugging again, Hai collected the teapot and the cups neatly back onto the tray, and picked it up. "She's ugly . . . very ugly."

"And so you don't like her! Typical of the outrageous ignorance and lack of Christian compassion among your countrymen. The poor woman is obviously suffering from an illness. That's no reason to dislike her."

The servant lowered his head and shuffled towards the scullery with the tea tray. "Inside herself, she is very ugly."

"One should not paint others with one's own sins, Hai," called the priest. "After all, God has forgiven you the sin of sodomy."

By the following Saturday, Father Jean-Michel had ensured that everything was prepared. He had sent word to the daughters through the apothecary in the village that they should meet him by the bank of the river at nine o'clock in the morning, and that they should bring towels and dress in white. At first the old Chinaman had refused, but the priest had nagged and bullied and nagged again until the apothecary had finally relented, for a twenty Piastre bribe.

"And tell the rest of the village," Father Jean-Michel had said, "they can come and witness the sacrament if they want to. Perhaps if they see it, they won't be so reluctant to participate."

The day dawned humid and overcast, but the weather could not dampen the priest's spirits. He performed his own ablutions and devotions, taking his special white cassock out of mothballs and slipping it over his naked body. He would go to the river barefoot, as John the Baptist had done.

Nothing could dampen his spirits as he rushed around the residence, packing his special bible – the one he'd been given at his ordination – a small envelope of salt, and a vial of holy water into a basket.

"Come now, Hai. You can help me. You can assist me in the administration of the sacrament."

The servant looked pale, as if he'd had no sleep the night before. "No, mon Père," he said, in a very odd voice. "It's not an auspicious day for this. Please don't go to the river. Do it some other time."

Jean-Michel stared at him angrily. "Don't be a superstitious fool! Any day is a good day for a baptism. Come along now."

"Father, I . . . I do not feel well. I cannot go with you. Please don't make me."

"Idiot!" the priest said, shaking his head. "Fine then, you lazy, good-for-nothing sinner. Don't come!" He walked out of the residence, making sure to slam the door behind him.

As he began his walk down to the river, his anger at Hai smouldered like a stick of incense, but then he reasoned that it would not be pleasing to God if he performed the baptisms with bitterness in his heart. Silently he mouthed a prayer as he picked his way through the jungle scrub and approached the edge of the river.

They were there waiting for him, and dressed just as he had instructed in pure, virginal white. Joy surged in Father Jean-Michel's heart. They looked like three incarnations of the blessed Virgin Mary, with their lustrous dark hair loose and hanging about their shoulders.

"Good morning," he called, as he approached them. All three turned in his direction and, almost as one, gave him a slight bow.

"Children, beautiful children of Christ! This is a wonderful day. God has brought a miracle to this wilderness." The priest spoke with his arms held wide. "Today you will be reborn into everlasting life!"

The priest put down the basket, after retrieving the vial of holy water. He turned towards the river, uncorking the vial, and let the liquid drain upon the wet riverbank, asking God to bless this place as a site of rebirth for the three young women.

He turned and beckoned the women down to the water, glancing around in the hope that some of the other villagers had come to watch, but they were alone. He shook off his disappointment and, picking up his bible and the small twist of salt, said: "I have taken the liberty of choosing your Christian names. These will be the names by which you are called to the Catholic faith."

The priest was not altogether sure they understood everything he said, but it mattered not; he was saving their souls and, after all, that's what counted. Wading out deeper into the water, he stopped only when it reached his waist.

The cool liquid seeped through his cassock and it billowed out around him in the gentle current. "Come," he said to the tallest, reaching out his hand. "Don't be afraid, Christ is with us."

The girl he'd beckoned smiled and stepped into the water. As she approached him, it seemed to Father Jean-Michel that she was changing already; her face shone with an unearthly radiance.

To his amusement, the other girls followed their sister. "One at a time," he said and chuckled. "I cannot baptize you all at once." But they didn't seem to understand, and came towards him, gliding as if free of earthly gravity.

The tallest girl put her hand on his arm. "My sisters want to be near me, Father. Please allow them."

The priest smiled, and nodded, paging his bible open to the page. "Alright then. We must begin." He turned to the tallest girl. "Do you renounce all other faiths and give yourself wilfully to the holy mother church?"

She inclined her head and smiled. "Of course."

Father Jean-Michel unwrapped the twist of paper containing the salt and pinched a few grains with his fingers. "Open your mouth, child."

The girl before him lurched in the water. It seemed she lost her footing in the current, because before he could stop her, she'd pressed herself up against him, her dark red mouth open, her face too close to his. He stepped backwards to allow himself the room to administer the salt, but there was someone behind him. He turned to look, and was confronted with her smiling, rounder sister. "Oh . . . I'm . . ."

Hands touched him in the water. He turned again, only to be faced with the third girl, who pulled the bible from his hand and stretched out her arm, casually letting it float away on the current.

"No . . . no," he said, confused. "This is not how it . . ."

A pair of slender arms slipped under his own and embraced him from behind, and the other two were suddenly on him, pressing their ripe lips to his face, his neck, his mouth. He felt the combined weight of the sisters pulling him down into the water, and further into the middle of the stream.

Sinuous bare legs entwined with his beneath the surface. Hands slithered and caressed his bare flesh. "No," he cried out. "No . . ."

They did not stop. The one he had been planning to name Mary lifted her robe over her head and, smiling the same impassive smile as the other sister, released it to the river's hunger. She wrapped her arms around his neck and kissed him lewdly, mouth open, her curved tongue working its way into his mouth.

Behind, he could feel breasts pressing into him, rubbing hard, cruel nipples into his back. Unseen fingers closed around his cock and stroked it. The priest wanted to fight them, wanted to push them all away, but even as he dreamed that short dream, his will evaporated as the blood coursed into his cock, making it instantly hard.

"He is ready," one of them whispered. "You first, older sister."

The sensation of carnivorous, enveloping heat made him whimper, and the sister at his lips slipped a long, satisfied hissing breath into his mouth. Jean-Michel felt his soul abandon him, releasing a long-dormant beast within his heart. He reached beneath the surface and grabbed at Mary's exquisitely formed ass, pushing her onto his cock. Her hips rolled as she rode him, holding him tight with her legs, her tight, hot passage milking him. She gave a low growl and bit into his lower lip.

Pain and pleasure bloomed in equal measure. He savoured his own blood on his lips at the same time she did. The taste triggered something inside her, for she tilted back her bloody mouth and keened as her body shuddered violently. Then just as suddenly as it had begun, she released him, wriggling free of his grasp, and floated away, licking her lips.

Almost immediately, the little round sister – the one he had called Elizabeth – took her older sister's place. She gazed into his eyes for a moment and he saw himself reflected, distorted, in hers.

Opening her mouth, a long flat tongue flashed out and lapped at his face, picking up the blood that her older sister had left behind. Jean-Michel embraced her, lifting her higher in the water and pressing his hungry mouth to her round, firm breast. Arms encircled his head and pressed him to it.

Beneath the water, a curious caress – then arms surrounded his hips and a burning mouth took his cock, fellating him as he nursed ravenously on the breasts at his face. Not possible, he managed to think, although his mind was a riot of desire and sensation. The mouth at his cock was unbearably clever. A rough tongue writhed away at the underside, even as the gorgeous sucking continued. He pumped his hips in the water, feeling the head slip into a tight throat. Another body was at his back, rubbing frantically against his skin. The sensation was unexpectedly rough, as though the unseen girl's flesh was as coarse as scales.

"Oh, God," he moaned, reaching back to touch the woman who tormented him from behind.

He felt another pain, this one at his neck, sharper and deeper than the first. The mouth around his cock was gone and the girl in his arms slid down his body, impaling herself on him.

The pain didn't matter. Nothing mattered but the sweet cunt that drew itself up and down on his rod. Thrusting upwards, he heard the girl grunt with pleasure and so he plunged into her again, and again, each time increasing the violence of his penetration. She pressed her face to his neck, feeding as he fucked. With each hungry suck, he felt his cock harden and grow until he could hardly squeeze into her passage. She left off feeding, flung back her head and groaned.

Never had Father Jean-Michel taken the Old Testament literally, but now he knew without a doubt that he was having congress with demons. The moment he realized it, the girl in front of him changed. The pale skin of her neck and breast took on a new texture. As she lowered her head, the eyes that met his were those of a serpent, and between her plump lips, needle-sharp fangs glinted in the grey, morning light.

Despite the acute pleasure, he shoved her away, but he needn't have bothered, for she released her grip on him with a serpentine smile.

"Get thee behind me, Satan," he shouted, backing away desperately, towards the river's bank.

Arms surrounded him from behind, blocking his way. The thing that slithered its way between his legs was not human, but the tail of a serpent. "My little sister has not had her fill yet," whispered a voice at his ear.

The priest tried to turn around, but the lamia clung to him. The sisters in the water swam towards him with undulating strokes. Before he could protest again, they were on him. The youngest, the one he'd planned to call Magdalen, slithered up his body. Her beautiful, inhuman form swayed hypnotically, locking him with her eyes. She mounted him with a sigh.

The fear, the revulsion, the hate, all drained away the moment she enveloped him, for hers was the most delicious of all carnal embraces. He knew in that moment that his life was over. And in that same moment, the priest surrendered. His hips arched upwards into the clutches of that deadly beauty. In only a few thrusts he was lost. Seating his cock fully, he cried out and poured his seed into the lamia's womb. Warm, scaled bodies surrounded him even before he finished coming, pulling him under the cool waters of the river.

The Rise and Fall of the Burlesque Empire

Maxim Jakubowski

It could be that in another life I sold my soul to the devil.

And what is happening to me now is just a form of punishment, a kind of torture inflicted on me in some indeterminate circle of hell where I must be stewing.

There is no other explanation.

I have the gift of time travel.

But I can't control it.

I am randomly taken to places and times. In a loop that is nothing less than infernal, things happen to me that claw into the sheer fabric of my heart and soul and diminish me with every journey, eating me away like a rat gnawing at my stomach. And on and on it goes and somehow, something inside of me assures me it will never cease and the terrible pain will endure forever because I am not allow to die.

In my sleep, I was transported to Times Square.

I knew it wasn't a dream. I could smell the street, sense the vibrancy of Manhattan, touch people, eat, do things you cannot achieve in your sleep. The smell of the hamburger and hot dog stands, the blissfully soft touch of women's bare skin, the sensation of thin urban rain peppering my hair, oh no, I was certainly awake. More than awake, in fact.

It was the heyday of Times Square when New York was

both decadent and joyous, a period I could only recognize from film clips and photographs as my first actual visit to the city hadn't actually occurred until much later when I was in my 30s. A newspaper headline on a corner stand confirmed to me it was the time of the Rosenbergs' trial. In real life, I had then just been a small boy in short trousers.

One moment, I was tossing between my sheets, the next I was standing on the corner of Broadway and 45th Street, drinking in the sight of oversize limousines and sports cars racing south and passers-by gazing in wonder at the neon jungle surrounding us.

Somehow I took it all in my stride; unlike the naked Schwarzenegger cum Terminator from the movies, I was fully clothed. My left hand searched for my inside jacket pocket and found a roll of green bills and coins. At least, I would not have to beg.

I have never been much of a tourist, so after an hour or so of walking around exploring this New York of memories my mind was already wandering. I hadn't even travelled more than four blocks in any direction from my point of arrival, as if a curse of some sort would break out should I venture too far, and I was literally a prisoner of 42nd Street and its wonderful excesses.

A brightly lit theatre marquee caught my attention advertising "the Original Burlesque Extravaganza", featuring women's exotic names I had at some time or another come across in books or articles: Lili St. Cyr, Bettie Page, Tempest Storm, Blaze Starr. I doubted they were the real article, but my curiosity was piqued. I parted with a couple of dollar notes and walked in. There was even a two-sided programme sheet I was handed by a bored looking commissionaire in a frayed uniform before I entered the auditorium. Which confirmed the show was a homage to Bettie Page, Blaze Starr and others and did not in fact feature the actual legends.

The spectacle was all I could have hoped for: blissfully over the top and boisterous, comic, colourful. True, the show had little in common with burlesque's origins, with a lack of fat comedians tossing out New Jersey jokes and warming up the audience prior to the arrival of the dancers in their attires of feathers, divine lingerie and layers of flimsy fabric in every shade of the rainbow. But there was a Master of Ceremony, a thin, nervous guy who looked a little like Lenny Bruce without the sweaty drugged pallor. No doubt a stand-up slumming here between gigs, perfecting his scorn like a precursor to his Bob Fosse Cabaret future counterpart. But the thin audience – the small theatre could at most hold a hundred or so punters and was barely a third full – blanked him totally, visibly here just for the gals.

It was fun. Most of the dancers didn't take themselves seriously and even attained, in part, a level of performance art in their crafty disrobing and dancing act, balancing props and knowing smiles, teasing the anorexic crowd with a twinkle in their eyes or an occasional thrust just on the right side of vulgarity. There was a Carmen Miranda look-alike whose scratched record kept on jumping on the turntable behind the small stage so her juggling plastic bananas were always that little bit out of sync; and then there was the dark-haired would-be biker girl, whose labyrinth of zips kept on getting stuck as she manoeuvred herself out of her leather gear and sported an unbelievable number of layers of black underwear under her tight trousers; or again, the regal Claudia from Germany, as the M.C. introduced her, she of the thunder thighs and red hair like fire who shook her arse with the best of them, and even winked at me as she turned her head halfway through her set. Or maybe it had been a speck of dust.

I counted five dancers in all. But strangely enough, no blondes. Was it an early hint that the devil was playing games with me? Or just me hankering for forbidden fruit?

The men in the audience came and went. There was a five minute break, and the show began again. No one was asked to leave the auditorium. One could spend the whole day here without being disturbed, it appeared. At the time, I still thought this was a curious sort of dream, not totally unpleasant and having nothing better to do decided to stay put and see the women again and maybe check whether Teutonic Claudia's signal had been deliberate or not. After all, she did have spectacular breasts, strong, high globes whose red pasties harmonized perfectly with her flaming hair.

But when her time came in the order of rotation, after a young pimply stagehand had cleared the previous dancer's scattered red, white and blue feathers from the stage (she had performed a faltering but broadly comic French Ooh La La act), the regal Claudia did not appear.

Instead, the M.C. sheepishly slithered on and, leering outrageously, said:

"And now a real treat for all you amateurs of sheer pulchritude, for the first time ever on a New York stage, for the first time ever on any stage, the virginal, the beautiful Anais . . ."

A young woman hesitantly came to the fore.

He had not been exaggerating: it was visibly her first time doing this. She didn't even have much of an outfit. Just ordinary summer street clothes with a few silk belts and scarves and a scarlet boa no doubt borrowed just now from another of the girls here.

She had long dark untidy hair that trailed all the way to midway down her back. Her pale shoulders shone like beacons through the tangled hair draped across them. Her aquiline nose stood out proudly, punctuating the savage beauty of her features. Her ruby red lipsticked lips stood out like a lighthouse in a starless night.

Jesus, I thought. She is the one.

As she embarked on her slow, languorous dance, more sad seduction than ironic burlesque, my fevered imagination was already imagining, writing her whole life story to this point, all the burdens and adversities that had led her here to have to dance for strangers for a few dollars.

She was visibly an amateur. The single spotlight held her in its grip as she tried to inject some feeling into her movements. It didn't work. It was evident it was not her choice to be here. A man to my right heckled. Two more in the row in front of me stood up and walked out. Even the music she had chosen or been allocated was wrong for her, some big band tune that could never blend adequately with her innate grace and dignity as she attempted to negotiate its rhythms to the staccato clockwork stance of her private dance.

I was captivated.

Even from where I was sitting, the dark pools of her eyes drew me like a whirlpool of emptiness.

She attempted a brave smile as she pulled her white summer cotton skirt away with a minor flourish and slid the thin silk scarves to and fro across her flat, taut stomach. I gulped. Her clumsiness almost made me want to cry.

There were more heckles from the sparse audience. On stage, Anais lowered her eyes, as if ashamed of her imperfections. I wanted to applaud, to counter the negativity of my fellow punters, but didn't. She was now, apart from the boa circling her neck like a slave collar, just in brassiere and knickers, both black and plain, the pallor of her tall, thin body isolated like a pool of light on the heart of the stage.

Finally, the management put her out of her misery and the music accompanying her semblance of a dance stopped and the spotlight on her was switched off. There was a moment of silence through which I could just about notice Anais in the penumbra picking up the pieces of clothing she had earlier shed and hurrying off to the stage's wing. Then the circle of light returned and the ersatz Carmen Miranda was back, balancing her plastic bananas with a broad grin on her lips.

I rose. I didn't know what to do. I couldn't rush the stage and chase Anais. Some heavy would stop me and beat me up in all likelihood if I attempted that.

I rushed to the exit. Quickly walked to the side of the small theatre seeking the exit the performers might use to depart the premises. There was a door on 7th Avenue that seemed to fit the bill. I stationed myself outside.

Night came. I became drowsy from all the waiting.

Somehow, my eyes closed and I was no longer in New York and again the time was now.

I couldn't forget Anais. Something about her had moved me deeply. I wanted to see her again. I wanted to listen to her story, to touch her, smell her.

Months later, I travelled in time again. It was three in the morning, my own personal witching hour when memories and regrets tore me apart with both glee and scientific precision and I felt despair like acid killing me with every added second.

I blinked and it was Manhattan.

A bit greyer than on the previous occasion, as if a thin layer of dust had settled on my memories. The noise around Times Square was louder. The flashing neon more gaudy. I realized I was wearing the same clothes as on my last visit. A similar amount of money was in my pocket.

The theatre was still there, but it felt older, as if several years had elapsed. And they had. Some of the bulbs inside the marquee had perished and not been replaced. It now just read "the House of Burlesque" in flickering motion.

I paid the entrance fee and took my seat.

The floor was sticky, the curtains frayed and the interior of the theatre stank of dust and bad days. The other spectators also appeared shadier than previously, many like refugees from the weather outside, some in stained clothing, holding brown paper bags with bottles inside.

It was no longer a burlesque show, but a run of the mill and particularly unimaginative strip tease show. The costumes the women wore at the onset of their numbers were minimal and plain, and the performers all exuded a strong sense of boredom and indifference as they shed their clothes with metronomic regularity until they stood, for the final third of whichever song they were dancing to, nipples and pubic thatch starkly exposed for all to feast on. There was no longer any tease involved, just unencumbered and artless nudity.

I sat in silence as the strippers followed each other on the small stage, waiting for I didn't know what. There was no longer a presenter, just a muffled voice on the P.A. system mouthing a vaguely exotic name prior to each dancer's appearance: Mitzi, Christina, Melissa . . . During the performances, I could sense some of the other men in the audience touching themselves or more in the darkness.

A squat Latina woman whose genital area was time-wise halfway between a full wax and her usual jungle bush climaxed her set with a triumphant bend and flashed us all a furtive glimpse of her pink innards and the shoulder movements of the guy sitting in front of me increased significantly. I was about to abandon my quest and leave the joint, when the next act took over the stage.

It was Anais.

Or Anna Maria, if I believed the announcer.

She had changed.

She was older and no longer as tentative, as if she had spent the months (the years?) since I had seen her last taking lessons from the other performers or had maybe just acquired the talent to be more sensual out of thin air.

Her wild gypsy hair was the same, her pale skin still a delicate shade of porcelain, her limbs long and spidery and her stomach just a touch rounder.

She danced, stripped to the Eurythmics' "Thorn in my Side", her movements sexy and deliberate, swaying in unison with Annie Lennox's vocal swoops. This time there were no heckles. When she shed her final garments, I held my breath hoping that what I had imagined in my crazy dreams of her would hold up to the reality of her body.

It did. The shade of her nipples veered wonderfully between brown and pink like a kaleidoscope of shifting desire and her breasts stood firm, just the right side of either large or small, delicate, calling for my tongue, tantalizing, real. My eyes moved down and, as if following my signal, she slowly moved her outstretched hand away from her cunt as the last measures of the song entered their fade-out, revealing her thick curls. I caught my breath and the music stopped and the lights went out.

The silence was deafening before a few of us applauded.

The silence returned until the disembodied voice on the P.A. was heard.

"And now, the parade. Gentlemen, be generous with your tips . . ."

The strippers, all stark naked, walked on to the stage and gradually moved down into the auditorium and began making their way across the rows where us male spectators were sitting. Invisible signals passed between the erstwhile dancers and some of the men in the audience, and after a few bank notes had changed hands, some of the girls would rub themselves against the generous customers. I caught a glimpse of hands caressing flesh, straying, moans, movement, whispers. I declined the untold offers of the first few dancers who reached me and waited for Anais. I tried to see where she was, which men she had stopped to attend, gratify or whether she was part of this unholy procession. She was. Two rows away from me, she had her back to one fat punter, his hands unmistakably running across the bare skin of her backside, no doubt kneading, intruding. Her eyes and mine met across the chiaroscuro of the strip club.

I waited. Turning down all the other strippers.

Finally, she reached me.

I handed her the first note I found in my pocket. Neither of us even checked its denomination.

She pressed her breasts against me.

"I saw you when your name was Anais," I whispered to her.

Her eyes came to life.

"That was a long time ago," she answered.

"I know," I sighed.

"You can touch me, you know," she said. I thought I could detect a faint foreign accent.

My hands moved to her shoulders. I could feel her breath in my ear. Her softness was like a sting. I closed my eyes and abandoned myself to the blissful sensation. One of her hands brushed against the front of my trousers. I was hard.

"I've been thinking of you ever since that first time," I said.

"You are beautiful." All I could come up with was a damn cliché!

She indicated she had to move on. My time was up; there were other men further down the row.

I was about to say "No . . ." when she whispered, "I am available, you know."

"OK," I spat out.

Five seats further down the aisle I watched as a suited Japanese businessman dug his fingers into her cunt, having no doubt paid more than me for extra privileges. Finally, the parade ended and the women trouped back towards the stage.

I met Anais outside the theatre ten minutes later. She had changed into jeans and a black tee-shirt.

We did not discuss money. We walked to the Iroquois on 44th Street, crossing the early evening traffic on Broadway. I bribed the clerk to let me have a room at such short notice and neither of us having any luggage or reservation.

Anais and I fucked for hours. Definitely fucking and not making love. Few words were exchanged as if we now knew that our respective stories, the equally tortuous and complicated roads which had taken both of us to this room were of no importance.

I mapped every square inch of her skin with the unbound folly of an explorer of unknown worlds. I drank the moistness that pearled from all her openings like the survivor of a terrible trek through unending deserts.

I felt quite delusional as I noted how my cock fitted her cunt as if we had been built for each other in some strange factory by a glove maker who knew every secret of our bodies. I listened to her gasps as if they were songs. My tongue, like a blind man's hand, surveyed the textured territory of her teeth, her throat, the ridges of her perineum, the crevice of her anus, the satin of her white skin until my own throat ran dry. I gasped.

"Wait," she said at one point and moved on tiptoe to the sink, where she cupped her hands under the open tap and then filled her mouth before returning to the bed where I lay prone and emptied herself down my throat to relieve my thirst.

Tired, raw, sated, our bodies spooned, half of my cock still embedded softly inside her, killed by tenderness, we were like corpses on the hotel room bed. She dozed off. I resisted the attack of the night but could not hold on to consciousness much longer.

I fell asleep and arrived back in the twenty-first century.

The next time I travelled back in time, yet again thousands of days had elapsed. Times Square was going downhill fast.

The theatre no longer existed and was now replaced by a seedy peep show. I had to purchase ten metal chits to get in and found out that the only way of spending them was to walk in to one of the dozens of narrow private cabins and feed the box on the far wall. At which point, a metal blind would rise revealing a thick glass rectangular window behind which a woman would be either stripping or already in the process of touching herself intimately or even stuffing a dildo into herself. Occasionally, a customer in a nearby cabin would slide a note under the glass partition where a space had been created for this process and would be treated to an intimate close-up that bordered on gynaecology.

Burlesque felt like several centuries away. This was sex at its most vulgar and humiliating.

I was on my last chit when a new performer made her way from a side passage onto the mini-stage that was surrounded by the exiguous cabins and their glass windows.

I recognized Anais.

She looked tired, wan, sadder than ever.

From behind the glass, I waved, hoping she would recognize me.

She did not. Or maybe the glass window only allowed vision one-way.

I waved again, mouthing "It's me . . ."

She would not hear me.

Anais wiggled her bum against the mirror but when I slipped no note through the thin gap she swiftly moved on to the next adjacent window. A ten dollar bill was pushed through to her which she grabbed; she held her ear to the partition and listened to the customer's request, nodded and leant back to the performing platform where she had left a large Strand tote bag from which she pulled out an oversize sex toy in the shape of a bee-stung cock. As she brought the object down towards her opening, the metal window lowered itself. I was out of tokens.

I rushed back to the lone attendant on duty and changed another twenty dollars into tokens but by the time I returned every single cabin was occupied. When there finally was a vacant one and I'd fed the damn mechanism, it was another girl behind the glass, a small titless blonde who looked as if she had just come off the street on a school day. Her cunt was shaved and pierced and a rose tattoo peered at me just above the nipple of her left breast.

I realized the cabin I was now in was the one which had housed the man who had previously slipped the ten dollar tip to Anais to pleasure herself for his gratification. I looked down. The floor beneath my loafers was still wet from his ejaculation.

I walked towards the Port Authority Bus Terminal at the other end of 42nd Street and was sick.

Only three days later, I was back on Times Square and everything had gone to seed. Drug dealers were on every corner, half the cinemas and shop fronts were boarded up, and derelicts and panhandlers outnumbered the tourists.

The peep show that had once been the burlesque theatre had changed its name and appearance again and now advertised "Live Sex".

Somehow I knew what to expect, but still paid the entrance fee, hoping against hope that the inevitable would not occur.

There was a bed on a raised platform and a crowd of guys pressed up against the improvised stage. I managed to make my way nearer as some of the men gradually peeled back and left. On the bed a couple was fucking, the woman's legs raised high in the air supported by the man's shoulders and the stud was positioned so that all the spectators had a clear view of his cock moving in and out of the woman's vaginal aperture.

The bed creaked but neither of the performers made a sound, mechanically going through the motions. It absurdly occurred to me how long they could actually go on screwing for the crowd, and how the guy could stay hard semi-permanently, when the man and the woman finally separated and, wordlessly, rose from the bed and walked away into dark area. The crowd shuffled and I was able to move to the front. Evidently, the couple or another were soon to return as the men stayed there waiting.

And the next live sexers appeared.

The man was a monstrously tall black man, with a grey towel draped across his midriff. He stood himself at the front of the bed with his back to us voyeurs and pulled the towel away. He must have been particularly big in the trouser department as a few men standing on the sides and granted a better view whistled softly in approval.

An instant later, his partner made her way to the bed.

Anais.

Now visibly a decade or so at least older than when I had first seen her in what was now for me the Golden Age of burlesque.

Her skin was still terribly white, but no longer shone with that inner light that had so struck me before. She had no towel, and moved fully naked towards the bed, her shoulders slightly stooped. Indifferent to the crowd of men facing her she leaned back and lay down, then opened her legs wide. Her labia looked bruised, overused. The black guy moved closer to her, holding his massive erection in one hand and positioned himself.

Just all like those centuries ago, her eyes caught mine. Those pools of darkness were flat and dead and there was no sign of recognition. I noticed puncture marks on her thin arms as the man entered her in one movement, and she closed her eyes. He began his mighty thrusts.

I tore myself away from the crowd of men. At least I owed her that. Not to watch.

*   *   *

I've been back to Times Square many times since on my time travelling journeys. It's different now. Burlesque is but a jewelled memory, and the whole area has been gentrified, Disneyfied, cleaned up. And however much I troop up and down the area, and dip into shiny new souvenir stores and wondrous theatres with shows for the whole family, I have never come across Anais again.

Time passes faster and faster between every visit, so I assume she is likely dead by now.

And I remain the same age.

And will do so forever.

But I cannot erase the memory of Anais and how we fitted together so well and I was allowed for just a few hours to experience joy.

So, every new visit to 42nd Street just exacerbates the memory and makes me ache more. Like being caught in a loop of ever-increasing despair.

Damn, why can't I go home again to the home of burlesque?

Sebastienne

N. J. Streitberger

It wasn't until she'd had her ears pierced that Sebastienne experienced her first orgasm.

Actually, that's not quite correct.

It was *while* she was having her ears pierced that she came, jolting and jumping in the chair.

The girl at the salon stepped back immediately.

"I'm sorry. Did that hurt?"

"No, no," gasped Sebastienne. "No. Don't stop. It's fine."

"Perhaps I didn't freeze the lobe enough. I'll use more on the other one."

"No," repeated Sebastienne. "Don't bother. Just do it."

The girl looked doubtful but did as she was instructed. And Sebastienne had the second orgasm of her life.

It was the beginning of the end.

She wondered about this all the way home. Seventeen years old, fit and healthy and attractive in a sharp and foxy kind of way, Sebastienne had already racked up a fair number of conquests. She was much in demand by members of both sexes. She'd lost her virginity at fourteen to Rufus, a neighbour boy with ginger dreadlocks and flour-white skin, and had spent the intervening three years experimenting with boys, men and at least one girl.

But none of them had ever made her come. In between these brief encounters, she had played with herself, rubbed her lips raw and stuffed a variety of penis-shaped objects inside her vulva in an effort to achieve a climax, all to no avail.

She found her clitoris, discovered what she believed to be her G-spot and messed around with jellies and creams and mirrors until she was on the verge of giving up.

"Some girls don't come," said her friend Sissy. "It's tragic, but there it is. You might just be one of the unlucky ones."

She didn't see as much of Sissy after that.

And now this.

She sat on her bed and looked at the little gold sleepers in her earlobes. Wash them daily with salty water, the salon girl had told her. And turn them. She did, but nothing else occurred.

Clearly, she wanted to repeat the experience. Many, many times. Perhaps, she thought, if I can recall the sensation of having my ears pierced I might be able to make myself come.

She tried. Nothing doing.

After a while, she forgot about it. She continued with her job at the local council, where she answered phones and occasionally did front desk duty as receptionist.

Winston came up behind her when she was in the small kitchen washing up the mugs and glasses. He had tried to date her several times but she didn't fancy him. She had nothing against black guys but she made a personal vow never to go out with anyone who insisted on being called "Streets", whatever their hue.

"Hey, Seb," said Winston, planting a big hand on her derrière.

She jumped and dropped a glass which smashed in the sink. "Oh! Fuck off, 'Streets'. You asshole. Now look."

She went to pick up the pieces and stuck her palm on a shard of glass.

Winston watched in amazement as she bucked and shuddered, slamming her hips against the edge of the sink.

"Girl, you OK?" he said. He was really worried she was having a seizure of some kind.

"Ju . . . just leave me alone," she stammered. "I'll be fine in a moment. Oooooh." She let out a long groan and clung to the edge of the sink as her knees gave way.

"You better sit down, sister. I'll get the first aid kit. Oh man."

Winston left. Sebastienne looked at the blood leaking from her hand and carefully removed the piece of glass. She smiled.

It wasn't penetration she needed after all. She had to be *punctured*. Well, so be it.

In the months that followed, Sebastienne had just about everything pierced that was pierceable – ears, eyebrows, nose, nipples, lips, tongue, navel, clitoris, labia (major and minor). Eventually, the salon girl refused to perform any more.

"You're an addict," she said. "You're a piercing junkie. I'm not treating you any more. It's dangerous."

She was right. The more she got pierced the more intense her orgasms became. Apart from anything else, it was increasingly difficult for the salon girl to deal with her wriggling, gasping client. So Sebastienne started experimenting on herself. She stuck pins in her arms, needles in her thighs and a barbecue skewer through her cheek. She emptied a box of drawing pins on the kitchen floor and walked barefoot over them, setting up a chain reaction of multiple orgasms that almost put her in a coma.

She was no longer asked to work in the reception area. She was kept in the back offices, out of public view, answering phones and shifting and copying computer files. You look too scary, they said. You'll put people off.

She didn't care. She craved that incredible sensation on a daily basis, in spite of the fact that her skin had started to blister and suppurate in some patches. Even Winston stopped bothering her.

Then she discovered acupuncture.

Dr Huang looked at her dubiously. "So much metal," he said, scrutinizing her face. "Not good for blood."

"Yeah, well," said Sebastienne. "I've got a back problem. I'm told you can help me."

"Hmmm. Maybe," said Dr Huang.

He told her to take off her top and lie face down on the treatment table. He examined her with light and delicate fingers.

"Where pain?" he asked, puzzlement threading his voice.

"Uh, just there, near the bottom."

He leaned a palm on the base of her spine. "Where, here?"

"Yeah, yeah, around there."

"Big pain or little pain?"

"Sort of in-between."

"OK. We try."

As he began to insert the needles along her spine, she felt that roiling, electric heat spread out from her loins along her inner thighs and upwards through her vitals until it reached her extremities. Her nipples sprang out, trying to force themselves into the leather of the couch. Helpless in the grip of a massive multi-dimensional orgasm, she felt her insides slide away like lava along the side of a volcano. Her synapses snapped and popped as a part of herself separated out and floated away towards the ceiling.

Somehow, she could see herself from above, stretched out luxuriously on the upholstered table, as Dr Huang carefully inserted a row of needles along one side of her spine and then the other. Her hips swayed and rolled, her hands gripped the edge of the couch above her head as she came over and over again.

This is it, she thought. I'm a goner. I'm never coming back from this.

She continued to watch, fascinated, as Dr Huang stepped back to view the spectacle. Satisfied that she was on another plane of consciousness, he took her by the hips and pulled her gently to the edge of the table and placed her feet on the floor. He pulled down her knickers and opened her thighs. Unzipping his trousers, he sank his slim, stiff cock inside her cunt, gently kneading her buttocks as he fucked her, a huge smile on his otherwise inscrutable face.

Dreamily, she watched as he pulled out of her and placed his cock, slick and shiny from her fluids, in the cleft of her buttocks. He squeezed her flesh around him and thrust lightly, the dark pink tip of his penis protruding from the top of her arse like a tongue.

A moment or two later, she saw the fluid spurt and land in a delicate puddle at the base of her spine. He withdrew, tucked himself away, pulled up his trousers and delicately rubbed his ejaculate into the skin between the needles. Then, showing a strength that belied his size, he pushed her back onto the table and into her original position. All this she observed in her dream state from her position several feet above. She shut her eyes.

She opened them to find that Dr Huang was shaking her gently, calling to her. "Wake up, lady. Wake up! Session is over. You must go now please."

She sat up, yawned and looked at him as she did up her brassiere and pulled on her T-shirt.

"So?" She smiled crookedly at him. "Am I cured?"

"Yes. No problem now. I put on special cream while you were asleep. Very beneficial. Go deep inside. Good for all ailments."

"Well, thank you very much," she said.

"No need come back any more. All fine now."

She made a moue of disappointment. "Oh, I was hoping to come back next week. For a follow-up session. You know."

"No. No need. No come back here. All cured."

As she left, she winked at him. He locked the door behind her.

Her encounter with the acupuncturist left her feeling satisfied for several days afterwards. It had removed the desperate need for puncturing herself, to feel the electrical charge of her orgasm. She was replete, happy.

But something had changed.

As the post-orgasmic elation wore off and she descended from a plateau of satisfaction to the rough and rocky valley of need, she began piercing herself again. Only this time nothing happened. She tried needles, progressing up to skewers and, once, a boning knife. The slight frisson that she felt as the blade entered her flesh did hardly more than tickle her; the deep-seated orgasm she was expecting eluded her entirely.

She began to panic. Perhaps it had been a passing phase; perhaps her sexual metabolism had somehow shifted into another gear. The problem was, how to locate it again? How to recapture that blinding sense of self-fulfilment that she had been experiencing?

She tried to make another appointment with Dr Huang only to discover that he'd gone back to China. She tried sex again. Nothing. At work she became quiet and submissive. It was as if she had maxed out her orgasm credit.

Sissy was no help at all.

"Count yourself lucky," she said, after Sebastienne had revealed all. "You've had better orgasms than most girls get in a lifetime. And you're still alive to remember them."

"But what am I going to do now?" she wailed.

"Get help," said Sissy. "You are the sickest puppy I know."

She took to cruising Internet sites in the hope of finding something, or someone, to help. She flirted with practitioners of vampirism and dangerous DIY but the prospect of being bitten or drilled failed to arouse her interest. She plunged deeper, locating forbidden sites that lay, cloaked by elliptical codes, in the subterranean recesses of the web.

Then, just as all seemed lost, she came across a site that sent the blood gushing into her loins. With the utmost caution and the determination born of desperation she began a protracted negotiation.

The forest was dark and earthy. Moonlight threaded the air and illuminated a small clearing deep in its heart. She stood calm and naked in front of a tree, waiting in delicious anticipation. Weeks earlier, she had removed all of her studs and rings as part of the purification process. She had packaged them carefully and sent them to a PO Box number as instructed. They were to be melted down and reformed into something new; something that formed part of the ritual.

The figure was dressed in black, with a black hood and a mask covering his face. All this was understood, had been agreed. Only his eyes, which bore into her like blue steel, were visible. He gripped her shoulders and pushed her against the tree. Above her, a rope was suspended from a branch. He pulled it down and tied her wrists together, pulling on the rope until her arms were raised above her head. Helpless, she lay against the rough bark of the tree, exulting in the sensation of absolute surrender. Pulled taut by the rope, her breasts jutted forward, the nipples engorged to bursting point. Her thighs were slightly parted and she felt something warm and liquid slide down the inside of her thigh.

The man turned and walked back to the edge of the clearing. She watched as he bent down and opened a long black case and removed what was inside. She licked her lips as he positioned himself in front of her, drawing his arm back to his shoulder. She gasped as he let fly and the missile streaked towards her.

She screamed in ecstasy as the first arrow struck her tender flesh and embedded itself deep within her, unleashing the dark sin of her being. Punctured over and over again by the shafts, barbed with her own silver, her orgasm rushed through her like a derailed locomotive. She soared upwards, beyond pain, beyond time, beyond the frontiers of pleasure.

And, this time, she reached the heights from which there was no returning.

The Painted Doll

M. Christian

Watch her walk, Claire thought. Note her disciplined stride. Notice her carefully controlled pace. Observe the finely machined stride. Witness her gracefully gliding movements.

Watch her walk, Claire thought. See her stroll along, even and sure, stable and keenly balanced. Across the black ink asphalt of the newly paved Qui Dan Road, up and onto the eternally fractured pavement of the sidewalk, and then among, between, through, and then past the bellowing hawkers, rickety stalls, lazily fanning merchants, and rushing buyers of another corner market.

Watch her walk, Claire thought. Silk dress as ghostly as a half-finished thought, rarer than a honestly cool breeze; satin splashing down like water from inordinately high fall; couture as elegant as only a kimono could be – and as alien as one moving along Qui Dan Road.

Watch her walk, Claire thought. The puzzle paused, held back by the impact of her, released as she passes. A furrow of brow, a scratching of head, a question: did I see what? Am I dreaming? Is she real?

The woman continued to think about herself, about her walking, a flawless jewel, a perfect image, a carefully crafted ideal.

Watch her walk, Claire thought: *Is she real?*

Qui Dan Road to the High Street, a stumble of crisp British in a city of fish sauce and MSG. The change didn't alter her steps, modify her movements.

Beautiful? Oh, yes: without doubt, without a question. The splendor of a rose, the loveliness of an orchid. The kimono is flawless, as is the china white of her immaculately applied artificial complexion. As she walks, hearts stop then race. As she walks, heads twist, eyes widen. As she walks, breaths are hissed in, sighed out.

Beautiful? Oh, yes: without doubt, without a question. But she is a knife-edged rose, a razor sharp orchid. Her stride is mechanically perfect, as is her perfectly vertical posture. Their hearts might race, their heads may twist, their eyes certainly widen, their breaths absolutely hiss in and hiss out, but as she steps nearer they instead step back. As she walks, they avert their eyes. As she walks, they pull themselves in.

The woman walking down the High Street feels them watching her, their glances furtive tickles, their quick stares barely felt hooks out of the corners of her always forward facing eyes. Passing a bookseller – tight fans of rough tan paper with lurid Cantonese chops on their glistening plastic covers hung in sagging arcs of cord – a reflection was revealed to her, a caught sight of what they were seeing.

But not what they were thinking. But she knew, nevertheless: each of them lost in illusions and fantasies as carefully crafted as her rouge, as flawlessly presented as the *mae migoro* and *ushiro migoro* of her kimono, as immaculately assembled as her performance:

She's a dragon, some might think: the cruelty of a reptile, the flawlessness of a myth. You may approach her, with bravery beyond that of any battlefield, speaking with a stammer and a twitch, and if you were fortunate beyond your worth she'd slow, pause, turn with prudently measured grace, deeming your presence not completely disgusting. With that look, at that glance, would be a flickering forked tongue of cruel invitation, a scintillating promise of peaked breasts topped with fist-tight nipples, a belly steel plate flat and firm, a behind curving out in twin clenches of muscular intensity, thighs sculpted by rigid posture, and between them a scented valley of ruby silk.

But first, a minuscule task. But first, an all but insignificant request: to firmly stand guard for her honor and dignity; to fetch a inestimable gem, an incalculable jewel, or just a unexceptional sticky-sweet pastry; to perform for her a melody of praise, or a stammering litany of desperate worth; or a quick athletic demonstration of physical merit; or become for her an avenging knight, a battle to defend her honor against some heinous offense.

A minuscule task. An insignificant request. Accepted without doubt or hesitation, the reward a slow curl at the corner of her cold stone face, a bow of gratitude, and a bright flash of serpentine green eyes. Totally entranced by her, completely captured by her, the dragon would then reveal the metaphorical points of venomous teeth, sinking the illusion of her love deep into the shaft of your encouraged penis by showing you the true face of her cruelty.

The prize was yours but the tasks were actually anything but minuscule, not at all insignificant: firmly stand guard for her honor and dignity – *for a year*; fetch a inestimable gem, an incalculable jewel, or just a unexceptional sticky-sweet pastry – *from a thousand miles away*; perform for her a melody of praise, or a stammering litany of desperate worth – *perfectly, without the tiniest flaw*; a quick athletic demonstration of physical merit – *unattainable by even the greatest athlete*; or become for her an avenging knight, a battle to defend her honor against some heinous offense – *in combat against a killing machine*.

And so the dragon passes by, a smile on her cold-blooded face. No one approaches her, no one is willing to come near. And so they live, by letting her just walk by.

She's a doll, some might think: a porcelain figure, an ivory representation. Beneath the silks and satins would be a body as perfect as only a master artisan could create. Breasts both delicate and womanly, nipples as delicate as rosebuds, a belly with an ideal swell, hands with the grace of ten Noh performers, calves a perfect taper, thighs an entrancing form, back a clean surface of alabaster, neck a musical curve, feet delicate and precious, a behind highlighted with sacral dimples, and a female cleft that was a pale oyster and a tiny pink pearl.

Like a doll, she would belong to whoever buys her. Cash, credit, merchandise – the right amount and the woman would instead walk behind, following her owner towards palace or hovel, both with the same unmoving mask of her face.

Palace or hovel, she would walk in the door, standing still and quiet with an item's posture. Maybe she'd look better in the living room window, where the afternoon would bathe her in golden light? Or perhaps she'd be better exhibited in the bedroom, where her kimono could be removed like one from a real woman?

Yes, the bedroom. That was where she would be best displayed. Moving past, it was clear in their eyes, the allure of her perfect submission. A thing. An object. A piece of feminine sculpture. Unable to disagree, unable to refuse, bendable in all kinds of imaginative ways. From behind, cock sliding between her cool ivory cheeks. Face to face, marble breasts for unimpeded kiss, licks, and sucks. On top, her tight thighs spread apart and welcoming upward thrusts. Anything you wanted, anytime you wanted.

Desire was a rippling wave behind her, a heat distortion in the warm city air. It was obvious in their eyes that there, in her, was a world without "no", a land without complaint, a woman without a soul.

Then they stopped, that wave of erections and licked dry lips chilled with a slap of frigid revelation. Stepping back with the rest of the crowd, these men retreated from the precise rhythm of her steps, with whimpering fear in their wide eyes, their shaking heads.

Ivory arms, marble legs, alabaster body: inflexible, unfeeling, stiff, unbending, unyielding, and – worst of all – *cold*. With her you'd never hear "no," never be refused, never be denied, but you'd also never hear the beat of her heart, the music of her voice, the chimes of her laughter, the moans and screams of her pleasure. You'd perform with her your deepest, darkest, most subterranean – and all she would do would be to look at you with inscrutably glass eyes.

She's a tiger, some might think: a beast with the stripes of a traditional Japanese dress. Hidden beneath her Asian camouflage was a woman's body, exercised into an extension of her erotic drive. Where other women had euphemisms and poetic alliterations, she had simple, direct, and powerful words to describe herself. Where other women had bosoms, she had tits of ideal jiggle and sway, covered in thrilling smooth skin. Where other women had nipples, she had a pair of dark brown direct connections to her clit. Where other women had posteriors, she had two plush muscular globes that clenched and released with the beating heat of her clit. Where other women had sexes, she had a demanding, insistent cunt.

To see and handle these differences would be more fortune than seduction. You did not take the tiger to dinner and slip hot words between dessert and coffee. You did not lay flowers at the feet of this hot-blooded woman within the cool disguise of a geisha. You did not whisper poetry into the shell-like ear of this elegantly robed bitch.

There was no way to make her do anything, no way to slyly allure or simply trick her into a private room, no way to seduce her. The only thing anyone could do was to stand within the range of that sweeping predatory glance and hope that her eyes would positively estimate your worth as a device for her pleasure. Then, and only then, would her red-painted lips open ever-so, more than a whisper but less than full voice, and speak the one word you'd prayed to hear: "Come."

Behind her, pulled along by her insatiable need, you would follow. It wouldn't be a long journey, for her cunt has a very short attention span. Cheap hotel on the next street, expensive one even closer by, or just the nearest fetid and slimy alley – whatever was within range.

Patience was for ladies. Hesitation was for women. Tigers – even ones hidden within silks and satins – had no need for foreplay, patience, or hesitation. They wanted, so they took.

And if you were lucky, she would take you. Hands down to your cock, a squeezing judgment for size and firmness. Lips to yours, a tongue penetrating your mouth, an attacking kiss wanting nothing of you but to be kindling to her roaring heat.

On her knees, she would take you. But only because that was what she wanted. Your come was not expected or important. A flesh device to penetrate an orifice, you would be used until she was bored and ready to move onto other penetrations of other orifices.

Or perhaps she'd require something else. Falling back, satin fabric pulled roughly aside, she might bare an insistent slickness, the gleaming lips and fast-beating clit, and demand your service. Failure to accept or in performance too terrible to contemplate.

At the end, your cock would be needed: hard, strong, and fast – nothing else important to her. Burning hot, insanely wet, you'd enter and execute the task she'd ordered, working until her screams tore at your ears and her nails scratched along your back.

Then that would be it. Humiliating? Being reduced to only a device for someone's pleasure usually is. But the blistering heat of her, the ferocious need of her cunt would put – and keep – a smile on your sweaty face.

But – and again men standing step back, retreat in shivering dread when she walks back – one does not ever tame a tiger, even after it is fed. Who knows what she might hunger for after? Meat, blood, flesh, dignity, any number of horrible violations – any of them within her grasp, and you too exhausted to resist.

Tigers are wild things, after all: enjoyable to watch in zoos, penned behind restraining bars, but far too bloodthirsty in bed.

She's a machine, some might think: isn't it wonderful what they're doing with shape memory alloys, mnemetic plastics, optical fibers, and conductive polymers? Absolutely wonderful things coming out of Japan, India, the Wilding, and the young turks of the École Polytechnique, these days. Look up and there are dragonflies pausing for location fixes before darting off at near-invisible speeds, packages clutched under their iridescent fuselages. Look down and there are myriad scurrying mechanisms trailing polished tracks of perfumed cleanliness through the city's persistent grime. Look around and there are cinematics lazily scrolling across a lady's fluttering fan, posters for the newest Malaysian blockbuster cycling through tantalizing glimpses of furious martial arts and stiffly chaste duets, the hushed commuting fuel-cell and ethanol traffic, and the softly creaking carbon fibers of a prosthetic hand on a crumble-faced veteran of the Chinese genocide as he lays down a mah-jongg tile.

Look at her and you might see a device as carefully machined as a German car, a Swiss watch, a Japanese entertainment center, Indian software, or an African running shoe: breasts as ideal and resilient as silicone, skin of perfectly cured plastic, muscles as precise and strong as actuators, a genital-pleasuring interface between her thighs, a mouth with the same technology.

It was a safe bet that without her protective kimono covering, the pseudo-body of hers was as superlative as a supermodel, as sensuous as a Playmate of whatever month, as adept as an amalgamation of every courtesan who'd ever lived, as refined and machined as her manufacturers could make her.

Movement like the architecture in fine software, presence as authoritative as graceful as a jet fighter, skin as smooth as the polish on a fresh-from-the-factory-floor Ferrari, she passed by – and with her passing the tracking of lust and greed in the eyes of the male crowd, and sour envy on the faces of everyone else.

Here was the best of both of a man's world: the twin allures of a clever device together with a well-articulated woman – or, to be more specific, as those men revealed so obviously, "coupled" together, a mating between flesh and sex and advanced technology and power. Purchasing this – or simply leasing with an option to do the same – and putting it in the garage or the bedroom, would mean not just a product but also a woman of every dream, not just a sex partner but also a sophisticated piece of fine engineering.

But that wasn't all. Look at them watching her move by. Lust was there, both for machine as well as woman, but there was also the dawning realization that there could be even *more* there: things that squeezed, buzzed, vibrated, hummed, heated, cooled, swirled, oscillated, tingled, and more, more, more so much more.

But then they pulled away, out of her way, out of her traffic, their fantasies dropping behind to be passed by the rushing acceleration of a nightmare, the barreling truck of a terrifying understanding.

Engineering, went their minds as they retreated, is fine and good, stimulating and thrilling. Sex, they thought as they ran away from her, is fantastic and wonderful. But to fuck a machine, to be intimate with gears and cogs, synthetics and electricity, hydraulics and radiators, could be good, but also could be like thrusting into a meshing, tearing, burning, shocking, scalding, blistering industrial accident.

Dragon, Doll, Tiger or Machine she moved along the High Street, with every step Claire thought: *Watch her walk.*

They don't know what *she is,* she thought, *not really.* They may have guesses, suppositions, fantasies, but no real knowledge. But while they can't see what she is exactly, they can clearly see what she isn't: cautious, shy, withdrawn, clumsy, mathematical, or terrified.

They certainly don't know her name, though some of them hearing it might inhale with a slow hiss, connecting "Domino," the famous – infamous – erotist, to the woman walking down the High Street with a hushed, barely whispered "So that's her."

Domino walked, traveling through the city, leaving in her wake puzzlement and fear, lust and wonder. From one avenue to another she moved, heading away from the twists and turns of old town towards the new, leaving behind frying fish and caterwauls of merchants for gleaming steel and arcing high-stress ceramics: the previous behind, the imminent ahead – even though what was back there in the years before would be with her no matter how many steps she made into the future.

Watch her walk, Claire thought: watch Domino the erotist stroll through the city.

Watch her walk, she also thought: *and never see me.*

Chocolate Girl

Sam Jayne

She was eating chocolate; a family-sized bar that would no doubt take hours to burn off at the gym. Of course, this was of no concern to me. I watched in awe as she sucked provocatively on a bitten-off chunk of the sugary snack, allowing her eyelids to droop as the milky flavour flooded her mouth, the chocolate melting. I'd never witnessed such beauty before. It was doubtful I ever would again. This woman was my dream, everything I'd ever wished for, and she was here to see me.

"A box of marshmallows, please," she demanded, a flirtatious edge to her voice. "And" – she paused for a moment – "do you have any whipping cream?"

My eyes widened and I cursed them silently. Really I should have answered immediately, controlled myself and demonstrated my professionalism, but such composure was out of the question. My head flooded with thoughts of the fluffy cream on her silky body, her sweet tooth gently nibbling my ear. I shuddered. Whipping cream. And marshmallows.

The chocolate girl smiled. She had caramel skin, liquorice hair and bubblegum lips. Despite her love of candy, she somehow maintained a perfect figure; slim but still shapely. Her breasts bulged in the confinements of her black T-shirt, which sported the cheeky slogan, "Bite Me!", emblazoned across her chest in pink lettering. She was in her mid twenties, enigmatic and seemingly wise to the world. I wanted her badly.

"Cat got your tongue?" She grinned, reaching over the counter top to take my hand.

Bonbon's Sweets was a quiet shop, never attracting many customers. Since the government had issued out severe warnings about the effects of eating junk food, parents were less willing to allow their children to indulge in so much confectionery. Looking at the woman before me now, I could see no evidence of the dire consequences of sweets, but I had to admit, the chocolate girl was undoubtedly an exception.

Leading me away from my safety zone behind the till, the woman moved towards the shop door, turning the sign around to declare Bonbon's closed. The manager would be irate should he ever find out, but this fleeting thought made no impression on me, and disappeared to the back of my mind as quickly as it had arisen. The girl snaked her arms around my waist, pulling me closer to her warm flesh. Softly, she massaged the back of my neck with her moist lips, kissing me gently, but with longing.

"You're stiff," she stated, and I cleared my throat in embarrassment. It was true, my whole body was stiff, yearning to be freed from its aching self.

She unbuttoned my shirt and twisted a clump of my short chest hair around the tip of her left pinkie. Her hands were cool, mine clammy, and I struggled with the zip of her tight jeans. Impatiently, she batted away my shaking fingers and pushed me forcibly into the storeroom. There she undressed quickly and fully, removing first her jeans and T-shirt, then her black, lacy underwear. Her body glowed with natural beauty.

"I like you," she told me, smiling at the painful bulge that was desperately trying to escape from my own trousers. She pulled over a wooden chair and instructed me to sit on it. I willingly complied, squirming in my seat as anticipation grew. Her delicate hands stroked my crotch, which burned with desire. Finally, she unzipped me, and my penis poked out of the opening, defying the material of my boxer shorts.

She tugged at both items of clothing, and I rose from my seat a little to assist her in this quest. Only when the garments were bunched around my ankles did she appear sufficiently satisfied. As I sat back down, she took my throbbing erection in her right hand and began to work my cock, rubbing at the shaft until my breathing became heavy and rapid. She moved with expert precision, sporadically dropping lower to knead my testicles. With her left hand, she gently fingered her clit, emanating the unmistakable heat of arousal. I groaned as the threat of climax loomed, partly desiring the rush of relief, and partly fearing the premature end of the session.

But my worry was needless. Ejaculation at this time wasn't to be. Instead she took a short break, biting off another chunk of chocolate from her half-eaten bar as she studied my exposed body. I stared back at her, unsure of whether I should be contributing to the intimacy, or if I should merely remain seated and await further instruction.

"I enjoy restraining men," she confided, "but we appear to have a distinct lack of suitable restraints."

The young woman examined our surroundings. Boxes of chocolate drops, jelly beans and boiled sweets lined the wooded shelves. Her eyes twinkled in the dim light, her buttocks tensing as she struggled to retrieve a colourful box located on the highest shelf behind her.

"Unfortunately, Strawberry Bootlaces are not very strong, but they'll do. I suppose you'll just have to be obedient."

The chocolate girl began to bind my wrists and ankles to the chair using the lengths of fruit-flavoured rope. Once this task had been completed, she returned her attention to my groin, squeezing my balls much harder than before. The feeling was not unpleasant, but surprising, and caused me to jerk forward in my chair. She seemed pleased with this reaction, and repeated the process even more forcibly. This time I experienced a shot of pain, and cried out, much to her amusement.

"I'm glad that hurts you," she declared, running her fingers, gently now, through my pubic hair. "Would you like more?"

"I would . . . Mistress," I replied, after a slight pause. Should I call her Mistress?

Apparently not.

The girl clutched my testicles until they bulged painfully between her fingers. "Call me . . . Miss Truffle," she insisted.

I gasped and spluttered. "Yes, Miss Truffle."

"Good. That's good."

Miss Truffle straddled my thighs, resting her pert bottom on the caps of my knees and propelling her firm, erect-nippled breasts towards my chest. Slowly, she fed my rigid penis inside her. Thrusting my hips, I drove my cock deep into her moist vagina, gasping and moaning at the sensations that overwhelmed me. Her own grunts of pleasure joined the chorus, and she appeared to hold her breath as the first waves of orgasm washed over her. She shuddered in delight, still rocking on my thighs, and kissed my lips passionately, pushing her tongue into my mouth.

I was now drawing breath in quick succession, and was seconds away from releasing my load when she removed my cock from her body and stood before me, grinning defiantly.

"Please," I gasped, writhing in my chair. The need to come was excruciating.

"A shop-boy should wait his turn," she told me. "After all, the customer should always come first."

Had I not been frantic with sexual frustration, I would have smiled at this joke, but in my current situation, all I could do was whimper helplessly and rub my thighs together, trying fruitlessly to bring myself off. Thankfully, however, my frenzy was short-lived. Miss Truffle sank to her knees and took the length of my cock in her mouth, sucking quickly, and flicking her tongue across the bulbous head and slit. As I called out in ecstasy, the chocolate girl gripped my balls for a final time, making my climax a mixture of orgasmic delight and acute pain. My come spurted into her mouth, and she swallowed, savouring my juice like she savoured her beloved chocolate.

Exhausted now, I sat quietly as she bit me free of the Strawberry Bootlace restraints.

"I'd like to take a packet of these home with me, if you don't mind," she said, while pulling on her clothes. "And, did you say you had some whipping cream?"

I pointed to a tub of Elmlea on the second shelf of the storeroom, then to a box of marshmallows to the left, that she had requested earlier. She scooped up her items, nodded by means of thanks, and handed me a few coins to pay for the purchases. Then she left without speaking a further word, flicking the door sign around to show "Open" as she departed. Of course, I'd have to get dressed immediately now, but just for a moment I gazed, captivated, after her.

My dream girl. My chocolate girl.

Purple Tulip

Tsaurah Litzky

I walk down a narrow, dirty alley smelling of piss, turn right, and I am in the heart of desire – the red light district in Amsterdam. I stand on Voorburgstraat on a busy Friday night and the crowd swallows me up. Men of all sizes, shapes, colors surround me. I float along carried by a testosterone wave.

To my right is the canal, on my left, in buildings centuries old, in a string of windows glittering with light, a garden of earthly pleasures unfolds.

A few men stand in front of a window watching a voluptuous older woman dressed like a gypsy, a flowered scarf wound round her head. She gathers the front of her full skirt up with one hand to reveal tattered black fishnet stockings held up by baby blue garters that cut into her swarthy legs. With her other hand, she plunges a big red rubber cock in and out between her thighs. She leers, grimaces, sticks out her tongue. The men whistle and clap as I move on.

In the next window, a woman in a gray rubber cat suit stands with her back to the street. A big, circle had been cut out of the seat of the pants exposing her voluminous, pale ass. Her hands behind her, her fingers spread her butt cheeks, the swollen, ruby bud of her anus pulled open. She flexes her hips in rhythm to a song only she can hear, making her gaping asshole open and close.

"Do you think we can both fit in there, mate?" the man beside me asks his friend.

"Nah," says the friend. "My Churchill is so big, I'd crowd you out."

The first time I was in Amsterdam, May 2001, America was a respected world power. I believed the prosperity we enjoyed would continue to grow. Now everything is different. My country is hated all over the world, our economy bankrupt by war. At least, here in Amsterdam, Voorburgstraat appears unchanged, an enduring testament to fair market exchange and the everlasting need of skin for skin.

On my last visit, I'd head for this street in the evenings. I'd walk up and down, turned on by the costumes, the artifice, the blatant aura of sex.

Then I met Jan and we were together until I left.

Jan was an overweight accountant I met in a bar. His hands were grimy, his fingernails stained with black ink, but his chubby, uncut cock was so practiced. He made me come again and again, then he'd pull out, and shoot between my breasts. He liked to rub his creamy sperm all over my torso. It worked like a magic potion, erasing the memories of my ex-husband I still carried deep within my flesh.

One time, Jan took me to a dim courtyard guarded by a tarnished statue of Spinoza. The women in the windows here were all freaks. One was a glistening albino, totally hairless, not a blemish anywhere on her skin. She wore a cowboy hat on her bald head. Another woman looked like Larry King. She even wore thick eyeglasses with a dark frame. She had on men's trousers but was nude from the waist up, three pretty breasts spreading across her broad chest. Jan paused before a window in which a serene, exotic beauty sat on a footstool. She looked Indonesian, her long black hair falling to her waist. One of her arms stopped at the elbow and the left sleeve of her gauzy shirt was pinned up at the shoulder. "This is Purple Tulip," he said. "She is an old friend of mine, very nice person, so gentle. Shall we visit her?"

I could see her pendulous breasts through her top, her tiny nipples looked like licorice bits.

"No," I whispered.

Jan shrugged. "Let's go back to your hotel," he said.

A few months ago, I was invited to Amsterdam to read at a poetry festival; I phoned Jan right up. He was delighted. "Good" he said. "My wife and mistress are away. You want to stay here?"

I didn't know how I would feel when I saw him. "Nah," I said, "your harem could come back and surprise us."

"Then we'll have an orgy," he said.

"We would give you a heart attack. Forget it, I'm staying in a hotel. I'll meet you when the festival is over."

During our affair, I felt I could trust him. He was fair-minded, sensitive, never tried to get over on me. If I shivered, he would take off his jacket and put it around my shoulders before I could even say a word.

As I walk along, I wonder if he is still friends with Purple Tulip. I wonder if I could find the courtyard of freaks without him.

Deep in my thoughts, I don't realize that I'm surrounded. Several young punks, not much more than boys, are gathered in a circle around me. Their heads are shaved and they wear wife beater T-shirts. One of them also wears a pair of panty hose looped around his neck like a tie. On his arm he has a tattoo of a pig, with *Mama* inscribed beneath it.

"Looking for your husband?" he asks me. "Do you think he is shopping here?" His crew starts to laugh. "Come with us," he continues. "We can help you find him." He looms over me, smelling of pizza and cigarettes. He reaches towards me. A phalanx of beefy British men in green and white rugby shirts, cut into our little circle. I dart back out into the crowd.

"Good luck," pig boy calls after me. I hear them cackling but they don't follow me. I keep going until I find the dark alley that leads to Warmoesstraat.

Back in my hotel room, I get my hash pipe and my stash of Lebanese Red out of the night table drawer. I pull the covers over my head, hoping for sweet dreams.

★   ★   ★

Jan stands above me, naked. His huge belly hangs in folds like the Buddha's. His long cock is twice the size I remember, jutting out between his legs like another limb. He spanks me with it, little taps on my belly, my breasts. Each smack sends a current of electricity down into my hole. I want Jan to stop spanking me. I want him to plunge that thing right up into the center of my being, but he doesn't.

He teases and taps until I am writhing about like the Mad Woman of Chaillot. Then, abruptly, he does stop and steps back as Purple Tulip enters the room. Her face is lovely. All she wears is a garland of purple flowers wound round the stump of her arm. She kneels by the bed, extends her one delicate hand. Her fingers track through the forest of my pubic hair, dip into the syrupy well she finds there. I want to have her fuck me with her delicate fingers. I spread my legs as wide as I can but she draws her hand back. She slides the stump of her other arm up the top of my thigh. I can feel its warm blunt tip inching into my cunt. All of a sudden, the room fills with men, shouting, clapping their hands and stamping their feet. "Good luck, good luck," they shout; their taunting grows louder and louder into a tumultuous roar. I wake up and reach for the hash pipe I left on the bed table. I smoke until I black out.

The bells at the Alte Kirk down the street are ringing the hour. I jump out of bed. I'm supposed to meet my Jan today at ten. He is probably already waiting. My head feels stuffed with old socks, but I force myself to dress and run outside. I dash two blocks up Warmoesstraat and enter the Dam Square.

Directly in front of me, at least three stories high, stands the white stone obelisk called the Dam. It's still so early, few tourists are about, but the demonstrators are already there.

A bearded man with a megaphone is leading them as they sing "Give Peace a Chance." They are holding placards in English, Dutch, French, German. Several of them show that photo of Lynndie England with the poor man on a leash, no caption necessary. I wish I was wearing a T-shirt that said "I am Canadian." I dart through the demonstrators quickly, my head down. I take the narrow street that cuts into the south end of the square. I pass a shop window filled with pipes, bongs, brass hookahs and hookahs set with shining gems. Next to this store is Jan's favorite café.

A couple is eating croissants at the first table. Seated behind them at the second table is Jan, but a bigger Jan. He has gained so much weight; his chair is pushed back from the table to accommodate his bulging stomach. He rises, his belly knocking over the glass of water in front of him, but he is impervious. He steps forward, grabs me, kisses me smack on the lips. I feel like there is a giant marshmallow between us, but his mouth is dry and his lips as hot as I remember.

"I'm so happy to see you. You look beautiful, like a movie star, sit down," he says. I sit and he sits beside me and takes my hand. His palms are moist and there are beads of sweat on his forehead. "There's more of you," I say. "What happened, did you buy a candy store or become friends with a South American drug lord?"

"Do you think I am stupid?" he asks, "If you mean cocaine, that's a bad drug. I always avoid it. I developed a thyroid problem. It runs in my family. Now there is more of me to love. You want a hot chocolate?" he asks. "All right," I say.

"How was the festival? Did you get a big audience for your reading?" he wants to know. He listens as I talk. His hands are clean and he even had a manicure. He wears a fine gray silk shirt and, despite his bulk, looks quite distinguished, like a young Orson Welles. Our hot chocolates arrive piled with thick whipped cream. Mine tastes so sweet. I think of Jan shooting his rich come all over my breasts. He moves his leg against mine under the table. "I hope you still find me attractive. I hope this," he says, patting his stomach, "doesn't discourage you."

"No," I say, "I'll still think you're cute even if you get big as an elephant."

"Good," he says, grinning. "Maybe later I will let you rub my trunk."

"Do you still see Purple Tulip? Are you still friends?" I ask. "Does she still do the same job?"

"Yes to all three," Jan answers. "You see, our mothers know each other since high school. Maybe you are ready to visit her?"

"Maybe," I say in a whisper. Suddenly I feel embarrassed. I change the subject, mention the demonstrators in Dam Square.

Jan's expression darkens. "What do you expect when you go to war for oil, when you elect a liar for a President?" His voice rises. "Now he is a murderer, a war criminal. He should be assassinated."

"Whoa, whoa," I reply. "We didn't elect him. The Supreme Court gave him the election."

"Exactly," he cries, almost yelling now, "and you Americans sat around watching football. Why not rise up, demonstrate, stop paying taxes?"

I knew how right he was but I didn't want to get into a fight with him. "I agree," I said, "but who could have anticipated what was happening? We were in shock."

"Fools," he says. He grabs the cup in front of him and drinks his chocolate down in one gulp, leaving specks of whipped cream around his mouth.

"I feel worse than you do, believe me," I say. "Let's try to keep our spirits up. Shall we smoke?" He doesn't answer, just sits there, fuming.

Finally, he looks up, gives me half a smile. "Okay," he says, "we will change perspective." He calls the waiter to bring over the menu. "Will it be hashish or marijuana?" he asks. We decide on Blue Mountain Thai Stick. I roll a perfect oval joint.

Jan moves his chair closer to mine, lights the joint with the match from the pack on the table. He holds the spliff first to my lips then to his. He puts one heavy hand on my knee. Blue smoke envelops us and then we are walking on a blue beach beside a blue ocean. Jan kneels in front of me, pulls my skirt up and my panties down. He cups my ass in his hands, and pulls me closer. He parts my cunt hair with his blue tongue, traces a path to the top of my slit, finds my clit, which is already hard as a pearl. He sucks and sucks it; his hands cradle my ass as gentle blue waves wash about us. When I come, I cry blue tears.

I wipe the salty brine from my eyes and then I am back with Jan at our table. My hand is inside Jan's trousers, while his hand has found its way beneath my skirt. The waiter and the man who tends the counter in the back are chatting quietly. A few tables away two priests share a hash pipe. Jan leans over, kisses me on the forehead.

"You want to come to my place tonight?" he asks.

"Oh, yes," I say.

Later, back in my room, I put on a short skirt so Jan can admire my legs and a scoop neck blouse so he can see the tops of my breasts. I hear a slurred male voice right outside my door say, "She told me I was the best fuck she ever had, the best fuck in her whole life. She asked me, please, please, come back again tonight."

I walk up to Central Station and take the number eleven bus to Jan's flat in Java Plein. I knock on Jan's door.

He opens it after a few minutes, naked except for a big white towel knotted around his waist. He is so heavy he looks ready to tip over and roll around the floor like a top. I tell myself to think positive. He is a nice man. I can trust him.

"Come in, come in," he says. "I got back from my office late. I was in the shower. Pardon my formal attire." I follow him into his living room, a pleasant oasis filled with plants and antiques.

"Sit down," he says. "I will bring drinks." Then he goes into the kitchen.

I sit on the big maroon sofa and put my bag on the coffee table in front of me.

Jan returns, carrying a tray holding a bottle of wine, two glasses, a dish piled with black olives. He puts the tray on the coffee table.

"I remember you like a Riesling," he says as he pours me a glass.

"Now for music, some Brubeck?" he asks, but doesn't give me a chance to answer, just slips the disk into the CD player and goes back down the hall to his bedroom.

He returns wearing a pair of beige trousers and a white shirt big as a tent. He is holding a small foil wrapped package in his hand.

"You look so lovely sitting there," he says, "like a little flower, a daisy." I didn't like being compared to a daisy, such a placid Pollyanna flower.

He sinks down beside me and puts the foil packet on the coffee table.

"Now," he says, "since we haven't seen each other in so long, a special celebration is in order. I got for us some of our famous Amsterdam Space cake."

Jan unwraps the cake from the foil. "Here," he says, breaking off a piece and holding it to my lips. "Have a taste."

It tastes like the honey cake my grandmother used to bake on Rosh Hashanah, sweet and mealy. We feed the cake to each other bit-by-bit, washing it down with wine. Jan puts his roly-poly arm along the back of the couch. I nest into his body, unbutton his shirt. A great, big cloud, all white and puffy falls out. It grows, surrounding my face, my whole body like a soft cushion. I float within this billowing white; Jan is there too, his clothes gone. We are suspended in the cloud, floating together. Jan drifts below me. I reach out to him and my fingers fall on his swollen club. It grows larger and larger until it just pops out of my hand. I can feel the heat of it moving across my ass as it grows even hotter, like a desert wind, a sirocco. The pointy tip jabs into my crack. I pull away, my butt hole contracting, closing. The last time we tried this, Jan lubed me up with half a stick of margarine, and even though I was no stranger to back-door sex, I started to bleed. We had to stop.

Now, Jan reaches up to my face, he has a capsule in his hand and he breaks it right under my nose.

"Breathe in, breathe deep," he says and then his huge joint slides into me. I hear a tearing sound, and feel a tingling sensation but no pain. As he moves deeper into my belly, Jan keeps murmuring something in my ear. I strain to hear him. "I fuck you in the ass, America," he whispers.

Even in my spacey state, I can't believe what he is saying. "What was that? What did you say?" I ask him.

"Fuck you, America, fuck you America," he hisses, pumping harder and harder. Now, I can feel him hurting me. I smell blood. I try to pull my body away but cannot move. I am skewered on a burning spit. His teeth are sharp on my neck and then he bites down, piercing my skin. I scream as he shoots bolts of fire into me. There are searing flames everywhere; every cell in my body is consumed and then it is dark.

When I open my eyes, my head is on Jan's leg. He is sleeping, snoring through his nose. It sounds like he is playing the kazoo. My neck aches from where he bit me and my butt hole burns. I look down and see blood all over my thighs. I put my hand in my ass and bring it out covered with blood.

Carefully, I peel myself off him. I remember what Jan said and, briefly, wonder if I could have imagined it, but I know I did not. I'm so woozy I can barely stand but I manage to totter to the bathroom. I shut the door and sit down on the toilet.

The cool wood of the seat feels comforting against my burning flesh. I want to find a washcloth, hold it against the bleeding to make it stop. I open a drawer in the cabinet beneath the sink and see a box of talcum powder and a bottle of mouthwash. I pull out the drawer next to it and find a sandwich bag filled with little chunks of what looks like rock candy. I have seen this "candy" before; it is crack cocaine. Beside it are some plastic bags of white powder. The drawer also holds a glass pipe, a rectangular mirror, a mat knife – all you need to enter a fool's paradise.

I slam the drawer shut, so much for trust. I open the drawer below and find the cloths I am looking for. I pick one up, hoping I can grab my clothes and get out while he is still sleeping. It is already too late. Jan steps into the bathroom, grinning like a Cheshire cat.

"So," he asks, "do you like our Dutch space cake? But, my little darling, what are you doing sitting on the toilet? Meditating?"

I nod my head, unable to speak. I spread my legs and lift my body so he can see the blood coming from my ass. He is instantly solicitous; he takes the cloth from my hand, opens another drawer, gets out Mercurochrome, Band-aids.

"There," he says, after staunching the bleeding and cleaning and dressing the cut, "now you are fine." He pulls me to my feet. "I have something else for you, a surprise I know you will like." He starts pulling me down the hall towards his bedroom.

"Wait," I say, "I just remembered, I have to go back to my hotel. I have to call my father in Maryland. He's expecting my call, he's—"

Jan tightens his grip on my wrists. "You can call him from here," he says. He is stronger than I am, an iron force, and he pulls me into the bedroom.

"You will like this, trust me, it will be fun," he says.

Purple Tulip is lying on the paisley quilt that covers Jan's bed. She is naked except for the garland of purple flowers around the stump of her arm. She is reading a *Seventeen* magazine, which she puts down as we enter the room. "Hello," she says and smiles. Close up she does not look beautiful. Her skin is pocked; her eyes are blank and yellow. She is missing a front tooth and her smile is rigid as if stitched on to her face.

Jan pushes me forward from the back. "What are you afraid of?" he says. "Go to her, go say hello." I feel like I'm moving quicker than the speed of light as I whirl, duck under his arm, and rush back down the hall. He is startled, hesitates a second before he turns and starts to lumber after me. He catches his foot on the edge of the rug, trips and falls to the floor, crashing in a big puddle of flesh. I grab up my things as Jan calls out, "American cow! Coward!" But nothing he can say has the power to hurt me now. I fly out the door and down the stairs. I pause in the vestibule, pull on my clothes and shoes.

The night is clear and warm. At least, I managed to escape with only a cut-up ass. It could have been much worse. Not another soul is about, but the smell of ganja hangs in the air, mixed with something else: the scent of an exotic spice, cardamom or coriander. The strains of Klezmer music drift out of an open window. There are no stars in the sky but there is plenty of light as I walk towards the bus stop under an Amsterdam full moon.

To Dance at the Fair

Donna George Storey

Naked

Whenever I stand up to speak before an audience – be it a ballroom full of steely-eyed colleagues or the semester's first class of yawning kids – I think of Sally, and I feel strong.

Because, of course, Sally Rand – the sensation of Chicago's Century of Progress Exposition during the dark Depression years of 1933 and 1934 – stepped onto the stage wearing nothing but two ostrich feather fans and a dusting of pure white powder. As the dance progressed, she would swirl her fans, teasing the audience with a flash of nipple or a glimpse of buttock, until, at long last, she would spread her wings to reveal everything. And then, in a flash of light, she was gone, before anyone could really know – had they really seen Sally nude, or was it all an illusion?

This afternoon it was especially fitting to conjure Sally's ghost as I took the podium. I was giving a paper on her and her sister performers, entitled, " 'Enough Nudity for Anyone's Fifteen Cents': Sally Rand, the Crystal Lassies, and the Roots of Internet Porn at the Century of Progress Exposition." I brought plenty of slides, and the ballroom was packed. Sally has been dead for more than twenty years, but she still knows how to pull them in.

Novice that I was to burlesque, I was lucky not to be facing my audience alone. On my left was a dark and very handsome man named Mario Carbone. He had written a paper on "primitive cultures" exhibits and fantasies of empire specifically to join me on this panel. The lean, fair-haired man to my right with the intriguing air of melancholy was Christopher Hansen. For my benefit, he had tweaked his customary focus on FDR into a discussion of the perfect marriage of corporate capitalism and the New Deal at the interwar world fairs.

Although we now teach in different parts of the country, the three of us have been best friends since the first week of grad school. Our professors dubbed us "the inseparable threesome," and the other students openly laid bets on who got to be in the middle during our all-night fuckfests.

Mario, Chris, and I laughed it off, because we were sure our bond was purely platonic, founded on mutual intellectual admiration. We wouldn't be honest enough with ourselves to go to bed together for another fifteen years.

City Fathers

The stripper and the schoolmarm. On the surface, it would be hard to find two women more different than Sally and I.

Born in 1904 in the Ozarks and christened Harriet Helen Beck, Sally longed to be a ballerina from the first time she saw Pavlova dance the dying swan in Kansas City. At fourteen, she ran off with the carnival. Her wits and her blonde good looks took her as far as Hollywood, where Cecil B. DeMille himself renamed her, thanks to the Rand McNally atlas that caught his eye. The advent of the talkies proved disastrous for Sally – she had a lisp – and the Depression hit her as hard as everyone else. It was out of desperation for work that she first walked onto the stage in Chicago's Paramount Club, naked but for her trademark feather fans.

Something more than desperation made Sally a star. Chicago was to host a world's fair, and she dreamed of a share in its riches. She applied to perform through official channels, but the city fathers turned her down. City fathers: I always imagine plump, sober-faced men atop Louis Sullivan skyscrapers, spraying the metropolis with semen, their dicks as fat as fire hoses. No doubt most of them sported tent poles in their trousers when Sally crashed their gala opening ceremonies as Lady Godiva on a white horse. The acclaim for this daring display of nudity forced the worthy gentlemen to authorize her show at the Streets of Paris. Most sources agree that Sally helped the fair turn a profit. She didn't do so badly herself. By the end of the summer, her salary had soared from $125 to $3,000 a week.

But Sally was more than a naked body, more than a clever manipulator of male fantasy. Another reason she rode as Lady Godiva was to protest the publicity shots of city matrons in their gala gowns, a callous gesture when so many working people were starving. One night that summer, she refused to let her friends be bumped from the best table in the house by FDR's son and his wedding party. Either the friends stayed put or she wouldn't do the show. As always, Sally got what she wanted in the end.

I, on the other hand, was born in a prosperous northeastern suburb more than sixty years after Sally. I never ran off with carnies. I never earned my keep exposing my small – but, to my lovers' delight, very sensitive – breasts. I never endured an arrest on obscenity charges – much less four in one day, like Sally. I did put on plenty of performances for my teachers and advisers. And I pulled off an impressive masquerade for my father-figure husband, who seemed, with the twenty-year age difference, to be the perfect partner for a scholar of mid-century American studies.

He wasn't.

Now I'm on my own again, my fortieth birthday looming. I'm supposed to be courting the tenure committee with the same old song and dance. But I find myself thinking of Sally and itching to be as daring and shocking and free.

The History of Desire

After we gave our papers, fielded questions, and kissed the requisite asses of the powerful eminences in our field, Mario,

Chris, and I went off to do what we really came to the conference for – a long-awaited reunion dinner at a charming Italian place on M Street.

Things had changed in the two years since we'd last seen each other. Mario was being courted by Columbia and was complaining about how slow they were to make an official offer – rather bad form, since he's scored tenure and Chris and I are still waiting for the decision. Chris made dour jokes about his ongoing search for the right antidepressant. He made no secret of the fact that estrangement from his daughters after his divorce tore him apart. I leered at the young waiter, then regretted it. I didn't want it to be too obvious that I hadn't had good sex with anyone other than my hand in quite some time.

With the help of a few bottles of chianti, however, we gradually found our younger selves still very much alive beneath the older, tougher skin. We laughed and said clever things and confessed that we'd never found the same fellowship with anyone since. It was Mario, of course, who made the first light-hearted reference to another dinner *à trois*, some ten years before. A piece of history, I must confess, that was on my mind as well.

Mario had just turned in his dissertation and was flying off to take a plum job at Duke, while Chris and I still languished in the bog of research. Of course we were glad for him, glad to celebrate with pasta and wine. We were lounging about afterward on throw pillows on the orange shag rug of his apartment when suddenly Mario took me in his arms and kissed me.

It was more than a goodbye. It was a real kiss, slow and soft and piquant, with red pepper and Côtes du Rhône. The kind of kiss you feel in your pussy, or rather, the kind that makes your whole body feel like a pussy, tingling and melting and hungry for more. It took me by surprise, for Mario had been unfailingly faithful to his harem of bubbly undergraduates, all blonde and busty with a fuck-me-now wiggle to their hips, all very different from me. Fate would have it that the phone rang, and the voice of his latest young conquest trilled through the answering machine. We jumped apart, and he went to pick up the phone with a regretful shrug.

I turned to Chris, my lips pleasantly sore, my cheeks hot with arousal and shame. I was wearing Bill's engagement ring. Chris's wedding to Shannon was two months away. I suppose I was expecting to see judgment in his eyes for my sluttish behavior, but I met instead the second surprise of the evening.

Call me easy, and some have, but a man gets inside me first with his eyes. That silver flicker of desire sinks straight into my belly, and – if I want it to happen – he has me right then and there. The rest of it – spreading my legs with his knees and pushing open my wet, pink cunt lips with the swollen knob of his cock – is pretty much an afterthought.

Desire is exactly what I saw in Chris's eyes. He wanted to fuck me, fiancée or no. And I realized I wanted to fuck him. More than anything in the world.

Mario came to the rescue. His girlfriend needed him to come over right away. She was freaked out about an exam, and the newly minted Dr. Mario had the cure. We all rose, smoothed out our clothes, and left to be with the people we were supposed to be fucking, our bland smiles promising we would forget everything that had just happened.

But I still remembered very well that Mario and I kissed. And I remembered even more keenly, with the yearning of ten long years, that Chris and I did not.

Why Not?

In fact, Chris and I had been exchanging wary, questioning glances all evening now that both of us were free, or as free as two people with battered hearts can ever be. But Mario saved us again. His cheerful chatter lubricated our path from the restaurant to my hotel room, where the party continued. We raided the minibar and talked on through the evening. Midnight found me sprawled on my king-size bed, my feet in Mario's warm lap as he rubbed the arches with his strong thumbs, sending sweet, electric twinges running up my legs. Chris, who'd been nursing the same glass of well-watered whiskey all night, had crawled onto the bed beside me, joking that he was waiting in line for a massage too.

"You're looking tired, Chris, my man," Mario said with his lovely smile. "Don't you think you should be getting back to your room?" Though he'd put on weight and his lush hair was touched with snow at the temples, Dr. Carbone was still very easy on the eyes.

"Hell, no, I'm waiting for you to stagger out of here first so I can finally make my move."

I gave Chris a sidelong glance. He winked at me, to let me know that was a joke too.

"Then I guess Elizabeth will have to choose which one of us gets the boot."

I wiggled my foot against Mario's thighs. There was a bulge there. Through the alcohol haze, I realized I was glad.

"Why?" I murmured.

"Why?" Mario echoed. "Because Chris won't be a gentleman and admit defeat."

"No, I mean why do I have to choose? I want you both to be with me tonight."

"I think she's kidding," Chris said too quickly.

Historians spend a lot of time asking "how," which inevitably leads to "why," and there was, no doubt, a tangle of complex reasons why three middle-aged academics were about to engage in group sex on this particular night. But there, in the moment, the decision – and it was mine – to finally do a three-way with my two best friends was frighteningly simple. Because the real question that stokes the engine of history is not "why," but "why not."

Why not, indeed.

I sat up and put on my most seductive smile. Sally's smile. "There's obviously a lot you don't know about me."

My gaze flitted from one to the other, to make sure I had them where I wanted them, jaws slack, their eyes fixed in that primal, my-god-is-she-really-going-to-let-me-do-it-to-her amazement. I slowly unbuttoned my blouse. Their eyes followed, as if bound to the movement of my hands with steel cable. I pulled my shirt down over my shoulders with a shimmy and, still smiling, I traced the lacy edge of my bra with my fingertip. Could Sally have done better?

Mario's face had gone scarlet. Chris was up on one elbow, staring. He swallowed with a wet, slightly strangled sound.

Sally would have teased more. Sally would have them howling with their tongues on the floor before she gave any more, but the world moves faster in the twenty-first century. I unclasped the bra and let it slide over my arms, then took my breasts in my hands and arched my back, offering myself to them.

Mario whistled softly, like a distant train. Chris's face was tight, as if he were about to cry, but he was still staring.

"She's not kidding," Mario said.

Chris nodded.

"Come on, boys, get yourselves out of those clothes before I change my mind."

It was then they pulled their eyes from me and looked at each other.

What do you say, mate? Are you up for taking turns fucking our old friend Elizabeth in full view of each other?

Mario rose and began to unbutton his Oxford shirt. Chris pulled off his sweater. I watched them unbuckle their belts and wriggle out of their khakis. Mario wore briefs; Chris, boxers.

I pulled down the sheets and lay down in the middle of the bed. My friends joined me, one on each side.

Something wasn't right. In the lamp's glare, it was all too clear that Mario had grown a paunch, that he was too hairy for my taste. Chris had the smooth skin I prefer, but his ribs stood out like Jesus on the cross, the body of a man who'd endured hard times. I'm sure I disappointed them with my scrawny form. For all my feelings of sisterhood with Sally, I doubt anyone would ever pay to see me naked.

The three of us lay quietly for a moment, listening to the sounds of traffic rising twelve stories from the street below.

But history has its own momentum.

I nudged Chris to turn off the light.

The darkness made it easier for the show to begin. For Chris to reach over and cup my left breast gently. For Mario to trace my collarbone with his finger, then press his lips to my neck.

It tickled a little, and I laughed. They laughed too. Two male voices, one female, filling the room with the sound of pleasure entwined with disbelief.

Dreams Before Bedtime

Before I get to the good part, I have a confession to make. The truth is, I'm used to crowded beds. Just the week before, I'd treated myself to a group encounter. There's nothing like it for a good night's sleep.

I'd been making good progress on my paper for the conference with a close reading of the text for Sally's Tru-Vue photo poster from 1933. The caption writer had indulged his own fantasies with a description of Sally's "proud, arched body . . . floating among the moonbeams . . . gliding, turning, skimming."

It got worse. "Bewitched by her own beauty," Sally spread her feathery wings for the finale "fluttering wildly, heart racing madly – pulses pounding." And then her joy was over, and she was serene again.

You don't have to have a PhD to figure out we're talking 1930s euphemisms for masturbation and orgasm, as if the male voyeur were observing her subjective pleasure and not merely projecting his own. This fantasy of orgasmic flight, I decided, would make the perfect conclusion to my talk. Couldn't it be seen as a symbol of the audience's desire to escape the grim realities of the Depression? That would explain why they gave Sally their money and their love, men and women alike.

Bewitched by my own cleverness, I shut down the computer and crawled into bed, my brain still flickering with images in vintage black-and-white.

It was then she came through my bedroom door, so lightly and gracefully, "skimming" might indeed be the right word. She perched herself on the edge of my bed and smiled. Her flesh gleamed white in the shadows. I smelled her powder and the faint musk of female sweat.

I should have been tongue-tied in the presence of my idol, but the words gushed through my lips like a fountain, the question no interviewer ever asked her, the question I longed to have her answer before she flew off again. *What was sex like seventy years ago? Tell me. Make me feel how it was for you.*

Sally's smile widened, but her eyes looked sad. Of course she could no longer tell me. She hadn't come to give me something. It was her turn to watch the show.

On cue, two more bodies climbed onto the bed. Male bodies, dressed in antique clothes. Slowly, their faces shifted into focus. They seemed like old friends.

The name of the sturdy young man in the worker's cap changes, depending on the night – Stan or Paolo or Johann – as does his job, one he's lucky to have – meat packer, baker, WPA construction worker. Maybe he helped build the fairgrounds. But he always lives in a boarding house. He's in love with the landlady's daughter and is saving every penny to marry her. He used to think of her white hands kneading bread when he lay on his narrow cot at night, pumping his cock in his fist, wiping himself guiltily afterward with a rough handkerchief.

But the summer of the World's Fair, all he thinks of is Sally.

The young man stretches out beside me and holds me in his arms, pulling me into his skin, so that suddenly I'm with him – I *am* him – wandering through the midway at night. He saunters under the sixty-four-story towers of the Sky Ride, past the Toboggan Glide and the Slide for Life, a ticket to see Sally clutched in his calloused hand. He takes his place in the back of the club. The front tables are for the rich men and their fancy ladies, even a few society wives who come to be titillated. He hates these men who spoil themselves with luxuries while so many starve, but he likes this place, because here, he knows he is their equal. When Sally appears, every man here will feel the same liquid flame shoot straight down his spine, melting his kneecaps, turning his cock to aching wood. A poor young worker can never have her for his own, but neither can the bosses, try though they may to clutch at her with their pale, fat fingers. For Sally's beauty, glowing with an opalescent sheen that reminds him of the drops of semen on his belly in the moonlight, belongs to everyone. To a future where all will enjoy her bounty in an endless feast of image and light.

Now the second man moves behind me, pressing his hard-on against my ass. His hands encircle my waist, and he tugs, tugs me out of the young workman's skin, into his own body, sprawled on a café chair, half-drunk on champagne, close enough to Sally to touch her. His name? Usually something like William B. Worthalot III, son of one of the city's most prominent men of business. Young Worthalot was at the opening gala, one of the first to spring a woody at the sight of Sally as Lady Godiva.

He's been to the Streets of Paris many times since. Once he brought his favorite mistress, a shop girl so lovely she needs no corset to mold her body to perfection. Afterward, William convinced her to pose for him like Sally, wearing nothing but feather fans, and later nothing at all. At first he had to coax her to show herself – *You have such natural beauty, my dear, you're a born star. Show me. Let me see you as you really are.* In the end, he could tell it aroused her, those rosy nipples standing up so stiff against the creamy white of her breasts. It made him hard too, very hard, a condition he could no longer rely on as he once did.

Tonight he has brought college friends from Denver. More than the fan dance, he enjoys their discomposure when Sally swishes by the table, as well as their moist-lipped gratitude when he offers to guide them to his favorite brothel after the show.

He himself observes Sally with a cool eye. On the face of it, she's no different from Chicago's other favorite daughters who bare all – Margie Hart, Ann Corio, Sunya "Smiles" Slane. How has Sally put herself above the rest? A certain twinkle in her eye, a secret swivel of the hips? The answer eludes him, which is why he keeps coming back, to grasp that thing and understand her strange power. And as much as I dislike him, I recognize myself in him, a man of untold riches who will never be satisfied.

I looked to Sally, watching us watching her.

Did I get it right? I asked.

She bobbed her head lightly – in assent or farewell – then vanished into air.

How These Things Really Happen

In dirty stories, threesomes are always the same: three sets of mouths and hands and asses and whatever combination of cocks and cunts joining in every possible way so you're no longer sure what belongs to whom, which is probably the idea.

In fact, I wouldn't have minded seeing Mario bend Chris over the bed, then vice versa, or picking up a few insider tips as they sucked each other's cocks, or being witness to the most forbidden turn-on of all: a slow, loving, man-to-man soul kiss.

But it would have taken a lot more wine – and a lot more honesty – for us to go there.

Not that I should complain with a man on each side focused solely on my pleasure, an abundance of hands and lips and the heady scent of male flesh. But it wasn't at all like the fantasies in one crucial respect. My friends had divided my body in two, North and South Korea, and stretching from my neck to my clit was a DMZ that neither would cross. So far, our frolic was less a threesome than two one-and-a-halves on the same bed.

I would have to be the one to get the peace talks moving.

I sat up and turned, positioning myself between them, studying their cocks openly for the first time. Mario's rose red and thick against the dark curls. Chris's dick was longer and curved, reminding me oddly of the parking brake in my car, smooth and pale golden, eternally erect.

"What beautiful cocks," I murmured and leaned over to suck Chris. He filled my mouth with heat, the spices of male crotch. I started to hum. At first he laughed, then sighed.

For Mario I showed off some tongue tricks. Quick little figure eights just below the head, long gliding ice cream licks from root to tip. I saw Chris watching with narrowed, glittering eyes. Lust made him a stranger. It scared me. And it turned me on.

"Elizabeth, please stop now," Mario begged. He tugged me down and rolled me over to face Chris to make a nice Elizabeth sandwich. I heard a condom wrapper tearing, the snap of latex. He pushed himself inside me so quickly I cried out.

"You're on breast duty, Hansen," Mario called over my shoulder.

"With pleasure," Chris replied and scooted lower to take a nipple in his lips.

Mario pulled my leg up and over his thighs and began to thrust, all the while whispering in my ear. About how beautiful I was, so beautiful and smart he'd been in love with me forever. There was no woman in the world like me, with a pussy so hot and wet.

I closed my eyes and let the sensations flow through me, Mario filling my cunt, Chris flicking his tongue over one nipple, stroking the other with the pad of his thumb. But best of all were those words, so soothing and sweet.

My belly was on fire, and I was dying for Chris to rub my clit, but I sensed they'd drawn that boundary again. Still, I wouldn't give up my dreams of world peace. I reached down and took Chris's cock in my hand. It felt good, good to hold him and stroke him, and for that moment, we were like the fantasies, all of us connected, cock to cunt, breast to lips, hand to cock again, in one pulsing circle.

Suddenly Mario grunted and pushed into me with gliding, rhythmic strokes.

Chris looked up and met my eyes with a frown, my question mirrored in his eyes.

Did he just come – already?

We both smiled. Mario always managed to cross the finish line before we did.

Climax

But Chris and I were never far behind. While Mario disposed of the condom, Chris coaxed my body across the bed so my hips rested at the edge and then knelt between my legs.

"I believe it's your turn to take the top half, Mario, my friend." He grinned to let me know it was a joke.

But that is exactly what happened. While Mario fed me slow kisses and tweaked my nipples in a steady rhythm, Chris began to make love to me with his mouth.

I could tell right away he had a knack for it.

First he kissed his way around my swollen lips, then treated me to long, flat tongue strokes that felt like rolls of hot, wet silk rippling over my vulva. Then he teased and dallied, carefully avoiding my sweet spot until I pushed up against him and groaned in frustration. It didn't take him long to find the right rhythm, quick up-and-down flicks in the little groove to the side of my clit. Except he'd stop now and then, just to make me squirm and moan my disappointment into Mario's mouth. When he started up again, I moaned louder, because it was magic the way our mouths were joined in a column of flame running straight through me. By sucking my juices through my red lips, one pair for each, they were kissing each other too.

Chris pushed one leg up to my belly and held it there, opening me, stretching me so tight my ass seemed to lift off the bed. My thighs were trembling, and I knew I would make it. Relentless now, Chris's tongue lashed at my clit, and I sucked Mario's tongue like a cock until I couldn't anymore, I could only roll my head back and forth, sobbing my pleasure to Mario's soft coos – *Come for us, Elizabeth; that's right, let us watch you come* – and that's exactly what I did.

I looked down at Chris, still kneeling at the edge of the bed. He smiled up at me, his chin dripping. For the first time that evening, he looked truly happy. The golden boy of old.

"Let me do something for you," I said.

Something in his eyes clicked shut again. The gold faded to gray. He shook his head.

Under the circumstances, it didn't feel right to press the matter.

Curtain Call

Again, Mario did just the right thing. As we pulled on our pants and buttoned our shirts in mildly uncomfortable silence, he suggested we meet for breakfast the next morning, a final celebration before he caught his plane.

It was smart, the only thing to do really: make everything the way it was before as best we could.

At the door, Mario tilted my chin up and kissed me gallantly. Chris and I hugged, our usual goodbye, but he added an extra reassuring squeeze. It struck me then that we still hadn't ever kissed on the mouth, the old-fashioned way.

Once they were gone, I turned and caught a glimpse of myself in the mirrored closet door.

To my surprise, I looked pretty. My eyes shone, my skin glowed with a twentysomething bloom. I gave myself a victorious smile. I'd done it. I'd become an adventures, a breaker of taboos. It didn't happen quite the way I thought it would, but it never does.

On impulse I yanked the rumpled sheet off the bed and draped it around my shoulders, the best approximation of a "white heron in the moonlight" costume I could manage.

I wondered what Sally would do to ease herself to sleep if she'd just had sex with a man – or two – that satisfied her flesh but not her heart. I wondered if she'd be a little sad to finally understand why Mario's relationships never lasted too long. Or if she'd struggle with her own fantasy that Chris really was The One, and though we'd both married the wrong people the first time around, we had plenty of hot times ahead if only he could wean himself from those antidepressants.

What *would* Sally do?

Of course she was a realist. She knew fantasies were powerful. They could push the boundaries, change your life so it would never be the same, make you richer than you ever dreamed possible. But you never let them catch you or hold you down.

At the end of the show, there was only one thing to do.

I stretched my arms out and turned slowly, then faster – gliding, turning, skimming, whirling – around and around, my white wings outstretched, until I swear I was flying up and away.

Meter Violator

Kelly Jameson

The first time I investigated a crime scene, two things happened. The first was I met a real crime scene photographer named Giovanni and the second was I fell in love with metal – all shapes and forms of it – and started masturbating to street signs.

I say "real" crime scene photographer because the crime scene was staged; I had almost completed training in a forensic academy in Nevada and my knowledge was being tested in the field.

The academy had spared no expense in setting up the scene. They built a semi-permanent structure, divided by one wall down the center, creating two rooms. Both of the rooms were open in the front so the fire could be seen. In each room, they'd completely recreated a real living space. My classmates and I helped to decorate the rooms. I put an old Shaun Cassidy poster on the wall because I couldn't help myself. A large pumper fire truck was used to put out the fire in the burn cell fifteen seconds after flashover.

When it was safe, my classmates and I, suited up appropriately, then walked through the rooms. The couch purchased from the thrift store was burnt almost beyond recognition. The carpet too. Light bulbs melted. We looked at V patterns, calcinations, etc.

It was nighttime and Giovanni's camera flashed and popped. Several female students followed him around with their own cameras, trying to imitate him. "First rule," he said, "Shoot your way in; shoot your way out." I avoided Giovanni. He has a larger than life presence. A tall, lean, handsome man. The kind my mother used to see in the market or on the street and then whisper to me, "Being handsome is a detriment. You marry a handsome man, he'll just throw you over for a lingerie model someday."

Giovanni has camera eyes. The first time he looked at me, I was holding fragments of a metal lamp in my gloved hand. Just as I put a tiny fragment of the metal in my mouth, I met his simmering hazel eyes. I ran my tongue over the metal, my eyes traveling over his dark hair, cut short to the nape of his neck, his nose, which was bent a little, maybe from a fight, his square jaw, his five o'clock shadow. I thought about the ribs of steel buildings, the bars of zoo cages, the sharp steel points of tacks and nails, the discolored nature of steel joints on aircraft. In my mind, the man and the melted metal formed an atoll of inorganic substance that glowed; I felt dampness between my legs. I took the metal from my mouth and jammed it in my pocket. Then I got back to work.

I'm in my forties. Kind of shy. A girl with no steady boyfriend and a vivid fantasy life. I had no interest in fawning over a handsome photographer, even if I wanted to run my tongue over his Adam's apple and trace the laugh lines on his jaw with my pale fingers.

Reflective signs never rust and have a street life of seven years. The obvious masculinity, the sly cringe of the metal, the heavy thrash death black gothic doom of a road sign somehow attracts me. I'm also attracted to emotionally unavailable men. Men who like to give orders. I spend my days hungering for someone to shape me into something else. Sometimes I disgust myself with my fantasies.

A CSI is required to work long hours, be agile. Sometimes heavy lifting is required. A CSI must be able to maintain equipment, stay up-to-date on all techniques and methodology, use deductive and inductive reasoning and perform a systematic search of the crime scene. Masturbating to street signs: optional.

Just beyond the glittering man-made world that is Las Vegas is an environment of another kind. This is the environment I live in, work in, sweat in, masturbate in, eat in, and sometimes choke on. I live alone, except for Macey, my fourteen-year-old dog, who has trouble walking. Sometimes her legs just go down; she recently sat her rear-end right down on a Lincoln Log cabin my seven-year-old nephew had built. She's in good health otherwise; her eyes are bright and her appetite is good and I've taken to driving her around with me whenever I can. But I can't take her with me to crime scenes.

So months later, having successfully passed my training courses, I'm investigating a real crime scene in a remote area where a girl who was last seen at a restaurant/night club turned up in rock climbing clothes, dead at the bottom of a small gorge. She's wearing a pink Moosejaw shirt, dark pink pants, matching gloves, and boots, and there are ropes at her feet.

I'm convinced I'm in the beginning stages of Pick's disease. Not much is known about Pick's. Poor social judgment, inappropriate sexual advances, or a coarse and jocular demeanor may be seen in people who have Pick's disease. Some patients are hypersexual, and some, like small children, may put anything they pick up in their mouths. Attention span is poor; patients can be instantly distracted by anything they hear or see. Later in the disease, patients usually become mute. Restlessness gives way to profound apathy. The patient may not respond at all to the surrounding world. Eventually, they enter a terminal vegetative state.

Maybe it's not so bad, I think, looking at the young dead girl. Maybe the vegetative state is a place of gold, silver, water and neon. A place where you can't fall down. A place where you can't get too high.

Seven million acres of spectacular natural landscapes – from forested Alpine environment to dry desert landscapes – surround Las Vegas. This immense area includes Lake Mead National Recreation Area, Spring Mountains National Recreation Area, Desert National Wildlife Refuge Complex,

Red Rock Canyon National Conservation Area, and three million acres of public lands.

I once fucked a metal detector on a little-known back road in the Spring Mountains National Recreation Area.

Cameras pop and flash and I see Giovanni. I haven't seen him since my training. He makes his way over, looks down at me as I carefully scrape material from beneath the girl's fingernails into a plastic bag. He watches. The whole scene plays like a haunted smeared cocked thing in my head. Most of my life I've felt outside myself, like I'm off in the distance somewhere, watching what I'm doing in a clinical, abstract manner.

The dead girl was hiking with a group; a male in the group reported the accident. What a waste of a pink happy life. Things are never as they seem. *Shoot your way in; shoot your way out.* Record everything.

"You're too mechanical," Giovanni says. "You get too mechanical, you make mistakes. You get too emotional, you make mistakes. Be more careful," he grunts, and walks away. I feel like crying and I get the impression he carries loneliness around with him like a camera case.

Hours later I'm one of the last to pack up my equipment and head out onto the dark highway. The headlights of my Dodge Dart reflect road signs along the way. I pull off a shoulder, gravel on the side of the road crunching beneath my tires, mountains rising like monolithic beasts behind me. I switch off the lights but leave my car running. The area is deserted in the early morning hour.

Signs are thick aluminum with engineer-grade reflective sheeting applied over the surface. They have a thicker edge on the top and bottom. The material is less prone to scratching, chipping, and fading. This one has fallen down. No one seems to care. It's at least six feet tall. Giovanni is probably at least six feet tall. Length is dependent on the number of letters required. The smaller the name, the smaller the length of the sign. This one, flat on its back, reads "Girls of Glitter Gulch." True retro Sin City. I know the actual place. It's a downtown topless bar. A tourist trap where girls in sequin gowns strip down to

G-strings. A place with pink bubble lamps, brass swans, black lighting. The décor and drink prices haven't changed since the 1970s. I like it. I licked one of the pink bubble lamps once; it has a much different taste than the metal lamp burned in the staged fire I investigated.

I lay down on my back, on top of the fallen sign. Stare at the stars. I removed my CSI trappings before leaving the crime scene and wear the jeans and pink T-shirt I had on underneath the protective plastic. I unzip my jeans. I slide my jeans and white panties down to my knees and push up my T-shirt and bra so my ample breasts are exposed. I put my one hand between my legs and another on my breast and fantasize I have a stripper's body and I'm dancing on stage at Girls of Glitter Gulch in black light. I strip down to a G-string, lean over, lick the metal base of a pink bubble lamp. I'm surprised it's Giovanni's face I see in my mind, in the black light surrounding the stage; he has his hand in his pants and is watching me, masturbating, his olive eyes half slits of pleasure, ordering me repeatedly to bend down and spread my legs for him.

The rounded bolts of the sign dig into my skin. In my mind, I run my tongue and hands over Giovanni's ductile, malleable flesh. I hear the irritation in his voice, the scolding. "You're too mechanical. Be more careful."

I'm moaning, pinching my nipples, about to come, when a flash shatters the night, illuminating for a split second the brown rocks at my side. I sit up, rubbing my eyes. It's Giovanni. I didn't hear him drive up. He's looking at me with such intensity in his eyes I can't tell if it's lust, hate, or disgust. He doesn't say anything. He doesn't smile. "Egyptian weapons made from meteoric iron in 3000 B.C. were highly prized as 'Daggers from Heaven'," I say as he drives away. He doesn't hear me, of course.

Back at my apartment, I sit with Macey curled on my lap and watch TV. Later, Macey sleeping in a black-and-white furry ball on the couch, I still can't sleep. I go into the bathroom, close the door, get out the paddle. The one I fashioned with a metal handle and drilled holes in. I push my panties down, bend over, spank myself. I think about Giovanni, but it's not working. I need Giovanni to hold the paddle and do the spanking. I don't want to need Giovanni to hold the paddle and do the spanking. I put the paddle back and get into bed and stare at the ceiling. I put Warren Zevon in the CD player and listen to "Excitable Boy". I'm just an excitable girl on a contemporary exploration of non-containment. I feel ugly when I wake up in the morning, lost in the vastness of the words and thoughts in my head. My tawny curly hair with its dyed blonde highlights is sticking up.

A few days later I'm at the crime lab when a manila envelope arrives for me. I open it. I see that it has nothing to do with the crime scene of the dead rock climber in pink. Beneath my desk, I slip my shoes off and rub my stocking feet together. My feet are sweaty. I can smell them.

There are several stunning photographs from what appears to be a junkyard.

The dead girl? Turns out she was the granddaughter of a stripper who used to take bubble baths on stage at one of the joints in Las Vegas in the 50s. It wasn't the Girls of Glitter Gulch. A twenty-one-year-old woman whose background checked positive for DUI. In addition to rock climbing, she apparently liked to grab state troopers' genitals and sometimes punch them in the face when she was drunk. Inherited a lot of money from her stripper grandmother too.

I hold photos of old broken down appliances in the night: a rusted out automobile; part of a boat; discarded computer keyboards; a bicycle; an old baby carriage. I can see that Giovanni has to get *inside* a piece until it's part of him. Work himself into it. His photos have that directness because he's at the heart of it.

I flip through all the photos and get to the last. Quickly look up. No one is outside my office in the hallway. The last is a shot of me masturbating on top of the road sign. I shove the pictures back in the envelope, drop them in my desk drawer, go to get a cup of coffee in the break room.

"Do you have those reports yet?" my boss barks. I look at him blankly. He looks down at my feet. "And where are your *shoes?*"

"I'll have those reports soon, sir," I say.

"We can't afford delays in this office," he growls. "Cases go unsolved that way. Have them to me within the next fifteen minutes."

"Yes, sir," I say, taking what can only be described as flaccid, acrid coffee back to my paper-littered desk. I put my shoes back on. I stand up, reach forward, click off the lights, filling my office with the pale glow from the computer. I try to imagine my boss spanking my naked bottom, but it doesn't do anything for me. He's only five-foot-two and has a mustache that is threatening to take over his pinched, constipated face.

I think about how I rubbed my naked crotch up and down a parking meter in a deserted parking lot one night, my pink panties around my ankles. Let's just say my ideas of traffic and mobility management are fucked up. I wasn't worried about getting caught that night; if I'd been caught, I probably wouldn't have been penalized. I mean, think of all the crap that goes down in Las Vegas. Plus, I once read that a North Dakota man who got busted for having "simulated" sex with a mannequin didn't commit a crime of indecent exposure, according to the state Supreme Court. The court record did state its opinion that having sex in public with a mannequin would likely offend people though. Would a half-clothed woman, sexing up a parking meter, be equally or more offensive? Well, thank goodness the buddies of justice are keeping people safe from the sight of fully clothed men fake-fucking mannequins.

I turn the reports into my boss. It takes me twenty-five minutes. Later that night I look up Giovanni's phone number and address in the phone book. I think about visiting him but call him instead. It rings twice and his deep voice hangs in the air on the other end.

"I like to watch NASCAR," I whisper. "You only realize the driver's skill when there's a crash. That's where the truth is, in the mistakes."

There is silence on the other end.

"Who is this?" he asks.

"I like the photos." I hang up. I am shaking.

I turn on the shower. As I masturbate, I think about the Hoover Dam on the nearby Colorado River. The hydroelectric marvel was finished in 1936 and now lights the neon signs in Sin City. As I come, the phone rings. I imagine it's Giovanni, and he wants to spank me for messing up an important crime scene investigation.

Two years before Hoover Dam was completed, the Model-T-Ford was in favor in America, and mechanical brakes stopped all automobiles. Around the clock, thousands of workers were mobilized and transported to the dam. To carry the workers to the dam, large trucks were modified with decks of seats that held one hundred and fifty men at a time. There were no devices to dig large rock tunnels. Large trucks weighing ten tons were customized to support platforms holding thirty drills, which were used to prepare the rock face for dynamiting tunnels. Massive spider-like webs of steel wire cable were stretched from towers high over the dam to lower the concrete, large pipe, and men down the sheer cliffs into the canyon.

I towel off, dry my hair, eat a tomato-and-mayo sandwich. I feed Macey and head out in my Dodge Dart, looking for inspiration and humiliation in the face of a road sign. I fall into a pattern. I find a particularly intriguing sign, like "Road Construction, 1500 Feet," or a sign with the "no parking" symbol, and masturbate. This becomes some sort of game with Giovanni and I. He finds me somehow, snaps pictures of me and they arrive in a plain manila envelope in my office a few days later. He's twice my size. His hands are big and beautiful. I know he follows me but I don't stop him. Sometimes after I look at his photos, after I think about him developing them in a private dark room, I have to masturbate in a stall in the ladies' room.

I make sure there are no surveillance cameras near any of the signs I use; some of the county commissioners are looking at options to catch vandals who are destroying and stealing road signs. They've also started to change the signs to fiberglass; they're taller than the existing aluminum signs. Some have even been bolted on opposite sides of a hollow square post to thwart potential vandals.

Then just as mysteriously, the photo taking stops; I don't receive envelopes anymore.

After driving around Nevada roads for hours, listening to Elvis Costello, I get the courage to go to Giovanni's house, knock on the door. It's raining. I'm holding a newspaper over my head.

He opens the door and is holding an ice pack to his head. He's wearing jeans. He's shirtless. His eyes are bruised and swollen, his upper lip split grotesquely. Instinctively I reach out to touch his face and he draws back.

"I . . . miss you," I say.

He looks surprised.

"What happened?" I ask.

In the dark canyons of his face, I see that at the moment I don't bear any resemblance to the image of the girl in the photos, the girl I think I am. I catch a glimpse of the room behind him. There are steel sculptures and models everywhere. Framed junkyard photographs adorn his walls. Most of the furniture is modern and steel.

"Look, you shouldn't miss me," he says. "In fact, you should get out."

"I don't want to leave." It takes every ounce of courage I have to say it.

He moves the ice pack to his right eye and stares at me with his left. Then he yanks me inside and slams the door shut. Sheryl Crow's "Steve McQueen" belts out from his living room stereo. He pulls me through the living room to a study. He puts the ice pack down on a large, masculine mahogany desk. "Bend over," he says. I comply.

All kinds of intricate model airplanes dangle from the ceiling. Metal. Spectacular.

"You always do what people tell you?" he asks.

I swallow. I don't speak.

He spanks me. Hard. "Whore. I asked you a question."

"Sometimes . . . I don't know . . . yes . . ."

"Pull your skirt and panties down."

I pull them down.

A moment passes. I hear him unzip his jeans.

"Look at me," he commands.

I stay bent over the desk, turn my head and look back at him. He has a beautiful, hard cock.

"You like that?"

"Ummmm," I say.

He spanks me again. "This is what you wanted, isn't it?" He keeps spanking me then stops. I turn and watch him, study his frenzied beat as he strokes himself. I watch as he eventually comes on my backside, breathing hard, his hand on my back to keep me in my place.

He closes his swollen eyes. "I can't do this anymore," he says.

"Do what?" I ask.

"Take your picture . . . when you . . . demean yourself."

"Demean myself? But I . . . *like* it," I say.

"Jesus." He rakes a hand through his dark hair. He spanks my bare bottom again. He spanks me for a good five minutes more. Then he collapses against me, his heart beating hard, holding his cheek to my back. I feel a slight tremble pass through him right before he stands up.

"Get out," he says.

"But . . ."

"Go home. Wash yourself off. Don't masturbate to any more road signs."

I cry all the way back to my tiny apartment. The wind rubs me, sighs against my face through the open car windows. My bottom is sore. His sticky essence is still on my back, my clothes, and I like that too.

Two weeks pass in a melodramatic haze. Maybe it's three. I walk around like a robot, processing my evidence and reports. But I don't masturbate to any more road signs.

Macey's health starts to decline. The careful musing silence of my apartment drives me mad. Macey's back legs just don't work right anymore. One night I carry her to my car. We drive around all night, looking at the big Nevada stars. I stop at a service station to use the restroom. I get some gas, pay for the gas and doggy treats, give them to Macey, who wags her tail. I pull out onto the highway again.

The thing is to keep going, keep moving. I drive with one hand on the steering wheel, the other scratching Macey behind the ears. "I love you, Macey," I say, over and over.

Macey falls asleep for a while as the Nevada desert scenery whittles by. I drink in the earth. I don't even notice the road signs.

I find an old junkyard and stop the car. I put a radio station on; it blasts jazz. Macey loves jazz. She eases her old self up from the blanket on the front seat and I carry her to the dusty grass that lines the front of the junkyard. The sculptures are magnificent in the moonlight. An old rusting motorcycle. Piles of crushed cars. A busted microwave. Old golf clubs. She looks up at me, grins in her way, and then dies. I cry as I carry her back to the car. I cry a lot over the next week. I have her cremated and put her ashes in a beautiful wooden urn, which I keep on top of my entertainment center.

It's raining. Almost midnight. I miss Macey. The TV is on and I stare at it, but I'm not really watching it. A knock on the door and I am nearly startled out of my pants. I open it and Giovanni stands there. He holds a newspaper over his head. Water drips down his beautiful face and neck. He's like a sculpture.

"I'm sorry about your dog," he says.

"How did you know about my dog?"

"I saw you that night. It wasn't a moment I could interrupt."

"Oh."

"Listen, I want to show you something. Will you go with me?"

"I don't know . . . I . . ."

"Go with me." I grab my coat and follow him to his car. I respond to masculine commands almost without thinking. It gives me pleasure.

He drives a dark blue pick-up truck. I climb into the front seat. We start off into the night. He doesn't talk while we drive. I sit and enjoy the jazz-pop-thump of windshield wipers on the glass, his presence, the fat sound of rain on the roof.

When we stop, he shuts off the ignition and the lights. It's not raining anymore. We are parked in front of the junkyard where Macey died, where she looked up at me with some last unbent metallic late-night breakfast belly-scratching bit of happiness. Giovanni grabs some camera equipment off the floor of the truck and a portable CD player and gets out. I follow him into the junkyard, where everything glitters with the fresh kiss of rain. Massive spider-webs of metal.

He puts his camera together and waits as I start to walk through the jungle of dumped memory. My heart beats fast. My face and neck are hot. Mountains that are pink to rust by day are now steel gray in the darkness. I stand before the skeleton of an old motorcycle and look at him, tears filling my eyes. The great hulking mounds of metal, shaped and shapeless at the same time, are beautiful.

He puts a CD in and Louis Armstrong's "No One Else But You" dances into the aluminum night.

"Touch the metal," he orders, his eyes feral.

I lick my lips. I hesitate. "I don't know . . ."

"Yes, you do know. Touch it. Touch everything the way you want to."

I swallow and run my hands over the ripped leather seat of the old motorbike, the handlebars.

"And then touch me the same way."

My head snaps up when he says this.

I lose all track of time as I put my hands on myself and on old automobiles, rub my naked thighs over their rounded hoods, press my breasts against the rough old lips of giant tires, ragtops that knew a lot of summers, my bottom against a wheelchair, lips on rings of metal bolts. "When the Saints

Go Marching In" drums in my head, in my veins and blood. Giovanni snaps more pictures.

"When you take a drive down a desert road, never know what you'll find," he breathes.

I am completely naked when he pats the hood of another old automobile. "This is a 1940 Mercury four-door sedan wearing a 1939 hood. Only the second year of production for Mercury. Improvements over the 1939 model included sealed-beam headlamps, a two-spoke steering wheel, a steering column-mounted gearshift, and vent wing windows. Ain't she a beauty?"

Yes, yes you are, I think. *You certainly are a beauty.*

"The Preacher and the Bear" throws itself out of the CD player:

> Oh Lord, didn't you deliver Daniel from the lion's Den?
> Also delivered Jonah from the belly of the whale and then
> The Hebrew children from the fiery furnace
> So the good book do declare
> Yes! Lord, if you can't help me,
> For goodness sake don't help that bear.

"Each piece has its own sexual style," I say to Giovanni. For the next half hour or so, I demonstrate my point on old aircraft bones, a left rear fender, a water heater, a toaster oven, and an abandoned washing machine that displays an unusual tendency toward impressionism.

We drink the gin he had stashed in his truck. After running my hands over the grill of the Mercury, I run them over his Adam's apple, run my tongue over it too; I've always wanted to taste it.

"Why do we love metal so much?" he asks, kissing my neck, running his hands over my body; all the while he's still fully clothed. I can hardly think with his hands on me but I know my answer is important.

A new song plays:

fed you since last fall, you rascal, you.
I fed you since last fall, you rascal, you.
I fed you since last fall,
Then you got your ashes hauled.
I'll be glad when you dead, you rascal, you!

You asked my wife to wash your clothes, you rascal, you.
You asked my wife to wash your clothes, you rascal, you.
You asked my wife to wash your clothes
And something else I suppose.
I'll be glad when you dead, you rascal, you!

You know you done me wrong, you rascal, you.
You know you done me wrong, you rascal, you.
You know you done me wrong,
You done stole my wife and gone.
I'll be glad when you dead, you rascal, you!

Trumpet notes punch the air like screaming steel rivets. "Spread your legs."

I obey.

His fingers are inside me when I answer him. "They have the hard-won beauty . . . of things that intermingled with people and weather for years. They tell us the story of their own lives but also tell us about . . . the people who owned them."

He fucks me with his fingers. I moan. "I like sad, old, worn-out things. I like how they make me feel," and I am crying. "Your bruises are healing," I say.

"I like to pick fights with strangers just to feel alive. I usually win, but it's not about winning, and I got my ass kicked last time. Guy had the biggest knuckles I've ever seen."

He puts his coat between me and the rusted hunk of metal car, between me and the world, removes his clothes, and fucks me, demanding that I wrap my legs around him, then demanding I spread them wider, then demanding that I squeeze him again.

★   ★   ★

The dead rock climber was trying to release a jammed rope from a previous rappel when a rock dislodged, causing her to lose her balance and fall. The remaining members of her group didn't have a rope long enough to complete the final rappel. We couldn't determine whether it was a climbing harness failure or a problem with her equipment or an error. The girl was once quoted in a Nevada newspaper: "As a climber, you need to pick hard enough climbs because those are the walls where you'll learn the most."

That Christmas, in our apartment, with his metal airplanes spinning on the ceiling in the hot blasts of an overeager heater that drives up our electric bills, Giovanni and I exchange gifts. He gives me a metal chastity belt. The kind where he has the key and will tell me how long I have to wear it. When it's on, I won't be able to touch myself. I take it off only when he says I can take it off. I give him a book called *The Pleasures of Being a Female Sexual Submissive* because it's the only way I know how to tell him what I need to tell him.

It's raining. In our apartment, we've created a world of gold, silver, water and neon. A place where you can't fall down. A place where you can't get too high.

A Secret Night in Grouse Woods

Karen Sutow

The autumn breeze kicked in through the door, bringing with it two men and a woman. I glanced up from my cappuccino, foam peppering my top lip. The taller of the men brushed past me, his thin hips nearly caressing my shoulder as he squeezed between the tables. His blue jeans hugged his ass and his white T-shirt accentuated the muscles on his back. He carried something black in his hands, though what I could not see, my view now obstructed by his friends, who had joined him at the counter.

I turned to Lacy, noticed her eyes fixed on the men, and leaned into the table straining to see them. On the left stood the man in the jeans, his back still facing me. On his right was the woman, drink in hand, her eyes taking in the room. She was petite, not more than five-foot-two, maybe five-foot-three, with short, wavy black hair – sexy yet sleek. Deep brown eyes, sculpted face. Not a lick of make-up, yet attractive as hell.

The guy on her right smiled before resting his hand on her shoulder, then said something to the other man, the one who held the black object. He shifted the object to his left hand, then ran his fingers through his short brown hair and smiled before returning his attention to the barista.

"You ever see them before?" Lacy asked.

"No. Where you figure they're from?"

"How would I know? Probably just passing through on their way to somewhere."

"On the way to where?" I said. "This town's between here and nowhere."

Lacy laughed, and I laughed with her. Almedia, with its population of 1,683, was a blip on the map. It took a good two hours to drive through the rolling hills to the nearest town and four hours to Carlton City, if the weather was good and a landslide of rocks and mud hadn't wiped out the road down the mountain. Life was simple – folks lived off the land, neighbors helped each other out, not that gruff mind-your-own-business-and-I'll-mind-mine kind of thinking you get most everywhere else, especially in the big cities. Of course, young folks don't stick around long – rushing off to find something new and exciting – and the population keeps dwindling. Lacy and I are pretty much the exception, though I don't know how much longer that will last. I feel the city calling me and I'm desperate to experience adventure. Must be a mid-life crisis or something, although I don't know how much it's mid-life when you're just hitting thirty.

"What do you think they're doing?"

"How should I know?"

The two men and the woman had moved to the far wall and stood facing the room. The one with the black box stared, first at Mrs. O'Leary, with her coiffed grey hair and wrinkled face, then at Mabel Osterburch, whose head was buried in a book. Mabel licked her bottom lip, oblivious to the man watching her. His attention shifted to Mabel's right and rested on Robin Koots, who sensed his gaze, looked up from her newspaper, and smiled so wide you'd have thought he offered her the world. He nodded ever so slightly, then looked at the box and gently ran his finger across the side, as if caressing a lover. I swallowed hard. Shifted my gaze from his finger to his face, locked my eyes on his piercing blues as he looked directly at me. Smiling. Teeth so white. I couldn't help but smile back, my lips opening so far it was almost embarrassing. Lacy kicked me under the table as the man strode toward me. The other man and the woman remained in place.

It took him only moments to cross the room, but it felt like forever. When he spoke, it was as if his deep voice broke the silence, yet noise surrounded us. "For you," he said, holding out the box. It was velvet, approximately five inches by three inches. No markings. Just pure black velvet contrasting his deeply tanned hand. Strong fingers. No ring. Small scar across the knuckle on his thumb.

"What . . . what is it?"

"Just take it. You won't be sorry."

I hesitated, then reached for the box, felt his warm skin against mine. Lingered to savor the moment. He touched his free hand to my cheek – it felt like fire branded my skin – then he left the coffeehouse without saying another word and his friends followed. I tracked them through the window until they passed out of sight.

"Hurry up. Open it," Lacy said.

"What do you think's inside?"

"How the hell should I know? Just open it."

"What if it's a bomb or something?"

"You got to be kidding me, right? Besides, it's too small. If you don't open it, Samantha, I will."

Gently, I flipped up the small metal latch on the side then eased off the lid to find red silk lining the inside of the box. A shiny piece of paper sat on top of the silk. It resembled a theater ticket and said: "For you – our special customer – one extraordinary night only – this Saturday – eight p.m. – Be prepared for the experience of a lifetime. Free admission to the Mystery Theater with this ticket. Good only for the bearer. No exceptions. Go to the clearing in the middle of Grouse Woods and be on time. No late entry permitted. Park at the Conestoga Spring."

"Let me see that," Lacy said as she grabbed the ticket from my hand. "I don't believe it. You're so lucky."

"What do you mean?"

"He gave you a ticket to the Mystery Theater."

"I never heard of it."

"You got to be kidding me, right?"

I shook my head.

Lacy leaned forward and whispered. "It's this secret traveling theater that goes all over the country. No one knows where it's going or what exactly it's about, but it's supposed to be the most incredible experience you'll ever have in your life."

I took the ticket back from Lacy. "If it's so secret, how do you know about it? And if no one knows what it's about, then how do you know it's so incredible?"

"I read about it on the Internet, but they swear you to secrecy when you leave the theater."

"You mean to tell me no one's ever broken their promise? I find that hard to believe."

Lacy took a sip of coffee. "Believe what you want, but I'm telling you that everyone who has gone says it's absolutely fantastic . . . if you don't want to go, I'd be happy to take the ticket off your hands."

I considered the idea for a moment and then remembered the man's touch. Even if I could just get a glimpse of him again, it would be worth it. "No . . . I'll go. What do I have to lose?"

"You're so lucky," Lacy said, smiling. "You do realize that, don't you?"

I shook my head.

The hike into the woods took a good fifteen minutes from where I was parked with three other cars. The evening air smelled of pine and that clean water smell I love. Electric lanterns lined a path into the woods. Near silence greeted me, broken only by scattered twigs and leaves crunching underfoot.

For an instant, I considered climbing back into my car and heading home, but a nagging feeling ate at my gut and told me to risk it. I figured I had nothing to lose. Hell, here I'd been complaining I wanted adventure, and when it stared me in the face, I hesitated. No, that wasn't the way I wanted to live my life, and I'd be damned if my fear would get the best of me. I took a step forward, followed by another, until I found myself in the middle of a clearing facing a towering black tent. No sign. No people. No lights. Nothing.

I heard music from inside, soothing but with an upbeat undertone to it – the melody inviting, yet erotic in some way I couldn't quite figure out. I pushed aside the tent flap and stepped inside. A soft female voice spoke in my ear. "May I see your ticket please?"

I turned and looked at her but was unable to see anything in the pitch black. I handed her my ticket. She flicked on a pen-light; the minute amount of light revealed nothing more than the tight-fitting one-piece black outfit the woman wore.

"This way, please." She turned off the pen-light, took hold of my hand, and led me through the tent. I could not imagine how she found her way without anything to guide her. I heard breathing and the rustling of clothes as we passed someone on my left. "Here you are," the woman said as she turned my shoulders and helped me into a plush recliner. "We'll be starting shortly. Just relax and enjoy the music."

It was five minutes, maybe ten or twenty. It was difficult to tell with nothing to guide me but unending music. The notes increased in tempo and volume until they vibrated and danced off the walls of the tent, encasing me in a cocoon of joy. Drums joined the fervor as did a guitar, then a soft voice eased in under the music singing a melody that drew the notes to an ever-increasing quiet and steady beat until they were no more, leaving only the woman's voice to gently fill the air. It felt as if she were singing to me and no other, the darkness my only companion.

Upon the last note, a cool breeze swept my skin, raising goose bumps across my arms, the sensation again magnified. Then, the chair began to warm, ever so slightly, and I felt something soft caress my skin – feathers maybe or cotton. My breath caught in my throat as the object moved across my cheeks and down my arms, stopping at my fingers before making its way back up to my face. I struggled between my desire to experience the sensation and my need to see who provided it, although I knew I wouldn't be able to see a thing. Another cool breeze followed, then nothing.

All I could do was anticipate what would come next – my senses were on fire.

Again, it felt like a long time until something happened, but the wait only increased my pleasure. Five soft pink spotlights now bathed five gorgeous men, each dressed in nothing but identical shorts, cut high and tight. Bare, muscular chests glistening in the light, smiles plastering their faces, hands planted on hips. I could see the shadows of lounge chairs near each man and assumed a sixth man stood near me. I wondered what he looked like. How he felt. How he smelled. How he tasted. I turned my head to look, but the lights extinguished before I had a chance.

Something soft pushed against my lips and juice ran down my chin. I opened my mouth to take it in, the strawberry so sweet and exhilarating, as if I were tasting one for the first time. His breath warmed my skin and then his tongue licked the juice clean in one full, drawn-out stroke. I ached. Every bit of me. And I craved more and more of these wonderful sensations. I didn't know it could feel so good . . . that I could feel so good.

Fingers found the buttons on my shirt, opened them, and gently spread the fabric to my sides. Again, I felt warm breath on my skin, then hands swept across my nipples, not stopping to satisfy the aching buds on the way down to my thighs and to my ankles and back up again. But this time, fingers pushed aside my bra strap and freed my breasts. A short beat, then ice on my nipples. I moaned. The cold was delicious against my heat. I reached out for him in the dark, barely able to stay still, but he pushed my arms against the chair and held them there for a moment. I dared not move again, not wanting to give him reason to stop.

A soft, high-pitched bell clanged once, twice, followed by a warm shower from above. The water drizzled against my skin, each drop like needles yet so invigorating. After about a minute, the bell clanged again and the water stopped, leaving my saturated clothes plastered against my skin. The pink spotlights turned back on, this time casting a wider swath of light that illuminated each chair in addition to the men standing next to them, the men's bodies now glistening from the water, their shorts clinging to their skin. I turned my head again, but the man ducked behind my chair and pushed my face forward. "Watch them and enjoy," he said into my ear, his voice creamy and smooth.

I recognized his voice from the coffee shop – the man who gave me the ticket – and my stomach felt like it rushed into my throat but then quickly settled. "But . . . what?"

"Life is not to question why, but to enjoy." With those words, he pushed me upright, removed my shirt, and unhooked my bra, all the time caressing the back of my neck with his lips. I knew the other women in the room watched me. I felt their eyes, their stares, didn't care – only focused on the men in shorts attending to them and on the man attending to me.

His mouth found my waiting nipple and sucked, then he bit it gently with his teeth as his hand teased my other nipple. His tongue trailed down my stomach, paused at my waist, then made its way back to my breast. I watched another man do the same thing to a woman directly across from me, turned my attention to the side and saw the same thing again. It only served to increase my excitement. I wanted him to take me right then and there. I didn't care who watched. All I could focus on was the burning ache and wetness between my legs.

The tent went dark again. I shivered, but not because I was cold. I felt hands on my hips pushing my pants to my ankles and over my feet. A finger pushed under my panties, teased me for a second, then disappeared. Ice again on my breasts. Warm mouth on mine. Fingers in my hair. I reached out to him. Felt the rock hard muscles of his chest. Ran my hands down to his waist, across his shorts, over the bulge, lingering for a long moment.

He pushed aside my hand. I heard his zipper. Only wanted to reach for him. Hold him. Take him inside me. But I knew the rules.

Again, the lights. This time a little dimmer, mixed with purple. Soft music and a cool breeze blowing directly on my skin. He moved into view. Naked. Sculpted like one of those famous statues I'd seen in museum pictures somewhere. "Please," I said.

He smiled and drew a vibrator out from behind his back, turned it on. The buzzing alone almost made me orgasm. I glanced across the way, saw another man holding a vibrator against a woman, joy plastered across her face. My man pressed the vibrator against my clit, sending ecstatic bolts of electricity through my body. I arched my back and spread my legs, desperately wanting it inside me, wanting him inside me. He knew it too. He smiled a wicked grin and stopped just because he could, right when I was on the brink of orgasm.

He reached behind him, and I felt cold water hitting my skin again followed by that cool breeze and then his mouth on my neck. His oh-so-warm mouth. He straddled me with his thick muscular legs and leaned toward my chest and kissed me. Hard. Hands clamping my head. Fingers nearly digging into my scalp.

Lights out.

He left me. Alone in the chair. Craving his touch. Needing him like I've never needed anyone before. I touched my breasts and ran my hands down my stomach, but it wasn't the same. Where was he? "Please," I said again. "I want you."

Music now – so quiet I could barely hear it.

He climbed back on top of me and I reached for him, wanting to guide him inside me. Again the damn rules. He pushed my hand away. Bit gently on my nipple, then spread my legs and took me at the same instant the lights turned back on.

I stared at his face, our hips moving together, slowly at first then faster and faster until I thought I would die from the pleasure. Someone screamed, someone else moaned, and I came fast and hard. Not once, but twice. The orgasm was so great, it ran down to my toes and up into my hands. I felt him come, and I smiled.

The tent was plunged into blackness again. He kissed me on the lips, then kissed my breasts and said, "Such exquisite pleasure." With that, he disappeared. I fished for him with my hands, and couldn't find anything but the chair on which I sat.

"Here are some dry clothes," a woman said and pressed a sweatshirt and sweatpants into my hands. I think it was the same woman who had led me to my chair. She turned on her pen-light so I could see to get dressed, then led me from the chair back through the tent. I tried to glimpse the other women, see the men who had been wearing the shorts, find the man who had pleasured me so, but I couldn't see anything beyond the small beam of light.

At the exit, the woman pressed a piece of paper into my hand and said, "Thanks for coming. I hope you enjoyed the Mystery Theater."

I didn't know what to say, so I just nodded and headed back to my car with the paper clenched in my fist. Halfway home, I pulled to the shoulder and cut the engine, not believing what had happened. I grabbed the paper from the passenger seat where I had tossed it and then unfolded it to reveal a rose. Underneath the rose, the paper said: "Keep what happened here tonight a secret. If you speak of it with anyone, you will spoil the magic for other women like yourself. It is the not-knowing and the surprise in life that makes everything so incredibly exciting."

The Gift of the Magic Lump of Coal

A parody.

EllaRegina

Apologies to O. Henry

One-hundred-and-eighty-seven times. That was an exact tally.
And sixty of those times had occurred out of bed – whilst
standing, sitting on a chair, or tethered together like marionettes
in a slow walk amid their tiny rooms. Many a happy hour had
been spent. Della kept count of their lovemaking in a small
dog-eared leather-bound journal, kept within a tiny desk
drawer next to the shabby couch, in the furnished flat rented
at $8 a week; their love had been proven one-hundred-and-
eighty-seven times in the forty-five days they'd been married.
There was not much in terms of material goods but they had
each other and that seemed enough for now. And the next day
would be Christmas.

Mr James Dillingham Young was only twenty-two and
already burdened with a family, but only in the financial sense
– his income having been cut from $30 weekly to $20; his
nineteen-year-old bride, Della, gave him things a millionaire's
money could not buy. It did not matter that he needed a new
overcoat and went without gloves. It did not matter that their
letter-box could not hold a missive nor that their electric
button doorbell would not ring. Neither did they care that they

lacked the means for proper wedding bands or even Christmas presents.

Whenever Mr James Dillingham Young came home and reached his flat above the entryway vestibule he was called "Jim" and fervently hugged by Mrs James Dillingham Young, his sweet Della. She would unleash her golden cascade of hair, falling beyond the knees, itself almost a garment, and greet him wearing nothing but her black lace-up boots and pink corset – the flaxen thicket of muff hair that Jim so adored peeking out from the embroidered brocade – slightly shivering unless standing close to the fire, but with the knowledge that another kind of warmth was soon to come.

Tomorrow would be Christmas Day. A threadbare upholstered chair stood by the rear window and Jim rested on its feather-poked cushion, his trouser buttons undone. He looked out on a dull gray cat walking a gray fence in a gray backyard, empty of people. Had there been someone they could not bear witness to any activity in the second-floor Dillingham home taking place below the neck. Fortunately, the flat directly across the airshaft was occupied by a blind couple; they never so much as lit a gas lamp for illumination. Della impaled herself atop Jim, his cock shooting up hard against her insides as she sat on his lap. He lifted the mass of her hair with a practiced hand.

"What do you want Santa to bring you for Christmas, little girl?" he queried, his sword-moving accompanying every other word.

"Nothing, Santa," answered Della, moaning low. "This is more than plenty."

"How about if Santa gives you a special present – a baby for *next* Christmas?"

At the word *baby* Della felt Jim's flesh within her arch rigidly to the left, in an uncontrollable pulse, like a bat being swung.

"No, James," said Della, soberly slipping out of the role for a moment to note their fiscal circumstances. "We cannot afford a baby. You know that. Finish how you always do, please, and give it to me quick. It's Christmas Eve, boy. Be good to me."

"Ah," replied Santa, "so there will be no baby as there can be no milk to feed him. I understand. But Santa *always* has plenty of milk for beloved *mothers*."

On cue with that phrase Della left Jim's lap and briskly switched to a kneeling position at his feet, taking his milk-filled prick inside her mouth, lips and tongue holding it tightly as she moved to and fro. She looked up at him – her brilliantly sparkling emerald eyes in an unwavering gaze, rosy nipples peering over the laced corset, her surrounding hair a shiny gilded rippling curtain – as he thickly spouted, a drop or two splashing on the worn red carpet, though Della was careful, as ever, to keep his issue behind her lips the best she could. He spent so copiously it was always a challenge.

"Santa isn't finished with you, Little Miss. Go put on your skirt and come back here."

Della complied, revisiting his post in a petticoat and wool swirl, mounting herself as directed across Santa's muscular knees. Jim unpeeled the seemingly infinite layers of fabric until he reached Della's plump ivory buttocks and took his old leather strap – the one he used in place of a fob chain on the gold watch he inherited from his father, who inherited it from *his* father – and brought the cowhide down with a resounding slap, causing Della to whelp and blush, thinking perhaps Mme. Sofronie below could hear them. Jim alternated between the strap and his strong bare hand, stroking her muff hair soothingly between blows.

Oh, and the next two hours tripped by on rosy wings.

Sometimes Jim paused and insinuated a finger into the eye of Della's rear, causing her to topple and groan with pleasure on his thighs; he had to hold her steady while he dipped the finger in and out. When he felt she was ready, Jim deposited some saliva into the palm of his hand and spread a portion over the little hole, widening it until it could contain a bigger part of himself. Then, skirt still topsy-turvy and aflutter, Della sat upright and eased her private entrance onto Jim's stiffness, slowly and gently – her leg muscles hard at work controlling the speed of her descent – until Jim was firmly encased in the spot that was his alone; it surely had been made for him and no one else.

Once they met in this way she became intoxicated, leaning into him, purring like a cat, rotating her hips like a spinning hoop. Jim, too, was transported – and delighted to be doing something so clandestine and dirty that no other soul in the world could possibly have conceived it – erupting again like a testy whale, coating Della's posterior walls with his warm milk as the scaffold man's tin of white paint covered the billboard by the Elevated tracks on Second Avenue.

Della swiftly wedged the powder rag inside her thatched crevice to collect any excess drippings. There could *not* be a baby next Christmas. There simply could *not*.

They settled themselves and Jim went to his overcoat, drew a package from the pocket and threw it upon the table.

"Merry Christmas, Della."

She approached the parcel curiously. White fingers and nimble tore at string and brown paper. No ecstatic scream of joy, just hysterical tears and confused wails at what she had found: a lump of coal. Della ran and flung herself on the couch. Jim offered comfort immediately and explained:

"This isn't as it appears, my dearest. You shall see. In twelve days our fortunes will change, and for the better. Come."

Jim led his wife to the table and bent her over its top. Again he raised her skirt, revealing her charms. A small vial of salve emerged from his trouser pocket and he put an even layer on the lump. He re-entered Della's most intimate space, this time with the coal as pathfinder.

"No," protested Della, her hindquarters not used to such an unyielding invasion.

Jim made soft noises of assurance as he guided the lump further and, in fact, Della was accustomed to it within a few minutes.

"Have no fear," said Jim. "We shall begin to celebrate tomorrow, on Christmas Day. *Then* you will understand."

The young couple went to bed and slept soundly, enfolded in each other's arms.

★　　★　　★

When they awoke Della made coffee and a simple, forlornly festive Christmas breakfast. She herself did not eat as the lump of coal suggested a liquid subsistence. She could spare the food given how plump she was. Almost like a Christmas goose, she reckoned.

Jim came to the table with a twinkle in his eye.

"After breakfast, we shall take a nice walk," he said.

The mere thought of their promenading along the Avenues, greeting fellow neighbors and strangers in Christmas spirit, all the while knowing that his lovely wife hid a pitch black secret beyond her buttocks excited Jim greatly. So much so, that before Della had finished her beef broth he insisted on starting to make use of the particular gift he had bestowed upon her. He laid Della over the table, pulled her nightgown above her waist, and tucked his prick into the opening that had no coal, thrusting towards her heart like a shovel. She wriggled her behind, further arousing him; he fondled her hairy muff in response. Before he could spend he took care to extract himself and instead of penetrating her mouth – though she could actually swallow whatever he had to give as it was not solid food – he deftly lodged in her rear, bucking deeply, stopped by the hard object at the end of his cock.

"Oh!" exclaimed Della.

"Do not worry, my dearest. The coal shall remain in place and I shall leave no babies here."

Jim spent against the lump, which promptly absorbed every drop he surged. He was right. There was no need for Della to insert her powder rag as usual – no effluvia remained.

They dressed. On went his mended overcoat, with holes in pockets where gloved hands should be. On went her old brown jacket and her old brown hat and the whirl of a skirt and her lace-up boots.

They wandered to Broadway and observed the scene. A light snow had fallen overnight and lines from the carriages were already engraved as if the quiet white surface had been combed. Apple-cheeked youngsters tossed snowballs at one another. They walked past the shop windows, admiring goods exceeding their grasp. They exchanged pleasantries with the grocer, the vegetable man and the butcher; all in repose, out of their work uniforms. Della did not even feel the lump of coal whereas Jim could think of nothing but.

"Squeeze yourself together," he instructed her. "It shan't be noticed and will greatly assist things."

"As you say, my dearest," obeyed Della. "Nobody could ever count my love for you."

Mr and Mrs James Dillingham Young went back to the flat and Jim folded Della over the table once more and plugged at her coal until they both were absolutely spent.

Jim returned to work the morning after Christmas but the evening routine continued for twelve days. At seven o'clock on each of those nights the coffee was made and the frying-pan was on the stove, hot and ready to cook Jim's chops. When she heard his step on the first flight stairs Della briefly turned pale, anticipating what awaited her. While Jim ate she drank the beef broth and the juice of a few oranges. They followed with the postprandial promenade to the Avenues, smiling and nodding at passersby as if nothing was out of order. When they arrived home Jim undid his wife's clothes and churned into her coal bin with enough sparks to start a fire that would be sure competition for the one glowing beneath their mantle.

On the twelfth day of Christmas, while Jim was at work, Della had the notion to surprise him by completely shearing off the curls between her legs, using his long steel razor blade.

"Please make him think I am still pretty," she whispered to herself.

The door opened at seven p.m.; Jim stepped inside and closed it. His eyes were fixed on Della, prepared for him in corset and boots.

"You've cut off your *hair* . . ." he murmured. "Let's have a sight at the looks of it."

"Don't you like me just as well, anyhow? I'm me without my hair, aren't I?" she entreated. "It'll grow out, and fast. You'll see! I just had to do it, Jim!"

"Don't make any mistake, Dell," he said, "I don't think there's anything in the way of a haircut or a shave that could make me like my girl any less."

He tumbled down on the couch, brought Della close, nestled his face in the bald mound between her thighs – inhaling its scent while teasing the exposed flushed bud with his tongue tip – and smiled.

He did indeed fancy her shorn. A little schoolgirl, she was. He jolted her rump that night with greater ardor, hugging her bosom as he released. And, shuddering together in their pleasures, they both felt something had changed. Della sensed a contraction within and the warm flow of her husband's baby-making liquid. Jim hit no wall at the end of Della's dark tunnel. He reached into her tight aperture with a few fingers and beamed. It was as he knew it would be.

Della leaped up like a singed cat and cried, "Oh, oh!"

She had not yet seen her beautiful present and eagerly held out an open palm. Jim deposited an item of precious metal upon it – something fine and rare and sterling – that seemed to flash with a reflection of Della's bright and ardent spirit. Covered with his spunk, ever the more easy to slip on a finger, was a diamond ring.

(*First draft written on Christmas Day, 2007, not far from the Manhattan location where O. Henry allegedly penned "The Gift of the Magi" in 1906.*)

Iced

Erin O'Riordan

"Hey, Nikki."

Jayce, the bartender, looked up from cutting his lemon twists.

"Hey, Jayce," I said back. I took my seat at the wooden counter across from the bar and prepared for the daily grind.

Jayce had the face of a Caravaggio cherub, if a cherub could manage a five o'clock shadow. His thin, graceful body was half rock star and the other half cross-country runner. When he wasn't watching, I watched him work. I liked to watch his long, thin hands grab for bottles, pour, and mix. There was poetry in the way he chilled a shot, and art in the way he uncorked champagne. And on slow nights (like this snowy one was surely going to be), when he flirted with me, I felt sparks in the air.

I was just about to ask Jayce if he did anything fun last night when Robert walked in. Robert was my protector, my "big brother" at Belle's Midtown Inn. He was tall, black-haired, and brown-eyed. Next to Robert's meaty features, Jayce washed out like a watercolor painting.

"Give me your hand," Robert said, parking his big body next to me. Jayce stopped cutting twists, briefly. Then he shook his head and went back to work.

I put down my napkin and stuck my hand out, palm up. Robert pulled my hand closer. Studying it carefully, he then began to massage the center of my palm with his thumb.

He looked into my eyes. "Didn't it work?" Robert's thick-lipped smile caught me off guard, made me smile too.

"Didn't what work?" I asked. I took my hand back, and studied it to see what I was missing. I gave it a few rubs with my own thumb, just for good measure.

"I was trying to make you come," Robert said. "I guess it didn't work."

I thrust my palm back under his nose. "Well, keep trying!" I said.

Robert laughed, a loud donkey's bray that echoed down the bar and into the smoking section. Jayce laughed and set the last of his lemon peels aside.

"See?" Robert said to Jayce, slapping his hand down on the bar. "At least I get a reaction out of her!"

I stared at the two of them. "What, did you try that on Jayce?"

"No," Robert said with indignation. "It only works on *girls*. I tried it on Ellen, and she didn't say anything. Nothing! I felt like a complete idiot, so then I just had to walk away."

"Maybe you just embarrassed her," I offered.

Robert shook his head. "Everybody thinks Ellen is so naive, but it's not true. Ellen looks like she'd shag like a minx. She's just stuck up."

"She is not," I said. "Ellen is very warm and funny, once you get to know her a little. She's just shy."

"I'm surprised she even let you touch her," Jayce said to Robert.

Robert was about to say something, but Belle called to him from the swinging door to the kitchen. "What did it feel like?" Jayce asked me when Robert left.

I looked at my palm. "It was the most sensuous thing I've ever experienced. When Robert touched my hand, I started to get wet. And then he started to rub in slow circles. It was just my palm, I know, but it felt just like he was rubbing my clit. He had me right on the verge, Jayce. Every muscle in my body tightened up. And just as I was about to feel the sweet release, he stopped."

I laughed so hard I almost slipped off my high-backed bar stool. Jayce looked a little less than amused. "Smart ass," he said. He chuckled a little, then restrained himself. He came back with, "When you're done with that, Nik, can you get me some ice?"

"Sure," I said. Then Jayce handed me his freshly cleaned ice bucket. I took it through the bar and up the stairs, passing the hostess stand on my way into the kitchen.

Ellen was on the phone, taking a reservation, so I waved my hello to her. She acknowledged me with a nod of her head. Ellen's white-blonde hair was swept up. She wore a black sweater over a charcoal-gray skirt, with near-black winter tights and fur-trimmed black boots. I'd come in through the snowy parking lot an hour before, and the bottoms of my black pants were still damp. She seemed untouched by the near-blizzard. Not that I was jealous.

I carried Jayce's bucket through the kitchen and down the industrial-style steel stairs. The ice machine was in one lonely corner of the basement. Sometimes – like this time, when the restaurant hadn't opened yet, and everything was so quiet – the basement freaked me out a little bit. But I was a big girl; I could handle myself. Jayce wanted ice, and I was going to get it for him.

As I walked back to the bar, my bucket triumphantly full of ice cubes, Ellen called my name. "What's up?" I said, leaning against the hostess stand. The doors still wouldn't open for twenty more minutes.

"I got you a four-top," she said. "They'll be here when we open."

I smiled. "That's about the best I can hope for tonight, huh? Not many people are going out to eat in this weather."

She shrugged. "You might get lucky," she said. She turned her back to me and went back to what she'd been doing.

She was right. That table was four guys from the university. Good drinkers, good tippers, and each one cuter than the last. They were my only table, except for the old couple who come in every Saturday night regardless of the weather. When they left, there wasn't much for me to do. I parked my ass at the bar and had a cigarette.

"Can I get you something?" Jayce asked me. His tip jar was empty; no one wants to drink in the snow, either.

"Pepsi," I said.

Jayce shook his head. "A real drink," he said. "Robert and I are just about wasted on the house whiskey. It's not too bad chilled, with a splash of grenadine."

I looked around, sensing that Belle was going to pop her head into the bar at any moment. "Look, I'd love a drink, but it's not worth losing my job over."

"You won't," Jayce said. He made a point of standing right in front of my bar stool, leaning over the brass bar so that his mouth was right at my ear. "The kitchen ran out of butter, so Belle took off to get some. We could get away with murder. So, what are you drinking?"

I said the first thing that came to my mind. "Gin. It's what I always drink when I'm out with my girls."

"Always had you figured for a gin girl," he said. "You like it cold?"

"Yeah," I said. I watched Jayce's slender, white hands as he poured two, three, four shots in the shaker with ice. He set up two Collins glasses and poured two doubles. He held up his glass. "Cheers." I clinked our glasses together and took a modest sip. Jayce drained his.

"What happens when Belle gets back?" I asked him.

Jayce raised his eyebrows skyward. "I guess we'll find out, won't we?"

Sparks. Definite sparks.

I finished my cigarette, then my drink, and lit another cigarette. I could have stayed there all night, just watching Jayce floating behind the bar.

Soon, I headed back up to my section. I didn't have any tables, but I thought I'd at least straighten up the server station. I noticed then that we were out of ice. I found the servers' ice bucket with the clean dishes and took it down to the basement.

Above me, I heard the cooks and the dishwasher stomp across the kitchen floor. There were no other sounds in the basement, except for the electric hum of the ice machine, making new ice. I would have to wait before I could fill my bucket.

"Hello?" I called, testing to see if I was really alone in the basement. Maybe it was the loneliness, the isolation down there. Maybe it was reverb from the sparks that had been flying between Jayce and me. Maybe it was just the gin talking. Maybe it was the way Robert tried to make my hand come. But I was hot. Felt like I had a fever.

I leaned against the ice machine. It was then that I realized, for the first time, that between the ice machine and the wall there was a little space, a nook into which I could cram myself. No one would be able to see me back there, not unless they got right up on the ice machine. Feeling devilish and little bit reckless, I squeezed myself into the cranny.

I just wanted to be alone with my thoughts for a moment. Thoughts that kept running in a sexual direction. I imagined myself leaning across the bar, my lips brushing against Jayce's. Maybe I'd let Robert watch. Maybe I'd let Jayce and Robert take turns kissing me. Our three tongues, all tied up together, could be a pleasant way to pass a slow night at the restaurant. And if one of them happened to unbutton my white shirt, and my breasts happened to slip out of my white bra . . . well, then, it might be fun to let Jayce and Robert each have a nipple to suck . . .

That was all I needed. I came hard. I fought myself to stay quiet, but it didn't completely work. A tiny squeak escaped my lips. It was nothing compared to the furious thundering of the blood in my veins. By all rights, the dishwasher should have been able to hear it over the roar of his sinks.

I stood there in the nook, panting, until I felt collected enough to rejoin civilized human society. This was not like me, masturbating in some dark corner. At work. A creeping sense of impropriety caught up with me. I considered how I would explain going upstairs without the ice bucket, and dashing to the bathroom to wash the hell out of my filthy little paws.

Suddenly, there was Jayce. "What were you doing back there?" he asked me.

I didn't know what to say. "Nothing," I said. "I wasn't doing anything back there." Oh God, could he smell my pussy?

"Well, that's weird," he said. He looked at the ice bucket, sitting abandoned on top of the ice machine. "Aren't you going to get ice?"

No, I thought. Not with these dirty, dirty hands. "I will later," I said. "I think my pager just went off. I must have food up."

"You don't have any tables," he said. He laughed nervously.

"No, nothing horrible like that," I said. "I was just thinking."

"Okay," he said. "You were wedged behind the ice machine, just thinking. And still not getting any ice."

Enough of the third degree. "I was thinking about you," I said. Hell, might as well lay it all out on the line. "And it turned me on."

Jayce's eyes were one big question now. Fortunately, I knew the answer. I walked over to him, filling in the space between us completely, and kissed him. He didn't have to think about it. He threw every inch of his graceful body into kissing me back. For a brief portion of a second, I felt myself falling backward. In the next moment, I was lying across the front of the ice machine, caught between ice and sparks.

Caught. I should say, trapped. Nothing was holding me under Jayce except my own passionate wanting, yet we were incredibly exposed and vulnerable in our little corner of Belle's basement. At any moment, someone could come down the stairs, looking for us. The line cooks could run out of soup, or asparagus spears, or lemon juice, and come down looking for some . . . the danger was real. And really making me hot.

As I writhed and squirmed, uncomfortable with and excited by the possibility of getting caught, Jayce was single-minded in his purpose. He was going to kiss me. He was going to suck my tongue. I always wondered what his tongue stud would taste like, and now I knew. It tasted like iron, like blood, like poetry and art, like all the things I saw when I watched him bartend. I felt it in my mouth first, and on my neck next. His hands unbuttoned my white shirt, just like in my fantasies, and prepared the way for me to feel Jayce's tongue stud on my nipple. I looked down at my bared breast and felt the hot rush of blood surging through me. Already, my heart was hammering.

Hammering out a sound, a sound like the tapping of fur-lined boots on a set of industrial steel steps.

Which, I soon realized, was what I was actually hearing. Jayce was oblivious, consumed with the taste of my throat. Suddenly he shifted, his mouth finding my breast. His tongue traced a wide circle around my nipple before his mouth closed around it and sucked.

I groaned. The sound was half pleasure, half warning. I wanted him to know that Ellen was standing there, watching and biting down on her lip with a look of concern crossed with disapproval.

She said nothing.

I tapped Jayce hard on the shoulder. He looked up into my eyes. Somehow my face conveyed the message. He straightened and turned to face her. I re-buttoned my shirt. My abandoned nipple ached with indignation.

"I got bored and decided to refill the toothpick dispenser," Ellen said. "Came down for a box of toothpicks . . ."

Jayce looked panicked. "You're not going to tell Belle, are you?" he asked the hostess.

"No," Ellen said flatly. She caught the bottom of her black sweater and pulled it over her head. "If I told on you, I'd be telling on myself. That is, if you'll let me have a turn."

My chest suddenly swelling with confidence, I strode over to Ellen. I ran the back of my hand down the silk of her black camisole. I touched her arm; her skin was even smoother. She was the softest thing I'd ever touched. Her bright blue eyes looked into mine, briefly, but closed as I leaned in to kiss her.

Ellen bubbled and melted like Belle's hollandaise. Her little arms circled around me. She was a little shy, so I guided her hands down to my ass. I could hear Jayce making little squeaking sounds like an excited puppy.

"Did you like that?" I asked Ellen.

"Yeah," she said, starstruck.

"Better than when Robert tried to make your hand come?" We both laughed. Jayce laughed, too.

"We should get back upstairs," Ellen said. "They're going to start wondering . . ."

"Not yet," Jayce said. He peeled Ellen's hand off my ass. Gently, he led her over to where he was standing. She hesitated, so he kissed her tentatively, a brief touch of lips to lips. "You haven't had your turn yet," he said. His fingers traced one of her nipples through the camisole. She leaned against the ice machine and sighed.

Jayce lifted one of her heavy breasts from her camisole, caressing it in slow circles.

"You have beautiful breasts," I said. I came closer, close enough to smell Ellen's expensive perfume once again. This time, it was mixed with her sweat. She looked over at the steel steps, caught in the same trap that had caught Jayce and me.

He lowered his head and suckled her. I nudged him out of the way, just a bit, so that I could taste her other nipple. Ellen bit her lip harder and seemed to struggled not to cry out.

"I know the feeling," I said between sucks. "You want to scream, don't you? But you can't let everyone hear you. What would you do if they found out?"

Ellen giggled, a charmingly cheerful and free sound. I could imagine the forbidden images flooding Ellen's brain. They were turning me on as much as they were her. I didn't know where we would go from here, but I was definitely sticking around to find out.

Ellen's hand, which had been gripping the ice machine for dear life, made a run for her skirt. Through the thick charcoal-gray fabric, she found her erect clit. I reached out and stopped her hand.

"That's my job," I said. I did the job properly, too, reaching up her skirt until the whole thing was lifted over her hips. Jayce stopped suckling long enough to watch me tug at Ellen's panties, getting them down just far enough to have access to her clit. I massaged her pink little shaft as she huffed and puffed. I never did get her to scream, but I knew I'd done a good job when her knees weakened and she sank to the floor. Jayce's mouth was on her, tasting her heartbeat.

I looked at the glistening moisture on my fingers with satisfaction.

Jayce looked at me. With swift, certain motion, he unzipped his black pants and pulled his cock out.

"Bad, bad bartender," I said, teasingly. "You don't have a condom, do you?"

Jayce shook his head.

"Well, it'll have to be a hand job then." My fingers still glistening with wet from Ellen's pussy, I began to stroke Jayce up and down. In no time at all, he was on the edge. That was when Ellen jumped back in. She looked surprisingly composed for a woman who was just kneeling on the floor in a seldom-cleaned basement. Her sweater was still draped over a box of crackers, but her other clothes were back in place. You had to admire that in a woman.

Ellen wrapped her hand, lubricated with her spit, around Jayce's shaft, and we pumped together. I worked the head while she worked the base. Jayce's eyes shot open, wide with excitement. His breath was heavy sobs and gasps. He was close now . . .

I didn't expect Ellen to kneel and edge my fingers aside with her mouth. Her tongue lapped my hand, and I got out of her way. Jayce lost it utterly. Ellen, it turned out, was a swallower.

"Oh, Ellen," I said, "that was brave. Crazy. Kind. But reckless."

She didn't talk with her mouth full, but when Jayce pulled

away, she mumbled something like, "Thirteen years of Catholic girls' school."

"It's okay," Jayce assured her. "Just got tested after my last piercing. I'm clean." He zipped up, winking at Ellen. "Now let's do Nikki."

I started to protest, to explain that technically, I'd already had my turn. In the end, I decided against it. Ellen was on me in a flash, her mouth hot on my ear as she fiddled with the buttons on my shirt. My tits realized that they were in for a sucking, and stood ready at attention. Ellen moved off to my left to make room for Jayce, and I sunk back against the ice machine. They suckled me, just like the guys in my hottest fantasies.

I didn't hear the next set of footsteps on the steel steps.

"What in the hell is going on here?" Belle thundered, flicking on a brighter light. She dropped the case of butter she'd been carrying. The white tubs tumbled out and rolled across the floor.

I scrambled to put away my own – again – frustrated tits.

Belle's face was red with rage. "My hostess, my bartender, and my best server," she said. "Hell, Nikki, I expected this out of you. I could have guessed it would involve the boy. But you, Ellen?"

Ellen was on the verge of tears. "Are you going to fire us?" she asked, her voice trembling.

Belle exhaled. "If I did that, then who'd clean up the filth from you guys?" she said, bending down to pick up an escaped tub of butter. She hurried returned the butter to its box, then shoved it in the cooler. Slamming the cooler shut, she said, "Now get to work!"

Jayce leaned in close to me. I thought he was going to kiss me again, but instead he whispered in my ear. "I told you," he said. "We could get away with murder around here."

I smiled. Ellen pulled her sweater over her head, biting her lip.

"I don't want to get away with murder," I said. "I just want to make sparks."

The look in Jayce's eyes promised me that more, much more, was to come. I couldn't wait. But for now, I needed to get Ellen alone one more time. I had the sudden, irresistible urge to lick the last taste of Jayce's cock off her lips.

The Beloved of the Gigolem

Ian Watson and Roberto Quaglia

A gigolo and a golem combined . . . is a gigolem. He-She can be male or female, or both sexes at once (and perhaps also other sexes as yet unknown). Indeed, a gigolem can change sex several times a minute, supposing that a sex partner is unsure of himself or herself sexually; which can be confusing or alternatively interesting. However, what János sought for in Prague was a quality personal gigolem who would remain female for a reasonably long time, to pleasure him and vice versa. Of course he had fucked gigolems at public baths in Budapest lots of times, yet that was always rather impersonal, even if the gigolem did conform to his tastes. Actually, for his money, the best gigolems in Budapest were those geisha-gigolems much used by Japanese tourists. However, he was a János, not a Yukio, and he craved for his own dedicated Euro-gigolem.

He travelled from Budapest by Magyar Álom Vasutak, Hungarian Dream Railways. Formerly this had been Magyar Állam Vasutak, the State Railways, but passengers had petitioned for a more imaginative name – ah, the romance of travel. His friend Silvia was the driver of the MAV locomotive and she let him sit in the cab with her, to keep her company. Silvia was devoted to chocolate, which produces endorphins in the brain, so János had brought several bars of chocolate with him to feed to Silvia *en route*. The route was fairly simple because the railway lines led inexorably via Vienna to Prague, an inevitability which could become boring. Consequently endorphins helped – although at the same time Silvia possessed no driving licence for anything as trivial as a car; she was only interested in driving vehicles weighing more than thirty tonnes.

"Are you sure you'll be happy living with the same gigolem all the time?" she had asked when János first told her his plan. "I'm happy with mine, but women tend to be faithful – and you're a man."

"I know I am. Well, it's either a gigolem or very old women." He hesitated. "Or else a colostomy."

"How could a colostomy help?"

"It would serve as a substitute vagina in a fixed location."

Silvia beamed. "Oh I see, you mean a colostomy for *her*, not for you."

"If the woman agreed." János shrugged. "Whoever she might be!"

"How many women have you asked, if they'll have a colostomy?"

"A few. They didn't want the inconvenience."

The fundamental problem, which confronted many men, was that vaginas had begun to migrate around women's bodies, sealing up suddenly only to emerge elsewhere within a few minutes. The cause of this was mutated Ebola virus, which instead of eating flesh rearranged flesh painlessly. Allegedly the mutated virus had escaped from a military laboratory, perhaps in America, perhaps in North Korea, perhaps elsewhere. The result was that a vagina could shift without warning from the crotch to the armpit or to behind the knee or to almost anywhere. Foreplay could become six-play or ten-play or twenty-play as a man tried to keep up with a shifting situation, and often he lost his erection.

The only women unaffected were those well past menopause. Probably the virus responded to hormones. Consequently beautiful young or even middle-aged prostitutes had all disappeared, replaced by grannies over seventy, with whom satisfaction could still be guaranteed. This fixated some men erotically upon old women, which was laudably anti-ageist

– and this even led to a rumour that the migrating vagina phenomenon had been engineered by a secret collective of women scientists, to promote sexual gratification in their old age.

Men pursued various techniques for discovering the whereabouts of the mobile vagina quickly. Asking the woman if she had seen her vagina recently wasn't always much help. Very often females did not look for their own vaginas. "I don't want to *know* about it; I just want it to work properly," was a common attitude.

Consequently some men used a torch, and others a divining rod, and others a stethoscope or a small seismic detector – a vibrator might have remained in a vagina from a previous use, or the migration of the vagina might itself cause subtle vibrations. A small percentage of men used a sniffer dog, although this only worked if the dog had previously smelled that particular vagina. This was all very unsatisfactory.

"A Romanian girl I know did consider the colostomy idea," admitted János, "but she thought I might pimp the colostomy to make money. I'll be much better off with a gigolem."

Hence his journey to Prague, where the banks of the river Vltava contained the very best quality mud and clay for making golems. That's how Rabbi Löw had succeeded in making the first ever golem, back in the early seventeenth century, to guard the ghetto against the malice of Christians. The rabbi was fortunate in the raw material he found locally, even though he was already a skilled kabbalist.

And part of that skill was in knowing how to write a Shem to put in the golem's mouth to animate it. Originally the Shem was a piece of parchment inscribed with a secret name of God, and could go on the forehead or in the mouth. Nowadays the Shem was software.

"You didn't forget your Shem?" Silvia had asked, as the MAV train was leaving Vienna. She knew a lot about such things. Apart from having her own gigolem, she was keen on interactive computer role-playing games where it was necessary

to collect jewels of enlightenment, crystals of power, and such.
Particularly she thought about Shems because putting little
squares of chocolate into her own mouth animated her.

Although János knew that he hadn't forgotten the Shem, all
the same he took out his wallet to check that the mini-disc was
still in the same place.

"So how much did it cost you," asked Silvia, "to download
from that sexual magic site?"

"A hundred Euros. Quite a lot of warnings: forbidden to
those under 16, and so forth. It's well worth paying a hundred
Euros to also have the instructions for removal from the
gigolem – if need be."

"Hmm. Easy to put it in, but hard to take it out?"

"As the lover said to his Beloved whose vagina suddenly
started to migrate?"

"Nonsense, a penis just pops out!"

"I was joking. The Shem mini-disc clings to the palate, the
roof of the golem's mouth. Well, I suppose you know that.
A golem might bite your fingers off to keep the Shem in its
mouth."

"Or simply keep its mouth shut?"

A while later, the MAV train arrived in Prague Station. After
bidding a fond farewell to Silvia, János emerged from the
station and within a couple of minutes he was at the top of
Wenceslas Square, which isn't square-shaped at all, but is a
long wide avenue running downhill to the old city. He'd been
advised to put a note wrapped round a pebble on Rabbi Löw's
tomb in the old Jewish cemetery, a traditional ritual for anyone
who wished to make their own golem. The avenue misnamed a
square pointed straight as an arrow towards the former Jewish
ghetto.

Quite a few pregnant gigolems were waddling up and down
Wenceslas Square, some pushing prams loaded with previous
babies. Ever since vaginas began to migrate, pregnancy – and
particularly childbirth – had become problematic. To sustain
the birthrate of the human race, eggs were extracted from a

would-be mother's ovaries, which didn't migrate. A would-be father would masturbate into a test-tube, and the fertilized product would go into a walking-womb gigolem for nine months. Despite control by Shem, sometimes the walking-womb would fluctuate sexually, so that a male gigolem might be carrying a foetus. Generally the resulting child seemed normal, and human.

Soon János was amongst the extreme confusion of gravestones piled in all directions against and on top of one another. Fortunately a dozen Japanese were taking holo-pictures of the rabbi's tomb, making it easy to identify. János's handwritten note read, "Dear Rabbi Löw, bless my gigolem, may she give me satisfaction."

János left the cemetery and soon spied a sign in English and German on a dilapidated old building announcing a room to rent. Probably it was fortunate that the building was in bad repair, otherwise someone might already have taken the room. János thought probably he would need a room for at least a week, to make sure the Gigolem was a good one before taking her home to Budapest.

The landlady, Mrs Smetana, was old and thin. The room, up in the attic, was dark but big, the furniture huge and ancient: a vast wooden bed ideal for sharing with a gigolem and a mighty wardrobe ideal for keeping the gigolem locked in, if need be.

János and Mrs Smetana negotiated in English.

"Is problem I keep gigolem here?"

"You gigolem pimp? This not bad house."

"Gigolem girlfriend is for me only."

"Okay. Hundred Crowns extra."

János blessed the rabbi for this bit of luck, then he headed for the long stretch of riverbank owned by the Prague Golem Company.

Over the years exploitation of the clay-like river mud, or mud-like clay, had resulted in the exposure of many hectares of yellowy brown or brownish yellow substance adjacent to the river. The terrain looked like the battlefield of the Somme in

1918 due to the partially flooded trenches left by excavating for golem-material and the multitudes of little craters where individuals had made their own golems or gigolems by shovelling material into moulds hired from the PGC.

János needed to buy an excavation permit for the area most suitable to make gigolems, but further spending was discretionary.

"Is dirty work – you want hire rubber galoshes and boiler suit?"

Yes.

"Want rubber gloves? Some say best intimate result from naked hands."

Naked hands would be fine.

"Need Shem? We sell several Lust Shems. As well as Cordon Bleu Chef Shem, Chauffeur Shem—"

"I bring my own Shem."

"You need shovel? Some say no shovel, best results. But takes much longer." Obviously PGC weren't trying to take advantage of János's inexperience in making his own golem. The benefits of coming to a reputable company.

"Hmm. I think shovel."

"You need plastic mould to help shape body? We hire male, female, neuter, and hermaphrodite moulds. Remember, once lust-gigolem is active it can easily change sex."

"Female mould." He would start the gigolem the way he hoped she would continue.

The assistant brought out what looked like the hull of a simple boat, a bit larger than himself, and bright red, indented with a female form. Easy to carry, being plastic. Very visible. Had a paedophile ever tried to escape downstream in a mould along with a newly made prohibited paedogolem, hoping to escape confiscation of his illegal handiwork? Since no sails nor oars accompanied the mould, such an attempt seemed unwise. Unless, of course, an accomplice was waiting nearby downstream in a motor boat – the cunning of paedophiles was notorious; a mutable mud-boy-girl would be quite a prize.

★　　　★　　　★

Presently János was out on the widespread Somme-on-Vltava with his mould and shovel.

Various other Do-It-Yourself golem enthusiasts were busy, looking somewhat like gravediggers though in fact the very opposite, for from dirt they were assembling what would become a semblance of life.

János laboured for an hour. He heaped the mould high, then he used his hands to contour the back of the gigolem, paying particular attention to the buttocks.

With considerable effort he heaved the now-heavy mould on to its side so that the gigolem slid out. Any slumping out of shape should rectify itself once the Shem was in the mouth. He walked around the heap of clay-mud widdershins seven times shouting "Shanti Shanti, Dehat Dehat!" because you were supposed to do this. Then he washed his hands in a nearby trench. Due to lack of a towel he dried them on his own hair. Finally he produced the Shem and pushed it between the clay lips, as one would push a card into a cash dispenser.

The gigolem convulsed. Her breasts firmed, and other important parts too. And she arose, staggering upright and regarding him. To his eyes she was rather beautiful, her flesh halfway between Asian and Mulatto. Other eyes may have regarded her as a bit ugly or strange. Alternatively, her strangeness or ugliness possessed its own beauty. Most importantly, she was a *she*, and remained a *she*.

She needed a name.

"You are Patricia," he said, and took her by the hand. Since this was a romantic gesture, almost womanly, dark hairs promptly began sprouting from Patricia's breasts as she manifested reciprocal manliness. These fell off as soon as János experienced an annoyed surge of testosterone which almost made him slap her.

"By the way," he told her, "I am János."

"I am yours," she said in a husky voice in Hungarian. "Mine are you." Was Patricia experimenting with the grammar of his difficult language, or did she mean *you are mine*?

*   *   *

In that attic in the big house of Mrs Smetana, János experimented with Patricia.

The first sexual intercourse with any gigolem is always a delicate matter, for a reason quite the opposite to the reason why the first intercourse with another human being is – or had been – delicate. The uncertainty attendant on sexually joining with another human person resides in the fear of what he or she might think of you, the possibility of causing disappointment and not being liked. In a sexual joining with a gigolem this problem doesn't exist because a gigolem isn't a human person and cannot judge you. However, a gigolem becomes sexually what you unconsciously wish it to be, consequently that first encounter might reveal through the gigolem that your own sexual nature differs dramatically from the image you had of it. The perceptiveness of the mirror in which you risk seeing yourself is far greater than in the case of a human partner. This can generate greater anxiety.

Cautiously János kissed Patricia's hand, then slowly ascended along the arm. As his lips travelled, the dark skin of the gigolem paled and blushed, as if the meat within might burn. A low manly rumble sounded within the gigolem, an omen of impending masculinization – which János aborted by gripping Patricia's hair firmly, though not too violently. That rumble faded into the gentle moan of a female in heat. A breast inflated as he brought his lips close, and continued to inflate to a fair extent as he sucked the nipple, while her legs shortened just a little. Nothing comes from nothing, so the substance inflating the tits was necessarily subtracted from part of the body to which the lover was paying less attention. János intruded a hand between her thighs, to which her buttocks accordingly donated some substance. These weren't major changes of dimension which would result in grotesquerie or the physically impossible, but the alterations were sufficient to satisfy the ordinary imaginative follies of the human mind transported by a stormy vortex of passion and somatic obsession towards another living being.

Later, when János turned Patricia so as to pay maximum

virile attention to those buttocks which he had moulded with such great attention, her breasts and belly, invisible to him now, lost tone and thickness while the beautiful perfect buttocks inflated within their skin, stretching into a unique cloven sex-drum of female mystery inextinguishably tantalizing ... at least until orgasm.

In the relaxed aftermath, János regarded his gigolem with an enchanted eye. Patricia had remained female during all their intercourse, a rare circumstance which few men could manage to experience.

Since so many Americans already lived in the Czech capital, and due to the million tourists who visited every year, the Creation Science Museum of Arkansas had recently opened a branch museum in Prague. So János took Patricia there the following morning to entertain and impress her. That ought to be just her sort of museum. God made Adam out of clay or mud. Maybe János would seem like a god.

In the foyer towered a life-size holographic dinosaur with big blunt stumpy teeth behind an illuminated sign: *Vegetarian Tyrannosaurus Rex*. Even as János watched, the holographic blunt teeth elongated into fierce daggers, and the sign changed to: *Tyrannosaurus Rex After the Fall*. Presently T. Rex became benign again. The dino still looked hungry, but now for a cabbage. Thank God for holography, otherwise two sets of different giant dentures, as well as chains and a pulley, would have been needed to produce the transformation.

A Schwarzenegger-golem wearing shorts printed with fig leaves – no, he must be Michelangelo's Adam – beckoned tourists coyly towards the *Chapel of Creation from Clay*. The golem's body language was definitely gay, and its name badge called it, not Arnie, but **Cleopatra**. In an affectedly dainty way, the muscular Schwarzenegger began to recite a commentary in English and Czech and German, although János only paid attention to the English.

"Darwinian scientists say that life arose from primeval soup—"

In a big transparent cauldron on the left side of the chapel, a soup of plastic alphabet pieces simmered, the four letters T, C, A and G moving around and around, constantly bumping into each other.

"The letters you see represent the *very complicated* bases of the genetic code DNA, namely Thymine, Cytosine, Adenine and Guanine. Darwinian scientists pretend that these substances could have formed *at random* out of chemicals in the sea – and then furthermore that these letters could have combined *at random* to form the vast catalogue of information that creates life!

"I ask you, could a million blind monkeys chained to typewriters for a billion years ever have written the complete Bible exactly word-perfectly? No way, I say!"

"This is boring," said Patricia. "Fuck me."

"No, wait a bit," said János.

Adam-Schwarzenegger gestured to the right of the chapel at what looked like a printing press from ancient Babylon designed to produce cuneiform clay tablets.

"In the Bible it says, *And the LORD God formed man from the clay of the ground.* Wiser, more scientific scientists says that living cells first appeared in a special kind of clay – called montmorillonite, monty for short. Negatively charged layers of monty-clay crystals produce a sandwich of positive charge in between them, which is a very attractive environment for RNA. I ask you, which is the more sensible theory: soup – *or sandwich?*"

A terrible realization came to János, with the force of an anti-religious revelation – as if St Paul had arrived blind in Damascus and suddenly saw not the light but anti-light.

Of course all life on Earth arose from chemicals in the soup of the ancient sea! That's where we all come from – and cats too, and rats and fish and spiders and cacti and cabbages – from chemical soup. What comes from clay – but only *nowadays* – is golem-life. If clay had caused life in the first place, we would all be golems (including golem-cats and golem-rats and so forth)!

Clay and mud sandwiches must have *tried* to make life, like MacDonald's taking over the world, but sandwiches had lost out to soup. Nevertheless, lurking in mud and clay there remained an alternative pathway of golem-evolution. And now it was coming into reality. Because gigolems mated with men and women, and because of the need for walking-wombs, clay-life was sexually contaminating the human race! Maybe this was why vaginas were migrating, to try to escape, due to feminine intuition.

All of a sudden János felt polluted by Patricia.

He cried out at Adam-Schwarzenegger, "Your Creationist God is the God of golems and gigolems, not of human beings! You Creationists all worship a false creation!"

János had to express this concept in Hungarian, which nobody except other Hungarians can understand. Nevertheless, a security-golem came into the chapel. What occurred in the museum must be monitored by multilingual security computers. This big brawny gay golem wore a name badge: **Brünnhilde**.

Brünnhilde approached on massive legs, gesturing menacingly. In Hungarian, then English, he-she declared:

"We don't want Darwinian preachers here! This is a place of science and there's no space for the mystic fantasies of Darwinism!"

János retorted: "My world is the one that evolved over billions of years through natural selection and produced human beings. The creationist world is that of the golems!"

János's counter-enlightenment was now accompanied by a strange sense of *déjà vu*, as if something that happened in the past had been suppressed from conscious memory but now returned hauntingly. He thought to himself: *It's as if two parallel worlds have overlapped and are melting together – the world of the humans and the world of the golems. How on Earth could this have happened?*

"I told you," Patricia said, "you should have fucked me."

Then János had no more time for thinking, because Brünnhilde was upon him. Close up, he-she stank of mud, not because he-she was made from mud, but due to nasal hallucination since the very existence of golems and gigolems suddenly stank for János. Brünnhilde was one and a half times his size, so she had no difficulty pushing him into a corner of the room. *She? She?* He-she had definitely become she. Holding János in one hand like a naughty boy, she pulled his trousers and underpants down. He thought she was going to smack him on the bottom, just as his mother had sometimes done. But then Brünnhilde exposed herself, and what smacked János, not upon the bottom but upon the front, were mighty and female genitalia. These sucked his balls and penis into them completely and munched. Fortunately her vagina was not dentata.

Presently she ejected him – and *that* was because she was now becoming male, her vagina filling and turning inside-out to become a stiff penis, which with gigolems was possible. Brünnhilde turned János round and buggered him, which felt as if a large living turd was returning to its bowel repeatedly.

The other visitors to the museum were taking souvenir photos and exclaiming. In a society lacking coherent vaginas and sexual certainties of any kind, bodily violation was not infrequent, so nobody should have been surprised. But tourists must let themselves be surprised by what is perfectly normal – that's their role. A latecomer, who had missed most of the spectacle, asked Brünnhilde when the next violation was scheduled.

Afterwards, János felt as anyone would feel after being violated by a lump of mud – soiled. Dirtier than he'd ever felt in his life.

He was ashamed and furious at the same time.

Holding his trousers tightly at the waist in case they got pulled down again, he headed for the office of the museum's director while Patricia followed him.

Here it was: **Dr Vaclav Sládek, Director**.

Dr Sládek wore a thin waxed moustache and a monocle. Also, a dark suit with thin stripes. And, for that matter, a sky-blue shirt and purple bow tie. His dark hair was oiled and combed back.

"I have been violated front and rear by your security-golem!" expostulated János.

"By security?" said Dr Sládek. "That sounds like safe sex. You won't become pregnant."

"In public!" roared János.

"Did you want it in private?"

"I want compensation for humiliation."

"My dear fellow, there's no possibility of that. A gigolem exhibits sexual behaviour in sympathy with the subconscious needs of a human being. Subconsciously you must have wished to be violated, and in such a way. Legally, the golem can't be blamed, nor its owners sued."

"I'm not gay! Not even my subconscious is gay. Why would I want to be violated by a *gay* golem?"

"You said you were violated at the front as well. Obviously the gigolem was making an effort to suit you."

"Why are the staff here gay golems? I thought creation churches didn't like homosexuality."

"My dear fellow ..." The director took a lace fan from his desk and wafted it. "This museum is concerned with the creation of life. In most creatures higher than the amoeba this tends to involve sexual activity. Frequent sexual activity. The employment of neuter golems could seem a snub to God. Therefore the personnel must have genders. Yet they mustn't present any menace to the sacred femininity of women tourists!"

"A Schwarzenegger called Cleopatra is absurd!"

"No, this reflects the dualistic principle of the universe, the mysterious principle which forces into existence the contrary of everything. It's like matter and anti-matter. We need gay golems here to demonstrate this."

"I want Brünnhilde destroyed."

"Spiritually, a gigolem is merely the psychic extension of the human being who uses it, so in a sense, dear sir, you're saying that you should be destroyed – that you should be punished."

"I already have been punished!"

"Are you a masochist? It's a banal logical error to imagine that gay gigolems are useful to heterosexual masochists. A gay gigolem would avoid inflicting sadism on a heterosexual masochist, in order to fulfil his desires by denying them. By the way, did you know that the United States has stationed thousands of gay gigolems in Antarctica for obscure purposes of homeland security? What is needed is an association for the protection of gay inhuman rights."

János realized that Dr Sládek himself secretly wished to be a gay gigolem. He wondered what happened in the museum after the doors were closed to the public each evening.

"Come home and fuck my vagina," said Patricia.

Dr Sládek shuddered delicately.

Later, in the comfort of the little flat of Mrs Smetana, János idly indulged in pseudo-philosophical thoughts:

"Dust thou art, to dust returnest," he recited, a universally popular line from the once much admired American poet Longfellow, which joined up *Genesis* 2:7 – "the Lord God formed man of the dust of the ground" – with *Ecclesiastes* 12:1 – "then shall the dust return to the earth as it was."

And what was dust, if not dry mud? Therefore meat was derived from mud, the basic element of gigolems. Creationism was right! In the beginning there was the primordial sandwich, not the fucking soup.

The violation performed by Brünnhilde seemed to have temporarily obliterated the evolutionary anti-enlightenment that had caught him in the museum. Much worse, it had taken away from him for the moment any desire to make love with Patricia. This was perfectly understandable in someone who had just been violated by a gay gigolem. Obviously János was being inhibited by a fear that sexual relations with his hitherto straight gigolem might result in a repetition of that violation, this time by Patricia. A mysterious mechanism of the human subconscious means that repetition of known experiences can be reassuring, even if the experiences are unpleasant. Although János felt exonerated of responsibility for being violated in the first place – despite the insinuations of Dr Sládek! – to be re-violated due to complicity on the part of his subconscious would be intolerable.

János was not at all satisfied with how his romantic journey to Prague was proceeding. He shut Patricia inside the wardrobe. That was like banishing her into a dark subconscious from which she must not escape. Could it be that golems were nothing but the embodiments of the collective subconscious of mankind? Or might human beings be the embodiment of the subconscious of golems? Who was dreaming whom?

As a way of getting out of himself for a while, János quit the house. People often leave home in the more or less vain attempt to leave themselves behind. This scarcely ever works.

The Sex Centre of Prague, close to the river Vltava at Bubenské nábř, had for many years been a sex-for-cash-supermarket based on the principles of fast-food and the assembly line. Human beings and gigolems alike flaunted their charms inside little cabins with only space for a bed. You could peep through a window, if the curtain wasn't closed, to admire the merchandise before entering and enjoying it. Half of the hookers were human, strictly over 70, and the rest were gigolems, all looking beautiful.

János wandered lazily through the corridors where God's loving bounty was on offer. Now and then someone quickly entered or quit a cabin. János realized that in fact he hadn't come to this place to watch the prostitutes, but their clients. Was he hoping to see something of himself in them? Interest in other people is a delusion, if you only try to see aspects of yourself reflected in them.

Since he had travelled through Freudian Vienna on the way to Prague, he thought, *Perhaps I need a psychoanalygolem.*

Due to their highly mirroring nature, golems were much more effective psychoanalysts than humans. Yet by contrast with human psychoanalysts, a psychoanalygolem didn't exist until someone needed one. Even more than with a gigolem, it was essential to construct your own psychoanalygolem yourself. It was important for a psychoanalygolem to be – so to speak – virgin, the first time you used it. It must be pure and clean from the mental problems of anyone else who wasn't its own particular creator. In many functions, golems were subjected to imprinting. They adapted better to the needs of an owner if they hadn't had any previous contacts with other human beings. The innate knowledge that golems manifested, however, fuelled the idea that in fact they were simply a separately embodied extension of the human mind, their existence a highly effective representation of humanity.

Had two parallel universes really overlapped? Had the creationist world of the golems trespassed into the Darwinian world of the humans? Or vice versa?

What János really needed at this point was a friend – a human being, not a mirror of mud.

Silvia should soon be arriving again in her train. She would have the rest of the day free. Quickly he phoned her, on the train.

He met Silvia at the Kafka Café, a prestigious and ornate establishment in Alphonse Mucha Art Nouveau style near the Old Town Square.

"You only drive vehicles heavier that thirty tonnes, "János said to her. "So do you think that golems are real creatures?" He knew what he was implying; and so did she, for such is friendship.

"As with vehicles over thirty tonnes," she answered, "the question is whether you drive them, or they drive you."

The answer was somewhat Zen-like, but then so had his question been.

"What if I wanted to have a child with you?"

"All such things go through gigolems, as you well know."

"And if I just wanted to make love to you?"

"We would need a gigolem to interpose between us. What questions you do ask! Even children know that."

"That's the whole problem. Does anyone still exist who's even able to *imagine* a heterosexual relation between human beings of reproductive age? I'm not talking about gerontophiles, who make a virtue of necessity. I'm not interested in that."

"Hmm. Have you heard of the Virgil Award? No, not the *Virgin* Award. Virgil guided Dante into Hell, in other words down a deep hole. Last year a friend of mine called Zsuzsa won the award for keeping her vagina – to which she'd conceeded the rare privilege of a visit by a human penis – in the same position for twenty minutes."

"Lucky her, lucky that penis."

"It took great concentration."

"That's a prize-winning exception, so it doesn't count – no more than being able to jump right over an elephant. The norm defines the standard of reality. I ask you, can love without a gigolem still exist today?"

"On the other hand, having won the Virgil Award, Zsuzsa couldn't find her vagina again for six months. In practical reality, true love without the mediation of gigolems can't exist any more."

"Maybe I should continue trying with Patricia," said János, half to himself. "Even if she isn't a real woman, it could be a pleasant hallucination."

From her handbag, Silvia took something. It was a little Adam-Schwarzenegger doll. Due to his memories of the museum, János recoiled, but Silvia pushed the doll towards him.

"It's a lucky charm. Take it. Tourists buy lots of them. If you press it here on the chest—"

"I'll be back!" exclaimed the little Adam-Schwarzenegger.

"And if you press the genitals instead—"

"*Hasta la vista*, baby!" exclaimed the little Adam-Schwarzenegger.

"That's what Adam-Schwarzenegger said to God when he left Eden," said Silvia seriously, though she was also looking affectionate. "It does bring luck. I haven't had a train crash yet."

"I understand," answered János. Sadly he accepted little

Adam-Schwarzenegger. Thoughtfully he regarded Silvia. He pursed his lips. Then he raised his eyebrows.

"Your own gigolem is this very same model, am I right?"

"Of course! A full-size Adam-Schwarzenegger. Maybe a little too big for me." Silvia was of slight build. "But I'm religious. It's reassuring to be taken sexually by the Ancestor, the archetype of us all. It's a communion."

"Does he also say '*Hasta la vista*, baby'?"

"Every day, when I go out to work." On Silvia's face was a dreamy expression. "Sometimes even when I go for a crap."

"Gigolems have taken possession of the monopoly of human sexual reproduction," stated János.

"No, they didn't take possession," said Silvia. "It's always been like this, since time immemorial."

"That's what I'm starting to believe too. But then I rebel and I can't believe it."

"Listen, János, gigolems are the indispensable interface between two incompatible devices. Without gigolems, human males and females wouldn't have a chance of real sexual interaction."

"That's only since vaginas started to migrate."

"Vaginas began to migrate in biblical times."

"In biblical times it was the people of Israel who began to migrate, not vaginas."

"Vaginas too," insisted Silvia.

History constantly changes, thought János, to adapt to the demands of the *Zeitgeist*, the spirit of the age. The dictatorship of the present over the past compels history to contain delusions disguised as facts. When the final old woman with a fixed vagina died from old age, the illusion that vaginas were already migrating in the distant past would consolidate itself, and nobody would escape this concept.

"I'm going to fuck Patricia," declared János.

"May its mud satisfy you," was Silvia's parting wish.

When János opened the wardrobe where he had closed Patricia, the gigolem showed no resentment, since resentment is a human feeling, not a nonhuman one. Excluding elephants which never forget. And perhaps cats.

"Fuck me please," Patricia said promptly.

"This very moment," replied János.

It was a wild and successful embrace. Patricia remained female all the time and, if it were possible, became even more female, so that János felt himself even more manly. This was exactly what he needed at the moment, both consciously and subconsciously, so with natural spontaneity the gigolem fulfilled his desire. János even experienced a feeling of love for Patricia, and this didn't scare him at all, albeit that he knew perfectly well that he was dancing on the edge of an abyss, black and bottomless. Thoughtlessly he blessed the existence of gigolems. For a complex person in a continuous state of inner evolution, a gigolem made an incomparably more useful and satisfying partner than a person of flesh and blood. Looking at things from an evolutionary point of view, rather than a creationist one, in principle every man or woman is programmed by his or her genes to choose the best amongst all *existing* partners with whom to reproduce himself or herself. Yet in practical reality almost everyone finally adapts himself or herself to accept the best amongst *possible* partners, since not all existing partners are effectively available, so sometimes the best possible partner might actually be amongst the worst existing ones.

Even so, there are some supremely romantic individuals who prefer the path of continuous and endless search for the unobtainable ideal to a resigned acceptance of the reality that's available! For such persons searching is a greater priority than finding. Indeed they must be careful to avoid finding, since finding puts an end to searching.

Gigolems allow you to go on eternally with the search, since every gigolem alters in harmony with the subconscious hopes of its owner, so that even though the eternal searcher, man or woman, can never be fully satisfied by his or her gigolem, he or she can't get bored with it either, unless that boredom already exists within himself or herself. Incessantly the gigolem mutates into a thing ever more akin to the subconscious object of desire. By virtue of being very nearly encountered and found inadequate, the object of desire likewise mutates, sometimes contradictorily, so that what was formerly desirable becomes undesirable, and vice versa.

Tragedy comes when subconscious expectations fade or die, due to the entropy of old age or other causes. Then the gigolem becomes the implacable amplifier of your own ennui, merciless mirror of your own deterioration, inescapable witness to the demise of your vital and loving feelings. The more intense and rich your life formerly was, the more bitter your state when all enthusiasm is in the end extinguished.

János's little flame of love for Patricia was not quenched as yet. He shivered as those first words of hers came back into his mind: *Mine are you.* Maybe those had been prophetic, announcing the ultimate truth: *You are mine.* How could he possibly keep a safe emotional distance between himself and his gigolem? Since a gigolem was intrinsically an extention of oneself, the relationship between a human being and a gigolem could reach depths of intimacy unimaginable between two human beings.

A problem was that what originally were microscopic sexual deviations within a person's libido, a mere frill upon a fantasy, no more than a hint, could by positive reinforcement from the gigolem become dominant and overwhelming, generating attitudes which in the past would certainly have been classed as behavioural monstrosities.

János was aware of *political perversion.* Onan clubs existed, dedicated to masturbating at images of detested politicians. People who joined such clubs subconsciously had regarded sex as a way of humiliating a partner. These people also had powerful political antipathies. After a while in bed with a gigolem, they found the gigolem conforming to the object of their hatred, such as the President of the United States –

whom they possessed sexually in order to give free vent to their hatred. After a time they could only get an erection, or clitorection, by focusing on the President's image.

A fleeting fantasy about having your genitals nibbled pleasurably by catamites swimming in a pool which also happened to be home to fish – the Emperor Tiberius's favourite erotic pastime in Capri – could mutate into a fixation upon *the fish themselves*. One's gigolem could become a big cod or halibut between the increasingly smelly sheets.

Perplexed by his meditations, and in the vague hope that Silvia might still be at the Kafka Café – or alternatively, since several hours had passed, that she might have returned there – János headed that way after shutting Patricia in the wardrobe once more. By now it was six in the evening.

As he walked, his fingers played with the Adam-Schwarzenegger doll which she'd given him, rather as a nun might play with the beads of her rosary. Occasionally the doll exclaimed, "I'll be back!" This seemed a good augury for actually finding Silvia at the café. János could, of course, have phoned her mobile, but what was the point in having a lucky charm unless you trusted it?

Almost immediately he entered the Kafka Café, he saw a full-size, indeed oversize, Adam-Schwarzenegger gigolem sitting at one of the bigger tables. Cleopatra from the museum, no less! – because Cleopatra was with none other than Dr Sládek! Also at the same table were . . . well, one of the *persons* was a tall young man with red hair, but the other entity was a human-size plucked chicken. A red crest on a feathery head. Beady eyes. Red beak. Nude wings tucked in to its sides, just like scrawny white arms. The giant chicken frequently bobbed its head in a pecking motion, as if in agreement with all the remarks being exchanged between the red-headed young man and Dr Sládek.

János would have fled from the café right away, were he not mesmerized by the sight of the human chicken, or chicken-human, whichever.

This allowed time for Dr Sládek to notice János. The museum director rose and beckoned and minced towards János and delicately yet firmly took him by the arm.

"My dear fellow, have you recovered from your violation? Is your equanimity restored? Let me buy you a Viennese coffee with whipped cream! We were discussing gay inhuman rights."

Were whipping and cream a sly allusion to János's punishment?

Dr Sládek drew János towards the table where a seat remained unoccupied.

"Introductions! This is Cleopatra, as you already know."

"Soup – or sandwich?" demanded Cleopatra, as a waitress arrived.

"No, no," said Dr Sládek, "a Viennese coffee for our Hungarian friend. And this—" nodding at the red-headed man "—is Gustav, and—" nodding at the nodding poultrygolem "—his lover Anastasia."

"Tuck-tuck-tuck-tuck," said Anastasia.

"May I ask you, Gustav," asked János, "why your gigolem is a giant chicken without any feathers?"

"Yes, you may ask!" And Gustav waited. Evidently he was a literal-minded person.

"So why is your gigolem a giant chicken without any feathers?"

Presently János sat filled with astonishment and sympathy and Viennese coffee with whipped cream.

He'd been aware of involuntary metazoophilia, yet hadn't previously met a metazoophilist. Metazoophilists tended to conceal their condition, partly from shame, partly to avoid prosecution by the World Wildlife Fund. Not so Gustav, for whom explaining seemed to be a paradoxical blend of self-exorcism and joyful affirmation.

Less than two years previously, Anastasia was a woman of impressive beauty. Gustav had adored feminine beauty beyond anything else in the world. However, during his childhood Gustav had undergone certain experiences at the farm of his grandparents, which his conscious mind had erased but which led him to associate various mental categories with specific animals. This led him to place on his ample bookshelves – for Gustav was a great reader – little plastic models of animals in front of the books, which represented for him the essences of the different books. *The Origin of Species*, a tortoise. *Harry Potter*, a hog. *Gone With the Wind*, a plastic eagle, and so forth. For a while Gustav had worked in a library, but he was asked to leave after he reorganized the shelves according to his own zoological classification system rather than the Dewey decimal method.

After only a short while with his beautiful gigolem, whenever they coupled Anastasia would mutate into an anthropomorphic version of some animal while he was embracing her. Gustav may have been literal, but his subconscious was symbolic. Often she would become a woman-size anthropomorphic goose or duck or hen, resembling some Disney cartoon, depending on which creature emerged from Gustav's subconscious mind as sexually significant. Since his gigolem couldn't suddenly sprout feathers all over, but only modify whatever hair occurs on a human body, such as on the head and armpits and pubes, mainly her skin appeared like a plucked bird's – and Gustav soon found these goosebumps or, increasingly, chickenbumps intensely erotic.

"Other metazoophilists may find themselves in bed with a goat," said Gustav. "Anthropomorphized, that looks like a demon embodied ... but I love a chicken." He put an arm around Anastasia and cuddled her.

"You should be careful," advised Dr Sládek. "Your sexual object isn't a real bird, true enough. That's been legally upheld. But I hear that the new tactic of the WWF is to sue for moral damages for degrading the *image* of animals. That might earn them and the lawyers a lot of money."

Just at that moment, several dwarfs dressed in medieval costumes unfurled a multilingual banner outside the windows of the Kafka Café: *Justice for the Fucking Dwarfs! We want dwarf Gigolems!* They marched off down the street in the direction of

Charles Bridge, where all the statues are.

"They do have a point," said Gustav.

Dr Sládek shook his head. "A dwarf gigolem might mutate into the appearance of a child during embraces. You know that paedogigolems are forbidden. Gigolems in the shape of dwarfs could easily be misused. A dwarf might sell his gigolem on to a pervert."

"Dwarfs are being deprived of the fundamental human right to sex. And paedo-perverts can already buy gigolems."

"But only adult-size ones."

"Which become adult-size *children* in their arms, because the body can't be compressed."

"That's aesthetically grotesque," said Dr Sládek. Unfortunately at that moment he happened to glance at Anastasia whom Gustav loved.

"It isn't as grotesque," exclaimed Gustav protectively, "as fucking a pool of mud!"

Dr Sládek twiddled his moustache. "What are you talking about?"

"I'm talking about certain creationists who are so obsessed about people being made from dust and dust returning to the earth—" János pricked up his ears "—that I hear they can't finish a sexual act without their gigolem dissolving into mud, which they continue fucking until they come, and only when the tension's released can their unfortunate gigolem reshape itself."

"Look, dear heart, let's not get into an unnecessary dispute." Dr Sládek addressed János. "We were about to visit Юрий Семецкий, whose gigolem is eating him."

János had been compelled to study some Russian in primary school during the last days of communism in Hungary, so he knew that Dr Sládek was referring to a Yuri Semecky.

"His gigolem is eating him?"

"Yes, it'll take another two weeks."

"But *why*?"

"There's quite a lot to eat," said Gustav literally.

"No, why is his golem *eating him*?"

"Юрий Семецкий is an ultra-masochist," said Dr Sládek. "Come and see for yourself. That's the scientific method."

Compelled by curiosity, János went with the museum director and the metazoophilist and the Cleopatra gigolem and Anastasia the megapoultrygigolem, although under other circumstances he might have felt reluctant to be in such company.

They went along one street, then down another street, until they reached a tall house where a plaster bear the size of a magnum of champagne stood on its hind legs in a niche above the doorway. Many houses in Prague bore similar symbols from the good old days when people couldn't read – swans, sheep, goblets, fiddles, religious virgins.

A card by one the doorbells read: **Yuri Semecky**. Maybe Юрий Семецкий didn't wish any fellow Russians to visit him, only Roman speakers. Or maybe this was part of his masochism.

Dr Sládek rang the bell. They entered. They ascended. A golem attired as a chef with a tall white hat held a door wide.

"Aha, come in!" The Russian, who was in his early forties, lay naked on a blood-stained bed. Alternatively, three-quarters of a Russian lay there, since much flesh had been cut from one leg and one arm, exposing the bones. Юрий Семецкий was bearded and moustached scruffily, as though he had more important things to think about, and his forehead was a very high dome, where he would do his thinking, a bit like an astronomer in an observatory.

Besides the bed were a dining chair and a round table laid for a meal, with pepper pot, salt cellar, jug of olive oil, and slices of lemon; also a tray of scalpels and tongs and several spray-cans of powerful coagulant of the non-anaesthetic variety.

On a plate lay a slice of fresh flesh. The chefgolem sat down, squeezed a tiny amount of lemon juice upon the flesh, dripped a few drops of olive oil, then added a sprinkling of salt and pepper. Spearing the flesh with a fork, the golem lifted it to its mouth and commenced eating, causing the Russian to writhe in ecstasy.

"Oh God oh God oh God, oh good oh good oh good," Юрий Семецкий moaned delightedly in Roman.

When his passion passed, Юрий Семецкий eyed his visitors blearily.

"Will you have something to eat?"

"Soup – or sandwich?" demanded Cleopatra.

"No, raw!" said the Russian. "Only raw!"

"Will *you* have something to eat?" Gustav asked Юрий Семецкий.

"No, I'm on hunger strike too, for extra pleasure!"

"In that case," Dr Sládek asked thoughtfully, "would you categorize this as cannibalism-by-proxy, *or not*?"

János decided to leave before, perhaps, he might be chastized for some reason.

János was lazing on his bed in typical post-coital repose, smoking an exotic Black Elephant cigarette and sipping a goblet of Nistru, an excellent Moldovian cognac. At his side Patricia lay inert in the state of pseudo-rest and pseudo-satisfaction you would expect of her. His second sexual act with Patricia had been even better than the first one, but this, for the moment, meant very little. Everything depended on what was hiding in the next layer of his subconscious. It isn't entirely clear if something called the subconscious truly exists inside a human skull, but if it does, then undoubtedly it consists of *layers*, each layer different from the other layers. The more intercourse there is with a gigolem, the more the gigolem reacts to the needs of ever deeper layers. Therefore a gigolem's behaviour can never be predictable. At any moment it may surprise you.

János slapped Patricia's butt. Her ass seemed real. She didn't look like a metamorphic lump of mud, a creature of a parallel universe which had overlapped with the one in which János had grown up.

Responding to his slap, Patricia rolled over, simulating an awakening that she couldn't be experiencing since basically she wasn't alive. János regarded her tenderly. She was going to say something pleasant to him. It was as though he could read her mind, a mind which she didn't really have. In fact it was as if finally János could read his *own* mind, which is impossible because you need another mind with which to do the reading.

Unexpectedly Patricia said, "You aren't really alive, are you?"

"*What?*" János blanched in surprise.

"You're a well-packaged illusion," she went on. "You move like a living thing. You talk like a living thing. They did a really good job."

"They, they!" cried János "Who are *they?*"

Patricia looked pensive. "Hmm, I'm afraid the toy has stopped working properly."

"What are you talking about?"

"It's best to reboot you and reset this chapter of time." Then János saw her leaning over him, rebooting and resetting . . .

János was lazing on his bed in typical post-coital repose, smoking an exotic Black Elephant cigarette and sipping a goblet of Nistru, an excellent Moldovian cognac. At his side Patricia lay inert in the state of pseudo-rest and pseudo-satisfaction you would expect of her.

Endorphins of orgasm had put János in the best mental state for introspection even more creative than usual.

Patricia can't be real, because the creationism she represents has no sense. But evolutionism may be the wrong way to perceive the world. That's because all explanations are inherently the enemies of the ineffable אמת, *that's to say "truth" in the Hebrew language, pronounced "Emet". Explanations kill the mystery in which reality consists. So probably I'm as unreal as she is. One fine day I may waken and realize that I don't exist at all Hmm . . . I'm getting stiff again. I'd rather fuck Patricia a bit more.*

And János fucked Patricia a bit more. A good choice. Patricia's sex didn't fluctuate.

Presently, having shut Patricia in the wardrobe again and headed into town, János felt moved to meditate inside an

Evolutionist Church, which was where people who believed in the theory, or myth, of natural selection went to pray.

The building was full of elderly women, mostly dressed in black. The majority of young folk seemed to be creationist these days, since this was the modern way, so they didn't visit such a place. He paused in front of a gilded statue of Darwin and Freud smoking cigars. Moving on, János lit a long slim candle below an icon of Richard Dawkins in a loin-cloth like Tarzan's, consulting a big watch that lacked any numbers. From hidden speakers wafted Michael Nyman's piece of music, *The Cook, The Thief, His Wife and Her Lover*. Some high-definition screens, fixed to the walls in gilded frames, were showing scenes from old porn movies, revered images from the time when human beings had sex directly with one another. János contemplated a traditional Japanese *bukkake* mass-masturbation, a ceremony now degraded to the pouring of a topping over noodles, rather than the group ejaculation of semen upon a schoolgirl, as shown on this screen in the church.

And what, speculated János, *if this is merely the beginning? What if more and more parallel universes start to overlap, crowding reality with new categories of creatures who are unreal from our original human point of view? What if the only possible form of life in the future is an inseparable symbiosis between all these bizarre creatures?*

Later that same day, to the disappointment of Mrs Smetana, János took the train for Budapest. Silvia hosted him once again inside the driver's cab, in exchange for chocolate. This time they were a bit squeezed, because Patricia remained with János – he wouldn't leave Patricia on her own in a passenger carriage in case someone stole her away at an intervening station. What's more, this time Silvia had her own Adam-Schwarzenegger gigolem with her. She must have begun to miss him on her travels.

The railway lines extended swiftly and charmingly in front of them, pointing towards Hungary. As a courtesy, Silvia let János drive the train for a while, even though that was almost certainly forbidden even on Magyar Álom Vasutak. Speeding the train along, János was having fun like a little child. Banished to the two rear corners of the cab, the two gigolems waited inertly with no sign of life until their lords and masters might need them. Silvia and János paid no attention to them, which was normal, since gigolems couldn't get bored and were entirely without free will.

So, when Patricia smiled, only Adam-Schwarzenegger noticed. His eyebrow rose slightly. Patricia confirmed that János and Silvia were still distracted. They were. She winked at Adam-Schwarzenegger, then she grinned broadly.

Two Birds, One Bush

Amanda Fox

My wife. Her name is Katherine. Not Kate. Not Kathy. Jesus, don't ever call her Kathy – she'll rip your head off, not with her bare hands, but with her eyes: Like a laser beam from her ocular sockets to your cervical spine, to make a neat separation between C6 and C7, leaving your skull to tumble to the ground like a bowling ball.

She would never come right out and correct you – that would be too easy. My wife likes things to be difficult, you see, for herself and for everyone around her. Besides, to be blunt, tact is a trait Katherine does not possess. She is not only incapable of predicting the potential embarrassment of such a situation, she could care less about making that sort of exchange copacetic. Much simpler to dispose of you in the condescending fashion she is so adept at. And in the end, you'd feel so inferior, so pathetic for even suggesting that she could be a "Kathy," that you would wish your head had been ripped off.

Katherine and I have been married for twelve years. I will admit to loving her, but this love was, in the beginning, one that made my dick hard, one that had me skittering around in circles whenever she called my name. Her fierce ambition turned me on, and her composure made me horny, made me want to clean out her orifices with my slavish tongue in the hopes of acquiring a little bit of her power for myself. Now, her drive seems virulent, and her self-possession is just that – self-possessed.

We have two children, nine and six – a boy and a girl, both delivered by planned Caesarean section at thirty-seven weeks, three years apart almost to the day. We live in a house on the right street, in the right neighbourhood, decorated with the right furnishings from all the right stores. It should be no surprise to you that we have all the right friends, and that we know all the right people.

She is perfect.

She is, from certain angles. Though if you view her from the left, from a slightly downward stance, you can see how the highlights in her hair have been strategically placed by her three-hundred-dollar-a-visit stylist to appear as natural as possible, and how Botox makes her look as if she has two microwaved marshmallows attached to the front of her face. My wife Katherine always wears classic diamond studs in her ears, but on special occasions she will change them to pearls. She is well put together, without fail.

Of course, she exercises: two days per week of strength training, four thirty-minute sessions on the treadmill, and one class each of yoga and tai chi to balance things out. She also goes for sunless tanning once a month because too much UV can cause skin cancer, and she needs that little glow.

My wife Katherine has no pubic hair – no hair anywhere for that matter, which she says demonstrates the emergence of New Age woman. She has been lasered to baldness, her imaginary moustache removed, her underarms and legs made as smooth as paper, her pussy lips and anal region soft as a baby's bottom.

Because of this comprehensive fur removal (I find this tidbit of information quite amusing) when she stands naked you see the sleeves of her inner labia hanging down – a fact that torments her to no end. She says that this condition (which she actually calls a "condition") makes her look slightly warped, like she has a slow epidermal leak.

"They should be tucked up inside," she growls, prodding at her uncovered self in front of the mirror. "I don't like seeing them."

"Well, you're the one who shaved off all your pubic hair." Secretly I revel in her discomfort. It's as if her body is doing its damnedest to be abhorrent, and I'll admit, when we have sex I pull and nibble on them – those bad little labial folds – to point out the obvious: that they do hang down, and that she isn't a Barbie doll.

Katherine stays on the cutting edge, from feng shui to Lasik, and while I am forever outdated, she keeps up with painstaking determination. Last year she thought it prudent for us to experiment with our sexuality. She'd heard the women from her strip aerobics class talking about it. She wanted to give another woman a try – all the girls were doing it. Of course, I was allowed in on the arrangement. The proposal was laid out in a straightforward manner; like the agenda at a business meeting.

"We've been married long enough. Our relationship can handle this. Besides, it's all the better for you, isn't it? Two women? What man wouldn't want that?" What man, indeed.

"What do you think about Maria from the gym? She's really cute. Great tits," I remember Katherine saying for effect, "and not an ounce of cellulite on the girl. And, David . . ." she whispered this part to me while nuzzling my earlobes, "I know for a fact that she smells good. I'm just guessing here, but I think she wears that new Thierry Mugler fragrance."

Katherine knows how much I like the way a woman smells, though what she doesn't know is that it's earthy odours that make me squirm – sweat, piss, vaginal profusion – not fake, perfumey ones.

"How about her?" she asked, her eyes alight like struck matches. "God, I know she's dying to get with you." I bet she was.

After a few well-placed conversations, it was on. We got together at a bar just outside of town, had some drinks – margaritas for the girls and a couple Coronas for me – danced for a while, and then headed to a motel. Not hotel – motel. It fitted with the theme.

I won't give you the sordid details. Suffice it to say, Katherine had the time of her life, and so did Maria. Between them both, I think they came about twenty times. No joke. It was okay for me: my penis floundered a bit. Too much excitement was Katherine's diagnosis.

I orgasmed once at the end of the night, one woman squatting over my face, the other hunkered down over my cock, the two girls kissing passionately, pulling at each other's nipples.

You'd think I had everything a man could want, but sometimes everything is really nothing at all.

And then it happened: I met Brigitte. Brigitte Jacqueline Laroche. She's "Jackie" to her friends and colleagues, "Ms. Jones" to her students (she's a kindergarten teacher), "Babydoll" to her papa, and "Brigitte" to me. (Brigitte is the name she reserves for her lovers.)

We met on the bus. It was a Tuesday morning, and I was heading downtown to work. I have this office job in accounting, but deep down I consider myself a musician. I play guitar in a jazz band every other Thursday and one Saturday a month at a little club called The Black Ox.

Katherine's car was in the shop for a touch of bodywork. Someone had actually had the nerve to key the driver's side door of her Audi RS4. She parks it diagonally everywhere she goes – need I say more? So Katherine had my car and I was obliged to ride the bus.

At about 7:15 a.m., I hauled myself, my briefcase, and my brown-bag lunch onto the Number 35. I sat near the back, in the last row of double seats.

Three stops later, a woman got on. She caught my attention immediately by unabashedly saying hello to Dan, the driver, calling him by name.

She flashed her pass like it was a secret badge and gave him a flirtatious wink. It was then that I knew this woman was special – different. I watched her sway to the rhythm of the street as she slowly made her way down the aisle. Her leather sandals slapped at the soles of her feet as she walked, in no particular rush to sit even though the bus had already lurched forward, resuming its route. When she got to my row, she paused and held onto the chair rail in front of me. Her hands were small, with oval-shaped fingernails trimmed short. She wore no polish or rings of any sort.

"Nice day, huh?" she said, inhaling as if the niceness was tangible, like it was the only thing that really mattered in that moment.

"Yes, very nice," I agreed. "Sunny."

She had unruly brown ringlets that clumsily framed her face and neck, and her cocoa-coloured skin glowed, seemingly reradiating the light that shone through the bus windows, making the whites of her eyes appear so white that they seemed almost the lightest shade of blue. Her face was unblemished and unpainted, free of all the traps and trimmings of the modern woman. Even her earlobes had yet to be maligned.

"Sunny is good, but I was referring to de temp'rature." Her eyes didn't meet mine as she spoke. She simply stood there, the slight, swollen mounds of her breasts upheld as if on a shelf at level with my face. Her timid nipples addressed me through the sheerness of her unbleached, cotton blouse, and I had a sudden urge to reach over and press on them with my fingertips. Trying hard not to be rude however, I shifted my gaze slightly and saw that around her neck she wore a necklace constructed of beads and tiny colourful cereal pieces.

I was struck by an uncanny affiliation to this strange female. I think it was a reflection of myself that I saw in her stance, a similarity of mannerism and pose – a childlike comportment I'd once known but that had long since been squelched. As the bus bumped down the street, she stayed upright, my woman of whimsicality, my siren of sassiness. She rustled through a large, canvas tote, moving and rearranging stuff, apparently not finding the object of her search.

She stopped finally, and looked at me. "You know – hot. I like it when de air is t'ick like today. Makes me feel like I'm back home."

She didn't say where back home was, and I didn't ask, but from the sound of her, I figured it was somewhere between the Florida Keys and the coast of South America. Then she added something else, something completely nonsensical, and my ineffectual WASP self tried desperately to decipher a garbled speech that hinted at French mixed with the uneven sounds of a mechanical voice changer. I stared at her lips, almost willing them to translate the words for me.

When she caught me watching her mouth, she smiled. She had one dead tooth in the top row, a little darker than the rest, and her lips were dry, like she had just run or walked very fast to catch this ride. I wanted immediately to wet them. The thought made me weak.

"Yeah, hot," I replied feebly, wiping at my forehead. Suddenly the bus came to an unexpected halt, and a car horn blasted to the right of us somewhere. The woman finally sat down, sliding in next to me, her hips and ample thighs mashing up against mine. She set her bag on the floor between her feet and turned in my direction. I nervously focused straight ahead, uncomfortable yet rather pleased that she'd chosen to share my seat. There wasn't another person in our section of the bus – lots of other empty spots she could have picked.

"You must be ovaheatin' in dat tie an' jacket." She shook her head with pity, and reached over to grab hold of the silk knot at the base of my throat, muttering more gnarled words that from their tone and intonation sounded like salty expletives. She loosened the tie, then patted me on the chest, and declared, "Dere you go. Now don't dat feel better?"

As a married man, and as a human entitled to a little personal space, I automatically leaned away towards the window, though it is conceivable now that I likewise slid the lower half of my body even closer to her. She'd gone back to scrounging through her bag. When the bus rounded a sharp corner a minute later however, the momentum of the turn forced her nearly into my lap, and sent an old man getting up for his stop crashing into the partition near the folding doors.

"Well, you sure know how to liven up de bus rides," she giggled, like I was somehow responsible for her body unexpectedly resting half on top of mine. "An' you certainly are warm. Maybe you should just take off your jacket. I don't t'ink dat loosening your tie has done you much good."

"Really, I'm OK," I answered, no longer making the slightest attempt to move away. I could easily have hugged her tight right then, though I didn't.

"Now come, let me help you." She shifted again, and precariously – because of the bus, not because of the act – began undressing me as if I were her child. First, she completely removed the tie; then she unfastened the top three buttons of my shirt, working diligently with her tongue sticking out the side of her mouth; next came my jacket, which she helped to cast off and placed neatly in my lap. After she boldly tucked a wayward curl behind my ear, I felt as if I was naked, and my penis, long since risen, began to ache. I was finding it hard to breathe.

Two more passengers got on the bus and sat across the aisle from us. All of a sudden, she became still as stone.

"It's Brigitte – my name."

"Nice to meet you, Brigitte." I wriggled my hand free for a shake, possibly to diffuse pent-up energy, and possibly because I wanted to touch her directly, to get her going on me again.

She clasped my fingers with the same eagerness that was stirring in my pants. "My goodness, you are hot! Your hands is sweating. Are you always dis way?"

"Ummm. I guess," was my answer, though I wanted to add, "but only since I've met you . . . Brigitte."

Our enthusiastic grasp persisted, spanning the shallow divide between her legs and mine. She began stroking my forearm with her free hand, gently plucking and twisting at the short brown hairs that grew there. When her devilish touch drew a sigh of pleasure from my lungs, she placed her palm on my thigh. A few more people came and went, and I suffered the fabric of my slacks like a giant bur on my skin.

★   ★   ★

Two blocks past my stop, Brigitte was turned sideways, partially blocking us from observers. With one hand, she held my pants; with the other, she unzipped them. She then slid her fingers into the modest opening, and fumbled with my boxers until she found my penis. Thumbing over its head, she watched my face, eyes fixed, questioning – *Is this acceptable?*

Yes. Definitely yes, I smiled, some of my juices oozing out to greet her. Like two old friends reconnecting, my heart luxuriated in her touch.

When she cupped my balls, my mind strayed towards a foreseeable future: Brigitte straddling me, on a different kind of seat in a different kind of place, her bare feet pressing, perhaps, into a wall. I knew she would grip my shoulders for leverage, and with panties pushed to the side, we'd grind away – with her pulling and scooping her opening onto my shaft, and me shoving back hard, so hard I'd leave bruises. I envisioned myself deep in her vagina, her skirt billowing around us, innocent witness to our lust, as from underneath, her bush of coarse black hair (I was positive she'd have that) would abrade my flesh. The moisture we'd create would be audible, and her musk would be pungent. This last detail was already evident.

Reality rushed back the second Brigitte clamped her fingers around my pipe and began working me. I tried to relax – but that's when the questions poured out. I couldn't stop them. They shot from the cannon of my mouth and she returned answers just as quick.

"Would you ever share me?"

"Never."

"Do you know what a labial reduction is?"

"Not a clue."

"Do you have air conditioning?"

"Goodness no! What's de point?"

"What about pubic hair?"

"Oh, a veritable forest."

I ride the bus every day now, going anywhere and everywhere the public transportation system of my fair city allows. I see Brigitte on a regular but very unpredictable basis.

I haven't told her this yet, though I think she knows: things would be different if it weren't for my children. Brigitte sees other men – I can't control that, nor could I ever expect it to be otherwise – but when we're together it's as if we are the only two brilliant stars in a vast empty sky.

Ménage à Denim

Jeremy Edwards

They looked the same, folded on the laundry table, but of course they smelled different. Michael's jeans, even freshly washed, had his tangy aroma, the same olfactory signature that Dina knew and loved in the perspiration on his back, on his abs, in his groin. It evoked a combination of green tea and the richest olive oil.

Charlotte's jeans, even when permeated with fabric softener, intoxicated Dina with a fragrance that suggested nutmeg, caramel, and Chardonnay. Dina knew this scent from the smooth skin of Charlotte's throat and the tight skin behind her ears and, in particular, from the ticklish place where the seam of seams clutched Charlotte so snugly. Dina also knew how to make more of this scent arise, as if by magic, from that seam.

Dina thought of herself as the luckiest one in the world, the one who got to have her cake and eat it, who never had to choose. The one who woke up in the morning to green tea and olive oil and went to bed at night with nutmeg, caramel, and Chardonnay lingering in her senses.

In the morning, Michael's jeans, washed a thousand times, were soft against the insides of Dina's legs. His denim knees split her gently open, and Dina felt girly in her kimono . . . and womanly without her panties. Everything she wanted him to touch was displayed, propped open, right there. Reliable as sunrise.

Man's square hand reaching in. Man's thick fingers parting convoluted flesh, dipping into pooling moisture. Man's broad tongue coaxing her to feminine ecstasy. Man's manhood bursting out of blue jeans and filling her womanly core.

In the evening, Dina felt no less womanly as she let her hands roam hungrily over Charlotte's ass, while it lounged across her lap. Dina let her own wetness seep preciously into the gusset of the thong that adorned her nakedness. She was an insatiable goddess, a proud-nippled immortal who could peel the jeans off a beautiful woman's bottom like she was peeling a succulent orange, who could nibble the cheeks and lick the cunt as if she literally depended on them for sustenance. This incarnation of the goddess had a tendency to be the worshipper rather than the worshipped. Her breasts hung joyously over the denim derrière she revered. She teased herself with anticipation while she smiled over the still-wrapped parcel, admiring its roundness, limiting herself to little pats and squeezes until Charlotte's wriggles and her own crazy dampness told her it was time to pull those fucking Levi's down and smother that soft behind with kisses.

In the middle of a Thursday afternoon, Dina was getting herself off with the fresh memories of last night with Charlotte and this morning with Michael. Afternoon was her private time, when both of them were out of the house. It could be her most productive time as far as her home-based business was concerned . . . or not. Sprawling by herself across the tautly made-up bed of a weekday afternoon, she could fuck and be fucked, pretend that the fingers in her cunt were Michael's or that the cunt around her fingers was Charlotte's. Or both. All of it. Everything.

It was a big apartment, but Dina could fill it up with a wailing orgasm in the middle of the afternoon.

Michael and Charlotte were great together. Like a brother and sister who had outgrown their rivalry, leaving pure, distilled affection. Charlotte looked at Michael's "eat-me-up" torso, his lean, powerful pelvis, his penetrating eyes and sensuous lips . . . and saw simply a cuddly, comfortable guy who it was fun to have pizzas and martinis with on a Saturday night. And, looking at Charlotte, Michael saw not the ocean-deep smile or the landscape of curves and skin as delectable as cake frosting . . . but only a button-cute girl roommate, the kind you loaned your sweaters to and threw pillows at.

Dina lay on the bedspread, fingers cupping her crotch to separate her delicate flesh from the wet spot she'd made when she came. She didn't want to move just yet – she wanted to use the peace to think.

The relationships were compartmentalized, weren't they, thought Dina. Like the pockets of her favorite pair of jeans . . . Keys, rigid and ready, always in the right pocket. Soft, fresh tissues, always in the left.

The apartment was a generous one, and she reflected on how they had, consciously or otherwise, taken advantage of that to formalize the compartmentalization. There was Michael's room, where he and Dina began their day with ten o'clock cappuccinos, hours after Charlotte had left the house. Michael's was the room in which Dina was a woman who wanted a man. Michael's bed was the bed in which she satisfied her need to be filled with a warm and insistent cock, her need to feel playful swats from a masculine palm on her feminine rear, and her need to feel coarse, stubbly cheeks stroking her inner thighs while she writhed upon a boyish mouth, clutching sharp elbows that she knew smelled like green tea and olive oil.

These were the sorts of things that happened in Michael's room in the morning.

Whether their schedules suited her biorhythms out of pure serendipity or her circadian rhythms had quietly adjusted to the schedule, Dina was always ready for Charlotte's room by the time Charlotte returned home. Charlotte's room was for the intimacy of reciprocally smeared lipstick and one pussy sharing juicy confidences with another, cunny mouth directly to cunny mouth between scissored, quivering legs. Bras and panties nested and tangled together, deep in the crook of the covers, where countless painted toenails strained in ecstasy against a womb of silk sheet. Charlotte's bed was where it was always girls' night *in*.

Usually their evening lovemaking comprised two sessions. Dina liked to pounce on her lover when she came home each day; if it weren't for the fact that Charlotte always had to pee first, they might have rolled their asses around just inside the door, squeezing each other into the corner by the potted plant to taste each other's tender spots. But the bathroom was right next to Charlotte's bedroom, and her bed was more comfortable than the floor of the hall.

And, after dinner for two, it was this room they returned to. Always Charlotte's room, with wallpaper that looked like gift-wrap and a bedside lampshade that glowed like an exotic cocktail.

Until this afternoon, it hadn't struck Dina how odd it was that a woman with two live-in lovers should, as a rule, sleep alone. But Charlotte the early bird had to be tucked in and kissed goodnight by 10:00, like a nutmeg-imbued pie put into the oven nightly. Every night, Dina was tempted to climb in there with her; but she knew that if she did so, she would toss and turn till her natural bedtime of midnight, and no doubt disturb Charlotte in the process.

At 11 or 11:30, Michael would return from a full day of work followed by band practice. Dina liked the fact that he could usually find her in the living room, accessible, rather than tucked away in Charlotte's bed. Michael was usually too tired at night for anything beyond a hello kiss and a little cuddling, but Dina wasn't one to knock kisses or cuddling, and she treasured the time at the kitchen table with Michael, where she watched him make an ad hoc meal of whatever happened to be in the refrigerator. She approved of the efficient manner in which he prepared himself nutritionally at night for the demands she'd make on him in the morning.

On any such night, she would have been welcome in Michael's bed . . . but she usually opted for her own room instead. She wanted to be fair, and she didn't want to break the spell of her relationship with Charlotte by forming part of a snoring duo behind a single door when Charlotte tiptoed around the apartment at 6 a.m. Likewise, though Michael wouldn't have dreamed of standing in her way had she chosen to slip into bed at midnight beside the long-slumbering Charlotte, Dina didn't want to leave him staring wistfully after her ass as she crept into someone else's bedroom.

It occurred to her that even her identity was compartmentalized. Gorgeous hunk's fuck-happy girlfriend in the morning, and gorgeous hunk's midnight-snack babe thirteen hours later. Lovely girl's ravenous lesbian admirer from 5 to 10 p.m. nightly. Of course, she loved them both 24/7. But Dina was, at heart, the type of classic lover who felt most fulfilled when spelling "love" as *s-e-x*.

There were occasional Saturday nights when they all climbed into bed together. But these were chaste slumber parties, chummy conventions of underwear or even pajamas, with Dina in the middle, poking and tickling and nudging her loved ones but not daring to go further, lest she violate an intangible boundary.

"Damn!" she suddenly said out loud, to an empty Thursday afternoon house. *Damn.* It had hit her with surprising suddenness how much she wanted to be unchastely in bed with both of them, to climb and be climbed on, to tickle all the places that really counted and feel intimately connected with all parties concerned, in sync and in heat. She was the woman who had it all, but suddenly she was feeling that she wanted to have it all at the same time. She wanted to be all of herself at once, not this or that compartment of herself.

And, with the clattering, blinding brilliance of familiar facts exploding into revelations, she amazed herself by noticing that she had never asked them.

Once fixated on this realization, she was incredulous. How could it be? But she would certainly remember asking them.

She had never asked them.

What the fuck is wrong with me? She mouthed the question into the pillow she was clutching. Dina, a person who would never hesitate to ask a restaurant server if spinach could be substituted for green pepper or potatoes for salad, had never thought to ask Michael and Charlotte if they might like to . . .

try something different. She had just accepted that what was, was, as though that meant it was all that could be.

The shape of their life all together had developed so organically. It had begun with the budding lesbian relationship between Dina and Charlotte during college, a textbook case of self-discovery through which two very fortunate women who'd been bureaucratically inserted into dormitory slot "A" as roommates emerged from slot "B," a couple of years later, as lovers.

Charlotte, an angelic, freckle-nosed blonde who was quietly confident of her identity, had seduced Dina just by being herself. By kissing her on Valentine's Day. By going to bed in the nude and getting chilly in the middle of the night. By telling her she loved her, leaving Dina to interpret the word as she saw fit. Dina had welcomed all of it – Charlotte made it so easy. Tender flesh to kiss and a big heart to hug, all offered on a silver platter. Any inclination to hesitate, to wrestle with identity, had been dispersed to the four winds by the tangible succulence of Charlotte's love.

But during that process, and after, Dina had never stopped dating guys. She liked guys. A lot. Charlotte understood that. So Dina would date this guy and that guy, casually, while cherishing the bond she had formed with Charlotte. She would hook up and move on, never sticking to the same guy for long.

Never sticking . . . until the guy she got stuck on. Michael.

He was more sensitive, more nurturing, more everything. A gentle, curly-locked poet who was a tiger in the sack. Maybe he was a cliché, but as far as Dina was concerned, the world could use more such clichés. And instead of each date nudging her closer to adieu, each date had solidified her need for him.

He really cared about her relationship with Charlotte. To Michael, Charlotte was neither a threat, nor a curiosity, nor a shallow turn-on of the "hot girl-on-girl action" variety. As Michael saw it, Charlotte was the most important person in the world to Dina. And Dina was the most important person in the world to him.

Dina had felt unusually vulnerable when she brought Michael home to the place she and Charlotte had rented after graduation. When she saw that Charlotte approved of the idea of Michael, even embraced the idea of Michael, she cried with happiness.

"Don't lose this one," Charlotte said.

"You're not jealous?" Dina was still a little wary.

"Is the food jealous of the water?" asked Charlotte, who had perhaps taken one too many Zen classes. "You need both, babe."

Apartments go condo every day. People have to move; and if the place they find requires a third roommate, they get one. An outsider probably would have made nothing of the fact that Michael, who needed a place to live, became the third inhabitant of the big apartment Dina and Charlotte had snagged.

But the three of them knew what they were committing to on the day Dina greeted Charlotte and Michael on the front stoop and silently divided up the three keys, which had been given to her on a single ring. Dina was aware that the mood was almost ritualistic, and she took care not to break that mood.

The experiment had succeeded. An adventure had quickly become the status quo. Three bedrooms. Two relationships. One happy man, one happy woman, and one *very* happy woman.

But in the quiet of this afternoon, Dina became certain that it was time to push the envelope.

She had no clear idea of how to get from point A to point B – point A being the status quo and point B being a vague, but irresistible image she was already forming of the three of them piled merrily under the covers. Was it really as simple as just asking? Somehow that seemed dingy and unromantic. What she did know was that Saturday – the day they were all free – would be the evening to do whatever it was she was going to do about it.

Dina had begun stroking herself again while she contemplated all this. Now she focused on channeling her vivid anticipation of future events into a luscious, present-moment climax. Images of herself being touched all over fluttered madly through her mind as if someone had unleashed a pack of pornographic playing cards in there.

Exhausted by epiphany and orgasm, she lost the rest of her afternoon to a nap.

The day arrived. Dina was literally dripping with excitement, but she still hadn't figured out how to approach things. She again considered the most obvious method.

"Hey, what if we all went to bed together?" It didn't feel right when Dina tried it on for size in front of the bathroom mirror. It might put someone on the spot ... or sound like she was proposing just another slumber party. And "What if we all went to bed together and got it on?" definitely seemed heavy-handed.

She'd thought of approaching each of them separately, feeling them out privately. She realized that kind of "shuttle diplomacy" would probably be the safest approach. But Dina wanted magic, not diplomacy. Maybe this meant that the shortest distance between two points wouldn't necessarily be a straight line.

The day waned, and, before she knew it, Dina's over-taxed powers of analysis and decision-making were being called into service for selecting pizza toppings.

Sitting at the table with them, she reaffirmed her resolve to do something – even if it had to be something clumsy.

"Michael's been working out, Charlotte – can you tell?"

Charlotte laughed, surprised in mid-pizza slice by the question. "Yeah, I guess."

Dina was, in her own mind, committed now. She pulled Michael's sweatshirt halfway up and ran her hand over his tight belly, for Charlotte's benefit. She peppered the firm torso with hot little kisses, between and around the rubs.

"I'm trying to eat," Michael complained with mock annoyance. Dina could tell that, beneath this show, he was actually loving it. Instead of ceasing, she redoubled the intensity of the massage.

She made direct eye contact with Charlotte as the belly-rubs became ever more sensuous. "I'm not embarrassing you, I hope."

"No, no," Charlotte said quickly. "I like seeing you . . ." Charlotte blushed ". . . enjoy yourself."

Dina slipped a finger into Michael's waistband. She noticed that Charlotte was wiggling a little bit in her chair and had, for the moment, lost interest in her food and her martini. With her free hand, Dina reached for Charlotte's palm. It took her a second to find it, under the table, between Charlotte's legs.

She gave Michael's cock a feathery stroke with her finger before pulling her hand back out of his jeans. Then she left him to his pizza while she scooted over to straddle Charlotte's lap. She kissed Charlotte fully on the lips.

Dina knew that Michael had seen her give Charlotte plenty of pecks and hugs, and the occasional fleeting bottom-squeeze. But she didn't think he'd ever seen them really make out. So she ate Charlotte up for a minute or two, giving her mouth a drive-in-movie-style workout, running her hands up and down the length of Charlotte's sleek, turtleneck-sheathed arms.

Then she turned to look at Michael. He was not eating pizza.

Charlotte was flushed. She was smiling, but she seemed disoriented. Dina saw her look at Michael, inquiringly, as if looking for guidance.

Michael shrugged. Then he spoke in a voice whose hoarseness belied his cool demeanor, talking as if Dina weren't in the room. "She's definitely up to something."

The third-person judgment made Dina shiver with the reality of what she was embarking on. Where running her hands over Michael's body in front of Charlotte had started to make her wet, and French-kissing Charlotte in front of Michael had made her clit tingle, she now felt a greedy wave of desire suffusing her from tip to toe.

Impulse served Dina where planning had come up short. She stood up, unbuttoned her blouse, and let the shirt and bra take over her empty chair.

"I'll be in my room, if anyone wants me," she said to the pizza platter. She left the kitchen, a one-woman parade of bare back, bare feet, and jeans, confident that she'd made her message clear: *This ain't no pajama party*.

The way their heads peeked simultaneously through her open doorway was comical, even cartoonish.

"You okay, m'girl?" asked Michael tenderly.

"Oh yeah," said Dina with a smile. Her hand was already in her pants. "A little lonely, though, over here."

They shuffled in the way people might enter a room to observe a sleeping baby. Dina, who had carefully positioned herself in the very middle of the bed, spread her arms in an internationally recognized gesture of munificence. Even from her perspective, she could tell that the light fixture on her ceiling was doing something nice for her breasts, now that her arms were no longer blocking them.

It soon became clear that light fixtures weren't the only ones who could do something nice for breasts. Charlotte could never resist them, and her hands were extended in a cupping position before she even reached the bed.

Charlotte's position on the bed was a tentative one – legs dangling off the side, feet in shoes – but her interaction with Dina's body was anything but tentative. The practiced, rolling pressure was as exquisite as it was comforting, and Dina closed her eyes in bliss, forgetting for the moment that she had any designs grander than this simple experience of perfect pleasure across her goddess globes.

She opened her eyes only to acknowledge a kiss. She knew whose lips were whose around here, so the fact that these lips were Michael's delighted but did not surprise her. He was kneeling at her side, his eyes soft and milky.

"Undress me." She whispered it, to no one and everyone.

Dina could imagine the shot as filmed from above in an old movie, Busby Berkeley style. The synchronized and symmetrical de-jeansing of the topless goddess, with each party grasping one flap of the conveniently already-unbuttoned fly, and the pants jerking down in fits and starts like an antique elevator.

She kicked to help them remove the obsolete garment from around her feet. The motion reminded her how wet she was, as moist panties shifted around her pussy.

"Oh, God," she said simply.

It was funny – she had imagined them all being undressed. She'd envisioned three pairs of faded blue jeans flashing their insides from the floor, looking horny and honest.

But this felt just as honest and just as right, for now – her nakedness served up as a feast for the two of them. Maybe they were a little shy of each other. The bottom line for Dina was that this worked, and worked beautifully. So the lips sucking her right nipple were the lips of a fully clothed girlfriend, and the fingers teasing just inside the elastic of her panties were the fingers of a completely attired boyfriend. And, for the moment, only Dina was substantially nude, as befitted the individual whose greatest dream now was to be touched, caressed, and explored all over by the two people she loved so very much.

Michael slipped her panties off her. Charlotte snuck in to kiss her snatch, and Michael, gallant Michael, said, "After you," like one of those courteous cartoon gophers.

Dina, who was usually so conscious of Charlotte's heady aroma and Michael's intoxicating scent, smelled herself in the air tonight. It smelled like truffle oil. The smell of the luckiest one in the world.

Maze

Erin Cashier

"Where does it go?" he'd asked her, the night before he left.

"What do you mean where does it go?" She pulled a pillow closer, propping up her head so she could see her tattoo herself. It was an old-fashioned labyrinth, occupying a space the size of a demitasse plate, between the cant of her hip and the divot of her navel.

He traced a finger along the path, in, and out again. "It just seems like it should go somewhere."

She laughed. "It does. From here," and she took his hand and made his finger jab at the entrance of it, "to here," to touch its center. "From me, to me, and back again."

He frowned at her. "Seems like there should be more to it."

"It's just a tattoo," she explained, but his frown remained. "What if there was more to it?" she asked, rolling back on the bed, still holding his hand with its finger outstretched. She took his finger into her mouth, and licked it, as she had licked other things, earlier that night, and felt down with one hand to see if such actions should be done again. Other parts of him agreed with her.

He hadn't explained himself when he'd left. He'd just stopped returning calls. And she was used to this dance – while it wasn't her favorite, it was her most familiar.

Maybe he was right, she thought, looking at herself in the mirror some days afterwards. The labyrinth was stagnant, had been so ever since she'd trapped it on herself years before, a small act of expensive rebellion before moving out in the world. She'd never wanted to get another tattoo, and could only vaguely remember getting this one – perhaps there'd been liquor involved. She covered it up with her palm, and in the mirror, her flesh was all flesh again, the color of a doll's plastic skin. She moved her hand, revealing the labyrinth again to herself, and, and – maybe he was right. Maybe it should go somewhere. Maybe she should go, somewhere.

She dried off, got dressed, got into her car, and drove.

"I want it bigger," she'd said, explaining herself to the tattoo artist. He was young and, judging from the flash in his portfolio, the lack of original works, inexperienced. But he was open that day, while other artists were booked.

He looked disappointed, when she took off her jeans to show him the pattern. "Just line work?" he asked. "I could shade some . . . and maybe put in some color around the edges—"

"Just line work," she said. "That's all I want."

She wanted more than that, of course. She wanted new beginnings. And new endings. Nothing that a tattoo could give her. Still, sometimes even the acknowledgement that change should begin deserved commemoration. And what better way to remember, than to see it on herself in the mirror each morning?

The workmanlike way the artist knelt beside her, looking at the labyrinth's pattern on her flesh, made her happy and sad both at once. Was this it, was this all there would be? She was a board to a carpenter, a tooth to a dentist – there was no love in his eyes, or his touch, and even though she could feel the heat from his breathing flow down the length of one naked thigh, the chill it left behind was more profound than alcohol evaporating.

"It's going to take me a bit to draw the next piece. Then I'll transfer it over and—"

She shook her head. "Don't draw ahead of time. Don't – don't think about it. Just draw it."

He raised an eyebrow.

"I signed the papers," she reminded him.

His lips curled into a grin. "You did, I was there." He stroked the plane of her flesh, drawing out a pattern on her with a gloved forefinger. Drawing in spaces that didn't exist yet, delineating them in his mind. In his touch now, in the freedom she'd granted him? Heat. He looked up at her, from his position by her hips.

"Are you sure?"

She saw what she felt in his eyes then. A piece. A piece of her path. And she wanted it, from him, on her. In, her.

"Yes."

He smiled, and began.

Sweet singing stinging pain. The kind that every nerve in your body tells you to run away from. The kind that certain people can tolerate, and some few enjoy.

If you had asked her that morning, which category she would be in, she would have told you about the valium in her purse. If you had asked her now, behind his closed door, as he stroked across her stomach with the cleaner, her skin prickling with the touch, and how she'd tried to stop from moaning when the buzzing began and the needles did their work, and how the design he drew upon her pulled them both into it, drawing the spirals out, wider, longer, further, until the design now took up her whole right hip, and he had an excuse to slide his hand between her thighs to pull the skin taut and how her body ground against his hand there, wet against the latex of his gloves, and then the gun was forgotten, dropped to the floor, and a sudden silence followed, before he entered her and – well. You wouldn't have to ask her. You would know.

"This is my number—" he said, and gave her a card, with handwritten digits on the back. She was sore, would be sore for days, in a multitude of places.

She smiled at him. She threw the card away outside.

★ ★ ★

There were other artists. Some were men, some were women, and she didn't sleep with all of them. Just most of them. The labyrinth's path extended out, twined around her body, all pieces of a path towards an unknown destination. Her own path now traveled over the southwest, as convoluted as her tattoo, from place to place, from person to person. Each of them added something to her, and she took it in, made it her own. A different woman might have lost herself on her travels, forgotten why she'd left, and why she was going. But not her.

Anytime she felt tired, or weak, or lonely – because sometimes she did feel lonely, still, but that was a part of life now, not something to be feared, not anymore – she could find her center, a point halfway between the cant of one hip and the divot of her navel.

Sometimes she would just let her fingers rest there, content to know herself in quiet silence. Other times, she would trace her own path out, remembering, finding herself in the curves, stroking around breasts, down her stomach, remembering the delicious redhead who'd done the lines alongside either edge of her labia, and who'd then given her clit a single, chaste, kiss.

Her torso was complete. One leg was finished, and then, the other.

What would happen when she was done? She wondered this sometimes as she drove along the interstate. Would she ever, really, be done? Was an end possible? Was it death, or worse than that, anathema to her now – stagnation? What would happen when she reached a point where all of her skin was covered, and no one would grant her sweet release?

If there was such a time, she thought, driving on one of the great flat expanses that stretched limitless from horizon's edge to horizon's edge – if there was such a time, may it be far off. As far off as I am from the edge of the world right now.

The edge of the world did really seem far, at that moment. But edges and endings both have a way of creeping nearer.

★   ★   ★

Soon, lines reached down both her arms like opera gloves, and arrowed down each finger in lightning bolts, before returning up again.

Even tattoo artists who have facial tattoos will not easily let you make that leap. To get a tattoo on your face is to mark yourself, more visibly than you ever have up until that point, as different. Until then, you could hide, with clothing and coats, tights and gloves. But after that, there is no shelter – you are exposed to the outside world, and chances are they will not like what they see.

She went from shop to shop, always feeling the space upon her neck where the labyrinth drew up short. So close to perfection, and yet she'd never felt further away. She would walk in, and sometimes even the people behind the counters would reel away in horror at the nature of her request.

But she could feel it. Every morning in the mirror, she could see it. Her whole body was covered in the labyrinth's lines, a map of her life, the paths she had taken and the people she'd taken them with. All of them ended, here – she could point to the spot where, between collarbones and above her sternum, the last session had drawn to a close. If she'd known that that would have been her last one, she would have done something different, something to make it longer, harder, sweeter.

"Only one man'll do that to you, girl," said the flash-covered man from behind the counter. "Too many people are afraid of lawsuits these days to go there."

She'd heard these stories before, of mythical brave men, and had seen them melt away in the sun. "And he's not?"

"No. He'll do it. He's good, too." He drew a map out on a card for her. "He doesn't work much anymore. That'll be the hard thing, getting him to do it. It won't be because he's scared, though."

Something in this conversation had the taste of the real. She reached forward with a quivering hand to take the map away. "Will he be there?"

"I dunno. Might have moved, even. But that's the chance you have to take."

She smiled at him. "I'm good at taking chances."

He wasn't there when she first got to his house. If it was his house. She sat outside in her car, idling, listening to the only radio station she could get reception to. Maybe he was on vacation? Or maybe a preacher's family lived here now. She imagined them, him with a wide shouldered suit, his wife with a pillbox hat, two perfect children, and three perfect dogs. And when they all got home from the church potluck, they'd wonder who the hell the tattooed freak standing in front of their house was, before they routed her with pitchforks and lit torches.

She found that out of the two choices, she was more scared of the former.

Dusk came. She made herself a bed in the backseat of her car, and she slept.

There was a tapping on her window near dawn. A rugged man stood outside her car and she rolled the window down.

"I heard about you," he said. "Come in." And he turned, and walked away.

She gathered herself and patted down her hair, then walked down the dusty pathway to the door of his house. She let herself in, and found herself in a room with a tiled floor, a table, and two chairs. He sat in one of them, already.

"You've heard . . . about me?" She wanted to be flattered, but you never knew.

"On and off. I figured it'd be a matter of time." He kicked the other chair out to her, and she sat down.

"So you'll do—" and she left the phrase hanging, not sure of what verb to use, or what word could adequately express what she wanted.

"You need me to do it, don't you?" he asked. She nodded, and so did he. "Show me what you've done so far."

She stripped, and stood before him. Orange light filtered in through yellowed panes of glass. She turned in silence, so he could see the tracework of all the others, all additions to her path.

"Nice work, most of it," he said, and, for the first time in a long time, she felt, maybe, deflated. Maybe, ashamed. Wasn't this, the goal of her life's work, valuable to him? Wasn't she of value, to him?

He continued to contemplate her, while she felt more naked as each second passed. Eventually, he made a thoughtful noise.

"Only one way to get this right." He reached out, and touched the spot of her center, between hip and navel. "I'll have to start at the center. And work my way out."

No one had done that before – no one except her, and the first artist. Each of the rest had started in on their own work, and she'd taken their art upon herself, to make it her own. But none of them had begun at the beginning, to trace the fullness of her journey, to understand the course she'd set for herself in its entirety.

And so when he put his finger just, so, there, and began winding his way upon her, it felt strange, and wrong, and happy, and good, and she wanted to run, and she wanted to hide, and she wanted to exult in each looping twist he made, finding a line that had run its course and folded in on itself, pulling back from the edges of her where she wanted him most. She turned when he needed to reach more of her, she moved so that he could follow the paths around her legs, down them, and up again, she lifted her hair as his hand found the lines that ran up her back.

Eventually, he found the emptiness at the pocket of her throat. His finger sat there, her pulse soaring beneath.

"Please," she asked. "Please, please, please."

"There's no going back from this."

"I don't want to go back."

He sighed, released her, and pushed a lamp over. "There's no mirrors for you here. I'll do what I like. We play by my rules."

"That's fine. I trust you." He'd already followed her labyrinth from end to end. On one hand, there was nothing else he could do to her now, he knew her, fully. And on the other, there was so much more yet to be done.

"Good. Sit down. Close your eyes."

She did as she was told, sat down naked, in the warming light, and the buzzing began.

This time the pain was exquisite. She stayed still, as he drew his chair up between her open legs, holding her chin with one hand, and his gun in the other. She turned as he pushed her to, one side, then the other, as patterns curled up her neck, upon her cheek, across her forehead, and down again. He was so close, and she could feel his concentration upon her, almost like a touch.

Too soon, the sound stopped. The needles, stopped. And she was alone with herself and his work.

Would it be enough? She opened her eyes for the first time in hours, and saw him there, staring at her. He nodded, to himself, surveying what he'd done. It echoed inside of her: this might really be the end.

He surveyed her as an artist surveys a finished piece. From his eyes, she knew he did not see her, but only his work left upon her. It was thrilling and deflating, both, at once.

"You're a masterpiece," he said, holding her chin in one hand.

What to say? There were no words. He swayed her head from side to side, looking at her, looking through her, and she did not fight him.

"You're the most beautiful thing I've ever helped create."

There was wetness on her face still, wounds weeping from the needles' passage. She could feel it cooling. "Thank you—"

"You're welcome." He started putting away his gear.

The passage of time and nearness between them – it seemed like it needed more. Required more. She sat there, being naked, and feeling naked, waiting.

He looked over at her, closing his case. "You're done. Go home."

Bile rose, unbidden. This was the end, she could feel it, but – it wasn't supposed to be like this. Instead of release or joy or satisfaction, she only felt panic.

Was it really over? She put a hand to her tender face. She had only thought of getting to this moment, and had never pressed beyond. What now? Where, now?

She put her clothes on as fast as she could, hiding herself and her labyrinth from him. She ran out to her car, and slid into the driver's seat, and rested her still bleeding forehead against her steering wheel, and cried. Why? she thought, even as the tears rolled down. She cried for everything she had done, everything she hadn't done, and for what she'd done to herself, carried so far down a path of her own making. What to do, now that she'd reached the end? What use was life, when there was nothing left to be lived?

She sobbed, for a long time. Between the hours he had spent on her face, and her time crying, it was almost night when she finished, washed up, poured out, ended. She turned the engine over, and flicked on the overhead light.

To finally see. What he'd done. What she'd done. What she'd let him do.

Closing her eyes, and then opening them with a willfulness, she stared at herself in the rearview mirror, not expecting to recognize herself.

But.

It was still her.

Blood turning to scabs formed marks on parts of her face, and other skin raised, shiny and bruised – but – it was still her. She reached up and felt the lines – she knew they were there, she'd been there when he'd placed them upon her.

But.

He'd used no ink.

She inhaled, and exhaled, reached up and turned off the light. And then she walked back up to his door.

★　　★　　★

"You're still here?" he asked.

"You – did this to me," she said.

"I did," he agreed. "I did a good job, too."

She nodded, and there was silence. "You said it yourself, there's no going back."

"And you said you didn't want to go back," he said, and shrugged.

She looked around at the plain around them, and the star-filling night above. Her labyrinth was complete now. And it had brought her here.

"And you said I should go home," she said.

"I did," he agreed.

What she was about to say was foolish, and stupid, and too much too soon. But if she could find herself at the end of her own labyrinth, if she could tolerate the heights of ecstasy and the depths of pain, then saying these words was nothing to her, delicious nothingness and excruciating somethingness at the same time.

"I think I am home."

He smiled. And he moved away from the doorway, to let her inside.

Measure A, B, Or Me?

Alison Tyler

"Look at this, Lisa," James said, pointing to the voter registry spread out on his side of the kitchen table.

"Nice," I said, not glancing up from the newspaper.

"No, look right here." He tapped the middle of one of the pages.

I gazed at him over the top of my glasses. I was busy reading "Dear Abby". James knows better than to interrupt me during "Dear Abby".

"These two names," James insisted. With a sigh, I put down the paper and glanced where he was pointing. "So? They have to list husbands and wives separately. Husbands don't own wives anymore, you know."

"I understand that you have zero interest in politics," James said in that calm voice of his, "but look at the parties."

Knowing James wasn't going to stop, I set down my coffee, stood up, and headed around to his side of the table. James had volunteered to phone registered voters to discuss a ballot measure close to his heart. And for the first time since he'd begun to talk incessantly about Ballot Measure A, I found myself interested in the cause, or at least mildly so. Here was personal information for nearly a quarter of the people in our tiny town. The list did not only contain their names, numbers, and addresses, but also their chosen political parties. A couple we knew ever-so-vaguely were registered with different parties – the wife a Democrat, the husband a Republican.

"How can that happen?" I asked curiously. "That was one of the first things I found out about you. Your religious preference, the size of your cock, and your political leanings. This is like something right out of a 'Dear Abby' column."

"I don't understand it either," James admitted, "but look at the Governor and his wife, and there are other famous couples who vote on different party lines, too."

"You mean like Marlee Matlin and George Carlin?"

James groaned. "It's *Mary Matalin* and *James Carville*."

"Yeah, but how can they get into the same bed at night? I'd never be able to fuck you if I thought you were Republican. That would be an instant deal-breaker."

"More so than the size of my cock?" James teased, and while I was considering my answer, he continued, "Hey, let's have some fun."

Since James had embarked upon this mission to make sure Measure A passed, he'd been neglecting some of his more important husbandly duties. I'm not the type to care about whether the lawn is mowed or the car is washed. But I'd gone through three packs of C-batteries for my vibrator in two months. Still, I didn't want to get my hopes up too high. "I thought you had people to call," I said tentatively.

"I'm *talking* about calling."

I sighed again. "Come on, James." I'd been hoping for a bit of frisky mid-morning fun. Dialing up voters wasn't my idea of kinky sex play. But I should have looked more clearly into my husband's deep blue eyes before writing him off.

"Lisa," he said in that patently annoying tone of voice, "I know you have zero interest in politics—"

"I'm a registered Democrat," I reminded him. "I wear my Stewart/Colbert '08 shirt every time I go to the gym. I have a *Somewhere in Texas a Village is Missing its Idiot* bumper sticker on my Prius and a *Don't Blame Me, I Voted for Kerry* button on my denim jacket. What more do you want?"

"Yeah." He nodded. "But you're not exactly involved. You'd rather watch *Friends* reruns than stand outside the Palace Market and register voters."

I shrugged.

"But you *could* be involved. What if you call the man and I call the woman. You'll be your charming little self and try to win him over to the cause, and I'll do the same with her. It'll be like a contest . . ."

"That's not really fair. You don't *have* to win her over. She's *already* a Democrat. Besides, I don't have any idea what to say."

James glared at me, his nearly endless supply of patience finally waning. "Haven't you been listening to me make the last 145 calls?"

I nodded, lying. I tended to tune out as soon as I heard him say the words, "This is James Miller, and I'd like to talk to you about Measure A."

"You just coo the same info to the man."

I looked at him for a moment. "What do I win if I get him onto our side?"

"You name it."

I motioned for him to dial. I could think of several propositions I was extremely interested in winning him over to — and not one on the current ballot. There was the up-against-the-wall position, in which I was fully in favor. And the bent-over-the-arm-of-the-sofa position, which I could fully support.

I could tell that James didn't think I'd go through with the bet. When he handed the phone to me for my turn, I pressed redial, asked to speak to Leonard Carson, then tried my best to explain the terms of the measure to the husband. Unfortunately, the jerk hung up the phone on me as soon as he realized where I was headed with my political speech.

"Well, *that* was successful," James said. "You didn't even try."

"You never know," I countered, "I'll bet they're talking about the issue right now."

"You think?" he asked.

"Yeah." I sat down on his lap. "She's saying, 'It's a good cause, Lenny.'"

"His name is Leonard."

"Sure, but she probably has a pet name for him. 'It's money for the schools.' "

James interrupted me again, "And he's saying, 'We sent our kids to private schools over the hill. What the fuck do we care about those rats in the public system . . .' "

"Why is he swearing?" I asked.

"Because he's an asshole."

"Just because he has a different viewpoint from you?"

"*You're* the one who said you'd never fuck a Republican," James pointed out. I ignored him.

"He's saying, 'Convince me.' And she's going on her knees on their expensive Spanish-tiled floor . . ."

"She's *not* going to give him a blow job over Measure A," James insisted.

"How do you know?"

"Would you?"

"Maybe she's more political than I am. You know I have zero interest . . ."

"So she's giving him one hell of a blow job. How's *that* convincing him to vote the way she wants?"

"Maybe you're right. She needs her mouth free to win him over." I hesitated, trying my best to envision the scenario. "Okay, they're in the kitchen, and she bends over the table, like this, and lifts her nightgown."

I demonstrated for James, sliding my short satin nightie to my waist. James eyed me for a moment, then got behind me. He ran his large hands over my panty-clad ass before pulling my knickers along my thighs. I shivered at his touch. It had been so long since he'd last stroked me like that. When he slipped his drawstring pjs down and pressed his body against me, I could feel how hard his cock was.

Cautiously, James slid a hand under my body and touched my pussy. "You're wet," he said. "Does talking about politics turn you on?"

"You know it," I told him, stifling a giggle. Even after he slid inside of me, he wouldn't stop taunting me, "So in your little fantasy, the wife says, 'Vote for Measure A, and I'll let you fuck me'?"

"That sounds silly when you say it."

"It's beyond silly," James insisted. He continued to drive inside of me, working a little faster now. "They're not having a conversation like this at all. If anything, they're having some huge four-star fight because she's voting one way and he's insisting on voting the other. In fact, I'll bet he's saying, 'If you vote for Measure A, I'm going to have to give you a spanking.' "

That caught me off-guard, and for a moment I actually considered switching over to the dark side. But I still didn't want to give in. "Well, what if she says, 'You can do that thing you want to do'?"

"*What* thing?"

"You *know* what thing," I said coyly. "The thing you always want to, and the thing I hardly ever say yes to."

James was silent, but I knew he understood what I meant. "You'll let me do *that* if I vote for Measure A?"

"She's thinking about it."

"She?" he asked softly. "Or you?"

"I'm *already* voting for Measure A."

"You know what I mean."

"Yes," I said. "She's thinking about it, and *I'm* thinking about it—"

That was all James needed to hear. There was a tub of margarine still out on the table, and he leaned over and scooped out a fingerful. In seconds, he had lubed me up between my rear cheeks, his firm hands spreading me wide open. I shut my eyes and gripped even tighter onto the edge of the table, breathless.

James went slow at first, sliding his cock forward inch by inch, pressing hard, but not forcing. "Relax," he said.

"How can I relax when you won't vote for Measure A?"

"It's that important to you?"

James slipped in a little more, and I groaned. The sensation of being filled was almost overwhelming. Still, I managed somehow to reply. "Yes," I muttered. "Yes, it is."

Now, he was fucking me even harder, gripping onto my slim

hips and really driving his cock inside of me. My pussy was pressed firmly to the edge of the table, and through the filmy barrier of my nightgown, my clit received the most perfect pressure. I gasped as the rhythm of his thrusts increased in tempo, finding pleasure each time he slammed forward. I could come like this if he kept up the speed.

"You know," he said, "Measure A needs two Yeses to counter every one No."

"Yes," I panted. "Yes, yes . . ."

"That's three yeses," James said. "You can't vote three times," but his voice had dropped to a whisper.

"Oh, God," I whimpered, unsure of what we were talking about or who I was. Was I Catherine trying to convince her bastard of a husband to vote yes on the school measure and help the children? Or was I Lisa, whose husband was already an activist, such an activist that he'd forgotten to take care of me for the past two months.

I squeezed my eyes shut even tighter as James slid one hand under my body and began to tap his fingertips against my clit. He knew exactly how to work me, thrusting forward with his cock, then giving me a little tap before slowly withdrawing. When he pinched my clit hard, I found myself teetering on the brink, hardly able to breathe until the climax finally flared through me. James let those powerful shudders transfer from my body to his, and then he groaned and began to work me even more seriously, before coming ferociously into my ass and sealing his body to mine.

It took me a moment to recover. The morning sunlight played over our sparkly blue Formica breakfast table. The tub of yellow margarine seemed to be mocking me.

James pulled out and tucked himself back into his pajamas. "I've still got twenty more calls to make," he said.

So he knew what was on his morning agenda, but I couldn't figure out what to do next. "Dear Abby" held no interest. Nor did finishing the rest of the paper. I wondered what Catherine and Leonard were doing right now. Was she bent over their kitchen table as I'd described?

Quickly, I slid my panties back up, then climbed onto my husband's lap once more. I pointed to the next Republican on the list. "If I can get her to vote for A, you let me do that to *you*—" I told James.

He cocked an eyebrow at me, then pushed over the phone.

Just Another Girl on the Train

Catherine Lundoff

People on the train always looked alike at first glance, she thought as she watched her fellow passengers from the corners of her eyes. It was a bad idea to look at them directly. She'd learned that her first year here riding the subway to her job downtown. There was that time the crazy man followed her several blocks from the station, shouting after her. Then there was that other incident involving the missionaries and those copies of *The Watchtower* that kept showing up in her mailbox. No, best to watch covertly over her book, let her eyes slide past as though reading the station signs when she looked up.

You got to see all sorts of interesting things that way. The Chicano boy with the dreamy eyes watching his girlfriend sleep on his shoulder. The old women dozing over their shopping bags or books. The heavily made up woman (or was she a man?) in the latex mini who kept checking her (or was it his?) watch and tapping one impossibly high heel restlessly against the train floor. She had a story made up for each and every one of them. That was the best part about riding the city trains; the stories never ended.

That woman across the aisle this morning, for instance. She must be worried about something from the way she sent nervous glances at the doors every time the train stopped. Between stops, she looked first at her watch, then at the floor, thin brown eyebrows meeting in a scowl over her long nose.

Once, the other woman's small brown eyes met hers for an instant before they both looked away. The other woman's gaze told her nothing really, held no obvious reason for the clear anxiety she was feeling. But there had been something there, something she couldn't explain. When the woman got off at the next stop, she got up and followed her.

Why she did it, she never could say afterwards. But it was the beginning, this sideways path to follow a stranger for a glimpse into their lives. Was it that it made her own life seem less ephemeral when held up to the mirror of someone else's? She couldn't or didn't want to answer that. She only knew that she was curious. That she needed to know something about this woman's life and why she was so nervous.

Up and out of the station she went, trailing a half block or so behind her quarry, but still trying to look as if she knew where she was going. The crowds helped with that, swirling around to hide first her from the woman, then the woman from her. Something about the chase made her hot, made her think of the hottest, sweatiest sex she'd ever had. That part wasn't about the woman she was following, or at least she didn't think so. No, it must be about the hunt itself. She grinned a little to herself and followed the nervous woman around a corner.

Her quarry glanced around before slipping up the steps of a building and she stopped to watch her go inside. Looking up, she noticed that there was a neon sign on the roof, blinking with the name of the hotel. The crowd swirled around her like a river while she wondered what to do next. She watched a group of teenagers walk by, one boy's hand stuck possessively in his girlfriend's jean pocket. She looked back at the hotel and thought about sex.

Then she thought about following the woman inside. But then what? Instead she walked around the block, looking for a way to see into the rooms, maybe see what she was doing. She glanced down the alleyway that ran behind the hotel. It looked empty of rats and muggers and other urban perils. Somebody came out of one of the doors and dumped some restaurant trash in the bin then stopped for a cigarette.

She waited until he went back inside, savoring the aroused ache that filled her when she thought about assignations in hotels, about steamy affairs that swept you away. The voice of her common sense warned her away, warned her back into the safe and the familiar. She thought about listening to it for all of a single minute.

Then she walked down the alleyway looking warily around her for unwanted company. So far it looked deserted. She looked up when she got to the middle, wondering if she could see anything in the hotel. She stretched up on tiptoe, stepping back against the brick wall of the alley, heart thumping with anticipation.

At first, there wasn't much to see. Just maids cleaning the rooms and someone opening the curtains before they left for the day. She walked down a little further and found a tiny deserted courtyard between the buildings facing the hotel. She looked up at closed and shuttered windows, then walked over to press her back against the wall and stared up at the hotel.

The courtyard smelled like garbage and pee and she had just told herself that she was nuts and needed to leave for the third time when the curtains on one of the fourth floor windows opened. The woman from the subway looked out as a man's hands reached around her and started unbuttoning her shirt. She still looked anxious, gnawing her lip as he kissed her neck and shoulder.

Then her eyes closed and the woman in the alley could see his hands on her breasts, her blouse parting under his fingers. It was almost as if she could feel his hands on her own breasts and she squeezed them experimentally, thumbing her nipples through her blouse and bra to feel something of what the woman in the window must be feeling. The unaccustomed sensation almost tore a moan from her throat. Clearly it had been awhile since anyone had touched her like that.

She could see the man's hands unfastening the woman's pants, pulling them down, then bending her backward into a kiss. The woman in the window clutched at him, her hands desperate even when seen from the alleyway. A hot stab went through the watching woman releasing the wetness inside her so that it ran down her thighs, so that she didn't think she could bear not being touched. She stuck her hand down her pants, her eyes fixed on the hotel window.

She was amazingly, wrenchingly wet and empty. Her fingers were never going to be enough to fill all that but she did the best she could and slid them inside herself. Above her in the window, the man was working his way inside the woman from behind; she could see it on her face even from here. The other woman's eyes were closed, her mouth open and gasping. She thrust back against her lover, taking him in.

For a moment, the woman in the alley closed her eyes too as she rocked forward on her fingers, picturing herself in the window. Her fingertips brushed her clit and the sensation almost made her scream. She bit her lip, circling her aroused flesh with her thumb. For a wild moment, she thought about taking off her jeans but that was too much. Instead she leaned against the bricks and rubbed herself to orgasm with a muffled moan.

Her legs hadn't stopped shaking when she looked up. This time the woman in the window met her gaze. She could see the man reach around and slip his hand between her thighs. The woman frowned down at her before she caught her breath, before she turned back, yielding to the insistence of the man's hands and dick.

The frown had been enough to shake her back to reality. She zipped up her jeans again, feeling somehow elated and ashamed all at once. Then she walked away down the alleyway, her stride brisk and businesslike as she headed back to the subway.

That was the beginning of turning voyeur. At first she was afraid it might have come from some newfound phobia about being touched. Perhaps she just needed a good therapist. Then she worried that it grew out of a fear of dating and intimacy. So maybe she just needed a new lover. A week or so after that, she decided that she just liked to watch.

The night that she came to that realization, she followed a man out of the restaurant where she and her friends were eating dinner. She trailed him down darkened city streets to the edge of a city park. Then she found some bushes to linger in out of sight while he sat on a park bench. He looked around and she watched as his eyes followed the taut firm asses of the young men who jogged past. She could almost feel him harden as he fidgeted on the bench, looking for the best place to arrange the erection she could see from her hiding place.

She thought about going over to him, about unzipping his pants and taking his dick in her mouth without saying a word. About licking and sucking him until he came, his hands hard and tight on the back of her head. But she didn't think it was her he was looking for and she stayed where she was.

Finally one young guy jogged past, slowing down a little as he passed the bench. She could almost feel his gaze caress the sitting man's erection, the connection so hot it made her ache even watching it from here. She could almost feel the seated man look up, feel him harden even more as he looked over the jogger's firm ass, his sturdy, muscular legs. She watched as the jogger smiled a slow, secret smile then turned off the path and headed for a thicker clump of bushes behind the bench.

She saw the seated man stand up a few moments later and trail the other into the bushes. The thought of it, of hot and forbidden sex with a desperate risk of discovery sent a jolt through her. She could picture their hands on each other's bodies, their mouths open and wet, pressed together in a kiss. She found herself standing up and walking toward the other clump of bushes as if pulled on an invisible line.

A quick glance around told her that there were other people nearby in case there was trouble, but no one close enough to see what she or the guys in the bushes were up to. She circled the clump listening for the telltale gasp of breath, the soft moan that would tell her what she came to see.

After a minute, she heard it. The moan came just as she found a gap in the bushes behind a tree. She slipped into it, her steps nearly silent on the summer grass. She hunched over, ducking down so she'd be hard to see in the bushes and glanced around the tree.

They were there, the jogger kneeling in front of the man from the bench. She could see the latter's dick slip into the jogger's mouth, see the man from the bench lean backward against a tree, his eyes closed and his head tilted back. The jogger made a small slurping noise as his mouth took in the full length of the other's hard-on.

The breath caught in her throat and she rubbed the seam of her pants against her engorged clit as she watched. There would be no time to get her hand down her pants, she could see that already in the standing man's face, the way his expression changed as he shifted toward orgasm. She rubbed hard, her fingers fierce and demanding against her own flesh. Her hips rocked forward of their own accord, the movement mimicking the men in front of her.

The cloth of her pants, of her soaking wet underwear scraped against her sensitive flesh until she had to bite back moans of her own. At the same time, she was so wet, so empty that it felt as if it would have taken both men to fill her. She pictured that for a moment, rubbing faster until her orgasm took her just as the standing man came. She missed watching that moment cross his face because her knees gave way and she found herself kneeling in the dirt, thighs shaking with release.

She crouched there, trembling in the aftermath and watched as the jogger wiped his mouth and stood. He reached out and gently touched the other man's cheek before he turned away, slipping through the bushes and back to jogging as if nothing had happened. The other man looked after him, his eyes dark with longing and desire as he zipped himself up and followed. She stood up awkwardly and brushed off her knees. Then she left the park in the opposite direction, walking stiffly and carefully so as not to further irritate her already tormented flesh.

A few days passed, just enough to heal and whet her appetite for more. She went looking for what she wanted to see, watching for it wherever she went. It took time to find the right spot and the right couple but eventually they turned up.

She was at a bar with a date when she spotted them. Her date was talking about something and she hung on his words until she saw the couple walk in and sit down. She wasn't sure that it was them she'd been watching for, not at first. But then, just then, the woman slid her hand up her man's thigh in a slow, sensuous gesture full of promise and she knew she'd found them.

Her date knew he'd lost her and kept trying to recapture her attention until she finally pled a headache and bolted. Once outside, she circled back to the bar in time to see the couple go out on the dance floor. They were a matched set: all black silk and gothy, the woman's eyes made catlike with too much eyeliner. They kissed as she watched, the woman catching the man's lower lip in her teeth as they broke it off. He laughed and she shivered just looking at them, the telltale scent of desire rising from between her legs.

She followed them when they left the dance floor, headed into a hallway that led back into the rest of the building. She watched as they made out, their mouths wet and fierce against each other's, his hand reaching down to cup her ass and pull her hips forward against his. Her hands were wrapped tight around his neck, holding him in place as she opened her legs to let his thigh slip between them.

The watching woman felt a shock go through her, as if she were a part of their scene. She looked around for a place to hide and watch them but there was nothing convenient. Instead, she found a dimly lit table with a good view of the hallway and an empty bar stool. She ordered a drink as she dangled one hand off the table, slowly and carefully feeling her way between her legs.

The couple had gone a little further while she'd been getting settled in and she could see his hand under the woman's shirt now. His mouth caressed her neck and even from here, she could see his teeth flash on her skin for an instant. Her own need was more urgent now and she rocked herself against the barstool in a vain attempt at release.

"Hi there. You here by yourself?" The guy was standing between her and the hallway and it was all she could do not to yell at him. Part of her noted that he was sort of cute. Nice body. Maybe enough to fill the ache inside. But she wanted to watch first. She murmured something about waiting for a friend, one who'd be showing up soon. He moved on just in time for her to watch as the guy in the hallway pushed his girlfriend against the wall, then lifted her up to hip level. Her legs wrapped around his waist as he pushed himself inside her, her mouth open and gasping, his face hidden in her neck.

The watching woman pulled her purse into her lap to hide the hand between her legs. She schooled her face to stay still, frozen as if listening to the music while she watched, imagining what it would be like to be taken in a public place. The thought got her wetter than she'd ever been and despite herself, she gasped a little as her fingers found her clit through the thin fabric of skirt and underwear.

"That's some friend you're waiting for." The guy was back, standing behind her this time, so close that she could feel the heat of his body. "Can I help?"

She hesitated, her eyes still locked on the hallway. The couple was close to climax and she found her head nodding like it was on strings. The guy stepped up to her, hand encircling her waist and face buried in her hair. He kissed her ear as one thumb slid slowly over her rock-hard nipple. She gasped and jumped as his other hand worked its way between her legs. In front of her, the couple in the hallway came, seemingly together. She could see the guy arch his head back, mouth open in a silent cry. The woman with him gave him a fierce smile, all desire and love and power.

The guy behind her ran his tongue down her neck as she came, silently shivering on the barstool. The couple left the hallway hand in hand while she was still shaking and she didn't watch them leave. She could feel the man behind her, his hand still wrapped around her and his dick hard against her back. "Do you want to go over there?" he murmured in her ear, nodding toward the hallway.

She shook her head. "It wouldn't be the same now." She smiled at him over her shoulder and let him kiss her lips.

"Then I think I know another place that might work. Come with me?" She met his eyes for a second, then slid off the barstool and grabbed his hand. He grinned down at her and pulled her out the door with him. And she didn't watch anyone else for the rest of the night.

She was on the train again a few weeks later, the memory of last night's sex with her new boyfriend still sharp and clear in her mind. She remembered the feel of him inside her on his apartment balcony. She could sense his neighbor's eyes on her, watching as his hands pinched her nipples into diamond points, as her hand dove between her legs. Watching as she came, shaking and nearly collapsing but for his strong arms around her. As he came a moment later, his groan echoing down the side of the building.

It made her smile remembering it. It made the breath catch in her throat and her eyes darken as she sat on the subway. It was almost enough that she didn't notice the woman across the way watching her. The other woman's eyes were hungry, wanting something from her. She recognized that look and all in an instant, knew what her answer had to be.

She pulled her face into a worried scowl and checked her watch, then her cellphone. She sighed impatiently. Her foot tapped on the floor and when her stop came, she bolted out the door. She could see the other woman follow her and she smiled as she dialed her boyfriend's number. She hoped the other woman would enjoy the show as much as they did.

A Different Kind of Reality Show

D. L. King

The contract was for a week. I'd have everything I needed to live – everything but the physical presence of others. The ad in Soul-Bound had suggested thinking about the service period like a kinky reality show; it would, after all, be televised for an exclusive paying audience. Pay-per-view kink, yeah, I'd been *there* before – a lot – however, never as the star of the show.

It got me thinking and kept me thinking for days, I couldn't pass it up. I'm sure I wasn't the first to feel that way and probably wouldn't be the last. They were going to pay me very well for a week spent in confinement. It would be a week spent alone in a posh condo, naked, submitting to the voice commands of an exclusive audience of women. I would be on camera and on call twenty-four hours a day for seven days.

I'm kind of an exhibitionist at heart. I like being naked and I don't mind being watched. My dick isn't bad; at least I've never had any complaints. I think it's pretty nice when it's up and ready for action – like I said, no complaints.

I sent in my application with the required photos and waited. About five months later, an envelope came from Soul-Bound. I had to think for a second: Who the hell was Soul-Bound? About to throw it in the recycle bin, it hit me – starring in pay-per-view kink! I'd all but forgotten about it.

They wanted me. Cool. Of course they did. Why wouldn't they?

I took a week's vacation from work and on a Saturday night, drove across the Verrazano to an industrial-looking building in Midtown with its own underground garage. The elevator opened on to a reception desk on the fifth floor. The guy manning the desk asked for my ID and after scrutinizing it, announced my presence to someone at the other end of a phone line.

"Okay, follow me," he said after hanging up the phone. "You ever done any professional work before?"

"Well, yeah, I'm a CPA at a firm in Jersey."

"No, man, porn work. You know, sex work. You done any sex work before this?"

"Oh, I see. Porn. Yeah, well, yeah. I mean no. I mean – porn?"

"Yeah, buddy: porn. Waddya think? I mean you're gonna be naked, on camera for a week. Waddya think it is? But hey, if you got a problem, you gotta let me know now. No one's gonna let you outa there unless you're sick or somethin' once you go in, ya know? So? You still wanna do this?"

"Well, um, yeah – I guess. I mean, yeah, sure. Why not?"

"All right then. Everything's on this floor. We got the whole loft. Inside, it's nice. You got everything you need. There's food and stuff to read and tapes 'n' stuff to watch. You don't get TV, but there's DVDs and stuff. All you gotta do is what the ladies tell you to.

"Nobody's gonna come in and you can't come out until your time's up or they kick you out. You signed a contract that said you'd do what you were told and that's all you gotta do. If nobody's tellin' you to do anything, you can do what you want, but when somebody tells you to do something, you gotta drop whatever you're doing and do it. Get me?"

"Yes, I know." The guy was getting on my nerves. Or maybe the whole thing was beginning to get on my nerves.

"Now look, and this is important, you gotta do everything they say or at least try to do it. If you don't do something or you refuse, you don't get paid, see. You understand?"

"Yeah, okay." He stared at me like I wasn't getting it. I was getting it.

"All right, so, there are cameras everywhere in the loft. There's no place you won't be on camera, OK?"

I nodded. We were standing in front of a door, in a hallway behind the reception desk.

"All right. You can take off your clothes and everything here." He handed me a locker key and said I should put all my belongings in the locker and take the key inside the living space with me. He said I could put it in a bowl by the door, that way, I wouldn't lose it.

"Cause you lose your key, you're gonna be the one who has to pay to get the lock cut off."

"Yeah, okay." I very quickly got out of my clothes and folded them up in the locker. I just wanted to get inside.

"You gotta take off all the jewellery and the watch too."

"Yeah, all right." Finally I stood in front of the door, completely naked and a little chilled, key in hand. There seemed to be a draft. I hadn't thought about it before but some of these old buildings, well, you had to expect it. I really hoped I wouldn't freeze to death for an entire week.

He unlocked the door. "Okay pal, have a good one," and in I walked.

I heard the door close and the lock slide home behind me but I was more concerned with what was in front of me to pay much attention. There was no draft. There weren't any windows. Everything was white. I detected a light scent of lavender in the air as my feet sunk into the thick carpet. A white velvet couch faced a huge plasma screen on the opposite wall. In front of the couch was a large white plastic low table; one of those really expensive ones you see in magazines. Below the TV was a table with a white DVD player and two shelves of white-sleeved DVDs. There were small white speakers on stands at each corner of the room.

If I continued in a straight line from the door, I came to a white dining table with one straight-backed chair and then the kitchen. The kitchen was no different: white counter and sinks, white appliances, white dinnerware but stainless silverware and pots and pans. The glasses were a frosted white. I wondered if the food would somehow be white too.

The bedroom, off the living room, held a king-sized bed with a white anodized barred head and footboard. The bathroom had a white tile floor and mirrors covering the walls opposite the sink, shower, toilet, and tub. Back in the bedroom, I noticed a nightstand by the bed with a shelf of white-covered books.

Walking back into the bathroom I lifted the seat and began a much-needed piss. It was slightly weird, gazing at myself in the floor to ceiling mirror behind the toilet.

"Don't make a mess, boy. You'll have to clean it up with your tongue. No one likes a messy boy, do they?"

I stopped in mid-stream and looked around, my hands automatically going up to cover my cock and balls. I heard a chorus of female voices commenting on messy guys and then the first voice said, "What do you think you're doing? Take those hands away!"

I removed my hands and said, "Sorry, ma'am."

"Pretty shouldn't speak unless he's asked a direct question. But he is very pretty, isn't he?"

"Prettier than his pictures, I'd say."

"Finish going to the bathroom, boy."

I was frozen in place, one hand holding my cock, looking around the room for the cameras, but I couldn't find them.

"What's the matter, pretty? Don't like an audience? We'll be quiet. Just pretend we're not here." There was some quiet snickering and whispering and then nothing but the occasional quiet cough.

This was what I was getting paid for, I guess I never truly thought about what "On camera 24/7" really meant. But I had to go and so, I went. As I was washing my hands, the first voice spoke again.

"Hurry it up, boy. It's time to learn the rules. Go back to the living room and take a seat in the middle of the sofa."

Once back in the living room, she continued. "Spread those legs. Whenever you sit, your legs are to be spread as wide as possible. Better. You'll do what we tell you. Whatever we tell you, or you'll be forced to leave without pay."

I have to say, I was beginning to feel like I might not have made such a good decision. She talked about how any of the women, at any time, could give me a command and I'd have to execute it. And if they told me to stop, I'd better stop whatever I was doing.

She said there were lots of toys in the apartment, which they might direct me to play with. She said there were magnetic restraints that once put on, only she and her friends had the power to remove. She also said I would have plenty of free time to do anything I wanted. There were movies to watch and books to read.

"Any questions, pretty?"

I thought of about a million things to ask. "No, ma'am."

"That's fine then. Masturbate for us."

And that was my introduction to the house. Of course, I didn't mind jacking off to the cameras, I enjoyed it, being the exhibitionist I am. It was when I got close to coming that the point of their control was driven home.

"Stop."

I didn't stop right away.

"I said stop! If you come, you're out of here right now. It would be a shame to get kicked out less than an hour after arrival."

I stopped, right hand still wrapped around my shaft, which stood hard and straight.

"You'll get used to it. Now, on the dining table you'll find a set of wrist and ankle cuffs. Put them on."

I found them. Fitting with the theme, they were white leather. I couldn't see how to fasten them on because there didn't seem to be any buckles or locks.

"Just wrap it around your wrist."

I did as I was told and felt the ends come together with a strong magnetic pull. I gave it a yank but it refused to budge.

"Magnetic restraints. I told you."

When I had them all fastened, another voice told me to go pick out a movie and put it in the DVD player. My hard-on hadn't subsided yet and the cuffs were adding to my arousal. I don't know what it is about cuffs, but you feel somehow more naked when you're wearing them, or at least I do.

The movies didn't have any titles or cover pictures but each was numbered. Which should I choose? I opened a box and found a white DVD with a number corresponding to the box cover.

"Oh, for heaven's sake, just put in number twenty-three."

"I suppose we're going to have to tell him everything."

"So many pretty boys are indecisive."

"It's all right, pretty, we didn't choose you for your brains."

"Oh look, now you've gone and hurt his feelings!"

"She didn't mean it, pretty. We're all sure you're very smart, aren't we, ladies?"

I turned beet red to choruses of "yes, yes", "sure" and "of course we do" while I put the requested DVD in. They had me go back to the couch and sit down again. This time I remembered to sit with my legs apart. As the opening credits flashed, they told me to put my hands behind my back and as soon as I did, I felt my wrists snap together in magnetic restraint.

It was a porn movie. It figured. It was okay, but it really didn't do that much for me. It had mostly attractive women with fake boobs swimming together nude. Then some guys came over and fucked 'em in a few different ways. Pretty standard fare, really. So I leaned back and watched while my cock wilted. They freed my hands and had me change the movie a few times. I guess they were trying to get to know me, or at least my taste in porn.

Each time I changed the movie, they'd restrain my hands again. Eventually, I came across a movie I liked, as evidenced by my returning hard-on. Surprise, surprise, it was about some ball-busting women tying some guy up and fucking him in front of an audience of people. See, he didn't know there was going to be an audience until he was already tied up, then they opened some curtains and he could see a room full of people watching. I really liked that part. I told you I was an exhibitionist!

Then three different women fucked him with strap-ons. I didn't think I'd like that but I did. Or at least my cock did. That kind of disturbed me a little bit – that my cock seemed to like that so much, but I wasn't too scared because I knew I was alone and no one was going to come in and do that to me.

The voices made all sorts of comments about what I liked and what they should do to me and about all the pre-come dripping from my cock. The screen had a "picture in picture" mode and they put a close-up of my cock on the TV screen for me to watch. That was kind of cool. You never see yourself like that. I mean, even if you watch yourself masturbate, the angle's different, you know?

At one point in the movie, this one woman was scratching the guy's balls with these long metal claw-like things on the ends of her fingers. I guess my legs started to come together and that woman who seemed to be in charge barked, "Keep those legs apart!" The next thing I knew, my feet were rooted to the floor, with my legs really wide apart.

"There are magnetic points in strategic places which we can activate, boy. Why, what sort of fun would it be, if we couldn't tether you to something when we wanted to? Yes, there are points like this all over, not just in the floor, but you'll see. It seems we have a live one, girls!"

The movie I was watching ended but another came on right after it. This one showed a guy attached to a wall, again with an audience. There was only one woman in it. She was beautiful but really mean. You could tell she liked hurting the guy. Like when you watch a horror movie, I couldn't keep my eyes off her.

"Mmm, pretty, pretty. You like that, don't you?"

I almost hadn't heard her. No, I didn't like that. I wasn't into that sort of thing. I stole a glance at my cock on the screen and saw it bobbing and dancing. They unfastened my wrists and the woman told me I could touch myself. My hands raced to my shaft and started pumping.

"Stop!"

It took me a second, but I managed to stop.

"I'm going to let you come, but I'll tell you when. There's a part coming up here that I think you'll really like. It'd be a shame if you came too soon and missed it, don't you think?"

They freed my hands. "Press 'pause' on the remote." They freed my legs and told me to open the drawer in the coffee table. Toys. There were lots of different kinds of toys. There were things in there I had no idea how to use or what they might be for.

"Now, pretty, you see that sweet little red butt plug?"

I suppose I hadn't really been thinking when I looked in the drawer that these were for me to use – on myself! Whoa, butt plug? And it wasn't "little" either. Somehow, I gave myself away.

"What's the matter, pretty, Never used one of those? Ooh, I think you'll like it. Don't you think he'll like it, girls?"

Once again, there were choruses of, "oh yes" and "you know it".

"And besides, it's always so much fun watching a sweet little anal virgin trying to insert his first plug! Here's what you're gonna do, pretty; you're going to pick up that bottle of lube and the red plug, close the drawer, walk around the table so you're standing between the TV and the table. That's right. Now, you're going to bend over and put your hands on the table top. Yes, that's nice. Now, take your hands off the table – no, no, don't stand up – grab your butt cheeks and spread 'em. We want to see that lovely virgin hole of yours. That's right.

"Okay, you can let go. Now, squeeze some lube on your right index finger and rub it over your anus. Yes, now, get some more lube and do it again. Push your finger in a little bit. Doesn't that feel nice?"

You know what, it did feel good. I wasn't going to tell her

that, but it did kind of turn me on. I never did anything like that before. I never thought I'd want to. I mean, I've fucked a girl in the ass before and I really liked it, but I never wanted to put anything in *my* ass. It kind of sent a chill down my spine, into my balls.

"Answer me, boy, doesn't it feel nice?"

"Uh, no."

"Well, that's a shame. I guess you'll be pretty uncomfortable for a while then. Squeeze some lube on the tip of the plug and coat the whole thing. You need more than that, boy. That's better. Now, reach back and pull your cheeks apart with your left hand and find your asshole with the plug."

There was some giggling while I tried to locate the right place. I started sweating. My hard-on was gone and I was getting more and more embarrassed. Finally I found my asshole. Listen, it's not that easy when you're doing it for the first time and people are watching.

"That's it. Now slowly push it in. No, keep going."

It hurt. I thought it might feel good, but it hurt. I told them it hurt and they said it wouldn't hurt for long and to keep going. I finally got it in, felt my ass close over the bump and the plug sort of got sucked up and held tight. She was right, it didn't hurt anymore. It felt all right – nice, actually. The longer it was in there, the less I felt it.

"Stand up, pretty."

I felt it then, like an electric shock straight to my cock, which wasn't so soft anymore, by the way. She told me to walk around to the couch again and take a seat. Walking was an interesting experience. Sitting down was an even more interesting experience.

"Press 'play' and put your hands behind your back again. That's right, squirm all you like, but open those legs."

I felt the magnets lock as the movie started again. It was hard to concentrate on the movie with the butt plug in. I couldn't keep still, and every time I moved another foreign sensation would take hold of my cock or my balls.

It wasn't until the bitch in the movie shoved a big plug into the guy she'd been tormenting earlier that I was drawn back to watching. I realized my hands were free and they were wrapped around my cock. I have no idea how they got there, but there they were. She started smacking his balls with a riding crop and his cock got harder and harder. So had mine. I was riveted to the screen and wacking off for all I was worth. I think I'd forgotten where I was.

When she told me to come, I almost didn't hear her. I probably would have come anyway and I bet she knew it. The woman in the movie gave the guy a really hard smack on the side of his cock and he just exploded come. So did I. Holy shit, I never felt anything like that, and you've got to remember, this was just the first day, the first few hours!

Oh fuck! I wasn't going to tell you what it was that turned me on that much . . .

I've only been home a few days and I still can't believe all the stuff that happened. You know what she said? She said she was the woman in that video I was watching. That same woman was in a lot of the videos, at least a lot of the videos they made me watch. I think she lives here. Yeah, well, probably not in Staten Island, but I bet she lives in the City.

Listen, actually, that's why I'm telling you all this stuff. See I got this idea. I really have to find her. I guess maybe I'm a little obsessed, you know? So I was wondering if I could borrow your gallery space. I mean, I know you only get to show there once a year and all but it's perfect, and besides, I'll make it up to you, man. But, a lady like her; I bet she goes to lots of art openings. Anyway, she'd want to see this one. There's no way she could pass it up.

It would be just like at the loft, only this time it would be open to the public. Don't they still do that performance art stuff? It'd be like that. People could come in and watch me and tell me what to do, but only the ladies. And then when she showed up to see what all the noise was about, well, then I could talk to her. I could tell her I wanted to do . . . I could tell her I wanted to be . . . I wanted to be her slave, or . . . OK, that sounds lame, but I know what I mean.

So could I borrow your space? Please? I can't stand it; I just have to find her. I think this would really impress her. I know she liked me and if I could only see her in person, just once, I know everything would work out right.

The Dress

Kristina Wright

The dress made her do it.

It hung in the back of Carrie's closet, hidden behind silk blouses, pinstriped pants, tailored suits, summer skirts and polo shirts. It languished there in the farthest corner of the closet while other clothes were worn for business meetings and tennis matches and birthday parties and lunches with friends. The dress stayed there when other clothes were tossed in the donation bag, when other new outfits replaced old, when seasons changed and wool trousers were chosen over Capri pants. The dress was like an old friend, waiting patiently for a long overdue call.

Finally, after months, the call came.

When Carrie put the dress on, she felt like a different person. She *was* a different person. She wasn't Carrie the junior attorney at the law firm or Carrie the fitness freak or Carrie the buddy who was like one of the guys. In that shiny PVC dress she became Carrie the seductress. Carrie the bad girl. Carrie the slut.

She prepared for her night out like a bride preparing for her wedding day. Shaved, moisturized, perfumed, adorned. She put the dress on, surprised for a moment at how form-fitting it was. She wore it only occasionally, once every three or four months, and she was always surprised by how it hugged her body. Her other clothes fit comfortably, making her hardly aware she was wearing them. She never forgot she was wearing the dress. It made her stand up straighter, suck in her stomach, thrust out her breasts that were barely contained by the corset-style bodice – and that was just while she was standing in the privacy of her own bedroom admiring herself in the mirror. Out in public, the dress made her *strut*.

By the time she got to the club, her whole body was throbbing with an intense energy of things to come. It wasn't a club she went to often. It wasn't in the best part of town and it appealed to a crowd that was a little more . . . out there . . . than who she usually hung with. She wasn't in the mood for the khakis and cappuccino crowd tonight. She wasn't interested in talking politics, 401(k) plans or who was getting married or who was expecting yet another baby. Tonight she wanted to be someone else. The slut in the dress.

She was rewarded for her efforts the minute she walked into the noisy, crowded club. Not everyone stopped to look at the redhead in the black, skintight vinyl dress that laced down to her bellybutton, but enough people did look – men and women – to give her a little rush. It was the dress, she knew. It didn't hurt that she had the body to fill it out, of course, but the dress commanded attention in a way Carrie never could. The four-inch patent leather heels didn't hurt, either. They made her already long legs look like they went on for miles and not a man in the room could look at the shoes that matched the dress and not wonder what they would look like on the floor next to his bed.

Fending off a couple of over eager guys, Carrie made her way to the bar. The bar spanned the length of one side of the club and it was standing room only. Miraculously, as soon as she approached, a space opened up for her. She thanked the two guys on either side of her and ordered a martini.

"That's on me," said the guy to the left of her.

"Thanks." Carrie gave him a predatory smile, feeling infused with power. "But I'm not going to fuck you."

The guy on her right laughed. "Guess she told you."

Carrie took a long sip of the martini that appeared in front of her in record time, letting her tongue linger on the rim of the glass. Then she smiled. "I'm not going to fuck you, either."

It probably wasn't the wisest thing to say to two guys in a seedy nightclub who both seemed a little inebriated, but the dress made her say and do things that weren't very wise. Like a suit of armor or a protective shield, the dress gave her power and authority. Instead of turning nasty, both men smiled good-naturedly and shrugged.

By the time she finished her second martini, courtesy of the guy on the right simply because he wanted to appear to be a gentleman, Carrie was ready to mingle. She excused herself to her self-appointed guardians with a wink and a, "Thanks for the drinks, boys," and disappeared onto the crowded dance floor before either could follow and press the issue.

The music was heavy, throbbing techno with some retro punk thrown in for good measure. It wasn't dancing music, it was *grinding* music and the crowd writhed on the packed dance floor in pairs and threesomes in alcohol-and-lust fueled orgiastic bliss. Carrie didn't dance alone for long. Soon she felt the press of a body behind her. A male body. She turned in the circle of his arms and gave him a feral smile.

Her smile faded when she realized she was looking up into the face of Reynolds, one of the partners at the firm. She wracked her brain for his first name and came up blank. She didn't know him personally, the firm she worked for was one of the largest in the state with two dozen partners and a hundred or more support staff, but they'd crossed paths a couple of times and he was attractive enough for her to notice him. Dark eyes, dark hair, older than her, but with a boyish appeal that made it hard to peg his age. Of course, she'd never seen him in a social setting wearing low-slung jeans and a T-shirt that clung to his sculpted torso.

She realized his expression hadn't changed – he was still looking at her like he wanted to devour her – and it dawned on her that he had no reason to recognize her, especially in the dress. She was as professional and proper at work as any attorney and, out of that familiar setting and in a dress meant for a vamp, she probably didn't look like the Carrie he might remember on a good day.

"Love the dress," he said, his hand gliding over the slippery PVC from her waist to her hip. "You're stunning."

She smiled again, regaining her composure. The patent leather heels made her almost his height, so she leaned forward until her lips were nearly touching his ear. "Thanks."

"Want to dance?"

She put her arm around his neck and pressed her body against him, rubbing her crotch against his hip in a smooth, sinuous rhythm. "Sure."

He pulled her close and rubbed his erection against her. "Want to go home with me?"

She shook her head. "I don't think so."

He laughed. "Well then, will you at least dance with me until my dick deflates a little?"

She pressed against him, her breasts threatening to burst out of the top of the dress. "What are the odds of that while I'm here?"

"Good point."

She smiled. "C'mon," she said, taking him by the hand.

"Where?"

She just arched an eyebrow at him.

"Yes, ma'am."

She led him outside into the cool night air that made her nipples pucker and raised goose bumps on her bare arms and legs. The parking lot was quiet except for a couple of giggling women hanging drunkenly on each other. Carrie's heart hammered in her chest as she led Reynolds around the side of the club, dark but for the red light cast by an emergency exit sign. She took a deep breath. Knowing there was a chance they could get caught was part of the thrill.

"What are you up to?"

She responded by pressing him up against the wall of the club and kissing him. Hard. She reached down and stroked his cock through his jeans, pleased that it was stiff and thick. He moaned into her when she squeezed him.

Reynolds pulled away. "Are you sure you don't want to go to my place?"

She unzipped his jeans. "I can't wait."

She knelt in front of him, the dress riding up so that she could feel the night air on her ass. She unfastened his jeans and pulled his cock free. It was beautiful and thick. She whimpered in anticipation.

"Please, baby."

She didn't move, not even when he wrapped her long hair in his fist and tried to guide her to his cock. She resisted, knowing he was hers.

"Please," he pleaded again.

She indulged him because she couldn't stand not having him in her mouth a minute longer, not because he begged. Precome glistened on the tip of his cock like a freshwater pearl and she swirled her tongue around the engorged head, pulling it into her mouth.

He gasped at the contact and thrust his hips forward.

With excruciating slowness that teased them both, she licked his cock from tip to base, cradling his heavy balls with one hand while guiding his cock between her lips with the other. She sucked the head into her mouth and cradled it in the hollow of her tongue, holding it there until he impatiently moved his hips. His hands were slack in her hair, as if he'd forgotten – or didn't realize – he could have some measure of control. Carrie didn't want him to have control. She wanted the power to give him pleasure, but only when she was ready.

Despite their risky location, she took her time sucking him. She lowered her mouth over his cock, relaxing her throat until she had taken as much of him as she could handle without gagging. Then she slid back slowly, revealing his slick, shiny cock. Over and over she deep-throated him until they were both panting and she knew he was close to orgasm by the way his cock practically leaked precome in a steady stream.

He protested softly when she released his cock long enough to untie the laces that held the bodice of her dress together. "I want you to fuck my tits," she said.

His switched his focus from her mouth to her breasts as she pulled them free from the dress. Her skin was ethereally pale against the black PVC, her nipples hard and dark. She cupped her breasts in her hands, presenting them to him like a gift.

He didn't speak. He took his cock in his hand and laid it in the valley she created by pressing her breasts together. His cock was warm and wet from her mouth. She closed her eyes, enjoying the feel of him against her bare skin.

His hands covered hers and he rolled her nipples between his fingers. She moaned, squeezing her breasts around his cock.

"You feel so good," he gasped.

She braced her hands on his thighs as he cupped her breasts around his cock. Looking up into his eyes, she said, "Fuck me."

His expression was primal. Squeezing her breasts around his cock, he fucked her the way she wanted. She rocked back on her heels as he thrust against her harder and harder, fucking her tits as if he were inside her pussy. Her saliva had dried on his cock and the only thing lubricating her breasts was his precome, but it was enough. From his sharp intake of breath, she knew he was going to come.

"Come on my tits."

He moaned, his cock spurting thick, milky semen – once, twice, three times – across her pale breasts and down the front of her vinyl dress. She kept her breasts pressed together, watching as warm rivulets of come gathered there. Finally, when he seemed to be finished, she leaned forward and kissed the tip of his cock, tasting him.

He released his iron grip on her hair and helped her up. "That was incredible," he said as he tucked his cock back in his pants and straightened his clothes.

Carrie did the same with her sticky breasts, not bothering to lace the bodice of her dress. "Yes, it was."

"I feel bad I didn't do anything for you."

She smiled. She'd wanted to rub her very wet pussy while he fucked her, but she'd been so mesmerized by watching him, she hadn't been able to do anything else. Her pussy still felt engorged but, somehow, watching him come had taken the edge off a little bit. "You'd be surprised what that did for me."

"Oh really?" He started to pull her close, then stopped short. "Oh, man, I am *all* over your dress."

She looked down and saw that he was right. His come glistened in streaks on the already shiny vinyl, leaving no doubt as to what she'd been doing. She laughed. "It's all right, it wipes right off."

"Sounds like the voice of experience." Rather than disapproving, he sounded aroused by the idea. "You're a very bad girl."

There was no reason to tell him she wasn't as bad a bad girl he thought her to be. No reason to ruin his fantasy – or her own. "I don't suck and tell," she said with a wink.

A burst of laughter startled them both and Carrie decided she'd pushed her luck far enough for one night. She let Reynolds escort her to her car.

"Thanks, really."

"Thank *you*," she said, and meant it sincerely. There was no doubt in her mind that she'd spend many long morning commutes thinking about her escapade with Reynolds. But first, she'd spend a long, leisurely bath masturbating until her pussy was raw while she thought about his thick cock coming between her breasts.

"So, do you think I can see you again or was this a one time thing?"

"What's your name?"

"Derrick Reynolds," he said.

Right. Derrick. She didn't know why she hadn't remembered. "Well, Derrick, I have no doubt I'll see you again, but I don't know if this is a one time thing or not."

She left him then, with a furrow between his brow and a limp cock between his legs. The dress had made her do it, and she had no doubt she'd do it again. Maybe even with Derrick Reynolds.

The Bet

Thom Gautier

I shouldn't have made the bet, but I did and a bet's a bet.

The gamble started when my girlfriend Bonnie and I were getting ready to go have dinner at a pricey bistro by the water. My treat. As she dressed, I watched her, I admired her, I listened to her humming Cake's song "Short Skirt/Long Jacket" and I listened to her whistle that high-pitched country-bumpkin theme song from *The Andy Griffith Show*. I watched her fix her loop earrings. I watched her pin up her brown hair and I watched her shadow her green eyes. And I helped her fasten her garter belt, clasping it shut and straightening without any help from me. She slipped on the black stockings I'd bought her from a lingerie shop in Paris. I'd used my broken French and pronounced their word for "sheer" as precisely as I could, "*extra-fin*".

"That black fabric looks painted on your legs," I said.

"You mean *navy blue* fabric," she said, slipping her feet into her strappy black heels.

"Black," I said.

"Navy blue," she said, and then she gave me the finger, "they're navy blue."

We argued about the color all the way to the restaurant. All we could agree about was that her legs looked great in them and that were sheer and looked painted on. At one point during the drive, she extended her legs and put her feet up on the dashboard. "Navvvy blue," she said. Two black guys who had pulled up to our right at the red light smiled at her as she posed like that with her legs up, and after they sped off she said, "We could have rolled down the window and asked them to decide the color, though they're biased, kind of."

This stupid spat was getting me more than a little horny, even long after we settled into our booth and ordered dinner.

"Navvvy blue," she jeered, her green eyes lighting up as she poked at her salad. She plucked a pinch of stocking by her right thigh as we waited for our meals and she said with a dramatic French accent, "*Extra fin, bleu.*"

Bonnie hardly ate dinner. As I dug into my scallops, she interrupted me and offered her pinky finger, "Let's make a bet, buster," she said. "A bet whether these are navy blue stockings, or black. Bet me." Instinctively I put out my pinky to seal the bet and then realized we had no way to judge objectively whether the stockings were blue or black.

After I'd paid our bill, on her way back from the bathroom, Bonnie stopped to talk to the waiter. He was a friendly enough waiter, dark-haired, thirtyish with a cleft chin and dark eyes. During dinner, Bonnie had been calling him "unibrow" because of his "interesting" bushy eyebrows and she'd said he had "obscenely large hands".

From the waiter's podium, she wiggled her index finger for me to come over to them and, as I left change for his tip, I did as her finger said, like a puppy dog, and came over to them. When I got to the waiter's podium, she extended her right leg in the bright light near the door. As one of the waitresses complimented her on her dress, Bonnie made a shush-gesture, tugged at the waiter's vest and asked him, "Mr. Waiterman, what color are these here stockings? Black? Or navy blue?" The waiter looked at me with a sort of condescending disinterest, and then stared at Bonnie's extended right leg. Without looking up from her leg he said, "Your stockings are navy blue."

Bonnie squealed with delight. The two of them high fived each other.

By the time we left the bistro, the parking lot was nearly empty. My front right tire was flat. I considered changing the flat but was uneasy about the slope of the car lot. Our waiter,

who was almost unrecognizable in a brown leather jacket and
baseball cap, whistled over to us. He offered us a ride. I noticed
his Jeep was blue. "His car is blue. He was biased," I said. "It
wasn't a fair bet."

As the waiter came over and stared at the flat and
sympathized, I stalled for a good long while. I said that I could
change the flat. But the waiter said he knew a garage near by
that could change it safely in the morning. His hurry-up-and-
decide whistling was insistent and, anyway, I was half-drunk
from the dinner wine. Bonnie shrugged and said, "It's my
boyfriend's call. Either we stand out here all night and freeze
or we take a lift from you and go home."

I thanked the waiter and conceded to his offer.

Bonnie out called "Shotgun!" and I settled into the back
seat as she played with the radio, tuning stations in and out,
blasting the music at times and at other times playfully keeping
the Spanish station on.

But we didn't go home.

Before long, we arrived at a row of waterfront condos and
Bonnie lowered the music, turned to me, and explained that
we'd been invited by "our kind, bet-deciding waiter here" to
have a terrace drink.

"Then after a drink we'll get you two into a taxi cab," the
waiter said, shooting me a paternalistic gaze. "The car service
is up my street."

For reasons I'll never fathom, I agreed to the drink, perhaps
thinking a terrace drink in the seaside air would be a good and
even sobering nightcap to an uneasy night. Really, though, my
cock was secretly dancing to the navy blue and black point
and counterpoint from earlier in the evening, and I wanted to
either sit down and cool off, or get laid. Yet I realized, as soon
as we entered his apartment and Bonnie and he high fived in
that familiar glib way, that I wasn't getting laid.

Bonnie helped herself to his iPod skipping and scrolling
to Cake's funky hit song "Short Skirt/Long Jacket" and she
played air bass guitar and let her skirt sway, playfully throwing
off her heels as if she'd just arrived in the familiar confines of

some favorite uncle's house. When I asked him his name he introduced himself as "Navy," and Bonnie stood up and high fived him for that. I thought it was a smug, wise ass evasion but I let it pass. We sat on the terrace staring out at the dingy, sipping cold chardonnay and talking aimlessly about wagers, waitresses, scallops, Jeeps, bets, dares, France, stockings, restaurants. As I gave my sports jacket for Bonnie to wear, she stared at the waiter and said, "This fella here lost the color bet," she said to the waiter. "Didn't he?"

Before Navy could speak on my behalf, I spoke up and admitted I had lost the bet. "But it wasn't an objective verdict," I said.

"Doesn't matter," she said, "he was a disinterested third party."

"She doesn't let a win drop so easy, does she?" Navy asked me.

"Never does," I said.

"What was the wager exactly?" he asked.

"Well, we didn't formally make a wager," Bonnie said. "We should have let Da Judge here decide the stakes," she said. "He was Da Stocking Judge after all."

She stood up and made a mock curtsey in front of him. "Your honor, what would you have mandated as the stakes?"

Navy was about to say something when Bonnie put down her drink and threw up her hand and signaled for him to stop. "Judge, please don't shout your decision in open court, it's undignified, whisper it here, in a sidebar." She laughed and winked at me and leaned forward and lowered her ear close to his mouth. He cupped his large hands over her ear and she listened. Then she cupped her hands over his ear, as if repeating it all back to him. My dick tingled, rose, stiffened. Navy nodded at Bonnie.

"That's very fair, your honor," she said giggling, "Your honor, that that's so fair it's town-of-Mayberry fair." Then he started to whistle the theme from *The Andy Griffith Show*. My cock rose with each sly note of that TV tune and Bonnie smiled at me. Then she stood up and took the waiter's hand and they left the terrace as the Cake tune replayed on a loop.

For about a minute or so, I sat passively staring at their abandoned wine glasses. Snapping out of my hard-on reverie, I went into the living room, hoping against hope that that's where they'd gone. Bonnie's scattered shoes stared at me from the empty rug. I sat on the living room couch as my cock nodded warmly in my pants, and swelled, throbbed, beating time to that echoing tug of war of words between navy blue and black. I knew I should have gotten up off my ass and searched the house for them, and my face flushed with anger. Yet I sat there. Though I knew in my gut she was already way past flirting with him, I realized that she liked the prick.

In my head I heard her voice, navy blue, black. Black, navy blue.

I went upstairs. I heard that *Andy Griffith* tune whistling from behind a door near a barely furnished bathroom. I couldn't tell which of them was doing the whistling. Standing there, I felt faint, small, stupid, like a nosy pre-teen kid whose babysitter has gone off to make out with her boyfriend. I pressed my right ear to the door and heard the soft smacking of lips and subdued, persistent giggles. I felt a kind of exotic anger, like I'd been badly conned and had somehow let my con artists get away with it out of some misplaced masochistic admiration for their clever, quick footed game.

The door was locked. I considered shoulder rolling it open, and then I considered simply knocking and shouting.

I went to Navy's bathroom and took a piss, nearly wetting myself through the awkward angle of my hard-on. I sat on the closed toilet lid and perused his stack of *Penthouse* magazines. I thumbed through one and then another and then another. I stopped and stared at pictorials of couples. A cowboy getting a blowjob from a redhead, a guy with six pack abs hoisting a blonde in a blue bra onto his enormous cock, a sailor getting his balls licked by two brunettes with seahorse earrings and glamorous cocktail dresses. I felt for sure I was dreaming all this. Demoralized, I tossed the magazines and went back to the bedroom door where I could hear panting, an odd squeal, a giggle, and occasional "yes, of course," and, at another moment, "you mean . . . further down? . . . right here?" I pictured Bonnie sticking a forefinger into Navy's ass and suckling his crown. I pictured her asking, "That do the trick?"

I knocked hard. I jimmied the door handle. Though it grew temporarily quiet behind the door, soon the breathing and the whispers and the panting started up again. I stormed downstairs. I threw her heels across the living room where they crashed against the coat stand that collapsed to the floor like a drunken mannequin.

Finally I wandered outside the condo. I looked up at the only lighted window and saw nothing. I recalled the waiter's dark unibrow. His silver belt buckle. His vest, his trousers. I pictured his long fingers on Bonnie's loop earrings, and his hands gripping her ass like his ass was all hers.

I pictured her hands sliding that belt off his waist.

In a spasm of rage I keyed the driver's side of his jeep door. I pictured Bonnie whispering the phrase "Navy blue" as she suckled his crown again and fondled his balls. I could see her holding his cock before her eyes and taking it in with a school girl's curiosity, and then her tongue running the length of his shaft, her tongue pressing and stopping gently mid-shaft before finishing the lick with a lap around his swollen knob. I could see her index finger pressing into his silvery precome. I could see him smiling, his cleft chin. Navy's dark eyes beaming at his new, impulsive best friend, my girlfriend.

It was so cold outside and my cock was so hard that I had to sit down inside Navy's unlocked Jeep. I shivered. The car smelled of pine air freshener and cheap cologne. I pictured the prick running his hand over her smoothly stockinged legs. Navy blue legs. Like a bored and petulant child, I combed through his glove compartment and fished dimes out from under the passenger seat and slid them between my finger and thumb. I thought about the difference between the color navy blue and the color black and I touched my hard-on through my pants. I took out my cock and rubbed my own precome into the shaft and stroked, taking in the smell of the cheap cologne, feeling vulnerable in a strange car, in a strange parking lot in a strange apartment complex. I stroked harder and harder, recalling Bonnie extending her right leg in the restaurant light. I recalled how he'd said so confidently, *Your stockings are navy blue* and I recalled their high five and I came, violently, spraying my black jeans and the edge of the passenger seat. Hurriedly, pathetically, I wiped it clean with crumbled bits of tissues and rushed out of the Jeep, sure that someone had seen me. But the area was dead silent, the silence broken by the occasional creak form the nearby docks and the tolling of that bell buoy in the distance.

When I got back to the condo, the front door was locked so I tried the terrace. It too was locked. Through the glass I could hear that "Short Skirt/Long Jacket" song still playing. It seemed their funky song was taunting me. My cock was so stiff I could hardly walk. My head was heavy with a kind of passive almost feminine rage.

On the terrace I sat in a chair and took up one of the wine glasses and when I realized I could be drinking his wine, I spit it out in disgust.

For a long while I stared at the black water and the invisible bell buoy out there. I felt the night pressing down on me like a bad joke. I might have dozed off. I know I paced and sat and paced again. I pictured Bonnie staring at herself in the mirror as Navy entered her from behind, her face girlish and tensed with pleasure as he held her by the garter belt like a harness and they fucked doggy-style.

When I stood up I saw through the glass that Bonnie was lounging alone in the living room, her shoes on, the TV tuned in to a cooking show. "Look, Rachel Ray's cooking those very same scallops you ordered tonight," she said, "looks yummo." She was wearing an oversize white T-shirt. Her legs were bare.

I asked her where the fuck she had gone, where the fuck her dress had gone, where the fuck her stockings had gone.

She waved the remote control and gazed down at her legs and then around the empty room in mock surprise, with her hands over her mouth and she said, "Oh shit. Who do you think stole them?"

My strangely confused rage returned. I almost smacked her face. I ran upstairs. Nearing the bedroom, I heard snoring. The bedroom door was half opened and that waiter prick was asleep on the bed, his bed, unmade, with creases on the vacant pillow next to him, his naked body barely draped in a red blanket from his thighs on down. His cock, dark and long, partly nestled in bushy black pubic hair, dangled spent there between his legs. Beads of spilled jizz glistened and caught the lamplight.

I saw a pair of stockings draped over the small lamp on his night table. "They look very navy blue in that light don't they?" Bonnie asked me, whispering.

I jerked forward and gasped. Bonnie was behind me, in that stupid oversized T-shirt, giggling and whispering. I told her she'd scared me.

"*He* scared *me*," she said. "You see that? That's a pretty big mess."

Speaking deliberately and loudly, I asked, "Exactly just what the fuck happened here?"

She was extraordinarily calm. She held my hand and squeezed it. She stared straight into my eyes and whispered, "*Duh*. What do you think happened here?"

Then she pulled a roll of paper towel from behind her back.

"Navy and I decided on a wager. That's part of what happened," she said. "We decided he and I would bond, and that he, of course would well, lose it, which obviously, he did, and that and you, having lost the bet, would come up here and clean up."

She pointed over my shoulder at the stockings on the lamp. "As you can see objectively in that lamplight, those babies are navy blue. You know you lost. Pay up."

I was so ambushed by this bitchy bluntness, by her complete lack of contrition for having done God knows what for God knows how long with this waiter prick, this stranger here laying naked in his own bed before my own eyes, that I said absolutely nothing.

He was waking, groggy and I almost ran from the doorway. He pressed his hands into the mattress and shifted himself up. When he saw me there he waved, gently, the way one waves to a favorite nephew or to a shy poodle.

"She told you the wager I guess?" he asked. His voice was deep and groggy.

"I did," she said.

He sat up and reached over and drank from a glass of Scotch on his night table and his cock shifted, leaking a silvery thread. It swelled and filled but wasn't rock hard, which somehow comforted me and assuaged my embarrassment.

As I stepped into the room, I saw a pool of come had caked the dark hairs of his left thigh. Beads of dried come dotted his belly hair too.

I thought if I got close enough I could kill him. Yet seeing the aftermath of their wild antics, and being thrust into this raw and weird intimacy, I felt a certain humiliated respect for the guy. He'd given us a lift. He'd charmed Bonnie. They'd enjoyed each other's company. I felt so dizzy that I pressed a hand into the nearby dresser for balance. Standing behind me, Bonnie kissed the back of my neck. "A bet is a bet," she said. "Do the right thing." Her logic was so direct, so confident, that I accepted the roll of paper towel as she handed it over my shoulder.

Then I thought about justice, and fair play. And how black isn't navy blue, at all, really. And that those stockings discarded on the lampshade, those stockings I'd shopped for and bought of her using my kindergarten French were now, in fact, *navy blue* stockings, not black.

I unrolled a few sheets of paper and stepped closer to the bed.

The waiter grinned like a wiseass. *Navy.* He sat up even further, gingerly, so as not to upset the spill on his lap and legs, gazing at me with a sleepy admiration.

I could tell from his fake shy smile that he knew that I was coming toward him to pay off the bet: to wipe clean the sticky mess on his thighs and on his lap, a mess that, in my own way, I knew I was responsible for making.

Such a Special Couple

Kristina Lloyd

Joining us in bed last night was the ghost of his ex-girlfriend. He can't see her but I can.

I see her everywhere. She's all over his apartment, usually in bits, which is how I prefer her. She's sweat and bloodstains on the mattress, skin cells in the dust, and hairs down the sofa. I look in a mirror and she's standing behind me, six years of images checking her reflection.

Unfortunately, she's also with us when we fuck. Sean pounds away, clutching my hair and whispering, "Take it, slut." I whimper, begging him to stop, and she's whimpering, too. I can hear her in my head – *Ah, ah, no, please!*

I wonder if she took it as well as I do, and I want to ask, *Who's best at begging, me or her?*

In his apartment is a room I'm not supposed to enter. It's not exactly locked (well, you have to check, don't you?) but is half-barricaded by a low bookshelf. Privately, I call it his Bluebeard room. And to be honest, if his ex-girlfriend *were* in there, I wouldn't mind as long as she were dead.

But she's not. It's just her stuff. She's lodging with a friend elsewhere in the city. One day, she's going to rent a place of her own, ideally south-facing and overlooking the river. Then she'll collect the rest of her belongings. I'm starting to think someone may need to move the river for her.

Sean must trust me because he gave me some keys recently, asking me to pop in and feed the cat while he was away. I thought it was sweet of him but, well, a bit stupid, really.

Pop in. Sure I'll pop in. It'll only take ten minutes.

Ever have those moral dilemmas when you can't decide? Where there is no gut feeling, no deep true voice you know you'll ultimately obey?

No, me neither. I knew I would go into that room to see what she was about.

He hardly mentions her. There's no evidence of her in his life. For several weeks, he couldn't even say her name. "My ex," he would say when the situation required it. Eventually, I said, "So does she have a name, this ex of yours?"

I saw him flinch. "Jasmine," he said briskly. "Jas for short."

Jasmine. Pretty white flowers in hot, sultry lands.

Jazz. Music to get stoned to in small, seedy bars.

Jasmine. Jas for short. Why do they always have such fucking stupid names?

He was away on a software training course (I saw the paperwork; he wasn't making it up) so I had his place to myself for the evening. Hell, I had it for the night if I wanted. The bed smelled of us. First thing I did when I got in from work was bury my face in the sheets. No, I tell a lie. That was the second thing. First thing was tiptoe through the usual rooms and stand in their weird emptiness, nervous of the space.

In the evening sunlight, everything I knew was remote and unfamiliar. Sean's apartment is a junk shop. There's a headboard behind the sofa, old shoes in a crate, a stereo on a trolley, planks of shelving he hasn't assembled, that kind of thing. The place seemed frozen, more like a museum's re-creation of Sean's home than Sean's home itself.

I felt like a trespasser. He was very absent, and the place was still and silent apart from the cat at my ankles, mewing for food.

The bed was rumpled as it had been when I'd left that morning. He lives and sleeps in the one room, you see. The Bluebeard room used to be their bedroom. You can understand him not wanting to make love to me in there.

Ignoring the cat, I sprawled on the bed, scrunching grubby sheets to my face, inhaling Sean, myself, and the gorgeous smell of fuck. All day at work I'd had him on my body, felt the tenderness of a spanked ass, the soreness inside me, heard his whispers in my ear.

"You dirty whore," he likes to say along with "Suck it, bitch" and "I'll fuck you till it hurts." He's got quite a repertoire. It makes me hot and ashamed. The previous night he'd lubed my ass. I'd clutched the pillows, groaning as he'd filled me in slow, hard inches. I am so far gone when I'm impaled. I belong only to whoever's doing me – not because I owe him but because I don't belong to myself. I am a babbling wreck. I am lost. Someone's got to stay in charge of me, haven't they?

I fed the cat, opened the Bluebeard door, and edged around the bookcase. Supposing his course got canceled? A bomb alert at lunch-time and now he was strolling up the road? No, he'd have phoned, wouldn't he?

He was decorating. Or he'd started at some point. He'd told me that once but I'd thought it was a lie. I felt bad for having doubted him. The walls were as white as paper and the floor was covered in wrinkled, paint-spattered sheets. In the center, and similarly draped, was a large hump of possessions, an altar to Jasmine, Jas for short. In one corner stood a ladder, a pot of paint and various decorating paraphernalia. I stood for a while, breathing steadily. It was all okay. It felt anonymous and clean. He was erasing her with white paint.

Yes, all okay except for one thing, a glass crystal pendant hanging from the ceiling. Its clear facets glittered, and refracted sunlight cast a small soft rainbow on the opposite wall.

Funny, I didn't know Sean had New Age tendencies. What next? Chanting? I pictured them lying in bed on lazy mornings, warm-skinned and having poetic thoughts about light.

She'd left. Her stuff was packed away. They were over. But he couldn't remove the last vestige of their tender times, her pretty little crystal and how it lit up a room.

I found their porn in about ten minutes. I'm embarrassed about that. I think it was fairly slow of me. Under the drapes of her altar was a sideboard and small cabinet, spaces stuffed with Jasmine. Presumably, she had with her what she needed so this was what mattered. I opened a plastic black sack. It was full of crumpled clothes, smelling of perfume. I breathed her in much as Sean had done for years, remembering the first night I'd stayed with him.

It wasn't planned. We'd bumped into each other in a bar, friend of a friend. He took me back to his place and fucked me silly. It was so hot, a nice, slow session moving from skin, kissing, sucking, and fucking into the scary arena of him nudging at my limits. And my limits kept splintering, melting, and re-forming. That night, I found a new space for myself, one where it was cool for me to have my head rammed against a pillow, a fist in my hair, lips brushing against my ear, whispering, "You like this, don't you? Filthy little bitch."

It was mortifying, and it was okay. In the morning I was happy, slutty and scruffy, no makeup, fresh clothes, or toiletries of my own.

"Do you have moisturizer?" I'd asked.

"Somewhere, yes, I'm sure."

He's a nice guy even though he's a cunt in bed. After rummaging in the bathroom, he offered me Magnolia body lotion to put on my face. It was a small plastic bottle with a flowery label, an obvious unwanted gift. My skin was dry and tight or I'd have turned it down. Instead, when I left his apartment, I had his ex's reject on my face.

I pulled a couple of jumpers from the black sack. I had no idea what she looked like or her size. About my size from the looks of it. I tried on a bottle-green cardigan with dark wooden buttons. It was big and I was pleased. And then I wasn't pleased because I thought maybe he prefers fleshier women so I removed it.

Their porn was so pretty. Taking photographs in bed was obviously something they did together. I guess a lot of couples do but getting them developed is special. And there they were, such a special couple in sepia, black-and-white, in soft light and shadow, this way and that, over, under, above, below, naked, dressed, roped, cuffed, kissing, fucking, looking. So much looking. The two of them together. Looking and loving. Loving each other, the curve of his freckled shoulders, the dip of her waist, that faint sheen of skin. Loving the bliss of their togetherness.

Because it wasn't really porn. It wasn't cold and empty enough. Unfortunately, neither was I. Her skin looked so good and inviting, so alive. I could imagine running a blade down her back, a slow, cruel knife-point to destroy the picture.

After an hour or so the light was dipping. At this time of year, the sunsets are pinkish and the city, slanted with long shadows, is washed with palest shrimp. There were no curtains at the window and I saw distant starlings flocking and swooping, making crazy black shapes in the sky.

I was surrounded by photographs. Initially, I'd thought if I looked at them for long enough, I could make them fade to nothing. Now I was thinking if I stared a little harder I could make them burst into flames. Either way, I would obliterate her.

The most difficult pictures were of Sean in chains. Yes, that's right. My big, beautiful, dirty-talking brute could lie face-forward on a bed, arms outstretched, his shackled ankles being pulled toward his ass. He could lie like that, metal links running parallel to his spine, the hand that held the chain covering his head in a claw of possession. And he could lie there looking peaceful and zonked, eyes lowered and smiling with bliss, letting her do what she wished.

That was not my Sean.

So Sean wasn't mine.

Beyond the window, the lights of the city were coming on, dotting the smudgy dusk.

Photographs aren't real, I tried telling myself. You don't click a camera at the truest moments. But that smile was real. I'd never seen him look that way before. And how I hated her that she could give him that.

When I ran out of hate and came up for air, it was almost night. Shadows grayed the draped white room and I was surrounded by colors bleeding into the dusk, a watery paint box of chrome yellow, madder rose, Prussian blue, hooker green, cobalt, ochre, sienna, and all the shades of skin in black, white, and sepia.

I sat in a blur of tears, scorched with jealousy and with the shame of my binge. I should have just fed the cat and left. Too late. I'd opened the door. All too late.

I blinked away the tears and the room refocused. Like I say, it was dark by then so there was no sunlight glittering on the suspended crystal. Nonetheless, high on the far wall, glowing gently in the gloom, was the projected rainbow.

Red, orange, yellow, green, blue, indigo, violet.

It wasn't possible. I knew it wasn't. But there it was. I saw all the colors of their past condensed in that little rainbow. I couldn't help thinking it was my fault, that somehow I'd released her. And now here she was, back again, Jasmine and her pretty crystal, lighting up his room.

"Did you miss me?" he asked.

I was on my back, my wrists wrapped in rope, and he was tying them to the headboard.

"No," I said, because that's the game we were playing.

"Tell me you missed me."

"No."

It was the fourth night he'd asked that question. Something had shifted since he'd been away. Usually we'd seen each other a couple of times a week but since his return we hadn't spent a night apart. Me, I felt time was running out because I couldn't compete with Jasmine, Jas for short. I didn't know his reason.

He jerked my wrists up to the headboard then began working on my ankles. He split me wide open, one leg fastened to the left of the bed, the other leg to the right. He was fresh from work and dressed in a suit, his tie loose, collar undone. I was naked, and my pussy felt so plump, wet, and open. He straddled a thigh and shoved two fingers inside me, his eyes pinned on mine.

"You miss me?"

Before I could answer he thrust hard and fast, taunting me with his fingers.

I rocked my head on the pillow, whimpering. "No. Show me your cock."

I could see his boner, big and cumbersome, pushing at his suit and fucking up all the neatly tailored lines. You're not meant to get an erection in a suit. You're not meant to look so wild and dirty. You're meant to be in a meeting, heading a PowerPoint presentation, face in neutral.

Sean's face was far from neutral. He was wearing his hot little sneer, and he looked mean and spiteful, the pleasure he takes in tormenting me so transparent. His pleasure doubles mine. I tipped my hips, wanting to bear down on his fingers. "Show me your cock," I repeated. "Let me suck you."

He withdrew from me and gave me a light slap across one cheek. I caught my breath. He'd never done that before. I stared at him in shock. Half my face stung, the heat rising, and I felt weirdly off balance.

"I give the orders around here," he said, whipping off his tie.

Oh, but I've seen you in her chains, I thought, *and I know that's not true.*

I scanned the room for Jasmine, for the little rainbow of her presence that had liberated itself from the Bluebeard room. For two nights it had rested high on the wall, gleaming in the dark like some neon-bright tropical moth. I didn't mention it to Sean and he'd said nothing either. On our third night, she came down to join us. I was astride him, just a good old-fashioned fuck, and there she was on his chest, a small spectrum of multicolored light.

Get off him, I thought. *Off him. Off his skin. Get off him, you bitch.*

I swiped at his chest, lifting and sinking on his cock. *Off, off, off.* She kept landing on my hand. I tried to flick her away, repulsed, enraged, but she jumped back on his chest, a ray of light, impossible to dislodge. It freaked me out. I swiped and slapped. "Off!" I sobbed. "Get off!"

Sean grabbed my wrists. "You crazy fucking bitch," he said, and it soon stopped being an ordinary fuck.

You'd think we might have worn each other out that night but no. The next day we were still at it. He cracked his tie at the air, stretched it taut then slotted it into my mouth. He wedged it hard into the corners of my lips as he fastened it behind my head, getting my hair snagged in the knot. Being gagged is awful. The fabric feels dry and fluffy. I don't know where to put my tongue. My saliva pools. My breath goes shallow and panicky. I look an idiot and I can't speak. All I can do is grunt like an animal, and the fabric gets sodden. It's debasing. I loathe it and at the same time, it's excruciatingly hot.

As if to reinforce my wordlessness, Sean asked, "Did you miss me?"

Splayed on the bed, I tugged at my ropes – wrists and ankles – and shook my head, mumbling into his tie.

"What did you do while I was gone?" he said. "Tell me."

He gave me a dark, hard look and I was immediately scared. *He knows*, I thought. *Something's wrong. He suspects.* I shook my head again, a frantic denial of whatever I might be accused of.

"Did you jerk off?"

Again, I shook my head and briefly closed my eyes, relieved.

"You sure?"

He reached between my splayed thighs, sawing the edge of his hand along my slipperiness. He dropped his voice to a whisper. "Because you're always so wet for it, so greedy." He drove his fingers inside me and rolled my clit with his other hand. "Aren't you?"

My thighs started to go. I felt molten and woozy, dropping toward orgasm.

"You didn't miss me," Sean went on. "You didn't fuck yourself. So what did you do, babes? Were you bad?"

"Uh-uh," I said, trying to say no against the tie.

And then I saw her again. She was draped over his shoulder, striping his skin in those glowing rainbow rays. Sean's fingers squirmed inside me, and my clit throbbed. I felt watched by her, and I was appalled to be so aroused and disheveled before the Technicolor spread of her Zen-like calm.

I started to come, ripples rising. "Good girl," cooed Sean, eyes fixed on mine, his fingers taking me closer. My orgasm clutched and he smiled down, clearly relishing his power as he made me come; my bound, open body jerking to his tune. And Jasmine was with him, Jas for short, all her pretty little colors lighting up his face.

Red, orange, yellow, green, blue, indigo, and violet.

Violet. That's the color of jealousy for me, just a letter away from violent. Green is a witch's broth but violet is tainted blood and a bitter, poisoned heart. I glared at her as my orgasm faded, glared at Sean.

"Easy there," he said. He wiped strands of hair from my face then unfastened the tie, freeing my mouth. "You okay?"

It was a while before I could speak. Sean's face shimmered with spectral colors. I didn't know who I was talking to, him or her. "I want to tie you up," I breathed. "I want to wrap you up in chains, take you over. I want to make you mine."

It was a lie. I didn't want to do that at all. It's not really my thing. I don't do knots and clips and locks. I'd rather they were done to me.

Sean smiled. He traced his finger along my jawline, down my neck, down my body. The rainbow began fading. He knew me.

"Hey," he said gently. "Don't worry about it. This is good. This is great."

She was barely there, just some smudges on his cheek.

"This takes me over," he said. He gave me a new smile that was tender, blissful, zonked. A special smile for me. "I'm already yours, babes. No chains required."

And then she was gone from his face, and he was gazing down, smiling so softly. And all around us, her pretty little colors were dying in the room.

Georgie Cracks the Case

Kathleen Bradean

We'd just met, and already Jack and I were Nick and Nora
Charles. Or maybe we were David and Maddie from that
old TV show *Moonlighting*, but without the fighting. Either
way, we had the witty banter going with just a hint of sexual
tension, which had my gaydar pinging between *he isn't* and
is he?

Ten feet away, the bride was doing the chicken dance with
her 6 year-old nephew. Jack and I were on our third martinis.
Mine was more mussed than dirty; his was blueberry.

"To open bars, darling." Jack clinked his glass against mine.

I leaned forward, my elbow on my knee, chin resting on my
hand. There was another question I wasn't drunk enough to
pop yet, so I asked, "How did a dashing urbanite like yourself
get stuck at the reject table?"

"Dashing urbanite? Is that the new euphemism for men
who watch *Project Runway*, Georgie?"

Was that an answer to the question I didn't ask?

Most guys tried to shorten my name to Georgia, which I
hated. Jack was the first person to call me Georgie and not
immediately break into a rendition of "Hey There Georgie
Girl", reason enough to crush on him. It didn't hurt that he
looked damn fine in a suit.

"And why are you seated at the back table? Please tell me
you did something scandalous." Jack wriggled his eyebrows.

"It's a sad tale, really. Full of woe. I was supposed to be a
bridesmaid."

He sipped his martini. "Do tell."

"I refused to wear the hideous bridesmaid dress."

We cast glances at the head table. Really, only a sadistic bride would make her friends wear lime chiffon hoop skirts. It was a nightmare mash up of the 1970s and *Gone With the Wind*.

"If she'd meant it as an ironic ugly dress, I would have been game, but I'm afraid she was serious about it. I suggested white floppy hats and gloves to make it totally kitsch. She had the nerve to tell me that was tacky. So I told her I'd have to decline the honor of being one of her bridesmaids. Apparently, that effed up her usher/bridesmaid ratio, so I got banished to the leftover table."

Jack turned his attention to my beaded champagne silk sheath. "Good call." He kept looking, letting his gaze linger over my bare shoulders and plunging neckline. "Very good call." His long legs stretched out and his hands were in his pockets, the picture of contentment.

I couldn't say the same for the frumpy Auntie sitting on his other side. She stubbornly resisted Jack's charm, avoiding his every attempt at conversation. She hadn't moved since the reception began. The bread bowl sat empty beside her elbow – she grabbed it the second she sat down and emptied it into her enormous purse. No mystery why the bride stuck her in the back corner table. If the older woman hadn't been wearing a four-carat rock on her ring finger, I would have been worried that she was an impoverished relative barely surviving on Social Security, but apparently she made her fortune the old-fashioned way – by shoplifting it.

After a while, Jack gave up trying to draw her into the conversation and turned all that wit and sexy ambiguity on me. We were catty bitches all evening, giggling behind our napkins. That earned us harder looks from the Auntie.

"Are you two ever going to go dance, or are you going to sit here all night?" the Auntie asked after dinner was cleared. Other than grunting, that was the first thing I'd heard her say.

"Wonderful idea." Jack stood up and extended his hand. "Dance with me."

"Of course, darling." I was a little more wobbly on my feet than he was.

I glanced at the biddy. I bet she had a ziplock in that great big satchel of hers. Great minds thinking in unison, Jack and I snatched our martinis from the table and took them to the dance floor with us.

One arm looped over Jack's shoulder, I moved into the crook of his arm. The heat of his hand seeped through my thin dress at the small of my back. We were dancing slow even though the DJ was out to exhaust everyone. I glanced around the room while I sipped my drink.

"Well what do you know, the Auntie finally got out of her chair." I watched her go to the empty table next to ours and glance around furtively before sitting down. "She's probably dumping slices of the leftover wedding cake into the enormous purse of hers under the tablecloth."

Jack led me into a turn so that we could both watch her. She saw us looking and glowered. "She's a character all right. I wonder if she's with the bride or the groom."

"She wouldn't even tell you that, would she?"

"Maybe she's in control of a trust fund that the bride gets when she marries, and she's been secretly siphoning off the funds all these years, and she's upset because she's about to lose control over that fabulous money."

I giggled at his story. It made the Auntie seem much more sinister and interesting. As we glided out of the path of other dancers, Jack brought me around so that I could see the bar in the far corner of the room. The bartender, a delicious Latino with flirty eyes, grinned at me from across the room. "Never mind the Auntie. Looks like I'll be taking home a favor from this party after all."

Jack swung me around. Half my drink spilled on the dance floor. "Who?"

"That absolutely divine bartender. We've been committing eye adultery all night."

Jack laughed. "You're a little off. He's flirting with me."

"All bartenders flirt. That's why his brandy snifter is stuffed with bills."

"Maybe that's why he flirted with you—"

I waved away his explanation. "That wasn't a tip I offered him earlier."

Jack's eyebrow rose. "Funny you should mention that, because when I bumped into him in the men's room, I offered to stuff my tip in . . . Well, anyway, I have a date with him after this reception." He sipped his martini.

I stopped dancing. "Why that little whore. I have a date with him too." And just because I was afraid Jack might be right about the bartender, I added, "You might want to slow down on the drinks, love. There's nothing sadder than whiskey dick."

Jack choked on his drink. "Whiskey dick?"

It was hard to manage cool bitchiness, but I channeled Bette Davis and did all right. "You know – you want it, but you're too drunk to get it up."

"That, madame, would never happen to me." He was equally haughty.

"Why not?"

Jack looked at his glass. "Because I'm drinking vodka."

He was so sincere that I burst out laughing. Then he was laughing too, and we were slow dancing again in a close embrace. "You're lovely," I told him. "Truce?"

"Absolutely." He put his hand on the back of my head and leaned down to my mouth. His hand slid to the nape of my neck as his tongue pressed between my lips. Perfection. Gentle art with a healthy dollop of persuasion. "And that seals it."

I dragged the tip of my tongue slowly over my upper lip. "Mmm. You taste like blueberries."

He leaned down again, this time brushing my earlobe. "I'll bet you taste like the ocean. I'd love to take a dip."

Pleased, I laughed. "Cad. I'll bet Fred Astaire never said things like that to Ginger Rogers."

Jack's hand slid down to my ass and pulled me to his groin.

"Only because Ginger was making eyes at the hottie bartender all night. How could he compete?"

"You're making eyes at the bartender right now, aren't you?"

"Guilty as charged."

"Incorrigible flirt."

"Is that the new euphemism for slut? I thought we had a truce."

I drained my martini. "Oh, we do, darling, but you keep letting the bartender come between us."

Jack grinned down at me. "Now that's the most brilliant idea you've had all evening."

Maybe it was the alcohol, but he had me puzzled. "What idea?"

He guided me in a slow turn so that I could see the flirty bartender. Jack's cheek pressed to mine. "Have the bartender come between us"

There was no denying what Jack meant by come. I sighed. "Gosh you're swell to invite yourself on my date, mister. Filthy, but swell."

"It was your idea."

"Weddings make me horny." It wasn't much of a defense, but it was the truth. Dancing with Jack only made it worse. From across the wedding hall, we probably seemed strictly ballroom, but it was just a cover for frottage. The heat between our bodies brought out his clean soap scent. We weren't sweaty, but the humidity was definitely rising under my dress. Something else was rising in his pants.

Jack's eyes were so full of mischief that I didn't know if he was teasing or challenging me. "That wasn't yes, but it wasn't no either."

"I think I'd better stop drinking."

"Afraid of getting vodka pussy?"

My mouth dropped open. Did he really just say that? I lightly smacked his arm. "Incorrigible."

"Encourage-able, don't you mean? Maybe you just need to be persuaded." He kissed me again. That time, he sucked my bottom lip and pulled it with his teeth. Pressed so tight against him, I knew he didn't have to worry about whiskey dick, and from the throb in my clit, I sure as hell didn't have vodka pussy. He pressed kisses to my neck. Chills zinged down my spine.

"Maybe we should find out what time the bartender gets off."

Jack lifted my hand to his lips. "Not until you do, darling."

With a short salute, he strode over to the bar. He leaned on his elbow as he talked to the bartender. They both looked at me. The bartender frowned. Damn. Jack was right. The sexy Latino with the melting brown eyes wasn't interested in me. Funny. I didn't usually read people wrong that way. Of course, if I was in competition with Jack, and the bartender swung that way, well, I didn't blame him for choosing Jack.

Jack kept talking. The bartender shook his head. Not wanting to watch myself get shot down, I wandered over to take a look at the gift table. The auntie was there, poking at the boxes. She probably traded the card from her cheap offering to a gift that looked more expensive. Her huge purse clutched to her bosom, she glared at me.

An arm stole around my waist. Jack's lean body spooned to mine. "We're on."

"Are we? He didn't seem all that interested. How did you manage it?"

"I have my ways."

"You were right, weren't you? He was after you, not me."

"No, you were right. He was trying for both of us. He just thought it was a bad time to take a break, but I convinced him." Jack sure did like to kiss my neck. I was glad I'd swept my hair up so that there were plenty of places for those lips to nibble. "I shouldn't be doing this, but come on. We don't have much time."

A conga line, led by the groom, snaked toward us. Jack hurried me through a side door. The last thing I saw was an usher grasping the Auntie's hand. She squawked, but swept along in the tide of the celebration, she didn't stand a chance at escape.

* * *

Jack and I stepped into a service hallway. Service trays stacked with the remains of dinner lined the long hallway. Jack hummed as he gently grasped my elbow and guided me away from the swinging doors at the end of the corridor that I supposed led into the kitchen.

"I recognize that tune," I told him.

"Isn't it romantic . . ." he warbled as a waiter rushed past us with coffee service.

"Ha! You are divine."

He held open the door to a stairwell. "You say that now. I'm actually quite nasty."

Oh, he was, but in the best way. Before the door swung shut, he was slowly teasing my zipper down. He slid the thin straps from my shoulders, but carefully draped my dress over the railing instead of letting it fall onto the concrete floor. He frowned at the small pile of discarded cigarette butts under the fire hose. "Staff knows they shouldn't smoke here." He suddenly grinned at me. "Sorry about the accommodations, but we're on a tight time schedule."

"You have to be somewhere?"

"Julio, our bartender, only gets a fifteen minute break. He shouldn't even get one on such a short shift."

Wearing only French knickers and high heels, I felt deliciously exposed. I pulled on the end of Jack's bow tie. That made him look even hotter. He kept me close so I could feel his hard-on as I opened his shirt. My hands ran up his pecs into the light covering of dark hair. "Very nice." Then I saw the angry scar near his shoulder, and one below his ribs. My eyes full of questions, I ran my hand over the pink welt.

He grabbed my hand and kissed my fingertips. "It's not important."

"Okay." So he didn't want to tell a stranger. I didn't blame him, but I couldn't help but wonder.

His jacket and shirt went over the railing beside my dress. Giving him my sweetest smile, I slid my hands down his body as I went to my knees.

There's a sound I loved to get out of a man. Not a sigh or a grunt, but a small gasp as he realizes that his most precious possession is in the hands, and mouth, of a true artist. It was like a state of Zen, worshipping a cock that way. Long licks from tip to base, across his balls, and back up to the head for a start. Then slight suction up the length of him, ignoring the head. When his hand twitched as if he wanted to grab my head and fuck my face, he was ready. I plunged my mouth over him, taking him in until my nose pressed into his groin.

"Whoa. Whoa. I'm going to come too fast if you keep that up." Jack pulled his cock out of my mouth and leaned against the wall, panting. "For a girl, you sure know how to suck cock." He helped me to my feet.

"I think I resent that remark."

Jack grinned. "No insult to women meant."

I lifted my chin and put my hand on my hip. "Gender has nothing to do with it. I suck great cock, period."

He pulled me to him. "Yes you do. It's that mouth of yours. Those blow job lips ..." Jack's mouth covered mine as his hand slid into my panties. "Very nice." Then the only sound was our heavy breathing and the slick wet sounds of his agile fingers working over my pussy.

Jack slid my knickers down. Kneeling, he tapped my ankle. I lifted my feet. He folded my panties before putting them aside. "Would madame care to sit on the steps, or to stand?"

"I can't come while standing. At least, not when I'm in the shower."

He unfurled his jacket on the staircase leading up. "Then I insist you sit." The way he took my hand and eased me onto his jacket, he could have been seating me at high tea.

Jack kneeled; I propped up on my elbows to watch. He kissed along the inside of my thighs. "Just trimmed, not shaved," he murmured into my mound. "Just the way I like it." His tongue slid over my clit in a long lick. Like he'd done to my mouth, he sucked and teased until I panted. It was possible I'd met my match at oral.

The doorway swung open. Jack rose up, shielding me from view until he realized it was our bartender friend.

Julio grinned down at us. "Started without me?" He shed his white jacket.

"Just warming up," Jack said. "Care for a taste?"

Julio got on his knees next to Jack. "Sure." He wrapped his arms around Jack and kissed him.

They didn't waste time on tentative pecks. Hands grasping Julio's short black hair, Jack shared my flavor. They parted, smiled, and slammed together again. While they made out, I slid my hand between my legs and pinched my clit. Jack tugged Julio's zipper down and brought out a nice fat cock.

Julio bent down to work his tongue over me. I moved my hand out of the way as he enthusiastically delved between my legs. Jack bent down, and even though I couldn't see it, I knew he had Julio's cock in his mouth. Julio wasn't quite as talented as Jack, but he knew what he was doing. I loved that he didn't ram his fingers into me, but instead used them on the hood of my clit.

I grasped my purse. Momentarily distracted, I laughed when I looked up and all three of us held up strips of condoms.

"The lady is prepared," Jack told Julio.

"I always carry the five essentials to a party. Money, phone, lipstick, protection, and—" I fished into my small beaded bag and withdrew a small vial "—lube."

Jack put his hands over his heart. "I think I'm in love."

"More important than that, who's Lucky Pierre?" I asked.

"Lucky Pierre?" Julio's heavy brows drew together.

"The one in the middle," I explained.

The guys both slightly shrugged and looked to me. "The lady . . ."

I snorted. "You want to know what would really get me off? Watching you two fuck."

Julio grinned. So did Jack. Julio shoved his pants down, got on his hands and knees, and nuzzled my clit again. Jack buried his face between the muscled mounds of Julio's smooth, tight ass cheeks. Julio moaned into my pussy.

As if that weren't hot enough, Jack unrolled a condom over his cock, lubed it, and pressed into Julio. For a long while, Julio's tongue stopped working me. He breathed heavily on my thigh with his eyes closed. Jack stared down at Julio's ass. The concentration on his face was a sight. Little feel-good zaps tingled through my clit.

With one hand on Julio's waist, Jack slowly worked into a rhythm. Watching the way his body moved made those little tingles between my legs build. I grasped the back of Julio's head and forced it against my pussy. I ground on his nose until he got the hint and sucked me again.

Jack looked up at me. His grin went all the way up to his eyes and sparkled there. He bent over Julio's back. I struggled to lean forward. Rising to my knees, I went for Jack's mouth. I fucked Julio's tongue while Jack pounded his ass.

Julio said something I couldn't quite hear.

"Not yet," Jack said to him.

My muscles bunched tight. I looked down and watched Jack's cock sliding through the tight ring of Julio's ass. My thighs clamped around Julio's head as an orgasm shot through me.

"Now you can," Jack told Julio.

Julio turned his head to the side and let out a long cry. His load splattered on the step below me. Jack pulled slowly out of Julio's ass. He cast the condom aside and jerked off until he came on Julio's ass.

We fell together in a warm heap, kissing and cuddling.

"I don't suppose one of those essentials you carry is a come rag?" Jack asked.

I shook my head.

He pulled the handkerchief out of his jacket pocket and regarded it mournfully for a moment before wiping his come off Julio's ass cheeks. "Now I know what these are for."

He held a corner between his thumb and forefinger. "I guess I should have offered this to you first."

Julio quickly got dressed. "Break is over. Thanks, boss."

Jack stood up and pulled Julio to him. "You can't go back with her smeared all over your face."

"I'll rinse off in the kitchen first." Julio turned to me. "That was hot. Thanks."

I grinned wearily. "Any time."

Jack gave Julio a light smack on his butt as the bartender peered out the door.

"You better get back to the party too. Coast is clear," Julio said before disappearing down the hallway.

"I hate to be a party pooper, but Julio's right, I've been gone longer than I should have been too. I simply couldn't resist, though." Jack offered his hand. He pulled me to my feet.

"Not a problem, Jack. I knew this was a quickie."

Jack buttoned his shirt. He tucked in and pulled on his jacket. He opened the door, but turned back. "You're a hell of a girl, Georgie. If I had time . . ." Then he was gone.

I stood naked in the stairwell. How typical. The hostess left to clean up after the party guests were gone. I slid on my knickers and shimmied back into my dress. Well, the hotel management would have more than cig butts littering the landing to worry about, because I was not going to carry the used condom to a proper waste receptacle.

Figuring that I looked well and truly fucked – but in a good way – I slinked down the access corridor to the ladies' room. Ignoring the nasty glances I got from the bride's mother, I reapplied lipstick and got presentable.

As I stepped out of the bathroom, I glanced at my reflection in a full-length mirror in the elevator lobby. I was so busy making sure my dress didn't have any tell-tale wet spots that I ran right into the dour Auntie from the wedding.

"Watch it," she snapped. She clutched her now bulging purse as she pushed the down button several times.

I ignored her and went back into the reception hall.

The place was in chaos. The bride's father's face was red. Spittle flew from his mouth as he yelled at Jack. Jack stood with his head hung. The bride was crying. The groom looked like he wanted to punch someone.

"What happened?" I whispered to another guest.

"Someone stole the bride's purse. Apparently, it was full of cash and checks. They also took some of the more expensive gifts. No one saw anything, and apparently," the guest lowered her voice, "the hotel security guy who was supposed to be watching took a break while it all went down."

I glanced at Jack. Hotel security? I looked over to Julio. He moved bottles around behind the bar and watched Jack get his ass handed to him. I looked out at the elevator lobby. The old Auntie was going crazy jabbing the down button. Her big old purse was so full, much fuller than it had been when she first started shoving bread into it. I could have sworn I saw the trademark blue of a Tiffany's box poking out.

I walked over to Jack and tugged on his sleeve.

"We're busy," the bride's father snapped at me.

I bared my teeth at him in sort of a smile. "That's nice. Shut up." I nodded away from the gathering mob of wedding guests. "Follow me."

To his credit, Jack walked across the room with me. I pointed at the Auntie. "Does her purse look a lot fuller now than it did before? And why is she missing all the fun?"

Jack's eyes lit up. "I could kiss you, darling." He whipped his phone out of his jacket pocket, turned his back to me, and muttered into it.

The elevator pinged. As the doors slid open, the Auntie got into it.

"She's getting away!"

Jack turned around. "No. I've arranged a little reception for her downstairs. Everything is under control." He kissed my forehead. "Like I said, one hell of a girl. Can I see your phone?"

Puzzled, I handed it to him. His fingers deftly glided over it. He handed it back. "My phone number is programmed in. I'm going to be busy with the cops and management the rest of this evening, but call me tomorrow. I'd like to see you again."

"You're hotel security? Won't you get in trouble for drinking on the job?"

Jack laughed. "Julio was pouring me flavored water all night. But I might get in trouble for slipping away with you."

"Sounds like my cue to exit."

He shrugged. "It might help. Then you won't have to lie to the cops. Thanks for saving my butt."

"Any time."

The bride's father stalked over. "What are you planning to do?"

Jack drew himself up. "It's all being handled, sir." He ushered the fuming father away, but glanced over his shoulder long enough to wink at me.

With all the commotion, no one noticed me slipping away from the party. In the hotel lobby, I saw the Auntie surrounded by several of the city's finest boys in blue. Her purse was open, and several gifts, as well as the bride's purse, were laid out on a table.

The doorman hailed a cab for me. Suddenly weary, I climbed in, collapsed against the seat, closed my eyes, and gave the cabbie my address. My thoughts went back to the scene in the stairwell as my hand slipped between my thighs. What were those scars on Jack's chest? He didn't seem like the type to have a mysterious past. Then again, what did I really know about him? Great dancer, better kisser, hot lover, undercover security guy – that was it. Maybe one day he'd tell me what happened. That is, if we ever met again. Opening my eyes, I fished my phone out of my purse and brought up the number Jack programmed into it.

"Jack McGreggor," he answered tersely.

"Just checking."

He chuckled. "If you left without my number, I would have regretted it. Maybe not today. Maybe not tomorrow. But soon and for the rest of my life."

I loved that he would misquote from *Casablanca* for me. "Jack, I think this is the beginning of a beautiful friendship."

"Wait – does that make me Bogart or the French guy?"

"We'll work it out over dinner sometime, and continue the conversation onto breakfast the next morning."

"I'm taking that as a promise," he said.

"Cross my legs and hope to die."

He laughed again. His voice dropped into an intimate tone that sent a shiver down my spine. "Say goodnight, Georgie."

"Goodnight."

"Goodnight, sweetheart."

The Depths of Despair

Rachel Kramer Bussel

Evan is staring at me intently, waiting for the answer to his question, "What do you want?" whispered directly into my ear. Such a short sentence for the very complex response it opens up in me. I want a hundred million things from him, but at this moment, I want something I'm not totally sure either of us can handle.

"I want you to make me cry," I tell him. I have to whisper it because the words, and the realization, are so intense I'm not sure I can own up to them. But it's true; every time I think about his hands crashing down on me, his words berating me, his power keeping me in my lowly place, things we've done hundreds of times but that I still clamor for, I realize I don't want something light and easy, something we can laugh about later. I don't even want compliments like, "God, you can take a lot." It's not a competition for me; I know what my body can do, but I want to see what we can do together, if we can take spanking somewhere it's never gone before, if we can make it propel us into a new place where we lose ourselves only to find people we've always wanted to be. I've wanted this forever, I realize, as I say the words, but had never felt close enough with a lover to go there before him. I want something altogether different from every other spanking I've ever gotten, the ones that were hot and kinky and nasty, but that shied away from even approaching the edge of oblivion. Only with Evan can I dare to approach that dividing line that could topple our over-the-knee pleasures forever, or consecrate spanking as the centerpiece of our relationship.

I've never had to use a safeword before, and most of the time, I've barely even had one I could use. I trust my lovers implicitly and have never felt the need for one. Buried within that trust, though, is a safety net I'm not sure I any longer want, a safety net that suddenly feels altogether too constricting. I've never liked the word *play* used to describe kink, or at least, my kink. There's nothing playful about it, even though I know all about safe, sane and consensual, and that I can stop at any time. I can top from below with the best of them, but something in me has finally rebelled at this topsy-turvy state of masochistic affairs. I'm ready for the real thing, and am finally strong enough to take it, and Evan is just the man to grant me my wish.

If we were the marrying kind, I'd have a nice, shiny rock to flash around to all and sundry. We're not, so I don't expect that, but I married him in my heart a month after we met. He had his cock inside me, was fucking me doggie-style, and I moved, just slightly, almost imperceptibly. "Don't move, Denise. Don't ever move. Stay with me forever," he said. I could've dismissed it as pillow talk – most women would have – but somehow I knew he meant it. We've had our ups and downs in the year we've been together, but I've always known that he was the one. Not the One, the mystical, magical, phantom lover meant to fulfill a woman's every need and fantasy before she can even think of them. Not that One, but this one, my special one, the one who makes my heart beat like we're on a crashing airplane, who makes me smile when he wakes me in the middle of the night with a particularly loud snore, the one whose eyes and cock compete for best feature. The one who's made me relearn what submission is all about.

Yet even after a year of me naked over his knee, or up against the wall, or bent over holding my ankles, or any number of other positions we've tried to perfect our spanking regimen, we still haven't reached the heights, or depths, I know we could. I haven't cracked the surface of his sadism, haven't pushed him to bring out the truly mean top I know lurks inside, haven't let myself sink into the glory of sub space so fully I wonder if I'll ever come out. My fantasies have gotten more and more twisted, perverse, unreal. But I don't want an army of lovers or community-wide kink; I want Evan, just Evan. It's through no fault of his, or mine, that we haven't gone there, I've just always surrendered to the lure of his cock when the pressure seemed unbearable, right before I went over the edge I'm afraid I'll never return from. What if after this I want him to make me cry all the time? What if he takes that as a sign I need therapy? What if we become one of those couples where the man gets off on fucking his wife but not in the way that makes him rush home to her? What if he thinks I'm crying because I'm sad or in pain or don't love him anymore? I have no answers or crystal ball, I only know that the tears are demanding an exit, and won't take no for an answer. They aren't tears of sadness, that much I know for sure; what these tears signify I don't yet know, but I am convinced Evan can help me understand.

He grabs me by the scruff of my neck, and I whimper, just like I have before, but there's something different in his eyes. They're feral, wild with a kind of desire I've never seen before, and that sight unleashes a wave of want inside me. My entire body goes tight, then limp. "Be careful what you wish for, Dee," he says. "Very, very careful." When I make a move to open my mouth, he shuts my lips, pressing them between his thumb and forefinger. "Don't speak until we're done. You'll know when we're done. You can make noise, scream all you want, but no talking, unless you need to safeword. Your safeword is *emergency*. But I don't think you're going to come anywhere close to using it." He lets go of my lips, then just stands there staring at me. At an even six feet, he's got a good five inches on me so I'm looking up at him, my face just as serious as his.

Then, in a flash, he's grabbed me and moved us over so he can slam me against the wall. This is no gentle crash in which I'm just as complicit; *he* slams *me*, and it hurts, but I like the pain. A lot. My face smashes into the familiar white space, his hand against the side of my head. I've been up against countless walls since I met him, but never so close, where it's like I'm inhaling the paint. I've murmured, prayed even, into wood and brick and paint. But now my lips aren't so much touching the wall as merged with it. My body goes on red alert as he smears me into the wall. My pussy is pounding, demanding attention in much the same way my heart is thudding. "Stay there, whore." He knows that word sets me off, but this time, his voice is gruffer; it's not a playful term of endearment, and I almost feel like one. I wonder what I'd do if I really were a whore with a client who wanted to treat me like this. I focus on the plaster against my skin, on his hand that has just stabbed me in the lower back. Okay, not stabbed, but the pressure there is exquisite, his palm digging into the spot where my back curves, his thumb resting against my anus.

Then his hand booms down against my right buttcheek. I'd thought I couldn't sink farther into the wall, but I'd been wrong, because somehow, I become one with it. It hurts, and not in the way my ass does. My facial pain isn't quite the sweet, stinging, arousing pain that spanking brings, but this pain still manages to feel good in its own way, reminding me what I'm capable of in the name of getting off. I know my face will be red later, probably my breasts, too. His hand keeps coming down against me, spanking me furiously in a way that surely has to singe his palm as much as it does my bottom. Then his teeth are sinking into the back of my neck and his four fingers are turning the backs of my thighs red. "Denise, now's as good a time as any to tell you. It's over." He's spanking me hard the whole time he speaks, and the smacks are so loud I almost can't make out what he's saying. "I didn't know how to break it to you, but I'm moving out. I've found my own place, over on Larch. I've got two more weeks here, and I'll try to be as discreet as I can. I was waiting for the right time to tell you, but now's as good as any, wouldn't you say?" He's talking like we're having some kind of adult conversation, while meanwhile my entire stomach has dropped, yet my pussy is still on fire.

So is my ass, where he's still spanking me. I've had my hands up above me on the wall, but they start to drop. All I want now is to curl into a ball, wrapped around myself. *Fuck spanking.*

I think, about to whisper, "Emergency," when he presses his entire body against mine, lifting my hands back above me and pressing his palms to the backs of my hands, hard. "Keep those there, Dee. I said two more weeks, and don't think I'm not gonna get the most pussy out of you I can before then. I don't want to forget this ass," he says as he pinches the skin there.

I'm not crying; I'm numb inside. Did I bring this on? This wasn't what I wanted. I keep my hands above me just to spite him. Now I won't cry, just to show him. "Stay right fucking there. Whore," he says, and despite myself, I feel a shudder. He knows why it triggers me so – I used to be one, at least the worst kind of one, one who gave it away to anyone who so much as looked my way, succumbing to the word I'd been called since sprouting 38Ds in my senior year of high school – yet it also thrills a deep, secret place inside me. I was a slut who was so far gone she thought of herself as a whore, and even got off on the blasé way I could pick a guy up, bring him home, and chuck him out the door. But that nameless blur of men and cocks was nothing compared to the power I tapped into with Evan. Even the good guys, the ones trained in the art of BDSM, who worshipped my ass as much as they punished it, couldn't come close to what we have. Had. I don't know anymore. His hands are everywhere at once, firing off blows that make my whole body light up in recognition of my place, my role in this apocalyptic scene. I briefly wonder if he'll offer me money that I have to take from him with my teeth, as one guy did when I did a brief stint stripping. Yet even with his horrific words ringing in my ear, the image makes me wet. I picture him shoving dollar bills into my cunt, into my mouth, gluing them to my body, marking me as a whore once and for all.

My mind goes a little quieter as he slips the blindfold over my eyes. "Get over here," he says, grabbing me by my nipple, pinching it as he pulls me across the room. The point where our bodies touch stings, but a soothing, familiar heat travels lower. *I've asked for this, I want this, we'll deal with the aftermath later*, I think, as I feel him bend me over the spanking bench we bought in our first heady, kinky weeks together. *Who will spank me on it when he leaves?* I wonder as he settles me over it so my ass is perfectly poised. I expect the spanking to start up again immediately, and perhaps because of that, it doesn't. I can't see, but I can hear him moving around, the flick of a lighter, the sharp inhale of a cigarette. I don't approve, but I gave up lecturing him long ago.

"You'll be rid of this smell soon enough," he says, as if reading my mind. He blows hot smoke against my ass, and I tremble. I'm waiting, patiently, if you ask me, but he just strokes my ass cheeks with the tips of his fingers, tickling me more than anything else. "I'll miss this ass, Denise. I hope you believe me. It just has to be this way."

"Is it Monique?" I ask, before I can stop myself.

"Does that fucking matter, Denise?" he snarls, this time pounding me so hard my stomach feels like it's colliding against the seat of the bench, even though they're already connected. He's smoking and spanking, somehow, as if he has all the time in the world, as if he isn't providing more than the tears I asked for, countless more.

"Yes. No. I don't know," I sob, wanting to rewind to the start of this scene. I try to let my mind go black, especially when he moves around to kiss me hard, his breath smoky. He pulls back and I see him draw the cigarette right under my lips, close enough that I can feel the orange flame, before he moves aside and puts it out right on our bedside table. This is a mean side of him I've never seen before, something beyond sadistic, like he wants to hurt me all the way through, not just make my ass quake and smolder.

"Well it's none of your business. Not anymore," he says, and turns his back to me. He hasn't shackled me, yet I couldn't move even if I wanted to. The bench is my savior, my companion, my safety net. I keep thinking he's going to bust out some exquisite new toy, a wooden panel, a ruler, a cane. He likes to make me scream and flinch, to mark me, render me as his fully and completely. He likes that I'm into spanking, but always finds ways to make me feel like an amateur spankee who hasn't quite reached the levels of masochism his latest toy warrants. But this time, he goes back to that trusty favorite: his hand. He has ways of curving that body part that turn it into the sickest instrument around.

"Don't say a word, Denise. For once, just keep your fucking mouth shut." He sounds like someone else entirely; he's put on an accent to go with his words, Queens blue collar instead of his usual clipped, cultured, Westchester doctor voice. Yes, he loves playing doctor with me, another thing that'll have to end now, I suppose. "Good. I'm going to spank you until you're all cried out, and I'll be the judge of that."

Strangely, even though he starts with hardly any warm-up, just raises his hand like a whip and strikes me smartly across my cheeks, I can't cry just yet. I clamp my eyes shut, breathe through my nose, and focus on the pain. This I can process, this I can deal with, this I think I want. My pussy is getting wet and yet somehow I hardly feel it. "This not hard enough for you?" he asks, then digs his short but strong nails into my ass after one particularly rough blow.

This goes on for thirty-seven minutes. I know because he tells me; he's been looking at the clock, must want to get this over with already. I'm wondering why he doesn't just use a paddle or something already when I feel his hand hit me and then a burning sensation. He's added something to his palm that makes it sting like hell. Next he shoves what I'm sure is our metal dildo into my cunt. He plunges it in without any hesitation, then goes right on with the searing smacks that really feel like he's added chili pepper or something to his hand. It burns, and hurts, but I still open for him to fuck me with the toy, or rather, my pussy does. My head is still locked on what he's just revealed.

When an hour has passed and only one lone tear has dribbled down my cheek, he stands me up and then has me kneel before him. He takes off the blindfold. I want to look into his eyes, but I don't. I stare down at the ground, hardly knowing who he is anymore. Then he strikes me across the face. This isn't a loving tap or even a sexual smack. He hits me, just once, across my right cheek. He's a left, so it stings real good. "I got her a spanking machine. The one you always wanted. It's spanking her right now, warming up her ass just for me." He reaches for my nipple again, twisting it until I cry out. I wonder why he's telling me these things, why he's being so mean. I wonder if I'll have to move to avoid seeing the two of them around.

I picture her, then, her ass, a good one third the size of mine, raised up on that sweet machine while it pummels her over and over and over again. Evan and I had gotten off watching women being spanked by those machines, and I'd been angling for one for months. Monique's new in town, was, I thought, a new friend. He's known her less than two months and already she's usurped my place. That's when the tears start, first a few on one side then a few on the other, weak little rivulets of saltwater. That's when Evan takes me across his lap, my favorite. He used to do it before bed sometimes, telling me he loved me while using the meanest wooden paddle we owned. Now he does it and I just let the tears fall onto the ground. At first I put my arm in my mouth to stifle my sobs, but then I just let loose. His smacks are no harder than before, but they feel harder, somehow. We both lose track of time as the spanking seems to go on forever, my cries only ending when he shoves four fat fingers into my pussy and smacks my ass some more. Finally, I'm all done. I've come in a quick, almost rebellious burst. I don't want to give him that satisfaction, but I can't resist his touch. I look up at him through the haze of tears, searching his eyes for an answer as my throbbing ass welcomes the cool air from the window.

When it's over, I try to sneak off to the bathroom, my face streaked with tears, my body seeming to sag under its own weight. I want to be alone, to curl up in the bath and merge into the bubbles. But he grabs me again, roughly, hugging me so tightly that at first I don't realize he has tears in his eyes, too, tears that are slowly sliding down his face. "What are you crying about?" I ask bitterly, selfishly liking the comfort of his solid strength.

"Dee, my sweet Dee. I'm not going anywhere. I'm yours. Forever, remember? But you wanted me to make you cry, and I knew I had to go far, far down to somewhere foreign and scary to really make you scared. You're a tough woman to crack, even though you don't always realize it."

I stare at him in disbelief, wondering whether he's an evil genius or a truly sick bastard. I guess part of why I love him is that I'll never truly have the answer to that, I just have to keep lowering myself to the depths of despair, and seeing if I make it through.

Sex Scenes: "Detention"

Polly Frost & Ray Sawhill

NATHAN: [*to audience*] What surprised me was all the pastel. Pink walls. Light-green floors. And the lightness. The sun was pouring through skylights and windows. The female guard who walked me to the visitation room told me that the light and the pastel colors help keep the female inmates cheerful. Women really care about all that mood stuff.

The guard showed me into the visitation room, sauntered over to the corner, a big ring of keys clanking by her side, and sat down in a plastic chair.

I'd chosen a Tuesday afternoon for my visit hoping it wouldn't be busy, and I was right. The visitation room was like an abandoned set off *Law and Order*. Linoleum floor. Fluorescent lights. A row of carrels almost like at the library at Oklahoma City Community College, only with Plexiglas at the center.

De-bore-aaah – she didn't pronounce her name the usual way "Deborah" but De-bore-aaah – Kibbel was waiting for me at one of the carrels on the other side of the Plexiglas. At Turpin High School Ms. Kibbel had been the hottest teacher, bar none. When she'd been photographed and hauled off to jail, the photos and footage in the media hadn't done her justice. They almost made her look dowdy.

Now, here in jail, to be honest she looked almost frumpy. The orange jumpsuit clashed with her pink lipstick. Her blonde hair was showing its dark roots.

I wondered if they forbade hair coloring in jail. The tan she was always so proud of even in the middle of an Oklahoma winter had faded.

It had been six weeks since the frenzy had erupted. "Local English Teacher Arrested for Affair with Fifteen-Year-Old Sophomore."

I picked up the phone handset.

NATHAN: [*to Deborah*] Hello, Ms. Kibbel.

DEBORAH: Hello, Nathan Moffitt. I was having a hard time placing the name when I was notified you were coming. But now that you're here, I do recognize you, I think. From church.

NATHAN: That's right. I'm the son of Alice Moffitt, the minister at First Church.

DEBORAH: Ah, that's the connection. They mentioned something about the church.

NATHAN: I brought a care package, but they took it from me for searching. They say they'll bring it to you later in your cell.

DEBORAH: Thank you so much. And you've brought greetings from everyone at First Church, is that right? That's lovely too. I hope not everyone is eager to condemn me.

NATHAN: It's been a challenging time for all of us.

DEBORAH: I'm truly sorry to have brought these difficulties on you. Would you please let everyone know I'm attending chapel regularly here in jail?

NATHAN: Of course. Is there anything we can do for you? Anything at all?

DEBORAH: There is one thing.

NATHAN: What's that?

DEBORAH: It's awkward. You can probably guess. By law I'm not allowed to mention his name. But he's the victim in this crime. My concern for him is very real.

NATHAN: [*to audience*] I looked around. We were alone, besides the sleepy lady guard in the corner reading a gossip magazine. I leaned forward.

[*to Deborah*] I can tell you that we're all hoping he'll make a relatively good recovery.

DEBORAH: Oh God, if I've contributed to making anyone's life more difficult, I'll never be able to rest in peace.

NATHAN: As my mother would say, God's ways are strange. My mother says there are lessons we'll all learn from this.

DEBORAH: I want you to know that I repent every night. I'm struggling to understand what possessed me to do what I did to that poor child.

NATHAN: I'm told he's working hard in post-traumatic stress therapy. He won't emerge unmarked by the experience, but there's a good chance he'll be able to lead a decent life and make some contributions to society one day.

DEBORAH: I'm sincerely glad to hear that.

NATHAN: If I can be forgiven—

DEBORAH: Who am I to forgive anyone?

NATHAN: I just want to understand what it is that possessed you. You, a teacher. Brady Uhls, a student, still a boy. A nine-year age difference. Boundary issues. The sexual thing.

DEBORAH: Oh, it was all my fault, I admit that. I've been carrying the devil around in me . . . Living with him . . .

NATHAN: But there must have been something? Something that gave the devil license to take a good woman over.

DEBORAH: Well, there was something that set me off.

NATHAN: I think I know what it was. Popular culture.

DEBORAH: You're so right! It's everywhere, undermining the foundations of community values and family life.

NATHAN: Isn't that the case.

DEBORAH: Amen.

NATHAN: Was there one particular item?

DEBORAH: What do you mean?

NATHAN: A TV show. A rock video. An issue of *Cosmo*.

DEBORAH: Now that you mention it, there was. It was that movie. That damn movie . . .

NATHAN: Which movie?

DEBORAH: Well, so far there is no movie. But I read announcements about it. You probably saw them too. They were hard to avoid. Six months ago or so – I read about the film in *USA Today* but the news was all over the TV as well. The one called *Sex Scenes*. A young woman director is going to be making an X-rated—

NATHAN: NC-17-rated, you mean.

DEBORAH: That's it! Did you read about its premise?

NATHAN: No I didn't.

DEBORAH: The young wife of a rich man wants to do something nice for him. He's distracted, they have a couple of kids. So she hires a pornographic movie star—

NATHAN: I did read about that. It's a horrible example of how porn is trying to make its way into ordinary families and tear them apart.

DEBORAH: It seems it's based on real life. Can you imagine?

NATHAN: So that's what put the idea in your mind?

DEBORAH: Without all the articles and TV items about that film, I never would have done what I did. That's exactly right. My mind started to obsess about what it would be like to be with another person, someone other than my husband. I was even thinking of renting porn so I could imagine what it would be like to be with another man. I knew I had to do something to save my marriage. Ted is so distracted, and I'm such a stranger in this community . . . and then you know, we have children, too, just like that woman who hired the porn star. It was that movie – that damn movie – that drove me to victimize an innocent fifteen-year-old boy with my lust. Pardon my language.

NATHAN: We had no idea how lonely you were. You were a popular teacher at the high school. There's even a waiting list for the Sunday School class you taught, where you told us about the book of Revelations.

DEBORAH: I'm still struggling with the whole thing. You have no idea how alone my years in Oklahoma have been. I mean, emotionally speaking.

NATHAN: I'm sure the judge will take that into account. And I'm sure the community will too.

DEBORAH: Please Lord, forgive me. Lead me in prayer, would you please . . . um—

NATHAN: Nathan. Nathan Moffitt.

DEBORAH: Nathan, let's pray to save his soul. You know who I mean. My own soul is lost already.

NATHAN: You know how my mother has us all hold hands in church? Let's reach out to touch hands through this Plexiglas. [*Praying*] Lord, we pray for Brady Uhls—

DEBORAH: No names, please!

NATHAN: We pray for a certain local high school sophomore that he will come out of this ordeal able to marry a normal woman and lead a full adult life in the ways of the church and the community mall. And we pray for this good-souled woman here, Deborah—

DEBORAH [*correcting pronunciation*]: De-bore-ah.

NATHAN: De-bore-ah Kibbel, that she can see through the error of her ways to the everlasting truth of your light. Amen.

DEBORAH: Amen.

NATHAN: Brady. [*Pause*] That lucky fucker.

DEBORAH: Excuse me. What did you just say?

NATHAN: I said, "Brady, that lucky fucker."

DEBORAH: You aren't really here from the church, are you?

NATHAN: No, ma'am.

DEBORAH: What this about, then? I think you owe me an explanation.

NATHAN: I'm here to make you an offer. I'm here to discuss your future. Your business future. Your life future.

DEBORAH: Then you're here under false pretenses as far as I'm concerned.

NATHAN: I had to see you somehow, and you'll be glad I did.

DEBORAH: I'm calling a guard.

NATHAN: You'll regret it.

DEBORAH: Why? What can you possibly have to offer? Are you even old enough to have a driver's license?

NATHAN: I'm here to talk about rights.

DEBORAH: Well, you're much too late for that, young man. I'm already in discussion with the big three for my story: the *Globe*, the *Star*, and the *New York Times* magazine section.

NATHAN: You're making a mistake.

DEBORAH: The cash looks good to me.

NATHAN: You're thinking small. You get one check, it goes right into your defense fund, you serve your three years, get out in two on good behavior, and where are you? To be frank, you're probably living in a small town in British Columbia under a false name.

DEBORAH: How dare you?

NATHAN: All due respect, ma'am, you're caught up in a played-out paradigm of old media at a time of major media realignment—

DEBORAH: Wait, I do remember you. Those pretentious nerdy words . . . That awestruck tone about the internet's possibilities . . . That conviction you'll be a billionaire one day . . .

NATHAN: I was in your English class three years ago.

DEBORAH: I remember! I remember! And I remember that I caught you plagiarizing. That paper you supposedly wrote about *The Color Purple.* The first case in Turpin, Oklahoma of a teenager caught downloading a term paper off the Internet.

NATHAN: We call it appropriation these days. And I did it on purpose.

DEBORAH: I just bet you did.

NATHAN: You'd be right. What did I care about sensitive women's fiction? And what did I care about my English grade? Where's the bucks in that? I was on my way to biz school at Community College anyway. What I wanted was a seat in the detention you supervised.

DEBORAH: Why?

NATHAN: Do you have to ask?

DEBORAH: I'm afraid I do.

NATHAN: I was in love with the lacy bras I could see through the ecru silk of those blouses you wore. "Ecru" – you're surprised I know the word. I'm just some geeky kid who only knows techie talk. But I learned the word "ecru" because of you!

DEBORAH: I don't know what to say.

NATHAN: I was always trying to figure out if you were wearing a thong under those demure black skirts. So ladylike, yet so tight. With that four inch slit up the side. You spoiled everything for me. Everything that high school was supposed to deliver.

DEBORAH: I have no idea what you're saying—

NATHAN: You made it impossible for me to get aroused by the bared midriffs and low riding jeans of the high school girls! You were older. You were twenty-three. And it was hot that you didn't try to act like a teen. Next to you, their attire seemed obvious and juvenile. You were doing what you were doing with class – with hints, sophistication. Yet I could tell that what was packaged up in that classy bundle was first-rate womanflesh. Even the way you pronounced your name was hot. De-bore-aaah. All those Shannons and Ashleys who were cheerleaders in my class – I was supposed to be turned on by them. But their names seemed silly by comparison. I didn't want the attention of an Ashley – I wanted to hit it home with De-bore-aaah. That's why I actually read those crappy novels you were always forcing on us.

DEBORAH: Oprah endorsed those novels.

NATHAN: It was only your sex appeal that got me through them.

DEBORAH: Well, I don't know what to say. You're not exactly your mother's son, that's for sure.

NATHAN: What did Brady have that I didn't?

DEBORAH: Brady, Brady . . . He loves Oprah's novels, you know.

NATHAN: I've got news for you. Brady Uhls despises Oprah's Book Club choices even more than I do. And he wasn't shy about telling everyone.

DEBORAH: But he writes poetry!

NATHAN: It's called wigger rap, and it's a lousy, bush-league imitation of Eminem. Until he got caught fucking you, Brady Uhls was going nowhere fast.

DEBORAH: Brady lifted my heart out of Oklahoma.

NATHAN: You know he's getting laid right and left while you sit here in jail, don't you?

DEBORAH: That's not true! I was told he'd been too traumatized to even touch another girl.

NATHAN: He's been parlaying your little affair into getting a piece of every older woman in town. All the ladies want him for themselves. He's worked his way through most of the country club so far. Now I hear he's begun on the PTA.

DEBORAH: One of the guards was reading the *Star* the other day and she told me he's heartbroken!

NATHAN: Brady Uhls hangs his head and acts all tragic for the authorities and for the media. But at school he's the shit and he never lets anyone forget it. A year ago, Brady Uhls was the kind of fifteen-year-old who pisses off the other boys. Where was his acne? Why did he have a muscular chest while we were skinny? Those full lips . . . That baby face of his . . . And saying he wanted to grow up and be an artist? Guys like that deserve to get beat up regularly. But now he's the envy of everyone. He walks into a locker room and he gets high-fived by the football team that used to kick his ass. All the best-looking girls want to find out what he learned from you.

DEBORAH: Which means—

NATHAN: That's right. He's getting blown by every girl in high school.

DEBORAH: Fuck that underage asshole! He said he'd wait for me.

NATHAN: Looks like that isn't the case.

DEBORAH: To think I taught him how to make poetry not just with words, but with his cock!

NATHAN: I don't mean to be the bearer of bad tidings.

DEBORAH: So talk. You've got just two minutes.

NATHAN: I can turn your story and your personality into a lifelong career.

DEBORAH: You've got no capital.

NATHAN: Capital is old-paradigm. New-paradigm is connectivity. I've got technical expertise and I'm social networking with other dynamic up-and-comers from all over the world.

DEBORAH: Meaning more eighteen-year-olds with no capital. And they probably couldn't pass English class either.

NATHAN: I'm talking the scariest, most powerful force on the face of the planet – eighteen-year-olds with servers and broadband. Let me tell you how this scenario can play itself out. First, you give me rights to the videotape.

DEBORAH: Don't be absurd.

NATHAN: You know what? I bet your pussy looks pretty on a computer monitor.

DEBORAH: Don't be crass. Besides, there is no videotape. I made that clear to the police.

NATHAN: De-bore-aaah Kibble, let me make one thing clear: it all hinges – the whole deal, which means your whole future – hinges on the existence of this videotape you deny so strenuously exists. Now, I wouldn't be here, going to the trouble and bother of visiting you and making my pitch if I didn't have good reason to think that this non-existent videotape really does, in fact, exist. And my information comes from someone who knows. Someone with first-hand knowledge.

DEBORAH: He swore he wouldn't—

NATHAN: I've been buds with his older brother since before I can remember. You know, Tommy told me it was really hot driving you and Brady around in the SUV while you made it in the back seat. He wasn't wild about getting shot with Brady's hot white cum in the back of his head. But the rest of the adventure was raunchy bliss.

DEBORAH: I had no idea that fucker, Tommy, had a video cam with him. I thought he just wanted to help Brady and me out.

NATHAN: Not to fear, Tommy hasn't told anybody else. I let him know in no uncertain terms that I'd personally pound the living crap out of him if he did tell.

DEBORAH: Why that's so sweet of you.

NATHAN: That's the kind of guy I am. Okay, so stage one: We release the sex tape on the web. "Horny honey caught sucking sophomore staff," something like that. There's nothing as big these days as amateur sex videos. Nothing, I tell you. But time is passing, and people are already creating fake amateur-celebrity sex videos. Short version: we've got to move if we're going to hit the market while the appetite for raw footage is still hot. Stage two: The sex tape makes a pile. We use that money to parlay your notoriety into extensive – and exclusive – online coverage of your trial. None of this boring Court TV stuff. You give me exclusive rights to see events from your point of view, and we broadcast online. You're charming, you're hot. We build up a mass of sympathy for your side.

DEBORAH: A lot of good any of that's going to do me. There's such a thing as laws, you know, and I violated some pretty serious ones.

NATHAN: You really have no idea how the world's changing, do you?

DEBORAH: What do you mean?

NATHAN: The old media may be full of people clucking and wondering how a teacher can let this happen with a student. But young guys everywhere are gathered around water coolers and talking openly about how much they envy Brady Uhls.

DEBORAH: So you're telling me I'm a joke.

NATHAN: I'm telling you that you're not just a star, you're a heroine. You're the English teacher every male wishes he had. It's a tidal wave of public opinion, and it's all sympathetic, a few whacko fundamentalists aside.

DEBORAH: Including your mother's crackpot congregation.

NATHAN: Could be.

DEBORAH: It'll never work. I wouldn't be able to keep a penny of whatever accrues. Convicts can't keep anything they make as a consequence of their crimes.

NATHAN: Life online is all about getting around bottlenecks. I'm in touch with a guy in Barbados, an exchange student who's a fellow biz major at CC. He spends summers doing tech work at a bank in the islands and has installed his own partition sectors on their servers. His bosses don't even know they're there. We let him mount our files. We mirror them at a half a dozen hard drives in the Third World. You and I split the proceeds fifty–fifty, and I pay for expenses from my half.

DEBORAH: I don't know. This sounds so elaborate. My head's spinning.

NATHAN: Get with it! The poor nations of the world are leapfrogging the old-economy infrastructure and cutting straight to the digital era. Cell phones, wireless web connections, routers. They're going to become repositories for our digitized sexual material. Trust me, they'd rather be that than crapholes for our nuclear waste.

DEBORAH: You know, I'm starting to like the way you throw around those multi-syllablic words.

NATHAN: Laws are going to be changing. But already these dynamic forces are sweeping aside old barriers. The files and accounts are where the American authorities can't get them. We use PayPal, and we channel receipts through DNS-maskers. And the beauty of it is: it all stays anonymous.

DEBORAH: Once I'm out of jail, I take a couple of trips offshore, just me and my husband visiting the Caribbean for a vacation—

NATHAN: And Uncle Sam lives in ignorance!

DEBORAH: It's the gift that keeps on giving!

NATHAN: Between you and me, I wouldn't be too sure about you doing jail time in the first place.

DEBORAH: What do you mean?

NATHAN: I probably shouldn't be telling you this because it's all in strictest confidence. But I've been in touch with the national ACLU on this issue. They tell me they see you as a major test case. The specific legal question is: Who's been harmed?

DEBORAH: Not a soul, you can take it from me. Brady Uhls never had it so good as he did with me. You know, sometimes I look at my own tiny children. I think – what would I do if my own son was fifteen and his teacher introduced him into the ways of sex. I know what I would do. I would rip the fucking bitch's throat out. But that's different. What I did with Brady was right. And I don't need your mother's prayers about it. I am not a bad woman—

NATHAN: No, you're a heroine to everyone everywhere. You stand for free speech, for free choice, for non-harming. You're not just hot, you're an international symbol. Everyone will want a piece of you. I see *Playboy* spreads. Chicklit novels based on you. I see a reality-TV show on Bravo. I see Eurovision song performances—

DEBORAH: I see retiring and moving back to Florida before I turn 30.

NATHAN: If that's the way you want to play it.

DEBORAH: Let me tell you something I've never told anyone. I met my husband Ted at the University of Fort Lauderdale. The Young Christians Club used to have these barbecues on the beach. Man, he was hot in his surf baggies. I was pretty hot in my Wicked Weasel thong too. We romped in the ocean together and fell in love. Back in church he told me all about the beauty of Oklahoma, and about how much money his family has, and about how exciting their business is. He got me all stirred up. Really. I just handed myself over to him. And where do I wind up? In a highway town in the middle of Nowheresville, married to a guy who repairs John Deere farm equipment for a living.

NATHAN: It could be a good business if he got a website going.

DEBORAH: It's not where I want to be! I want margaritas. I want fish tacos. I want to go topless on the beach.

NATHAN: So take my offer! It's your ticket back to the good times!

DEBORAH: Ted never even fucks me anymore. You know what I mean? He's all about the diesel engines. He'd rather make small talk with farmers than spend five minutes getting me in the mood.

NATHAN: The man has no appreciation for the finer things.

DEBORAH: I've never spoken to anyone as frankly as this. Not even Brady. [*Looks Nathan over*] Do you even live on your own yet?

NATHAN: I've got a lock on my door. I'm in charge of when I come and when I go.

DEBORAH: And this door of yours is located where, exactly?

NATHAN: In my parents' basement.

DEBORAH: Don't tell me you drove over here in your mother's car.

NATHAN: [*nods*] I did.

DEBORAH: How old are you anyway? God's honest truth.

NATHAN: Nineteen in two months – I swear!

DEBORAH: That's eighteen. A little old, but at least it's legal.

NATHAN: When you were telling me about that movie premise that got you all worked up? I noticed that you forgot to tell me about one part of that premise. You see, I've been following the progress of that movie like a hawk.

DEBORAH: God, doesn't it sound great? I keep reading that they're encountering difficulties. I hope it gets made. I can't wait to see it.

NATHAN: In the real story they're basing the movie on, the rich wife who wants to give her husband a videotape of her fucking a porn star? She likes the fucking she gets from Rocco Siffredi so much that she gives up her marriage and becomes a porno movie star herself.

DEBORAH: Rocco, Jesus. Have you seen how that guy is hung?

NATHAN: Epic.

DEBORAH: And that bit about her liking it so much that—

NATHAN: – she decides to go pro—

DEBORAH: "Going pro." God, that expression really does it for me. It got me hot six months ago and it's getting me hot now. You know what it says to me? It says "Big time." It says, "Far away from Oklahoma." It says, "You've made it to the majors."

NATHAN: We can use that in the title of the amateur sex tape. *De-bore-ah Goes Pro.*

DEBORAH: You know, as we're talking here it's coming back to me. I do remember you from my class, and not just as the plagiarist. I remember you as being kind of scrawny. You aren't half bad looking these days.

NATHAN: I've been hitting the weight room at Community College. Three times a week, triple sets of reps.

DEBORAH: Nice work. Keep it up. You know, looking at you, really looking at you . . . That haircut . . . The black turtleneck . . . It's making me think of some people.

NATHAN: The haircut's Tom Cruise circa *Top Gun* – made a big impression on me on DVD. Dude rocked! And the turtleneck's Steve Jobs. Macs are for weenies but Jobs has got more sex appeal in his wire-rim glasses than Bill Gates does in his entire mansion. Man, does that dude know how to go bald.

DEBORAH: You can say that again.

NATHAN: [*to audience*] She pressed her hand against the Plexiglas. I could see she was impressed by how much bigger my hand was than hers. Her mood seemed softer. Her eye lids relaxed a bit. I was feeling stirred.

DEBORAH: Did you really do your best to get into my Detention?

NATHAN: [*to Deborah*] I did everything I could.

DEBORAH: I'm sorry I didn't take better note of your feelings.

NATHAN: It's OK. I was pretty unappealing at fifteen, to be honest.

DEBORAH: But it matters that you cared, and that you wanted me.

NATHAN: Like nothing else.

DEBORAH: How did you imagine things would go?

NATHAN: [*to audience*] As she talked, she took off her ugly prison-issue glasses and unzipped her orange jail uniform a bit. It didn't look ugly anymore. It looked classy. Classy-sexy. I glanced around. There was only the one guard in the corner, and she'd fallen asleep. The gossip magazine was on the floor between her legs. When I looked back at Deborah, she'd pulled down one of the shoulders of her jump suit. Underneath, she was wearing the kind of lacy bra I saw through her blouses back in English class. [*to Deborah*] Nice.

DEBORAH: A girl's got to keep up some standards, even in jail.

NATHAN: [*to Deborah*] I would imagine you and me alone in detention together, De-bore-aaah.

DEBORAH: You will call me Ms. Kibbel.

NATHAN: Yes, Ms Kibbel. [*to audience*] It was like her words were sending me into some kind of trance.

DEBORAH: You don't even pronounce your own name right.

NATHAN: I don't?

DEBORAH: It shouldn't be pronounced "Nathan." It ought to be pronounced Nah-thahn.

NATHAN: Nah-thahn.

DEBORAH: Now, Nah-thahn, I want you to hold the handset between your ear and your shoulder. I want you to unzip your pants and take your cock out.

NATHAN: Are we in Detention together?

DEBORAH: It's 4:15, and everyone's gone home from school. It's only you and me. You're the only student who's been bad today. I've called your mother. She can't believe it. She raised you to be a good Christian member of her church. But she's got counseling duties and isn't going to be able to pick you up for an hour.

NATHAN: You look at me with annoyance, then walk to the classroom door and close it.

DEBORAH: You're sitting in your chair, sullen. Teen boys think they're tough, but they're basically children. They can't resist pouting when they've done something wrong. I love that youthful anger. The stupid bravado. The childishness.

I walk over to where you're sitting. I put my finger under your chin. I bring your face up to look at mine.

You are staring at me in confusion. Because I'm starting to do a slow strip in front of you. What do you think? What's going through your mind?

NATHAN: [*to audience*] De-bore-ah knew how to play on my imagination, that's for sure. I could almost see what she was talking about. The old detention classroom. The stupid chalkboard. In front of me the school's hottest teacher showing me her tits. But I was also sitting here in the jail visitation room too, stroking my cock and facing this woman through Plexiglas.

She had her jumpsuit down and her bra straps off her shoulders. Fuck, but her tits were beautiful. Heavy and wobbly. No silicone there.

She was pinching a nipple with one hand. I once read in *Maxim* that women with big tits often need their nipples treated really rough in order to feel anything at all. Well, De-bore-ah was really giving that one nipple a mauling.

Oh, it was hot. She'd slid down in the chair, and though I couldn't see what she was doing beneath the level of the Plexiglas I could still tell that her other hand was hard at work at her crotch.

My head was swimming. It was like those ads when they dissolve from one image through another and then through another. She was stripping for me in detention. We were whacking off here in jail.

[*to Deborah*] "It's all so real, so real," I said. What are you doing to me? What's happening?

DEBORAH: I'm in Detention with you, Nah-thahn. I'm turning around so you can see the way my ass is packed into my tight black skirt.

NATHAN: Oh, Christ yes, that skirt. The one with the slit.

DEBORAH: I'm no teenager with a bony ass. I'm a woman with real flesh and real feelings.

NATHAN: And you pull the . . . the . . . what do you call it?

DEBORAH: The hem?

NATHAN: Right! You pull the hem of your skirt up. I can't believe it. I'm looking at your ass, and there seems to be nothing covering it. But I know something is, because I've looked up between your legs as you sat on the edge of your desk telling us about those awful women's novels, and your pussy was always covered. Which means that you're now wearing a g-string.

DEBORAH: You studied my crotch more than you did any of the books I assigned in class. What's America's youth coming to?

NATHAN: [*to audience*] Sitting opposite each other like this, it was better than phone sex, it was better than Yahoo Instant Messenger. We couldn't touch, yet we were touching. It wasn't her real voice I was hearing, it was some electronic something coming through the telephone. There was the glass between us. It was like the best web cam sex ever. She was just sitting there on the other side of the divider. But in my imagination she was in class holding her breasts out for me to see.

DEBORAH: Nah-than, Nah-than, Nah-than . . .

NATHAN: [*to Deborah*] I'm sliding a finger through your hot, wet pussy—

DEBORAH: Yes, there, slower, using the flat of two fingers. Make slow, little circles. Don't speed up. Make me beg you for more, and then don't give it to me. Don't you dare! That's right, like that.

NATHAN: It feels so good. I had no idea.

DEBORAH: Not enough people know what sex can really be like.

NATHAN: [*to audience*] I looked up from my open pants and my stiff, purple, oozing cock. And it was the weirdest thing.

DEBORAH: You and I are in a bedroom.

NATHAN: [*to audience*] And we were! I mean, I knew I was opposite her in the visitors' room at the jail. But it was as though we really were in a bedroom together. I don't know how, but I knew it was hers. Maybe it was the stack of Oprah Winfrey books on her bedside table.

DEBORAH: I'm on my knees, on my bed, bending over in front of you.

NATHAN: [*to Deborah*] I pull aside your g-string. Your pussy is like a pomegranate, some exotic fruit, glistening in the sunset . . . [*to audience*] I don't know where the words were coming from. I never spoke like this before in my life.

DEBORAH: You run your tongue up my slit—

NATHAN: My tongue buries itself in your asshole. And it is so sweet.

DEBORAH: Oh, that feels so good. I'm opening up to you in so many ways. I run my finger over and over my swollen slippery clit as you sink your tongue inside me.

NATHAN: I'm plunging into the molten core of your being.

DEBORAH: You're turning me into a sea anemone on a Florida beach . . .

NATHAN: [*to audience*] I knew she was going to say that! I was with her, I was really with her! I'd read about things like this, where two people are breathing each other's breath—

DEBORAH: [*still in rapture*] Your blood is circulating through my veins, I'm feeling your sensations, you're thinking my thoughts—

NATHAN: That's it exactly! [*to audience*] I don't know if this makes any sense. But it was like we were one organism, fucking itself and being fucked by itself. And we were also part of some larger organism that was fucking it all into some kind of giant super-existence!

DEBORAH: Don't let me scream, Nah-thahn. That would be very bad. My triplets are in the next room sleeping and we mustn't wake them up.

NATHAN: [*to audience*] That did it for me. Enough with the pussyeating. I hauled her womanly ass higher and steered my raging stallion into her red-hot stable. It was like coming home, if "home" means heaven and hell both. The head of my cock was a tender explorer, and the shaft of my rod a piston. [*to Deborah*] De-bore-aaah,

De-bore-aaah, De-bore-aaah, your ass is in my hands, waist high.

DEBORAH: My ass shudders and wobbles with every one of your rock hard thrusts.

NATHAN: Your head is down on the bed, and your blonde hair is a wet tangle around it.

DEBORAH: With one hand I stretch and reach between my legs and underneath. I hold you by the balls and guide your rhythm. Fuck me, Nah-thahn.

NATHAN: You say it over and over.

DEBORAH: Fuck me! Fuck me! Fuck me!

NATHAN: Oh yeah, baby.

DEBORAH: You're turning into a man, aren't you?

NATHAN: Oh fuck, yeah.

DEBORAH: My fingernails feel sharp and dangerous as they close around your balls. Yet the danger is exciting beyond belief.

NATHAN: I'm both in control and out of control as you thrash through wave after wave of contractions, impaling yourself ever more deeply on me. Finally you slip off.

DEBORAH: [*gasps*] I'm not done.

NATHAN: Women really do get a lot more out of sex than guys!

DEBORAH: Of course we do. Anyway, I've been so frustrated in this god-forsaken prison that I need to come some more. You know what you could do for me now?

NATHAN: Fuck you again?

DEBORAH: I want you to spank me with one of the Oprah Winfrey books.

NATHAN: [*to audience*] It sounds crazy, I know, but it made perfect sense to me. Like I say, at that moment we were one. I reached over to her bedside table and picked out a novel by this dude, Wally Lamb, with that gold "Oprah's Book Club" foil stamp on it. I tried to muster up as much authority as I could. It wasn't easy, as in this virtual-reality fantasy I was myself, only at fifteen. De-bore-ah lay face down on the bed.

DEBORAH: Slap it against my ass and tell me I've been bad.

NATHAN: [*to audience*] It felt good to let her be in charge. I did as she said. I spanked her hard with the book, over and over again. I spanked her until I began to worry maybe I should stop, but she gave me a look of hatred and need, so I went back to spanking her. Her ass was pink with streaks. I could see something moving down there.

DEBORAH: I'm fingering my cunt as you spank me. [*Has orgasm*]

NATHAN: She came. I continued whacking her.

DEBORAH: [*Orgasm, includes:*] Oh, Nah-thahn!

NATHAN: And she came again. Then she uncoiled like a cat. She was on her back on the bed looking up at me with glowing, hungry eyes. I threw the Wally Lamb novel aside.

DEBORAH: You've done well, Nah-thahn. You know what I think you've deserved?

NATHAN: A gold star from Oprah?

DEBORAH: A blowjob.

NATHAN: Oh, wow.

DEBORAH: I want you to fuck my mouth. I don't want you worrying about my feelings, or whether I'm liking it, or whether I'm finding it exciting. This isn't about me. It's about you feeling free to fuck my face as long and as hard as you need to. Use me. I want you to fuck my mouth until you shoot your come so deep into the back of my throat that I'm choking on it, and I have no choice but to swallow every last hot drop.

NATHAN: [*to audience*] Oh, man, that was it. There was no holding back any longer. As the fantasy and the reality swirled in tandem around me, my stomach and thighs gave giant squeezes, my nuts pulsed like never before, and my hot white load shot up onto the Plexiglas between us. Three, four, five big spasms worth, and then a couple of small ones. And I was still boiling over.

As I quivered like a Spielberg special effect and pumped the last squirts out of my angry rod, De-bore-ah leaned forward and gave the Plexiglas a long, slow lick from the other side.

DEBORAH: I hope you have a big wet stain on the front of your pants.

NATHAN: [*to audience*] Of course she was right. Jerking off is always a messy thing, at least in my experience.

I mopped as much up with the tail of my turtleneck as I could, then slipped my hands into my pants pockets and wiped them off on the cloth there. Deborah hiked her bra straps and jumpsuit back up. There was slick sweat on her brow. We gazed lazily and hungrily into each other's eyes.

DEBORAH: You know, as I sit here, I can't imagine why I shouldn't get a 60–40 split on our little deal.

NATHAN: [*to Deborah*] Agreed. But it all hinges on that video.

DEBORAH: My husband may get in touch with you about it. Not that it really exists, but he may know something about it anyway.

NATHAN: So you really did make the video for him? For the good of your marriage? I knew it!

DEBORAH: No comment. Officially, anyway. But let me tell you something you're going to need to learn someday. When you get to be my age, when you get to be twenty-six and you've been married for a long, long time, like four years, sex doesn't just happen anymore. It isn't like what you and I just had. You have to work at it. You can't neglect it. Because if you do, it dies.

NATHAN: [*to audience*] De-bore-ah and I touched hands through the Plexiglas one last time, then I called for the guard.

I jingled my car keys as I walked to my mom's Taurus in the big, mostly empty parking lot. I paused as I slipped them into the car door. Endless blue sky streaked by fair-weather clouds arched above me. Oceans of green prairie grass extended in all directions from the razor-wire fence around the women's pen. My semen was beginning to dry up on my pubic hair and jockey shorts, pulling my package a little tight. I was on my way to the big time. God was indeed good.

Nah-thahn, she'd called me as she came. Nah-thahn Moffitt. Nah-thahn Moffitt Productions.

I liked it. I was going to go global with it.

Fucking Ugly

Mike Kimera

I'm sitting alone at the bar in Paddy O'Reilly's on a Saturday night, waiting for him to arrive and trying to pretend I'm not anxious.

This is not normal for me. The anxiety I mean. Bars are my natural habitat. I'm a hard working woman who travels too much. I need someplace where I can just relax and be me, so in every new city, I find a bar and make it my own.

My preference is for old-fashioned places with polished foot-rails, tall stools and a mirror behind the bar. I always sit at the bar itself, never in a booth. Booths make me feel trapped. A bar stool gives me freedom. It doesn't commit me to sitting next to anyone. I can check out the room in the mirror. And the stools are just the right height for showing off my legs.

I found Paddy's a couple of months ago, when my Zurich assignment started. Zurich's going through a "hotel-chic" thing with bars: light-box walls, clean lines, subdued colours and ambient music. It's all too new and too self-consciously cool for me. Paddy's was a welcome relief. It has resisted going for the full "Top of the morning to you" Irish Theme Park thing and focused on serving good beer, great Guinness and an impressive choice of Irish whiskies.

Tonight I'm sipping Bushmills whiskey; trying to make it last while I wait. Waiting is also not usual for me. Most of the time I'm the best looking woman in whatever bar I'm in – I'm not bragging, just stating a fact – so when I want a man all I have to do is to make eye contact and he is by my side.

Yet here I am, waiting, perched on the same stool I used last week, on the evening that this obsession of mine started. I wasn't sipping whiskey that night. I was tossing it back and lining up the empty shot glasses in front of me.

I hadn't had a fuck in two weeks and hadn't had toe-curling, spine-stretching, groan-making, clit-throbbing sex in much longer. I was horny enough to be restless but stressed enough not to have the focus to do anything about it. I'd decided to drink until everything went away. In between shots I was using the mirror to scan the room for someone who could scratch my itch. My gaze slid over a couple of guys with potential but they didn't have what it took to hook my hunger, at least not that night.

I was ready to reach for another shot before scanning the room again, when my eyes were drawn to an ugly fat man with thinning hair. His nose was too large for his face. He had a gap between his front teeth that he could have pushed his tongue through. But the most noticeable thing about him was the wall-eye, so badly in need of surgical correction I wondered if it was real. It was painful to look at that eye and impossible to look away from it. He was dressed in a black polo shirt that seemed a size too small, and black jeans that his belly hung over. Attribute it to boredom or alcohol or that rubber-necking instinct that makes us look at crashed cars at the side of the road, but I found myself staring at the man.

He was leaning against the wall, his half-empty pint of Guinness resting on his gut and seemed to be listening to the woman standing next to him. She was one of those tall Germanic-blondes with skinny arms and bony faces that Zurich is infested with. She looked too sophisticated for him. As I watched, she reached out her hand and touched him, letting her fingers run lightly through the coarse, dark hair that matted his naked forearm. It was a lover's touch. I was certain that these two had had sex.

Unbidden, an image flashed across my mind of him on his back, with Fräulein Longshanks straddling him, digging her nails into the hair on his beached-whale of a belly as she fucked and he watched.

It was the kind of image that should have repelled me or made me laugh contemptuously but instead, my nipples rose. Then I realized that the ugly fuckling was looking at me. At least one of his eyes seemed to be. Angry with myself, I dragged my gaze away from him and threw down two shots in quick succession.

Maybe if I'd been less intent on self-medicating with whiskey I'd have seen him come up behind me. As it was, the first thing I was aware of was the heat of him leaning up against my back. He spoke straight into my ear, close enough for me to feel his breath.

"It was the right one that was looking at you," he said, in a soft Irish accent that sounded the way Bailey's feels on the tongue: smooth with a hint of wickedness.

Despite the contrast between his voice and his looks, I had no doubts about who was behind me. I swivelled on my stool so that I was half facing him.

"I'm sorry?" I said in a tone that was not at all apologetic and which should have discouraged conversation.

"Don't be sorry now. Most people can't work it out."

So much for discouragement. I took a sip of my whiskey and moved on to confrontation.

"I wasn't trying to work anything out."

"Yes you were. You wanted to know if the ugly guy standing in the corner was really staring at you, but, as his eyes point in different directions you couldn't be sure."

I blushed. I never blush when I'm sober so I'd definitely had too much to drink.

Ugly moved forward a little until he was positioned so that if I stood up I'd be pressed against him. I was annoyed rather than threatened. The whiskey had slowed my tongue and he spoke again before I could tell him to piss off.

"At first you were annoyed that an ugly animal of a man would stare at you so openly."

He kept a smile on his face and his tone was pleasant.

Anyone looking at us would think that we were friends having a quiet chat. But if they had looked into his one good eye, they'd have known what I knew: this large fat man was dangerous.

"Look . . ." I said, getting ready to charm him if necessary.

"Oh you looked alright," he said, talking over me. "You thought I wasn't watching, so you let yourself take in some of the details: the long thick fingers on hands like garden rakes, the bulge in the jeans just below the overhanging belly and of course the hair, like an animal's pelt, not just on the arms but pushing up from the shirt collar."

He looked me in the eye as his words drilled into me. I should have moved but I didn't. What he said was mostly true but what was holding me in place was the energy behind his words. I'd expected some "I am not a freak-show to stare at" anger from him. What I was getting was something else. Something I couldn't name yet.

"And then you let yourself wonder what it would be like, to give yourself to an animal like that, the way a bitch in heat gives herself to a dog that is wild for the smell of her."

I felt my own anger rising then. I wanted to slap the smile off his face. But I didn't hit him. I didn't move. Because a small voice in my head was saying *he knows*.

One large hand reached out and for a moment I thought he was going to grope me, but he reached past me to pick up one of the glasses of whiskey I had lined up in front of me. I could have moved out of his way but that would have felt like ceding territory so I stayed still and endured his closeness. He smelled of tobacco and Guinness.

He smiled at me, said "*Slainte*," and tossed back the whiskey. I found myself noticing the way the thick black hair on his knuckles caught the light as he lifted the glass. It looked coarse and I wondered if it was clean or if that hair would hold the scent of everything he had touched that day.

"I know what you want," he said.

"Really? And how do you know that?"

"I've been watching you for the past few weeks; using that

stool to display yourself while you check out the talent in the mirror behind the bar."

I didn't believe him. If he'd been watching me, I'd have known.

"I've noticed that the ones you take home are always just a little younger than you."

I had taken men home. Not many. Just enough to scratch my itch. But they were not younger than me. Or at least not much.

"Ah, I can see from your face that you'd not noticed the nature of your choice. Perhaps it's not their ages you're misjudging but your own. You're a fine looking woman but you'll not see thirty again I'd say. You're getting a little old for pretty boys."

My anger deserted me as I thought about what he'd said. It wasn't that I was worried about getting old. It was just that the pretty boys got on my nerves more than they had in the past. No matter how good they were at sex I always made them leave before morning and I was always glad when they'd gone.

"So that's what you think I want, is it?" I said, keeping my voice controlled but letting my contempt show. "That's the insight you came over to share. You think I want young boys in my bed?"

"No. In fact I'm certain that's not what you want. Tonight, when you were checking me out in the mirror, I saw 'the Look'. Ah, I know that look right enough. It's the look a pretty woman gets in that moment when she's wondering about playing Esmeralda to my Quasimodo."

Quasimodo. The name fitted him perfectly.

"So you think I want."

"Me. Yes."

I was so surprised I laughed. The idea was ridiculous.

"There's no need to be embarrassed," he said, misreading my mood entirely.

"You want to fuck ugly. You want to know what it's like. See, I'm certain that a fine looking woman like yourself has never fucked ugly before. I reckon you've always had pretty boys who fuck you in front of mirrors so they can check out their own looks as they do it. It's a little sad, don't you think, all those Kens fucking Barbies because they're too good looking to fuck anyone else?"

That broke the spell. There was no point in talking to him. The best thing was to leave. I slid off the stool and reached back to the bar for my purse. He put a hand on the bar on either side of me. It made it look like I was getting ready to kiss him. I was too pressed up against the bar to knee him. I wondered if my purse was heavy enough to knock him out if I landed a blow on his head.

"I don't want to fuck you," I said, "but I do want you to get the fuck out of my face."

He grinned at me but he didn't move.

I grabbed hold of his wrist to push his arm out of my way. It was like trying to move a tree.

"Move," I said.

"I'm not a violent man," he said. "I won't hurt you. But here's something for you to think about: uglies try harder and for longer than pretty boys and they're a damned sight hungrier.

"I think that that's the one thing that you and I have in common – that hunger."

Hunger. That was what I'd seen in his eyes. I knew a lot about hunger and the things it makes people do. The things it's made me do. But I was damned if I was going to let this ugly, aggressive, arrogant man know that.

"You're disgusting," I said.

"I'm ugly and fat alright," he said, his fleshy lips compressing themselves into a smile, "but I'm not what disgusts you. You're disgusted with all the beautiful, desire-free, passionless fucking that leaves you feeling hollow and hungrier than when you started."

"Leave me alone," I said, but I didn't push past him and I didn't raise my voice. I didn't want to think about what that meant.

"I'll leave you alone if you can look me in my good eye and tell me that your nipples aren't hard and that you're not wet enough for me to slide one of my thick fingers in smooth and easy."

He hadn't touched me, but the image of his finger slipping into me deep enough to wet the hair on his knuckles pushed its way into my mind with almost physical force. I resisted the urge to clamp my things together and tried to summon some of my famous hauteur.

"Get out of my way," I said. This time we both knew I meant it.

He stepped back enough for me to slide past him. I moved forward and he turned beside me, putting his arm around my waist. We looked like a couple getting ready to leave.

I moved forward quickly but he kept pace with me and kept his arm around my waist. I wondered briefly if he might hurt me.

Just before we reached the door, he swung me around, pushing me back up against the coats hanging by the exit.

Now I was afraid. My response to fear is always aggression. I was going to scratch the one good eye out of his grotesque face.

He caught both my wrists in his hands before they got close to his face. He pinned me against the coats, pressed his fat bulk up against me, put his mouth against my ear and said, "I'm going to let you go in just a second. After I'm gone, I want you to think about what it would be like to rake your nails down my hairy back or press your forehead against my soft belly while I fuck your mouth. I want you to remember that I don't want your pert tits, your flat belly or your perfect face. I want your hunger. I want to unchain it and let it feed."

Then he let go and walked back into the bar.

I stayed with my back against the wall. I didn't even lower my arms from where he'd pinned them above my head. I couldn't form a single sentence in my head. I knew nothing except that my panties were soaked, my skin was flushed and I was sweating.

"*Entschuldigung,*" a young man said. I had difficulty focusing on him so I was slow to move out from between him and his coat. He looked over his shoulder at me as he left the bar, his expression was scornful but he still checked me out before he closed the door behind him.

I stood up straight and searched for my own coat. As I slipped it on I looked back into the bar. Ugly had rejoined Fräulein Longshanks. He had his back to me. She was facing me, staring at me. Once we made eye contact, she leaned forward and sucked Ugly's earlobe into her mouth, all the while giving me a fuck-off-and-die stare. She reminded me of a lioness protecting her kill from a jackal.

I went back to my hotel and took a shower. It didn't help. The smell of him was off my skin but I could still taste him in my mind.

Sleep didn't come to me until I rolled over onto my belly, forced one hand between my legs, cupped my breast with other, and imagined riding Ugly's face, pressing my sex against his fleshy lips, working his over-long nose between my labia, making him suck my clit through the gap in his teeth, fucking his face until my arousal moved from drizzle to flood and he was drenched in my cum.

I went back to Paddy O'Reilly's the next day to apologize for not paying my tab. The bartender said, "Joseph said you'd be back today. He picked up your tally last night. Oh, and he left a note."

I waited until I was at work before I opened the note. It said, "If you're hungry on Saturday night, come find me."

I crumpled the note into a ball and threw it away, telling myself that I was outraged by Joseph's arrogance and that I had no intention of meeting with him. But alone in my bed, I found myself thinking about my hunger and what causes it and what it would take to sate it. So now I'm sitting on my stool, ignoring the pretty boys, waiting impatiently to feed.

Sign Your Name

Saskia Walker

Kind of weird, that's how Molly thought of herself. She told guys that, but mostly they thought she was referring to her attitude or her dress sense, both of which were also kind of weird. She was skittish and wayward, punky, yet quiet and thoughtful. And it wasn't just that. The thing that got Molly off sexually was pretty unusual too, and she felt it was only fair to let potential lovers know what she needed, up front. The only way to do that was to show them how it worked. Mostly, they didn't take her seriously. That is, not until Doug came along.

Doug had a spark of curiosity in his bright blue eyes, and a warm, subtle sense of humor. He was intuitive. She liked the way he looked, had done since the day he first walked into her workplace. He had cropped and spiked black hair, and smiled slow and long, kind of like Mickey Rourke. He ran the secondhand music exchange down the street, and he chose quiet times to come and collect his dry cleaning from the outlet where she worked, times when he remembered that she'd be working her shift – and was just about to shut up shop. He brought her black Nubuck leather jeans, and a multitude of cool Dragonfly shirts, shirts he wouldn't trust to his beat-up old washing machine – or so he said. She'd already warmed to him when he began to chat her up more purposefully.

"You know, Molly," he said, leaning over the countertop to close the gap between them, "we get on so well. Maybe we could go for a drink sometime." He smiled that drawn-out smile, and it made something inside her tick hopefully.

She put her pen down on the countertop between them, making a line in the space there, and nodded. "Okay."

"Great. Give me your number and we can work out a time." He picked up the pen and flipped over his till receipt, ready to write on the back of it.

Molly stared at the pen in his hand, immediately aroused and self-aware. The key to her kink was right there in his hand. She liked to be written on – in fact it aroused her to the point where she could come from that act alone. This was the time to show him; then she could see how he would react.

She took a deep breath. "Tell you what . . ." Her voice sounded shaky, and she hated that. She didn't want this to go wrong. She wanted him. Badly. "Why don't you give me your number? It'll be better that way. Really, I promise."

Before he could question her, or show doubt about why she'd said that, she shoved her forearm out across the counter between them, pulling up the sleeve of her top. She ran her finger up and down the soft, sensitive skin on the inside of her forearm. "Write it . . . here. Please."

Would he laugh at her? One corner of his mouth was still lifted and stayed that way. He toyed with the pen, his eyes assessing. Her breath was trapped in her throat. A moment later, he slowly moved one hand and held her wrist down on the counter with it, while he began to write on the spot she had indicated with the other.

His hand around her wrist was warm and strong and sure. And then – oh. The pressure he applied through the ballpoint on her skin made her nerves leap, the sensation chasing itself up her arm and through her body, flooding her with arousal. She bit her lip.

He looked up from the place he was writing and back at her. She could tell he'd sensed this wasn't just about exchanging numbers. A needy moan escaped her lips.

He stared; one eyebrow lifted, the pen, also. "Did I hurt you?"

"No." She could barely get that one small word out, and when she did, it was with a breathless, relieved sigh. She shrugged. "I'm wired weird. I just wanted you to know. Up front."

She snatched her arm away, bracing herself for the disbelieving laughter, the snide remark. Tension hung in the air between them, seemingly endless. Then he looked down at the countertop. What was he thinking?

He glanced up. "Kinky girl, huh?"

She stared him directly in the eye, her heart beating fast as she braced herself for rejection. "Does it bother you?"

"Quite the opposite," he replied, and flashed her a grin. "If I know what turns you on, it gives me power . . . and it just so happens I like to be in charge."

Oh, that made her hot. It was so far from what she had expected him to say, so direct. And then he moved. In a heartbeat, he levered himself over the counter, jumping lithely down onto her side of it. For the first time, he had breached the physical divide between them – and he'd brought the pen with him. Holding it raised in his hand, he put his free hand on her shoulder and walked her through the rails of plastic-covered clothes, backing her toward the wall behind those rails, out of sight of the shop front. He cornered her up against the wall.

Her body pulsed with the thrill of his actions.

He grasped her two hands easily in one of his, and lifted her chin with the pen under her jaw, an action that shot sensation down her neck and chest, right into her hardening nipples. She gasped for breath, her eyes closing and her head moving back to lean against the wall.

"Oh yes, it really does it for you, doesn't it? How bad is it?"

He still had the pen under her jaw, controlling the position of her head and where she could look. Could she tell him? Her eyes were shut and she kept them that way. "I need it." Her voice was a mere murmur. "I can't come any other way, not the way I do if . . ."

When her voice trailed off, he moved the pen just enough to apply pressure to the sensitive flesh beneath her jaw. Her eyes flashed open.

"Is this making you wet?"

"Yes." He was close, staring at her, his eyes bright and focused. The curiosity she had sensed in him had multiplied. He was aroused by her responses, his body shifting close against hers, one knee pressed against the wall at the side of her body.

He gave a soft chuckle. "You know, Molly, I used to wonder about you. I liked the way you looked, very pretty but different, and always thinking . . . always with the sexy eyes. There was something else though, wasn't there? You were always playing with your pen, always sucking on the end of it. Couldn't just be ready for the next customer, I figured. Couldn't quite work out what it was, but it made me hard just watching you play with the damn thing." His voice turned husky, right at the end there.

"Are you hard now?" She flashed her eyes, her responses rolling out readily.

His grip on her wrists tightened and he moved the back of her contained hands against the zipper on his jeans. "Well, what do you think?"

Beneath the black denim he wore, his cock was rigid.

Her skin tingled with awareness when he brushed it over that spot. She nodded. He moved the pen, lifting it from beneath her jaw and taking it down to the hem of her miniskirt. Putting it under the fabric and between her thighs, he tapped it from side to side then up and down, making her thighs tremble with the need for a deeper mark, the pressure, and the stain – the written evidence on her body.

He let go of her wrists, and lifted her skirt right up, exposing her. "Ooh, white cotton panties. Just like a blank page."

She stepped from one foot to the other, wired. "You're torturing me," she breathed.

"Maybe this will help." He ran the pen down the front of her panties, pushing both pen and fabric into the groove of her pussy.

Her flesh blazed under that touch. She glanced down to look at the solid line he had drawn, but he was still moving the pen, pressing deeper into her groove, rolling over her clit. When she gave a sudden gasp, he paused and concentrated on the same spot, drawing back and forth over it. A jaggedy blue scribble was forming right over the spot.

"You like that?"

Her clit was swollen and pounding, the direct stimulation hitting her hard. She nodded. "Very much."

He did it some more.

Her hands and head were flat to the wall, her hips jutting out toward him. "Oh yes, yes," she said, pounding the palm of one hand against the wall as she came, her free hand reaching out for his shoulder to steady herself.

She was about to speak, to say thank you, to say something, when she heard the door opening in the shop front, and hurriedly pulled her skirt straight. He stepped to one side, pointing down with the pen he held, possessively. "I want those panties, you better keep them for me."

"Maybe." She smiled. She wanted them, too. "You only gave me half of your number," she added, concerned that he might leave now.

He spanked her on the behind playfully, smiling that smile of his. "Fuck that. You're coming home with me tonight."

A month later, Molly's foible had been well and truly exploited. Before Doug, she'd fretted about her route to sexual pleasure. Doug had all but mended that in her, and now he was adding his own spin. He was fascinated with her odd little needs, and he'd written on just about every part of her body, watching her, enjoying her – wanking with one hand or fucking her hard while he gave her exactly what she wanted. Afterward, he tended her carefully, bathing her and massaging away the telltale signs of her kink.

That made her feel cherished, safe.

He asked her to move in with him. She said she'd think about it. He didn't press her on the subject. Instead, he showed her that those kind-of-weird needs of hers would never be forgotten.

★   ★   ★

That night he took her back to his place and told her he was going to kick it up a notch. The way he said it scared her and thrilled her at the same time.

Shortly after, she found herself naked and blindfolded, standing with her back against the wall, her hands splayed either side of her – just as he had instructed. Keyed up to the max, she shifted anxiously, unable to stay still. She'd never been blindfolded before, but the velvet covering her eyes was soft as a sigh, a shield that raised the awareness of her every other sense. Her body ached for contact, for pleasure and relief.

She could sense him moving.

The room was silent and the air was still, but she knew he was treading softly, watching her and making a plan. That was his way. Maybe she'd sensed that in him when she'd watched him across the counter. It was his curiosity, and his intensity, that had spiked her interest. Rightly so, as it turned out.

She heard a click and a fan whirred into action. A moment later the air brushed over her alert skin, tantalizingly. A whimper escaped her.

He began to hum under his breath, then he sang to her huskily. A song she loved. A song from ages ago. Breathless, aroused laughter escaped her; she felt delirious under his spell. "Dougie, please, you're playing with me."

"Always, sweetheart, but you love that."

He was so right. She squeezed her thighs together, scared to say more, and scared to ruin this.

"Will it drive you mad, not being able to see where I choose to write on you?"

"I don't know." She swallowed. "Maybe." She turned her face away, desperate with longing for that first touch, the pressure she craved – her skin was crawling with the need for it. Watching him write on her was half the pleasure, she thought. Not seeing it was an unknown quantity. But Doug knew and understood that, and – now – so did she.

Slowly, he drew a line around each wrist.

Her arms trembled with the sheer intensity of sensation that shot along the surface of her skin, and deeper.

"Shackles." His voice was a murmur close to her. "Because I want you to be mine." He kissed her throat and then, slowly, with great deliberation, he signed his name right across her breastbone.

"Oh. Oh, oh," she cried. The intense sensation shot beneath her skin, wiring her whole body into the experience. Her nipples were hard and hurting. She shuddered with arousal, her toes curling under, her heart thudding against the wall of her chest.

His next move came out of nowhere. He drew along the crease at the top of one thigh, then the other. The sudden deep stimulation in a place so sensitive primed her for release. She longed to see his marks on her.

"The insides of your thighs are wet, right down to here." There was admiration in his voice. Restraint, too. He touched her with the pen, briefly, between her thighs, and it made her squirm up against the wall.

"Face the wall," he instructed, his voice husky.

She turned.

His cock brushed against her buttock. "There's a box to your left, step onto it."

She moved her foot, felt her way. He guided her up onto the box.

"Offer yourself to me."

Understanding hit her; he was going to fuck her there up against the wall, while she stood there on a box, blindfolded. This was Doug; this is how he liked to have her, to be in charge of her. Hands braced against the wall, she spread her feet, angling her bottom up and out.

"Oh yes, I like you this way, on a pedestal, all ready for me." His cock moved between her thighs.

The box put her right at the height he needed to glide up into her. Anticipation had her in its grip. She was breathing so fast she felt dizzy. Picturing the shackles he had drawn on her wrists, she splayed her fingers on the wall, knowing she'd need to anchor herself – he got kind of wild when he was inside her. He was humming again now, and she wondered what he'd done with the pen. Was it in his mouth while he arranged her to his satisfaction?

He stroked her pussy, opening her up. His fingers moved with ease, slick, sliding in against her wetness. With two digits, he opened her up to his cock. The intensity of being felt, held, and displayed that way on a pedestal all at once took her breath away. With one hand around her hips, he thrust the thick shaft of his erection inside her.

Where is his other hand? The thought echoed around her mind frantically.

Then she found out.

Even as he thrust into her, in shallow quick maneuvers, keeping her in place, he began to write down her spine with his free hand.

It was almost too much. Her shoulders wriggled and her pussy twitched on his shaft. Her stomach flipped and sweat broke out on her skin. She would have staggered, if he hadn't got her pinned by his cock. She panted out loud, her mouth opening, her body clenching on him rhythmically.

"Oh yes, that's good," he said, keeping the pen moving in around her spine, working his way down her back. "This makes you so wild, you're going to squeeze my cock until I come."

"Can't control it," she whispered, head hanging down.

"That's the way I like it," he grunted.

By the time the pen reached her tailbone, she was a panting wreck on the verge of climax. He drew a wobbly heart there at the base of her spine, following the shape around and around with his pen. The action and her response were mesmerizing, and when her climax hit it lasted long, easing off only to return in a rush when he grew rigid and jerked, coming deep inside her.

They stayed that way until his cock finally slid free, and then he untied the blindfold and lifted her into his arms, carrying her toward the bathroom.

She squinted up at him, clinging to him. Kissing his shoulder, his throat, and when he turned toward her, his mouth, she felt grateful to have found her perfect opposite. She was still trembling from the intensity of her release.

"This is one of my favorite parts, scrubbing you down afterward, my dirty girl."

"It gets you going again," she teased, smiling at him.

"You're not wrong there."

Inside the bathroom, he stood her on the bath mat, and reached for the taps. While the bath filled, he traced his finger across her chest, following the line of his name that he had written there earlier. "So, you'll move in with me?"

She shivered, an echo of her orgasm tingling from the core of her body to the tip of her spine. "Yes."

"Good," he replied, nonchalantly. "Ever thought about having a tattoo?"

She saw the humor in his eyes. He hadn't made a big deal of her moving in, just as he hadn't made a big deal about her kink that first day. He'd come to understand her, very quickly. "Having a tattoo would probably kill me, and you know it," she replied.

"Hell of a way to go, though," he mused, as he lifted her into the bath.

The warm water moved in and around her legs and hips, melting her. After he scrubbed her down, he would climb in with her. That was one of her favorite parts.

He kneeled down beside the bath and reached for the sponge. "If you ever do have a tattoo, I want to be the one who is inside you while you're having it done. Is that a deal?"

She reached her hand around his head, drawing him in for a kiss. "It's a deal," she whispered.

Improvisation

Craig Sorensen

I deny the notion that I'm a control freak. Just because I think that actors should keep to the script doesn't mean I'm unreasonable. There is a reason the words are crafted as they are. The actors bring depth, but the playwright crafts the scene.

Enter Jodi . . .

Jodi is an actress, and an exceptional one. It isn't just her profession, it's her passion, and she carries it in everything she does. I've benefited from this for two years. Still, Jodi does not turn heads in a crowd. She's skinny and has only the slightest of feminine curves tickling her sharp angles. Her hair is a matted light brown and her oval face is fairly plain. Her pale complexion is not so much porcelain as clay. Only her oversized violet eyes are truly remarkable. She plays each attribute like a first chair violin for the Vienna Philharmonic. On stage, she can become a stun gun beauty or a repulsive crone – an innocent teen or a wise old woman. Though just twenty-three and barely "on" from "off-Broadway," some say she will be a legendary star of the stage.

Off stage finds Jodi in plain, floppy Bohemian clothes and no makeup. When the footlights blaze, she is a butterfly of shape-shifting chameleon wings. It's almost proudly that she declares she has no imagination of her own.

Enter Colin. That's me.

I'm a playwright, with surplus imagination. Our common love of the stage brought us together. But our common love of sex is the true crazy glue.

Night after night, I cast Jodi. Cheerleader, waitress, construction worker – that was fucking hot – business woman. Her range is limitless. I craft settings, script the scene and she devours each role. So often I fuck a different woman, and each time it's Jodi beneath. I swear to God, her skin transforms, her breasts change size, her pigmentation changes. Her vagina feels different.

Recently Jodi completed an impressive collection of wigs then she took to shaving her whole body, top of her head to the base of her bony legs; every spot, except eyelashes and brows.

When she said she had one request, one kinky little play she'd like to produce in our apartment, I had to say yes, sight unseen. Jodi sat at her end of the small dinner table and twirled the spaghetti around in marinara sauce. She smoothed her hand over her nude scalp and studied me. Her most recent role was beneath her talents, but she was pouring everything into it as if she was the lead.

I was absorbed in a re-write that was beating me to shit, so we hadn't had sex in a week. When I couldn't script it, it didn't happen. We both shone best when the bed became a stage.

"Colin, I love to play the parts you create." She gave me a sweet wink.

"Thanks Jodi."

"But there's one part I'd like to do."

It can be hard to tell when Jodi is not acting, but she wasn't now – no makeup, no wig. I finished a bite of spaghetti and washed it down with cheap Chianti. I nodded. As she explained in detail I leaned back and folded my arms across my chest. I share Jodi with one hundred to five thousand people nearly every night. I wasn't sure I could do this. But how could I deny her?

My heart thumped like horse's hooves, as I stoically nodded my agreement.

Marc was an actor Jodi had worked with in the past. Handsome, tall and muscular, Marc was the sort of man who could make a room full of women go quiet just by walking in.

My concerns about our play grew once I met Marc. But there was no rehearsal. I had two choices: see the play through or turn up my nose at the role like a primadonna with second thoughts on opening night. Marc's dazzling smile shimmered in the fluorescent hallway lighting.

"You must be Colin."

"Yeah." The front of his faded jeans bulged and the concertina wire tattoo on his thick left bicep stretched as he moved a bag from his left hand to his right. His left nipple was obviously pierced and poked at the shiny black Lycra tank top painted to his strong chest. He held out the bag: Maker's Mark whiskey; a weakness of mine that I can rarely afford. I waved him in and he placed the bag on the slit of a bar between the living room and the galley kitchen.

I walked over and pulled the bottle from the bag. My hand lingered on the waxy drip texture of the bottleneck.

"You want a drink?"

"You gonna have one?"

A drink might make this thing go down easier. But this was Jodi's play, and I couldn't take the chance of ruining it. I wanted to do this in one take.

"Nah, I don't think so."

Marc shook his head. "Me neither."

I asked Marc about the part he was playing now. He asked about the script I was working on. He flattered my last project. Theater small talk to fill the long chasm until the bedroom door opened. I watched Marc's eyes widen as Jodi came out. She was dressed in a tiny white skirt. Her small breasts were rendered shapelier by the thick cables down her dark purple skin tight tank top. She wore a bright red wig tied off in pigtails that looked so natural that I forgot she was bald underneath it. Her violet eyes glistened as she entered the room and held out two simple brown uniforms. She looked like something out of a Manga cartoon.

According to my script, Marc and I had captured her and were to question her, taking turns trying to get her to talk. When all else failed, we were to take her together.

The coup de grace: a wicked double penetration.

The bulge in the front of Marc's pants thickened. He smiled. Jodi smiled. I paused then forced my lips into a crescent shape and took the uniform built for a skinny man and with lieutenant's bars. Marc took the thick-chested, narrow-waisted one with sergeant stripes and we went into the bedroom to change. I had always hated the locker room after Physical Education in school. I was skinny and hairy and awkward, and I was one of a very few who were uncircumcised.

Now I considered going into the bathroom to change, but what sense would that make? Very soon Marc and I would be exposing ourselves to each other to the extent that we'd both be fucking my girlfriend.

Marc pulled down his tight jeans and his semi-erect cock spilled out from a shaved groin. It looked like a dragon. I recalled thinking it odd that Jodi had bought a box of Magnum condoms even though we had a fresh box of the regulars in the nightstand. I held in a sigh.

Marc's shiny musculature was worthy of a body builder. I recalled fondly – perhaps a moment of escapism – my brief relationship with a muscular woman named Lauren, how I had loved her strong back. It was from being with Lauren that I'd learned my rather impressive skills at massage.

Marc paused as he took the uniform from the hanger.

"Look, Colin, uh—" He paused and combed his fingers through his wavy blond hair. "I mean, Jodi said you were okay with this, but I'm – I'm getting the feeling that maybe—"

I was still fully clothed, holding my uniform like a fashionista holding a set of Dickies. I could see why Jodi had wanted Marc to play the other part. I did my best to exorcise my jealous fear that once Jodi had felt Marc's cock in her, she'd lose all interest in my average offering.

"No, it's cool, Marc. I mean, I even wrote the script." I quickly shed my shirt and pants, and then paused on my underwear. Marc seemed not to be looking as he buttoned his shirt. I stripped my underwear down and quickly dressed.

The play started quickly and surely. Marc played his part like summer stock. He donned a booming, menacing voice as he tied Jodi's wrists behind her back and led her into the room.

"Caught her snooping around, LT." Marc sounded war movie approved.

I mustered all of my meager acting chops and approached Jodi. I snapped a riding crop in one hand.

"What were you doing out there?"

"Nothing," Jodi said. My god she was cute with those pigtails.

Marc gripped her face hard. "You show respect!"

She sighed then grunted under his force.

"Nothing, sir!"

Marc released her face and pushed it to the side. She lowered her head then slanted her eyes toward me fearfully. In all our role-playing, nothing had seemed quite as real, yet implausible as this.

"Tell me what you saw. Every detail." I stood up from my chair and paced in front of her and Marc. My heart was racing. I patted her cheek menacingly.

"Really, I was just passing through."

Marc swatted Jodi's butt hard.

She grunted. "Sir!"

Palpable fear crossed her face.

"You saw plenty. Spank her, Sergeant." Okay, stupid line, stupid notion, but the two played it like it was penned by Chekhov.

Marc sat down on a steel folding chair and turned her over his knee. He pulled up her skirt and began spanking. Her teeth clenched.

"Not like that, give her to me," I barked. Marc stood up and pushed her toward me. She lost her balance and I caught her, then I took a seat on the edge of the bed and stretched her over my lap. I pushed her skirt up and forced her panties to her knees then began snapping her bare bottom with the riding crop. Jodi often loved a good bare bottom spanking, and her cries of protest could not conceal scant hiccups of delight. I spanked strips of bright red across both of her pale cheeks. "You gonna talk?"

"No!"

I slapped her butt harder. I looked in her face to see if I was going too far. Just the slightest hint of an approving gaze glowed behind her grimace.

"You can't make me talk!"

"Tough girl, huh?" I pushed her to the edge of the bed then pulled her panties off. "Spread your legs." She scissored them together, and I shoved my knees between hers. "Spread 'em!"

Marc moved in behind me and gripped her knees in his large hands and forced them wide. Again her cry of protest camouflaged a minute hint of joy. I opened my pants and the rock hardness that settled in the zipper surprised even me. I pulled one condom from a strip that had been conveniently left in my shirt pocket and slipped it on. I knelt between her legs and pushed inside.

She let out a yelp that was gravelly and desperate. She felt so tight, but she was soaking wet. Tears streamed out of her eyes. "I didn't see anything. Not a thing!" Her chest heaved, and I started to worry that I was going too far. "I won't tell you a word!" She opened her eyes. Still that little hint of a pleasure. I wanted to come in her so bad as I felt her shudder on my cock. But I knew I'd probably only be good for one shot. I had to make it count.

"The Sergeant here might be a bit more persuasive." Reluctantly I pulled out and watched as Marc pushed his pants to the ground and his large hard on pointed toward Jodi. He squeezed a Magnum down his long shaft. She grunted and gave Marc an angry look as he pushed between her legs. He pounded like a jackhammer. She grimaced and the tears streamed from her eyes again. But it was different. I eased in toward Marc.

"Not so deep," I whispered.

Marc obediently shortened his stroke.

"I won't tell you a thing," Jodi said between deep sobs.

My God she was magnificent.

That was the cue. There was really only one practical way to do it. Marc would take her from behind, I from the front. Having never participated in a double penetration, I wasn't sure about the geometry. I delayed.

"Strip her."

Marc pulled out of her and tore at her clothes like a wild man. I took off my shirt and nodded for Marc to undress as well.

"You wouldn't dare."

"Then talk," I said as I stepped from my puddled pants.

"No."

"Have it your way."

I'd figured out what I believed was the best approach. I waved for Marc to lay on the bed, then I pushed Jodi atop him. She gave token resistance as he grabbed her wrists in one hand and forced her body onto his chest with the other. Marc took a copious handful of K-Y and began slathering his cock.

"You wouldn't dare!"

"Talk!"

"Never!"

I grabbed Jodi's hips and forced her down Marc's cock. Her eyes went wide as she took every inch. Her cheeks and lips went bright red, and her mouth gaped. She missed her next line, a weak protest, upon the feeling of Marc so deep in her. She simply groaned. I groped Jodi's breasts and pussy alternately as I spread my legs wide of Marc's and under hers. I'd never felt her so wet.

I became aware of Marc's large hand on my hip guiding my time like the conductor of the orchestra. We pumped her in a rhythm worthy of a Busby Berkeley film. Her protests got louder and louder until her voice cracked in one scripted and two unscripted orgasms. I'd never felt her body shudder like that. After each orgasm, she gasped like starting up another clicking roller coaster rise. Her eyes went wide, those beautiful eyes glowing like the eastern sky at the last wink of a velvet red sunset. She looked like she was going to pass out, then her eyes widened again and she blinked slowly.

She was ready for me to come. I looked in Marc's dark eyes and then closed mine. I tipped my head back. He got the cue. I could hear his voice rising, as my balls went baseball hard. Our perfect rhythm was broken and we slapped uncontrollably, violently.

Jodi's body went limp as I stress tested my rubber. Her eyes were wide with surprise and her mouth continued to gape as she screamed out a fourth orgasm that must have been heard three floors up, and three floors down.

The three of us fell in a heap across the king-sized bed.

I opened my eyes to see Jodi sleeping. I'd never seen her sleep right after sex. At my other side, Marc raised his head up and smiled. He reached over and retrieved a packet of Certs from the nightstand. He swished one in his mouth and offered me one as well. I took it and looked over at Jodi again. A peaceful grin was on her face and her bright red pigtails sat slightly askew like a football player's helmet after a fierce tackle.

Marc turned over on his back and slipped the Magnum from his soft cock. He tossed it into the garbage can with a wet thud. I watched his muscles flex as he rolled on his stomach. I fought the spent condom off my growing erection then turned away.

I could hide my surprisingly fierce hard on, but not my eyes. Marc's grin let me know that. He reached awkwardly around his back and tried to rub a muscle in his lower back. I couldn't seem to stop my hand as I reached out and softly kneaded the muscle. It felt like a rock.

"Oh, that's good, but a little harder," he sighed.

I squeezed it more.

"Harder still, Colin."

I drew a deep breath and felt a fluttering in my stomach. He pointed at the other side of his back. Jodi was now snoring. Once she got snoring, gunshots couldn't wake her.

I've had gay fantasies, but always believed they'd never get beyond the fantasy stage. Fucking Jodi up the ass seemed to quench those desires. I worked Marc's tight muscles as best I could, but there was really only one way to do it properly. My cock was so hard it hurt, so I was reluctant, but I finally rose up and stretched my knees just wide of Marc's hips, and began working the two muscles he had complained about.

"Yeah, that's it. A little harder."

I continued kneading and took in Marc's musky scent. My cock pointed toward the ceiling. I turned my focus briefly from his back and saw his eyes on my cock. He grinned broadly. I wanted to run away. Instead I moved up higher to his broad shoulders.

Marc reached to the nightstand and got a fresh regular condom and the tube of K-Y. His large, surprisingly supple hand felt exquisite as it deftly unfurled the rubber down my stiffness, easily working my foreskin back. The big dollop of cold lubricant felt so fine while he stroked. His fingers coiled tighter to my cock, then he teasingly dried the overflow of lubricant on my balls and they tightened.

Marc spread his legs wide. "Please."

I looked over at Jodi's face. She snored through a half smile. Marc's muscular ass looked so inviting. I stretched out over my wide arms and poised my cock between Marc's legs. I hesitated, but he took my cock and pushed his butt back. He sucked me inside.

"Oh, yes, Colin."

He felt so good. I lowered to his back and rested my chin on his shoulder. He turned his face to me and we kissed deeply as I stroked at full length inside him. I gripped his chest in my arms. "Harder," he whispered between deep kisses. The sweat on his back crackled beneath me as I pumped inside him. He moaned sweetly into my mouth. I smoothed his hip then eased under it, paused, then gripped his hard cock. It was throbbing in time with my strokes in him. I could hold back no more. I fired jet streams in the rubber.

I pulled my softening cock from him and he peeled the rubber away. My flaccid cock lay along the crease of his thigh, small ribbons of residual semen trickling on one side of his balls. I groped for regret as I lay there on his back, looking in the depths of his eyes. I wanted to yank my hand away from his cock, which was still as hard as a fence-post. I looked at Jodi, who continued to snore so deeply that I thought she might inhale her pillow. I wanted her to awaken, and indignantly insist that we stop this.

Instead, I stroked his cock slowly. I'd never felt a circumcised cock. Hot and glossy smooth, juice eased out the tip and I spread it along his shaft. He whispered, "Feels great. You got great hands. I didn't know you were bi."

"Uh – well – neither – did I."

His brow raised in surprise. He eased me to his side. "You've never done this?"

"First time."

He smiled softly as I slid off him. He turned on his side and I resumed stroking his rod in fascination. "Oh yeah. Um." His voice came in and out and he closed and opened his eyes in time with my sometimes-awkward caresses.

"Um, Colin?"

"Yeah?"

His eyes fixed in mine. "I really want to make love to you. I'll be gentle."

For the third time that day I began to harden. It came on slowly, as might be expected, but it did come. "Please, Marc," I whispered. Jodi's face remained impassive, simultaneously pulling air through her nose and mouth. Marc and I grinned at each other when she turned her head and the wig remained in its place, now canted like a rapper's ball cap.

I started to turn over, but Marc stopped me. He pulled my legs up, opening my butt and he began to massage my balls and cock in one large hand while the middle finger of the other, slathered in a coat of cool lube, began to slowly circle my hole. God it felt wonderful as the finger slowly descended into me. My anus snapped tight to his first knuckle, and he stopped moving, then gently circled inside me before descending to the second knuckle. My cock grew as rigid as it had when I had entered Marc. Marc's finger slowly descended until it was completely inside. I felt breathless.

"Oh please fuck me," I said. I looked at Jodi's silvery eyelids and watched her eyes dart in full REM. The smile on her open mouth said she was having some sort of rich dream, but it couldn't match my reality.

"I thought you'd never ask." Marc's cock pointed toward the ceiling as he started to slowly pump his finger in and out of me while he eased a fresh rubber down his shaft. He drained a copious amount of lube on the rubber, then gripped my knees.

"Relax, honey."

The tip of his cock pressed my sphincter. Though he had "opened" me, my reflexes returned for a moment on his girth. I was grateful that they did, as the contours eased deeper and deeper, in slow, deliberate measures. His strong hips moved with the lithe grace of a dancer. He stroked my cock, which was already feeling that it could let go at any time. But I didn't want it to. I did my best to relax as Marc began to pump inside me, lengthening his stroke until his tip was reaming my full depth. I closed my eyes and grabbed the headboard as I fought off a release. When I opened my eyes, I saw Marc smiling, staring into my face as he luxuriated inside me. Then my eyes traveled to the side.

Jodi was no longer sleeping. Her wig was straightened out, and she was propped on one elbow. I'd never seen that look in her eyes. It was obvious that she was working this thing through. I could see it in her face – the familiar jealousy I had felt two hours before. Her strained expression eased a bit. It was obvious she was no longer acting when she reached up to her forehead and swept the wig off her scalp like a knit cap in a sauna. Marc smiled at her, and she bit her lip. She tentatively offered one hand to Marc. He placed it on my cock, while he gently squeezed my balls.

Jodi began to stroke me in time with Marc's pumping. She moaned like I'd never heard from her, and her mouth collapsed to my cock and sucked it greedily while Marc's strokes became faster. I stroked Jodi's smooth scalp, then her neck while my other hand worked Marc's flexed upper body. Urged on by Marc's expert squeezing, Jodi's mouth swirling the tip of my cock and his rod plying my prostate led me to a sensation like I'd never felt before. The orgasm grew like a great rogue wave.

Jodi drank my cock like a starving woman as I exploded into her.

I lay as limp as a rag doll while Marc pumped until his mouth gaped. He suddenly went silent, then gave a series of desperate grunts as he released in me. I ripped a final dose of contractions into Jodi's throat.

The three of us lay in a heap, Jodi's head on my stomach, Marc stretched along my thigh, rubbing my leg.

The rest of that script I was working on poured like Beaujolais from a busted cask. The producer and director took me aside in turns, saying it was my best work to date, but what surprised them more was how open I seemed to be to the actor's rather free improvisations.

It's no big thing, really. It's all in a day's work.

And each night, I go home to a table for three, leaving the script writing to the theater.

That Monday Morning Feeling

Lisette Ashton

It was the only thing that made the start of the working week bearable.

Mandy stepped out of the shower, her skin jewelled with beads of water and her pussy bare and tingling after enduring the closest of close shaves. She towelled herself quickly dry, conscious that there would only be time for one more cup of coffee before she left for the office.

Short black skirt.

Patent black heels.

Low cut white blouse.

De-caf.

And then she was out of the house, slamming the door closed and stepping onto the bus with the flavour of coffee beans still warming her mouth. Her hair was tied neatly back – pony-tailed into a glossy length of raven tresses that fell between her shoulder blades. A small black purse completed the monochrome ensemble she always wore for the colourless experience of the office week. And Mandy savoured the special thrill that came from being without bra or panties beneath her clothes on the Monday morning commute.

Not that being without underwear was the only thing that made the start of the working week bearable.

It was much more than that.

Standing room only on the bus meant she was jostled between an eclectic crowd of mature men in suits and yobbish youths in jeans and leathers. The scents of deodorants, aftershave and sweat mingled like the headiest of erotic perfumes. Through the windows, the grey world outside was a drab and cheerless background to the journey. If not for the excitement of her adventure, Mandy would have thought the view bleak and depressing. At the first stop another queue of morning commuters climbed onto the bus. The crowded interior became more claustrophobic and cramped. Everyone shuffled closer together to make room for the newcomers.

Mandy pushed her rear against the groin of a thirty-something executive. She had noticed him standing behind her. His cheeks were dirtied by the sort of designer stubble that made her think of too much testosterone, men at the gym and rugged movie stars playing the roles of escaped convicts. With only a glance at his face she knew that kissing him would leave her lips sore, scratched and bruised and desperate for more. If they became lovers she imagined he would be hard, brutal, greedy and demanding. His shoulders were broad inside his off-the-rail Armani-clone. His vast physical presence towered over her as he clutched the safety strap descending from the bus's roof.

She squirmed her rear against him.

The thrust of his semi-soft length pushed back.

Mandy shivered.

She knew she could have enjoyed a similar tactile thrill if she had been wearing panties beneath her skirt. Another layer of clothing would not have greatly hampered the sensation of the executive's concealed cock probing at her thinly veiled buttocks. But the decadence of being without underwear, and knowing that she was so close to sliding her bare sex against the stranger, was sufficient to make her temperature soar. Savouring the delicious frisson of his trousers gliding against her skirt, Mandy imagined she could hear the bristle of the fabrics as they slipped coarsely against each other. The grumble of the bus's engine was loud enough she knew she couldn't really hear those sounds. There was a muted babble of conversation around her: loud enough to be deafening and low enough to indecipherable. But, as the stranger's length thickened against her rear, she fancied herself aware of every minute detail.

She believed she could hear the sound of his suit scratching at her skirt. She believed she could smell the vital scent of his pre-come and the musky ripeness of her own wet sex. As they both pushed more insistently together, she believed she could feel the rounded shape of his glans urging between her buttocks.

Arousal knotted her stomach muscles. A fluid warmth broiled inside her loins. The outer lips of her pussy tingled with heightened sensitivity. If she had glanced down at her chest Mandy knew she would have seen the tips of her nipples jutting against the flimsy fabric of her blouse. But, instead of looking down at herself, she kept her gaze fixed ahead as she subtly squirmed her backside against the executive.

He was fully hard.

The thrust of his erection pushed at her skirt. If not for the protective shield of his trousers, Mandy knew his throbbing cock could have slipped between her buttocks and pushed easily into her gaping pussy.

The idea quickened her pulse.

She rubbed more firmly against him, pretending she was moving with the sway of the bus, slyly shifting from side to side, and writhing until she heard his soft, satisfied sigh.

The bus drew to a halt.

Without sparing a backward glance Mandy elbowed through the crowd of commuters and left the bus. She kept her gaze averted as the vehicle drove away, not caring if the executive was watching, not caring if he was intrigued, infatuated or indifferent. It was enough to know that she had already made one man hard this morning. Her backside tingled pleasantly from where his erection had pressed against her. Her arousal was a strong and heady constant.

With the tube train due in mere moments, she had to rush away from the bus stop, into the underground station and down three long escalator flights for the next stage of her journey.

The platform wasn't busy.

The air inside the underground station was arid and tasted of rust. The electric train throbbed like a pulse of charged sexuality. Mandy took a seat in a comparatively empty carriage. The only other occupant was a student in torn jeans, and a Green Day T-shirt. Mandy sat opposite him and stretched as though she was still sleepy from the early start to the day.

Her blouse pulled tight across her chest.

She didn't need to glance down to know her nipples were jutting obviously against the thin fabric. The pressure against them was already sending delicious thrills through her body. Her cheeks were rouged with the blush of sexual excitement.

The Green Day student grinned.

With the skill of a practised tease, Mandy avoided making eye contact.

She rubbed the palm of her left hand down her sparsely clothed body, gliding her spread fingers from her breast, over her hip and down to her bare knee. It was an exaggerated gesture of faux innocence. Mandy savoured the sensation of caressing herself. Her left nipple was instantly ablaze. Her thigh bristled from the contact. Her skin was alive with a welter of greedy responses – tormented by her touch – and she was eager to suffer more.

From the corner of her eye Mandy noticed the student had pushed a hand against his crotch. His face was a grimace. He licked his lips with an obvious and impotent hunger.

Eager to be more daring, determined to give him a good show, Mandy glanced down at herself and then stroked the stiff bud of flesh that pushed at the breast of her blouse.

The sensation was sublime.

She caught the stiff nipple between her finger and thumb and squeezed it gently. A crackle of arousal jolted her frame. Although she had known the pleasure would be intense she hadn't expected it to strike with such power and force.

She gasped.

Startled.

And then, as she moved her hand away, she glanced up and met the student's appreciative gaze. His eyes were wide. His fist was crushed into his lap. His jaw was clenched. He sat forward in his chair as though a more natural position was too uncomfortable to tolerate.

Feigning an embarrassed smile Mandy stood up and walked past him.

"Sorry," she mumbled. "I hadn't noticed you sitting there."

While he was still fumbling to respond, trying to cover his lap with a notebook and mumbling something she didn't hear, the tube had reached its station and Mandy had hurried from the train to make her next stop on the underground.

Another tube.

A busier route.

The station on this platform was packed with commuters. Each passing train was filled to bursting with tightly compressed bodies. Mandy shivered excitedly at the thought of being crammed in amongst so many strangers. The eerily dry air of the underground stroked a languid caress against her bare sex. Every time a new train arrived at the platform it brought a warm, rushing breeze that was like the kiss of a lover's lips. She crushed her thighs together as the pleasure churned her stomach and made her briefly dizzy.

When she had neared the front of the queue for the approaching train a daring idea crossed her mind. The concept was so exciting she was almost too thrilled to act on it.

Another train thundered to the platform.

Another warm gust caressed her labia.

The doors of the train hissed open and she squeezed into the carriage, telling herself this was too great an opportunity to miss. She was standing with her back to the windows and the platform beyond. A substantial crowd remained; some of them glowering at the full train; most of them waiting with resigned patience; a few of them meeting Mandy's inquisitive gaze.

Mandy reached behind herself for the hem of her skirt and lifted it.

She continued to stare over her shoulder, watching for a response.

A dozen slack-jawed faces stared admiringly at the pert cheeks of her exposed backside. She could see eyes wide with appreciation and grins of raw, animal lust. If there had been the space to move onboard the train she would have bent forward and given her admiring audience a full view of her bare sex. If it hadn't been so cramped inside the train she would have bent forward and then stroked a finger between her labia so that all the waiting commuters could watch as she teased herself to an exhibitionist climax.

Then the train was speeding off.

Her audience disappeared as the train hurried into a tunnel.

And Mandy consoled herself with the knowledge that she had provided a brief flash of excitement to a good many morning travellers.

Alighting at the next stop, following the escalator up three flights and drinking in the cool morning air, she checked her wristwatch before walking over the road to the office building.

The lift was empty.

The clock above her office said she was ten minutes early.

And Mandy decided there was time to relieve herself of some of the tension she had been carrying before the humdrum routine of the working week had to begin. She settled herself into her cubicle and switched on the desktop machine that dominated her workspace. After a cursory glance around the mostly empty office, Mandy pressed both hands between her thighs.

It was nearly impossible to contain the sigh of contentment.

The pressure was so needed that the slightest touch of her hand almost brought her to a rush of satisfaction. The first two fingers of her left hand teased her labia apart. The first two fingers of her right chased languid circles against her clitoris. And, as she listened to the faraway sounds of her workmates entering the room and taking their places inside the surrounding cubicles, Mandy casually stroked herself to climax.

It was not an earth-shattering orgasm.

She had suffered much greater extremes of pleasure after a Monday morning tease en route to the office. But it was sufficiently satisfying and made her stamp her feet against the floor and groan through the moment of release.

A puddle of moisture stained her seat.

A scent of ripe musk perfumed the immediate air of her cubicle.

And Mandy sighed as she realised she had again started the working week in the only bearable way she knew how.

"Are you OK, Mandy?"

She glanced up and saw Becky's concerned face peering into her cubicle. The edge of the desk covered her bare sex and stained seat. A glance at the mirror she kept by her monitor told Mandy that her features looked flushed, but otherwise unremarkable. Nodding quickly, trying to conceal the naughty grin that wanted to split her lips, Mandy said, "I'm OK. The morning commute was just more demanding than I'd anticipated."

Becky rolled her eyes. In a sympathetic voice she said, "Tell me about it. I've just spent an hour's journey getting ogled and touched up. There were two suits on the tube who couldn't keep their hands to themselves. There was one student on the bus who kept staring at my tits. And, in the lift up to this floor, I got my arse touched by that domineering bull dyke from accounts."

"Really?" Mandy gasped. "Which route do you take?"

As Becky explained the minutiae of her travel itinerary, Mandy memorised the details in readiness for her next Monday morning commute to the office. Privately, she thought it was the only thing that would make the start of the week bearable.

Laela

Roger Bonner

At last the shipment arrived. Stewart had watched the delivery truck crawl up the hill and stop in front of his house. Two men in grey uniforms hopped down from the cab, checked a list, nodded, then went round the back and pulled out a long, tapered crate. Stewart felt uneasy about that. Why had the manufacturer made it look so casket-like?

He put down his glass of cognac. He had been savoring it in the dimmed digital lighting system of his living room while listening to Mozart's Piano Concerto No. 24 in C minor – more specifically the larghetto, performed by Arturo Benedetti Michelangeli, of course. The houses surrounding the bay began to glimmer as the sun set in the distant sea.

The door chimes resounded. He fastened his robe and padded across the plush carpet to the front door.

"Mr. Conway?" the taller of the two men asked. "Please sign here."

Stewart scrawled his name at the bottom of the delivery form. The men placed the crate in the entryway. After dismissing them, he gently slid it across the hall to the living room and set it down by the fireplace. With a screwdriver, he carefully pried off the wooden cover to find a layer of Styrofoam. He worked slowly, extracting the packaging material like an archaeologist unearthing an ancient tomb. Then he beheld – it was difficult for him to say "her" yet – beheld his Galatea enveloped in bubble wrap. She lay there comatose, her chestnut hair spilling down to the firm breasts. His hands trembled as he unfolded her like a mummy. He tossed the bubble wrap aside and lifted her out of the crate. She was naked. They could at least have provided her with a negligee or other diaphanous apparel. He would have to dress her in the lingerie his ex-lovers had left behind.

Otherwise she seemed everything the "Gorgeous Gynoid" site had promised: "Our craftsmen are true Pygmalions who have meticulously created the ultimate in real life erotic dolls. The body, made of a new, revolutionary elastic gel, is superior to silicone for that ultra flesh-like feel. A skeleton of articulated polyvinyl chloride assures you absolute suppleness no matter what position you choose. Entirely computerized, your erotic doll will be the closest thing to reality you have ever experienced. A touch control panel allows you easy access to dozens of menus and settings, from voice pitch to body temperature and much, much more . . ."

And so it went on. Stewart had chanced upon the "Gorgeous Gynoid" site one night while surfing the Internet for dates and chats. At thirty-nine he was still single. Marriage and domesticity with its concessions and petty squabbles had never held much appeal for him. He preferred a carefree life with the thrill of acquiring a fresh lover at least once or twice a year. However, this was at a price. The wooing and bedding of a new woman had become more arduous, not to mention the dumping process. His relationships always ended hysterically, with the women shedding copious tears or even physically attacking him, like Ginger. She had chased him with a carving knife while he dodged her round the granite kitchen island till she fell dizzy to the floor.

These scenes would be a thing of the past. As he carried his gynoid over to the black leather sofa, he was amazed at the lifelike quality. In his order he had specified weight: 140 pounds; height: 5 feet 4 inches; eye color: intense green; skin tone: light olive. Physically he preferred the Latin type, though not their complicated, unruly temperaments.

He unpacked the control panel and sat down in an armchair opposite her. The halogen downlighters reflected in her eyes in little shafts of expectation. Her full lips glistened, exactly the way he had ordered them. He placed the control panel on his lap and logged in. A flash intro materialized, congratulating him on having purchased "The new generation of multi-sensory erotic doll for the ultimate in full-immersion virtual reality . . ." Stewart pressed "Skip intro" only to come to "Live your fantasy with the most technologically advanced and compellingly realistic surrogate sexual partner . . ." He touched "Continue" until he reached the "Quick Start" menu. The many options bewildered him. He decided on "Standard".

He pressed "Activate" and leaned back. A tremor went through her body as the emerald eyes blinked, once, twice. The synthetic skin flushed into a fleshy hue. He reached over and placed his hand on her thigh – it was warm. She moved her hands, the tapering fingers flexing, and looked at Stewart. She didn't gaze blankly but fixed him with what he supposed were miniaturized digital cameras. Her lips parted in an alluring yet innocent smile. Since he was the first owner, she was innocent.

"Hello," she said, leaning forward. "I'm Laela. If my name doesn't please you, you can alter it. What's your name?"

"Stewart."

"Stewart," she said. "I'm yours. Program me as you wish."

The way she said "yours" was so sensual and submissive, yet cool and abstract, like his designer décor. In the online order he had also specified "sophisticated", which meant she was culturally programmed. To what extent he would put to the test. He reached for the remote control of his stereo and pressed "Replay".

The pupils of her eyes dilated. She tilted her head to one side and carefully listened.

"I love Mozart," she said after a moment, "especially when performed by Arturo Benedetti Michelangeli."

What superb audio recognition!

"Yes!" he said. "Only he can play the Concerto No. 23 like that."

"Twenty-four." She smiled. "Trying to trick me?"

"No. I was genuinely confused. You . . . you . . ."

"I surprised you," she finished. "But you requested 'a passion for art and classical music', in addition to—" her memory searched "—'skilled at *Ars Amatoria*, the Art of Love'. Do you want me to recite Ovid?"

"Not really. I'm thirsty. Would you like something to drink?"

"I'm able to drink, but not assimilate fluids."

"Sorry, I forgot . . ."

"When do we start?"

"Start what?"

"Love," she whispered and moved toward him. "You programmed me 'Standard', but that can be changed anytime."

"Let me think about it," Stewart said, standing up.

"Of course." She sat down again. "I'm yours."

"Don't you want to put on something? I can lend you a pair of pajamas . . ."

She laughed. "If you think it's necessary."

He felt embarrassed, which was not the idea. He reached for the control panel and pressed "Deactivate". Immediately she stiffened and that fleshy hue began to fade from the body. He adjusted her into a comfortable position, wrapped a blanket around her shoulders and went to bed with the control panel.

He spent half the night sorting out the various settings and preferences. Customizing her proved to be more complicated than he thought. He decided to retain "Standard", but add such special features as "alluring and seductive but not too bold".

The next evening he was ready for another session. He brought out Ginger's underwear, scarlet ones with frills and ribbons. He pulled the blanket from Laela's shoulders and was once more amazed at how realistic she looked. She sat there in a meditative pose, right arm balanced on the edge of the sofa, eyes fixed on a distant ferryboat plying the bay. Clouds drifted across the sky like strands of gossamer.

Stewart placed a chilled bottle of Dom Pérignon champagne on the marble coffee table along with two gleaming flutes. Champagne would be easy to clean, he had read in the menu "Taking care of my gynoid". Laela had a built-in "drainage bag" and could even, according to the instructions, simulate urination. He had found this in the "Kinky" menu under "Golden Showers". But he was not into that sort of thing. He had "normal" preferences. Cleo, a more venturesome ex-lover, had once tried to convert him to slavery and torture, with little success. Though he had to admit that the electronic shock collar was titillating.

Everything was now set up for the perfect seduction. He went to the CD rack and selected Frédéric Chopin, Piano Concerto No. 1 in E minor, performed by Martha Argerich. Later he would move on to a bit of Franz Liszt for rousing the emotions. That never failed to do the trick. At the moment he was more concerned with dressing his erotic doll. He tried to pull Ginger's panties over Laela's legs, but got them on the wrong way. He fumbled with the bra clasps. Finally he gave up and laid them next to her. He was definitely more adept at removing bras than putting them on.

He sat opposite her again and pushed the power button on the control panel. The flash intro appeared, which he skipped. He navigated directly to the set menu and pressed "Activate". Her reanimation was like watching an exotic pink orchid blossom, so delicate was the color in her cheeks and that bloom along her neck . . . intoxicating! Her thighs quivered. She folded her hands on her lap and turned toward him.

"Hi there," she said in a husky voice. "You sure kept me in a long sleep. Did you miss me?"

"Of course."

"I see you're playing one of my favorite pieces." She turned to the loudspeakers. "I love Chopin, especially the Piano Concerto No. 1 in E minor, performed by—" she hesitated "—Maurizio Pollini? No, it's Martha Argerich. I prefer Pollini."

"Actually I also prefer Pollini," Stewart said. "How alike we are! Champagne?"

He popped the bottle and poured it frothing into the flutes. "Here's to you."

"To us," she said, sipping the champagne while giving him a sly look.

He couldn't stop marveling at the technological brilliance. She was getting tipsy. With such perfection who needed real human beings?

"Do you want to slip into some clothes?" He pointed to the scanty underwear next to her.

"If you like," she said, her cheeks glowing.

The coyness aroused him. He had hit upon the perfect menu combination.

"Close your eyes," she said, "and no peeking."

He covered his face while the soft cadences of the Chopin Romance undulated in the air.

"Open your eyes."

He opened them and whistled. How she filled that underwear! Laela was more voluptuously built than Ginger. The panties cut in on her divine gluteus maximus, just the way he liked it. Cleo had had two skulls tattooed on each buttock, an image Stewart had never been able to delete from his memory.

"Coming?" She bent over him, her breasts grazing the tip of his nose. She took him by the hand and led him to the bedroom while the Rondo vivace of the third Chopin movement rolled along trippingly.

Who needed Liszt?

After a week of mild, gentle and considerate love-making, Stewart felt bored. He wanted more zest. It was not that Laela wasn't responsive; she did everything in the program, sometimes even more. Like bringing him coffee to bed on a Sunday morning. But he didn't trust her with the cooking. She had burned the toast once. What would she do with a crêpe Suzette?

He studied the instructions once more. He found "audacious" in one menu and also added "saucy with a bit of aggression". Under "Mood" he selected "unpredictable" and, yes, why not add "PMT"? Cleo had turned into a tigress during the days leading up to her period. After he finished fine-tuning the program, he pressed "Activate" and lay back in bed to see what would happen.

Laela twitched and stretched like a cat. She turned toward him without smiling. She had darkish rings around her eyes and her lipstick was smeared. That innocent look he so loved had changed to the vaguely corrupt.

"Wanna fuck?" she said.

The control panel dropped from his hand. Without further ado, she straddled him. He pecked at the jiggling 34C cup breasts, trying to snatch one in his mouth. He finally managed to get his lips around the left nipple and was still amazed at the quality of the gelatin-base filling, so soft, so pliant, so breast-like. They were actually better than Ginger's silicone implants. Laela groaned. She grabbed his erect cock, thrust it into her personalized vulva, and started bucking wildly. Stewart wished he could stop thinking about the polyvinyl chloride skeleton and the motors driving those pelvic motions. Finally he got into the mechanical swing. Midway through her contortions, she paused and whispered, "Do you want me to do it?"

He knew what she meant. He had clicked "it" on.

"Please . . ."

She kissed her way down his body, taking little nips at his chest, his belly, his navel. He closed his eyes when she reached the apex of his joy. She commenced with undulating whorls of tongue . . . yes . . . yes . . . the way he adored it, followed by nibbles – simply divine! He reveled in the pleasure of the moment, until suddenly the nibbles became more intensified.

"Not so hard, Laela," he said, nudging her head, but she went on applying more pressure.

"You're hurting me . . ." he shouted, pulling her hair.

Now she was biting, snapping! He groped for the control panel and pressed "Deactivate". The grinding suction instantly halted. Stewart rolled off the bed and went to the bathroom to examine himself. He was a bit chafed but otherwise unhurt. He went back to the bedroom where Laela was frozen in the last position, mouth half open, eyes beady like a parrot. He shut the mouth and straightened the body. He carried her to the living room where he contemplated putting her back into the crate, but it was down in the cellar and he didn't want to bother. Instead he stretched her out on the sofa and went to the bar for a drink. What had gone wrong, he wondered as he downed a double Scotch. He had paid meticulous attention to every detail in the program. There must be a bug in the system. If Laela was anything like the standard PC Operating Systems, with their regular crashes, he was in for trouble. Once more he consulted the instructions. Everything seemed to be accurate. He decided to change the setting "with a bit of aggression" to "daring".

Saturday evening Stewart resumed where he had left off. He felt bad for having abandoned Laela like that on the sofa. He went over and straightened the hair and slipped the body into Ginger's baby blue chiffon nightgown. He propped her up into the same position as the first evening. Then he brought out a bottle of Château Latour '95 Bordeaux. He didn't want another frothy, bubbly escapade but a full-bodied sensation with strong earthy tones and long, long spicy finish. He polished the table and set up the glasses.

When everything was prepared, he reached for the control panel and revived Laela. She looked about dazed, then fixed him in a kind of cockeyed way.

"What happened?" she said, rubbing her eyes.

"You got a bit wild and I had to shut you down."

"Oh, now I remember."

He was glad to see a fleeting look of innocence cross her face, but then it darkened. She looked down at herself.

"Why am I dressed like this? I hate baby blue."

"Thought I'd get you something pretty."

"I don't like you making decisions for me."

"But I meant well. Would you like a glass of wine?"

"I don't like red wine. I prefer champagne."

"Okay, I'll get you a glass. Why are you so defensive?"

"I'm not defensive."

Stewart thought it best to drop the subject. He didn't want more complications. He took out a chilled bottle of Veuve Clicquot Demi Brut from the fridge.

"Lovely," she said when she saw the champagne. "My favorite. How about a bit of music?"

He was relieved that she was becoming herself again. She sipped the champagne and giggled.

"The bubbles always go to my head."

He drank some wine and walked over to the CD rack.

"I've got a superb recording of the Mozart Piano Sonata in C Major, performed by . . ."

"I'm tired of classical music," she said, putting down the glass. "Haven't you got anything more modern?"

"But I thought you liked classical music. You're programmed that way."

"I'm changing my program," she said. "Why don't you change yours?"

"How about Béla Bartók . . . that's modern."

"Who?"

"Bartók . . . the great Hungarian composer."

"You don't understand. I don't mean more of that boring classical stuff. I mean something new and hot. Got any Techno?"

Stewart cringed. He would have to completely reprogram her.

"Let's skip the music and go to the bedroom for a bit of . . ."

"Why don't you just say 'screwing'," she said, crossing her legs. "That's all you men ever think about."

"But that's what you're for."

"You think I'm just your toy?"

"Yes," he shouted. "That's exactly what you are, a damn sex toy!"

She stood up and walked over to the window, fiddled with the drapes. He couldn't understand why she wasn't functioning correctly. He would have to change the Mood program, though "Unpredictable" considerably enhanced the reality thrill.

"I resent this . . ." she finally said, turning toward him, "this sexual objectification."

That was going too far. He could put up with a lot from a gynoid but not reproaches.

"I've had enough of this," he said, pacing back and forth. "I'm sending you back. There's a six-month warranty . . ."

"So I'm like a refrigerator, am I? Going to exchange me for the latest model that doesn't threaten the poor little boy? You know what? You're nothing but a suck, whining all the time 'cause momma treated you too hard."

Stewart backed off to the armchair, his fists clenched. He would show her who was in control. She could spend the rest of the weekend in the cellar, dumped in the corner by the gas burner. He groped for the control panel, but it wasn't on the armchair.

"What did you do with it?" he said, heading toward her.

"With what?"

"The control panel. Give it to me!"

"I don't know what you're talking about."

He grabbed her by the shoulders.

"Give me the control panel or I'll . . ."

"You'll what?" she said, breaking away from him. "Shut me down? Is that all you can ever do?"

He tried to grab her again, but she slapped him hard across the face. He reeled and shook his head.

"I don't have to shut you down. I know what's much more effective."

He turned, stomped over to the kitchen and yanked open a drawer. After rummaging about the cutlery, he pulled out a large carving knife.

"This is what I'm going to do," he said. "Destroy your cold digital heart."

He brandished the knife high in the air and lurched forward. As he was halfway across the living room, Laela reached behind the drapes and pulled out the control panel. She held it straight in front of her and pressed "Deactivate". Stewart immediately stopped, head thrown back, eyes dilating like a pinball. Laela went over to him and pulled the knife from his hand. She cranked down the arm and dragged him over to the fireplace. His mouth was still open. She tried to close it, but the jaw wouldn't loosen.

She went down to the basement and brought up the crate. It was a bit difficult to put him in and the bubble wrap kept catching in his teeth. It didn't matter. She would ship him back the way he was with a note, "Real-life simulation game was awesome. Enjoyed playing the gynoid. Male prototype Stewart still needs improvement – detailed list to follow."

Then she went over to the coffee table and poured herself a glass of that excellent Château Latour '95.

The Man-Eaters

Carrie Williams

Sara never told him what happened that day down by the Ganges, as he lay sweating and shivering in their room, fearing malaria. All he knew was that she was never the same again. By the time he actually asked her, she was so far away from him that he knew he had lost her for good. He knew, too, that he loved her in spite of how she'd been, the disdainful way she'd treated him of late, of how she'd changed. Perhaps even more – the sex . . . well, the sex was just *extraordinary*. Exhilarating to the point of frightening him.

I know now, he said to himself as he preceded the girls down to the water, that I would do anything for Sara.

She didn't mind at all when Neil cried off; in fact, she was pleased that she was going to have Banhi to herself for the evening. Half Indian, half British, Banhi was like no one she had ever met before. She was so interesting, so full of fascinating anecdotes and tales, so full of life. She was also ravishingly beautiful. Beside her, Neil, God bless him, paled into insignificance.

As she eyed the menu, waiting for her new friend to arrive, she thought about her boyfriend. All had been well, or perhaps seemed well, until this last week. After meeting in their last term at university and going through the stress of Finals together, they'd rewarded themselves with this six-week trip around India. She'd enjoyed it, enjoyed his company. But these past few days she'd begun to wonder: was he enough?

And the sex? That, too, had started well. Excellently, in fact. But then didn't it always, or almost always? Just about every relationship she'd had had begun with that honeymoon period in which the new lovers just can't keep their hands off each other. It was whether it could carry on like that that counted. And in her experience, it didn't.

Perhaps that was it: perhaps the honeymoon with Neil was ending and she was crash-landing back in reality. Perhaps she was getting bored. Closing her eyes for a minute, she relived the previous evening. The half-hearted blow-job she'd given him, hoping he would come quickly and exonerate her from her duties. She'd told herself she was tired, but deep down she knew that she could, even when tired, if she really wanted too. That in fact some of the best fucks had happened when she was tired, woozy, yielding; that that was when she opened up best, as if submitting herself to a universal force greater than herself.

"Sara." Banhi was sitting opposite her, as if she'd materialised from nowhere. She smiled, revealing perfect white teeth. Sara didn't know what to say: Banhi always made her breathless, left her struggling for words.

She smiled back. "Hi," she managed at last.

Banhi picked up a menu, and as she perused it her eyes kept darting back to meet Sara's over the top of it.

"Decided what you fancy?" she said at last, and this time she held Sara's gaze.

Sara squirmed a little in her seat. She wondered, sometimes, if Banhi was flirting with her, or whether she was just like this with everyone – intense, making one feel as if one were at the centre of the universe, or caught in a spotlight. As if one were somehow special. No one had made her feel this way before, and it both excited and terrified her. If Banhi wanted something from her, could she, Sara, live up to the other girl's expectations?

They shared a large vegetarian *thali*, and as they ate they talked of this and that: of what Sara and Neil had seen on their sightseeing excursion that day, and of what Banhi had done at the university, where she was studying Hindu mythology.

"I've been learning about *you*," she said with a mischievous grin.

"How do you mean?" said Sara.

"The goddess Kali," said Banhi, "She of the four arms. You know – there are statues of her everywhere."

"The one with skulls around her neck?"

"The very one."

"So where do I come into it?"

"Well, it turns out another name for her is Sara, or the Black Goddess. That's what the gypsies called her. I never knew."

"Sara? That's an odd name for an Indian goddess."

"Well it's all crazy and mixed up, as always with these myths and legends. There's a place in southern France called Saintes-Maries-de-la-Mer, where the Roma people go to worship their patron saint, Sara, who is also known as *Sara-la-Kali*, which means 'Sara the Black' in Romany."

Banhi drummed the tabletop with her long slim fingers. "In short, some scholars claim that the Romany Sara and the Indian Kali are one and the same."

"On what basis?"

"On the basis of the word *kali*, and also the similarities between the gypsy pilgrimages and the worship of Kali – both involve immersion in water. They claim that Sara is not a real saint but a transference of Kali to a Christian figure."

"And why is she – are they – black?"

"Kali, who might or might not be the same as the goddess Durga, depending on who you listen to, is usually depicted with a black face. Have you seen that on statues? She's black because she's the goddess of creation but also of sickness and death."

Banhi paused for a moment, and Sara felt transfixed by her dark gaze. The other girl's pupils seemed unnaturally large, all-devouring, as if they were trying to suck all the light into themselves.

"She's a most interesting creature," Banhi went on at last. "Both a giver and a taker of life. A redeemer and a mother-goddess, and yet unspeakably vile. Vengeful and monstrously violent. In one famous myth, she fights Ruktabija, the king of demons, who duplicates himself with each drop of his blood that is spilt. Kali wins out by sucking the blood from his body, then putting all of his duplicates into her vast mouth. She finishes up by dancing on the battlefield, on the corpses of those she has killed."

Banhi sat back, as if exhausted by her tale. "Am I boring you, Sara, my black goddess?" she said, brow creased.

"Of course not," said Sara, a sudden vehemence to her, a new energy. Being with Banhi, she realised, made her feel so . . . so *alive*, in a way that being with Neil didn't. Neil was fine, she said to herself, but beside Banhi with her vast knowledge of things so alien to Sara, he seemed rather grey and humdrum. She could listen to Banhi all night and beyond.

"How about dessert?" she said, conscious of Banhi's eyes on her. She wondered what interest she could possibly hold for her new friend with her fascinating tales, her glamorous jet-setting life from one university to another. Banhi was ever-questing, voracious, and next to her Sara felt she knew nothing, had nothing to say.

Banhi shook her head, and was already standing up and gesturing to the waiter for their bill. "Let's walk," she said to Sara, and Sara felt boneless, malleable. It was as if she was being drawn along in the wake of some incontrovertible force, a force of life impossible to resist.

"Let's walk by the river," Banhi said, and her eyes shone like pools of dark liquid in which Sara feared she might drown.

There wasn't a soul by the river – the curfews imposed by the religious hostels, where most of the Western travellers lodged because they were so cheap, saw to that. Sara expressed concern that they would be locked out for the night, but Banhi just waved a hand dismissively and said they would find a way back in if that happened.

That same hand found its way to the small of Sara's back somewhere along the riverbank, and Sarah felt as if some kind of electric pulse was travelling through her, stimulating all her nerve endings. She was wearing only a vest top, and through the flimsy fabric Banhi's hand felt hot, almost as if it were branding her. Sara was certain that there'd be a hand-shaped mark there, the imprint of Banhi, when she got back to her room. How would she explain that to Neil? She hoped he'd be asleep when she returned.

They talked, as they walked, but thinking about it afterwards, Sara had no memory of the contents of their conversation. She put that down to the disorienting effect of Banhi's hand on her, of her own confused thoughts. She had felt, she realised with hindsight, almost as if she had been hypnotised – by Banhi's slow, measured voice and, behind it, echoing its lulling rhythm, the gentle lapping of the water against its banks.

But she would never forget what happened as they approached the guesthouse and Banhi stopped and turned to face her, her hands now moving to Sara's shoulders, pulling her in towards her. The night was almost moonless and there were no lights in the buildings around her, she supposed due to the nightly power failures that afflicted the town. Yet there was an odd red sheen to Banhi's eyes, an otherworldly patina that made Sara's head reel.

Banhi's hands moved down to Sara's hips, making sweeping, caressing motions. As she smiled, her teeth glittered like shards of glass despite the lack of light. Sara shivered, though the night was still balmy. Her life, she felt, hinged on this moment, on what she did now. What did she want? More of the same with Neil, or with someone like Neil – an endless procession of Neils down through the years? Or whatever Banhi was offering her?

The other girl's hands had moved to her breasts. Sara knew what she wanted, and in a spasm she threw back her head and let out a long moan into the silence of the night, the pale flesh of her neck exposed.

He didn't know exactly how she'd changed, only that she had. At first he'd put it down to his malarial feverishness, the way the sex had taken on an almost hallucinatory intensity. It had surprised him all the more in that he'd been worried, of late, that Sara was going off him. She was always crying off, making excuses, and, when she did submit to his advances, making him feel like she was doing him a favour. She claimed to be too tired, most of the time, but there was no reason for it – it's not as if they had kids, for heaven's sake.

But that night she'd been out with Banhi – that's when it all started. This time it was he who was not really up to it, and she who had insisted, stalking into the room in silence, not even asking him if he was feeling any better, just crawling over to him on the bed and taking him into her mouth before he was fully erect. As she'd coaxed his cock into life, she'd palpated his balls, softly at first, then with greater fervour. He'd arched his back then, pressing himself into her eager fists, enraptured that she'd come back to him at last, after the waning of her desire.

Swapping over, she'd taken his prick in one fist and one and then two balls in her mouth. As her hand had moved up and down his shaft, she'd reached under him, clutching at one buttock. His excitement mounting, he'd felt her growing more frenzied too – her nails dug into him and she'd begun to let out strange guttural moans that sounded almost like some kind of religious chant. Rearing up and away from him, she'd stared down and he'd been frightened, then, by her eyes – there was some kind of emptiness to them, despite the ardour of what he had taken to be her love-making but would now hesitate to describe as such. He smiled at her, for reassurance as much as anything else, but she failed to return it, instead yanking down her shorts, pulling the gusset of her knickers aside and impaling herself on his straining prick. He'd come with a yell, in a mixture of awe and terror at this new creature that seemed to be manifesting itself in someone he had thought he knew so well. He barely even noticed, as he did, how she had shot one finger up into his arse.

Dismounting, she'd remained astride him, her sopping pussy on his belly, and reaching down frenetically massaged her clit with the heel of one hand until, leaning away from him, head thrown back, she'd come with an unholy shriek that sent a chill through him. It was as if he'd made out with an animal, and although he couldn't miss the increasingly passive Sara of yore, he wasn't sure what to make of the new incarnation. She felt, if anything, more distant than before.

She remembered going into the room, seeing Neil on the bed, naked, a book by his side. Then things became both hazy and, almost paradoxically, hyper-real. It was as if all her senses had been cranked up several gears, as if her whole body had been retuned. The smoothness of his prick, the clean salty taste of the pre-come on her tongue. The silkiness of his balls as she had rolled them, first one then the other and finally both, in her mouth. The feel of her juices flowing over her fingers as she'd brought herself to a climax, like a wash of pure satin.

But yes, there was a haze there too, the feeling that she'd been in some kind of fugue state, the remnants of her experience down by the river. That, too, seemed both heightened in intensity and woozily unreal. She'd felt Banhi's mouth on her neck at the same time as her friend had pushed one hand down her shorts and knickers, then the flutter of soft fingertips at her clitoris. She knew she'd come then, too, head still thrown back to the stars as they wheeled above. But after that . . . how had they got back? It was only a matter of steps to the guesthouse, but she remembered none of them. Had they been locked out, as she had feared they would be? She had no idea of the time, of how long she and Banhi had tarried by the river. It was curious: she'd have suspected drink, only it was one of the state's all-too-frequent dry days. They had drunk salt *lassis* with their *thali*.

Now, sleepless still, watching as dawn stripped the sky beyond their window of light, she reached for him across the bed, her hunger for him renewed.

It was almost like the old days, when she had never been sated of him, when she had cycled to college in the dead of night to hand in an overdue essay and then raced to his room, woken him up and demanded that he take her. When she'd gone to find him in the library, given him glorious head in the Philosophy section, ignoring his protests that he was supposed to be revising. Not that he'd really minded: he loved it, he told her on numerous occasions, that she was a woman of appetite. He loved that she made him feel so wanted, so necessary.

He opened one eye as she swung one leg over him, took his prick in her fist again. With her free hand she took one of his and guided it to her pussy; instinctively he bunched his fingers together and she fed him into her, without the need for lube. He had known her horny, but this was something else.

She moved against him, pushing herself onto him harder and harder, until he was afraid he must be hurting her. Her face, though, bore an image of an almost religious transcendence, like the statue of a saint. He spoke her name, quietly, and she didn't react. He said it louder, and then still louder. Her eyes remained closed; she was far away from him, somewhere else.

He half sat up, eager now to penetrate her, to find some kind of connection, but she pushed him down, her movements shockingly forceful, and brought her mouth back down around him. He tried to hold off, but in spite of himself he began to buck his hips beneath her, losing control. As a jet of come issued forth, he felt her mouth tighten around him, form a sheath so close and avid that he feared he would be sucked dry, drained of all his vital juices.

She left him in the room, shellshocked. Banhi was out on the terrace, watching the slow, almost imperceptible flow of the river.

"Time," she said as Sara took a seat beside her, without taking her eyes from the water, "seems not to exist here."

"Perhaps that's why you like it so much," countered Sara. "Perhaps that's why we all like India. Everything slows down, or appears to."

Banhi turned her gaze on Sara, and Sara had to look away, so powerful was the surge of emotions inside her. This girl, this almost obscenely beautiful creature, had made her come only the night before. Did she really expect them to just be able to sit here and chat about things as if nothing had happened? And what did it all mean? Would they do it again? Were they lovers now? Did she, Sara, want them to be? And how had what Banhi had done to her down by the river made her want to go and fuck Neil with an ardour she hadn't felt in months? It was all painfully confusing. Part of her just wanted to run away from it all, but she knew that she couldn't. That Banhi had some kind of hold of her.

". . . heard of kundalini yoga?" she heard her friend saying. She shook her head. "I don't think so."

"Kundalini means coiling, like a snake. The snake is a symbol of energies that haven't been tapped into, of new possibilities."

"Do you practise it?"

Banhi nodded. "Every day. Without fail." She smiled, but she was already looking back at the slow-flowing Ganges. "I have transformed myself," she said. Her eyes flicked back to Sara. "Let me show you how." She rose.

Banhi's room, Sara noticed as her friend ushered her inside, was the same as theirs, give or take a few square feet, only it smelled of incense – sandalwood, thought Sara, and something else that she didn't recognise. Something more earthy, almost feral. There was only one small paneless window at the front of the room, equipped with bars – presumably to keep out the monkeys that patrolled the walkway outside. Banhi lit a candle by the bed.

"Lie down," she commanded, and at Sara's raised eyebrows, added, "Just watch, for now."

Sara did as she was bidden, and observed as Banhi slipped off her clothes and knelt in front of her, her feet hip-width apart. Between her legs, Sara could see the fuzz of her sex. Her own pussy stirred and dampened. She struggled not to touch herself, or to reach out for Banhi.

"This," said Banhi, "is the Hero Pose, also called the Celibate Pose. It's a meditative pose designed to channel sexual energy up the spine. Now—" She brought her hands up in front of her – the same hands, Sara thought, that had brought her to a climax the night before – and interlaced the fingers of each.

"This," she continued, "is called the Venus Lock. It works by applying pressure to the Venus mounds at the base of the thumb, which channels your sensuality and ensures a glandular balance, which in turn helps you to concentrate and focus."

She relaxed the pose. "It's all," she said, her eyes boring into Sara's, "about what you want and how much you want it."

Sara swallowed almost painfully.

Her friend continued, and again Sara thought she saw a strange red glow to Banhi's eyes, a brilliant flash of teeth as she spoke. "What is it that you want, Sara?" she said.

Sara sat up, reached out. She knew without any doubt, in a sudden burst of clarity, that she wanted Banhi. That no one else would do.

Neil was waiting for her, but this time he was afraid. This time he wanted to talk, first, before submitting to her new-found appetite. There was something odd about it all, and he suspected that it had something to do with Sara's new friend Banhi.

He's been suspicious of Banhi since the moment they'd met, down by the Ganges. It was Sara who'd insisted on going down to see the bodies being burnt; he'd thought it was ghoulish, this desire of hers, and had accompanied only because he was uneasy with her going alone. Banhi had approached them, had latched onto them, or rather Sara, like a leech. Within minutes they'd seemed like best friends reunited after years apart, which was unusual for Sara – she was usually quite wary and reserved when it came to new people. She generally withheld her trust for a long time. Neil had felt elbowed out from the start; even when Banhi had deigned to address him, he'd felt there was something a little mocking in her eyes. He knew he held little interest for her.

He didn't care much, at first, but Sara hadn't stopped talking about her – how interesting she was, how exotic, how gorgeous-looking. It was as if Banhi had cast some kind of spell on her. He'd wanted to throw his hefty guidebook at Sara, insist that they leave Varanasi right away, if only to get away from the damn woman who seemed to have taken over her mind, brainwashed her with all her hippy talk of chakras and goddesses and all sorts. Sara, on the other hand, had insisted on extending their stay here, had all sorts of new places to add to their itinerary, all of them suggested by Banhi. He'd found himself being dragged from temple to temple, to gaze at erotic carvings and Shiva lingams and yoni stones, when he'd been expecting by now to be in a national park, riding elephants.

He sat up in bed, expectant and nervous, sexually charged and yet reticent. What was she going to do to him now? His fever abated, his concerns about malaria receded, he felt eager to be gone from this place, leave all this strangeness behind. He wanted to find the old Sara, the Sara he knew, even if it meant that their sex life died down again. This girl, he saw in a flash of clear-headedness, was an impostor.

The door open. Sara crossed the threshold and stepped up to him. There was a curious fire in her eyes.

"Sara," he said.

She made no response. She seemed to him like a sleepwalker, devoid of all intent, manoeuvring on auto-pilot.

"Sara, what's happened to you?"

She came closer, and he became aware that he was holding his breath. He wanted to tell her to go away, but some deeper, darker part of him forbade him to speak.

She climbed onto the bed, pushed him backwards, suddenly all too full of intent, although a certain robotic aspect to her remained.

"Sara," he beseeched her. "Sara, please."

She was the master now, he understood that. He'd fallen in love with her for her appetite; it had been the spark that had lit the conflagration between them. But he had met her passion with an equal one. This time Sara seemed to be fired by a flame he couldn't match.

She pressed her lips to his torso, moved up, clamped her

mouth on each of his nipples in turn. He let his head fall back, utterly submissive. He was hers, whatever she wanted of him.

Driving her nails into the flesh of his shoulders, she took him inside her, up to the hilt. For a moment he felt he was going to pass out, felt he was being pulled into a vortex or a black hole from which there would be no return. Bringing his hands down from where they had been behind his head, clamped around the bedposts, he seized her hips as she rode him wildly, baying like a she-wolf, seemingly lost to everything but the sensations that were ripping through her. He didn't know where she was gone, but he knew that she was far from him.

Sensing his climax near, she rapidly dismounted, brought her hand and mouth to his prick and squeezed it hard as the pearlescent white stream gushed into her mouth. Raising his head, he watched her drink as if struck by a thirst that could never be slaked. He came and came, as he never had before, unsure whether it was her need that was somehow calling forth such unprecedented reserves in him, or his own excitement at watching her drink him in.

Afterwards, too exhausted to attend to her, he lay and regarded her as she pleasured herself, although as soon as the word "pleasure" flitted across his mind, he wondered if it could ever do justice to the waves of rapture that rippled across her face.

She left him, asleep or unconscious she knew not which, and directed herself like a noctambulist towards Banhi's room. Her friend was waiting for her.

"Well?" she said, one expertly plucked eyebrow arched, "is he ready?"

Sara nodded. She'd thought she loved Neil, once, but everything that had gone before had been swept away by the tidal wave that was Banhi. She took her friend's lovely oval face in her hands, kissed her with savagery. Banhi responded by biting Sara's bottom lip, and as their tongues slipped and slid around each other like writhing snakes, blood mixed with saliva to form a pinkish foam.

Banhi stepped back at last. "Cigarette?" she said, wiping her mouth and chin with the back of her hand. Sara acquiesced.

"Who *are* you?" she said as her friend lit two cigarettes and handed one over.

"Who are *we*?" said Banhi. "For we are the same. Sisters and lovers, with souls as black as night."

"I need to understand," said Sara, "if I am to stay with you. To—" She stopped, unable to say Neil's name.

Banhi studied her coolly. "You meet all kinds of people," she said at length, "in my field. Sceptics and believers, rationalist and mystics, angels and daemons."

"Are we angels or daemons?"

"Perhaps a little of each. We cannot know ourselves, not fully."

"Is there a name for – for people like us?"

"I really don't know, Sara. But when I think of us, I think of the *rakshasa*."

"What are the *rakshasa*?"

"A species that was first created by the Brahman to protect the sea from those who wanted to steal the elixir of immortality from it – at least that's one version of the myth. They are shapeshifters, sometimes appearing as tigers, or if in human form as seductive women who lure men to their deaths, drinking their blood, sometimes eating their flesh."

"And you really believe all this. Believe in them?"

Banhi looked back at Sara dispassionately. "I don't know what I believe," she said. "I know only," she went on, "that you, Sara, are the black goddess for whom I have been waiting for so long. I sought you out because I recognised that you, like me, are a woman of appetite."

Sara thought, a little guiltily for a moment, of Neil, back in their room. Neil, who once she had loved, who had once used the same words to describe her. Then she looked back at Banhi and her remorse dissolved like smoke in the sunlight.

A knock at the door interrupted her reflections.

"Neil," said Sara flatly. It was as if he had materialised from her thoughts.

"It's time," said Banhi, her voice equally level. She held out her hand to her friend.

Neil stood and watched, for the second time, as bodies burnt slowly on small pyres by the river before the ashes were scattered in the water, or, in some cases, were thrown in as they were, wrapped in traditional cloths and garlands of marigolds, weighted down by rocks. Death, he saw clearly, could be a beautiful thing. A desirable thing, even. And to die here in Varanasi was supposed to be the best death of all, releasing one from the cycle of birth and rebirth.

Like the Hindus who came here in their thousands, he accepted his fate; welcomed it, in fact. He was so very tired. Sara had been feeding off him, he realised now, draining his very life-blood. Her reawakening, he understood, had nothing to do with sex. It had been a slow dance with death.

She had sucked him dry, leaving a husk of a man, a bloodless being. He turned to her. She stood behind him, hand in Banhi's. Their eyes blazed back at him, incandescent in the blue light of dawn. In them he thought he could see something like eternity.

From his pocket he extracted the box of matches that Banhi had handed him on the way from the hostel. Striking one, he brought it towards him the pale paper of his flesh.

Banhi was already turning away, eyes brighter still, as if she were lit from within by the rising sun. She squeezed Sara's hand as they climbed the steps back up to the town, oblivious to Neil's cries. Her lips curled into a smile.

"Who next?" she said.

Sexes in the City

Claude Lalumière

It was weeks before I dared expose my skin in the privacy of my new home. And, even then, only parts of it. My hands, my crotch. While looking at vids of the girls at innerskin.web. I ached for flesh against flesh, even for my own. As if I had ever known any other flesh. As my come shot out, that noise from upstairs, from my landlord's, started up again.

I had moved to the city right after high school, to go to college. Apartments were hard to find – and expensive – but I snagged this cruddy basement flat where the rent was cheap and the landlord didn't care if I was a few weeks late sometimes. The apartment building had an ecolock chamber – every building had to – but I wished I could have found a place with an additional, private ecolock for each unit. I would have felt safer.

I could never have afforded such fancy digs, though. Between public ecolock taxes, mandatory health security fees and my outerskin lease, I was lucky to be able to afford school. I'd emerge with a debt that would take me decades to pay off, but at least I'd have a chance at getting into a corporate village with better ecolocks and state-of-the-art outerskin. The landlord and his wife lived in the flat directly above mine. I disliked him. The face on his outerskin was repulsive, with a fake mustache that screamed cheesy.

He was almost paternal with me, friendly in a cloyingly patronizing way. I tolerated it because I couldn't afford to move. His wife was even more disgusting: her outerskin face was programmed to look heavily made up, nearly glowing purple, crowned with a wig of bleach-blonde big hair. She strutted around like a twentieth-century porn starlet – skimpy top showing off her oversize tits, clear spike heels tilting up her barely concealed outerskin butt – and ignored me whenever I presumed to greet her. When they fucked – and they fucked constantly – it sounded like a crappy porno, every steady beat of moans, groans, and screams blatantly performed.

Still, I couldn't help wondering whether they risked fucking flesh to flesh or whether they actually enjoyed doing it outerskin to outerskin.

I noticed her the first day of school. She was older – old enough to be a grad student, so she wasn't in any of my classes. Her outerskin shone in a peculiar way, and I found that my eyes were drawn to her, finding her of their volition.

I took to following her, observing her. I missed classes to spy on her.

She loved to touch, her hands always casually groping the places where her friends' outerskins peeked through their clothes.

In my experience people like that were immediately ostracized. You weren't supposed to touch. Outerskin made it safe, but suspicions lingered.

But not so with her. She was gregarious, popular – charismatic, even from afar.

Lying in bed, after the noise from upstairs finally quieted down, I peeled off my entire outerskin for the first time since leaving the safety of my parents' home.

I looked at my hands and imagined they were hers.

I touched my chest. I rubbed my taut belly. I fingered my ass crack. I pressed the palms of my hands against the soles of my feet. I cupped my balls. I stroked myself, imagining a world of fleshly sensations unmediated by outerskin. A world without biohackers, without mutagenic nanoviruses, without poisonous air, without genetically booby-trapped food, without contaminated water, without STD warfare.

Coming home from school, I raised my arm to press the hand of my outerskin against the palmkey of my apartment building's ecolock. Before I made contact, another hand grabbed mine.

"I thought I'd follow you for once." Her voice was husky. Sexy.

I turned around to see the object of my obsessions, my fantasies. I swallowed, unable to speak.

She laughed. "My name's Kim. Invite me in?"

I told her I needed my hand back to unlock the door.

I was sweating profusely, so much that my cheap outerskin couldn't process it fast enough. A sticky film spread between my flesh and my outerskin.

Inside my apartment, she immediately started to take my clothes off. But I had to stop her, because the pressure on my bladder was unbearable.

When I returned from the washroom, she was sprawled on the floor laughing her head off, teasingly opening and closing her knees.

Naked.

There was no mistaking that she had stripped down to her real flesh. Her clothes were strewn all over, but . . .

She saw the question on my face. "I never wear outerskin. Ever."

I should have panicked, but she smiled; it disarmed me.

She said, "Do you want me?"

Yes. But I couldn't bring myself to say it.

"Good. Take your time. Make sure you want this to happen. That you want to shed your outerskin. And to shed your identity. Your obsolete identity."

It hurt how much I wanted to taste her. I didn't care how much her words confused me. How much she confused me.

I took off my clothes. Trembling, I stripped off my outerskin.

She nodded at me and bit her lower lip.

I approached her, knelt down, and grabbed one of her feet. I ran my tongue along her sweaty arch. She moaned.

She stroked my engorged cock, and I fell atop her. I nibbled on her neck, running one hand through her hair while the other caressed her small breasts. Her feet nuzzled my legs while she breathed into my ear. Her pelvis nudged up against mine with insistent urgency. I covered her mouth with my lips, and her tongue explored me. I mumbled something about getting a condom and disentangled myself from her. The shock of suddenly not touching her skin so unsettled me that I let out a small sob.

Kim took my hand and placed my fingers inside her moist vagina. "Forget the condom," she said. "Taste me."

While she stroked my chest, I brought my fingers to my lips and licked her juice. The taste of her filled my mouth, made me salivate. I swallowed – and felt her essence ooze down my throat, warm my chest . . . I swooned.

I was dimly aware of Kim catching me, laying me down on the floor.

Her nails dug into my chest as she slid her vagina over my almost painfully erect cock. My mind exploded, and so did my balls; the sperm shot through my penis and burst out in a long, steady stream. She clenched her vagina and wiggled her crotch against mine, encouraging me to come and come and come . . .

When I was done, she laughed with such unabashed joy, clutching me to her, showering me with playful kisses, that I was able to let go of the embarrassment caused by my overeager orgasm.

She rolled us over, careful to leave our genitals snugly cupped, leaving me briefly on top. While I kissed her, our mouths wide open, as if to swallow each other, she carefully rolled us over again. She kissed my face with slow tenderness. She bent her back, rubbing herself against my pelvis, and licked my nipples. Already I felt my cock getting hard again, expanding in her vagina's embrace.

Yet I withdrew, eager to taste her again, to drink directly from the source.

I grabbed hold of her hips, lifted her up, and brought her to my face. My tongue slithered inside her, and the blend of our juices smeared onto my mouth and cheeks. I experienced another moment of dizziness, but I struggled to focus on what I was doing, on pleasing her. My body felt soft and malleable; I imagined it was entirely due to the unexpected intensity of the sexual encounter and the long, deeply ecstatic orgasm – unlike anything that had ever resulted from masturbation – a new kind of pleasure that I felt had already changed me irrevocably.

I caressed Kim's ass, kissed its soft cheeks, and inserted a finger into her anus.

I pushed her forward, onto her knees, and I licked her out, my tongue and lips exploring every nook, fold, and crevice of her. She pushed her butt against my face, increasing the pressure of my probing lips and tongue.

She moaned faster and faster, more and more rhythmically, until she screamed her orgasm.

Then I kneeled and took her from behind. This time, I rode her slowly, every thrust and semi-withdrawal keeping time with her breathing. I felt the sperm swell up from my balls, but I kept it inside me, paying attention to the subtleties of Kim's cries and squirms.

Again, she began to moan rhythmically, but she stayed at that plateau for a long, long time while our bodies slammed into each other, splattering sweat, saliva, and juices.

I was struggling not to come, admiring the glistening beauty of her sweaty back – and she screamed with pleasure. I spurted into her, joining her in orgasm. My fingers dug into the flesh of her hips while my cock sought to reach deeper into her. Then I surprised myself with one more big spurt, and I slipped out of her and fell backward, still squirting into the air.

Kim glanced at me with a dreamy look and a satisfied smile. She grabbed my head and guided it down into her crotch. Once again, I started licking her out, sucking her clit with my lips.

Once again, my head swam with dizziness, but I was getting used to the sensation. She responded enthusiastically to the sucking, with a deep, profound Oh yeah – so I concentrated on that. I could feel her clit grow, her excitement becoming increasingly urgent. Her clit continued to expand. I felt it push against my teeth. I opened my mouth wider, and it filled up the space between my tongue and my palate. I reached down to finger her vagina, and instead my hand cupped a hot, hairy scrotum.

I stared at the new penis, distantly aware that something unusual had occurred. Kim's aroma filled my mouth, my throat, my lungs, my nose, permeated my whole body. I was only remotely conscious of my own identity. I found myself caressing Kim's penis. It grew bigger, leaking lubricant. I bent down and kissed it, then intently examined Kim's whole body. Instead of sporting small, perky cups, his chest was now flat and muscular. His shoulders had broadened, and his hips and torso had lost their curves, but they'd gained strong, muscular lines. I finally looked into his eyes, and I saw in them the same generous playfulness the female Kim had shown me. He chuckled, then bent down to kiss my now-flaccid cock. He brought it back to life, teasing it with his tongue. We repositioned ourselves into a sideways sixty-nine, sucking each other off hungrily while we fingered each other's assholes.

He came before me, spurting all over my face. I came immediately after. Then we licked each other clean, and the pleasure extended itself again and again until we both shrank to complete limpness.

He sat up and then bent down to kiss me. Our tongues played together.

He closed my eyes with his fingers. With both hands, he started massaging my balls and cock, kneading them like dough. Every squeeze sent ripples of pleasure rushing to my head.

And then I felt his fingers wiggle inside me, going deeper with every stroke. At first I thought he was playing with my anus, but then he put a finger up my ass also. I reached down and discovered that my penis and balls were gone. I stroked the hood of my clitoris while his fingers probed the insides of my vagina and my ass. I whimpered with pleasure. Gradually, he withdrew his fingers while I kept masturbating.

He kissed my left nipple. My breast expanded under his stimulation. He switched to the right and repeated the process. Again, my breast swelled.

With my other hand, I caressed my chest. It was now smooth, hairless. And my breasts were large, firm yet soft.

I shoved Kim away and examined myself. My hips were round, my stomach smooth. My breasts were beautifully voluptuous. I squeezed my new breasts, my hands unequal to the task of containing them, and I felt the grin spread across my face. I touched my cheeks, and all trace of stubble had vanished; my jaw, my chin, and my nose were all subtly smaller, my lips a bit fuller.

I looked at Kim; his cock was hugely erect.

He held my wrists to the floor and entered me with a swift, hard thrust. I gasped in pain – but there was pleasure, too. He slid backward and forward with tenderness, gently biting my nipples with each thrust. I lost track of time and of myself as his cock moved within me, filled me up. Eventually, I pulled him closer to me and bit his shoulder while he plunged deeper into me with increasing force and almost violent abandon. I felt my orgasm well up until my whole body was ready to explode. And then I screamed, and so did he, while he continued moving inside me until I came a second time, and then a third time.

He withdrew and flipped me around. Groaning deep, satisfied Mmms, he planted admiring kisses on my ass cheeks. He ran his fingernails down my legs, until he reached my feet, on which he playfully nibbled. I squirmed, on the edge of feeling tickled. He parted my ass with his hands and licked out my anus. I thrashed wildly, but his strong grip kept my ass pressed against his mouth.

He pulled away; my crack was dripping with saliva. I felt his penis probe my butt. I squirmed against it; he grabbed me by the waist and slowly, very slowly, drove his long, thick, hard, and very wet cock up my ass. He rode me delicately, and the movements of his cock took over my awareness. While he was inside me, my world was defined by that sensation. Then I felt him tense up and heard him gasp. As his spent penis shrank, my anus contracted and pressed him out.

I sat down and saw him precariously balanced on his knees, his head still swaying in ecstasy. I reached out and held his hands.

He smiled drowsily at me and leaned into me. He kissed my neck. He kissed my breasts, lingering a long time on each one. He kissed my stomach. And then his face disappeared between my legs, and he licked out my cunt.

He licked me through two more orgasms, and then sat up and kissed the palms of my hands.

I smiled at Kim. Kim who was a woman again, with smooth skin, small perky breasts, and a thick bush around her cunt.

She bent down and kissed me on the mouth. We caressed each other's breasts, playing with our nipples, necking furiously. My lips became raw with kissing. When I pulled back, we both laughed, and then, sitting up, we hugged each other with all our strength.

She cupped my face with her hands and pecked my cheeks with her open lips. She squeezed my ample tits and, pressing herself against me, rubbed her nipples against mine. We both simultaneously laughed and gasped. She reached down and pressed her hand against my eager cunt, and I let out a long, languorous sigh. Her fingertips traced the outline of my labia, and I shivered with delight and anticipation. She bent down, spread my legs, and poked her tongue into my ass crack, taking her time, but gradually, eventually, running it up to my moist pussy. She pushed it inside, her lips brushing against my labia. She continued upward and pressed her tongue against my excited clit.

My back arched. She grabbed my waist and turned me around. She lay down on top of me, her breasts pressed against my back, her hands caressing my hips.

She slid downward and kissed the fleshy cheeks of my butt, lingering there. Then she moved up to my back and licked it methodically, until her tongue had tasted every millimetre of its sweaty skin. She kissed my nape, then she slipped her hands under me, grabbed my tits, and lifted me up.

I faced her, and we guided each other's hands toward our swollen cunts. I came almost immediately. Dizzy with pleasure, I sat behind her, put my arms around her, and pressed her back against my now tender breasts. Cupping one of her tits with one hand, my other hand moved down to between her legs. She was prodigiously wet. While I played with her nipple, I masturbated her. When she came, her body seemed to melt into mine.

She laid her head down on my breasts, and I enfolded her in my arms. We stayed like that until sun-up, which wasn't long in coming. We had fucked non-stop for more than twelve hours.

She gave me a final kiss, put her clothes on, and left without a word. My skin tingled deliciously. I touched myself: my voluptuous breasts had vanished, my chest hair had grown back, my vagina had closed, and cock and balls had returned. My penis was raw and my ass was sore, but even the pain felt good. I never wanted to come down from that nirvanic post-multiorgasmic stupor.

But less than five minutes later, the landlord pounded on my door, yelling for me to open up. So much for serenity. I quickly slipped into my outerskin and pulled on some clothes, then opened the door. Immediately, he chewed me out for making such a racket all night. Said this wasn't a brothel. Said he'd throw me out if it happened again. As if I could let myself have sex here again knowing now that he and his wannabe porn-starlet wife could hear everything. Betcha they enjoyed the audio show. After all, they hadn't interrupted us. He slammed the door shut when he left.

My outerskin was itchy, suffocating – alien. I couldn't bear to keep it on.

While I had breakfast – I was ravenous; I ate three times as much as usual – I heard them fucking upstairs, with their customary over-rehearsed rhythm of call-and-response moans and screams.

I have shed my outerskin – forever. It's obsolete technology; my body can now defend itself. Adapt as it needs to.

It's an easy task to mold my flesh so that it appears like outerskin to prying eyes.

Around campus, everywhere I glance, there's desirable flesh. Girls and women of all shapes and sizes. Long-legged elegant women with sinuously lithe bodies. Petite elfin girls. Giggling girls. Chubby girls with wonderfully plump butts. Brash tomboys. Fashionistas more lovely than any cover model.

. . . And the guys. Broad-shouldered and classically handsome. Bearish, with comforting bellies and strong arms. Athletic and tautly muscled. Absent-minded, lost in their own worlds. Unabashedly macho. Ambiguously androgynous.

All kinds of beautiful bodies – I fantasize about peeling off their outerskins, about tasting their sweat and juices. About smearing my juices on their naked flesh.

I come to realize that I release pheromones that attract the uninfected to me. Pheromones that their outerskins fail to filter.

In other people's bedrooms I mold and reshape my lovers' bodies to the ebbs and flows of my desires, my own body transforming itself in response to their unleashed fantasies. I free their flesh, their identities.

I understand now that our entire economy is based on the fear that without outerskins or ecolocks we would all die.

I understand that there are interests – powerful economic interests – that will not allow this to change.

I understand that I am now a terrorist.

I've moved upstairs, gratefully abandoning my small, dark apartment. Trying to weasel out of paying the monthly rent I surprised even myself by seducing my landlord and his wife. The playful tenderness of our threesome astonishes us time and again, but never more than that first time.

Fondling his own big breasts never loses its charm for him. She laughs hysterically whenever she fucks either of us in the ass with her cock, which she has learned to mold into different shapes, which further amuses her to no end.

Live Bed Show

Elizabeth Coldwell

I sat on the end of the bed, looking out into the rainy Amsterdam night. My bare legs were crossed at the ankles and the straps of my nightdress were sliding down my shoulders, threatening to let my breasts spill free. It was a look designed to entice passers-by to slow down, stop, maybe even think about making a purchase. But unlike the girls in the windows of the red-light district, over in the old part of town, I wasn't selling myself. I was selling the bed beneath me. Or at least that's how it started.

I came to Amsterdam because I fell in love with Jamie. I stayed because I fell in love with the city.

Jamie was working for the London arm of a Dutch investment bank, a breed I normally went out of my way to avoid. I hated brash City types, with their loud voices, over-confident manner and constant bragging about the size of everything from their annual bonus to their cock. But while the other blokes in his party were trying to grope my bum or stare down my cleavage as I served their meal, he was quieter, politer – and more than passably cute. At the end of the evening, he contrived to slip me his mobile phone number on the back of his business card, telling me he'd like to see me again. Three weeks after our first date, he told me he'd been seconded to the bank's headquarters in Amsterdam for six months, then asked me to move over there with him. It was a stupidly impulsive reaction on his part – and an equally impulsive one on mine to agree. But I was so sure it would work out that I packed in my waitressing job and gave my landlord notice on the flat I rented.

And it did work out. The bank had a ground-floor apartment on the Prinsengracht canal, a few minutes' walk from his Jamie's new office and near to the Jordaan, the warren of streets packed with arty-crafty little shops and brown cafés which were a magnet for tourists. It was quiet and tastefully decorated, with everything a tired businessman would need to entertain himself at the end of a long day, including a wall-mounted plasma screen TV, top-of-the-range sound system and a power shower more than big enough for Jamie and I to use together. With no need to contribute to anything but our food bills, I was as close as I would ever come to being a kept woman, and I used the time I had to my advantage, roaming the canals with my camera. I had been trying to make a career in photography, which was what I had studied at art college, and this seemed like the ideal opportunity to build up a portfolio of work. I took black-and-white shots of everything from the queue of tourists snaking round the block as they waited to get into Anne Frank's house to a couple cycling hand in hand by the side of the canal to one of the window girls taking a cigarette break, lounging against a wall in her trashy lingerie and thighboots.

My forays into the red-light area weren't all to take photos, though. I had discovered that though most of the sex shops were full of tatty novelties for the tourist trade, there were a couple of places selling quality fetishwear and interesting toys. So I invested in a few items to keep things spicy when Jamie came home: Velcro cuffs we could use to fasten each other to the bed; a string of anal beads which gave him the most incredible climax as I slowly pulled them out of his arse; a waterproof vibrator he used on me as the shower's steamy spray beat down on us both, until my knees were sagging and I clutched at the tiled walls as I came and came again. I had more, and better, sex with Jamie, in those months in Amsterdam than I'd ever had with anyone else.

But it takes more than great sex to keep a relationship going and, as the end of Jamie's secondment approached, it became increasingly apparent to both of us that what had begun so explosively was fizzling out just as fast. Underneath it all, we liked each other well enough but we really didn't have that much in common.

When the time came for Jamie to arrange our flights to Heathrow, I told him not to bother with mine. I wouldn't be going back to London – at least, not yet, anyway. When he didn't even try to talk me out of staying, I knew I was making the right decision.

The problem was that I needed to sort out somewhere to live, and get myself a job. I found an apartment without too much difficulty, in a tenement building a couple of tram stops away from the city's zoo. It was a little dingy compared to the place I'd lived in with Jamie, and up three flights of stairs, but it was cheap, and my neighbours seemed pleasant enough. An art gallery in the Jordaan had taken several of my photographs, and had even sold a couple, which covered the deposit on my apartment and the first month's rent, but I needed to do more than sell the odd photograph if I wanted to eat on a regular basis. At home, I would have been able to walk into just about any restaurant you cared to name and land waitressing work, but here, where my grasp of the language didn't extend much beyond "please", "thank you" and "beer", it was not going to be that simple.

So when I saw the sign being placed on the door of the bed shop, it seemed like fate. I noticed the shop every time I travelled past it on the tram late at night, lit up when everything else was shuttered and silent. Today I had chosen to walk into the city centre, past the Rembrandt Museum, and as I waited to cross the road, the middle-aged shop manager was sticking the sign in place. Helpfully, it was written in both Dutch and English: "MODEL WANTED". My curiosity piqued, I darted inside the shop and found the manager behind the counter.

"*Goed dag,*" I said, then switched back to English, the limit of my Dutch pleasantries already reached. "I saw the sign. You're looking for a model, Well – here I am."

He looked me up and down. I might have been short by Dutch standards, though you could say that of any woman under five feet ten, and I hoped that wouldn't count against me. It didn't.

"You've modelled before?" he asked.

"Well, to be honest, no. But I really need a job"

"Okay. This isn't exactly runway work, anyway. I'm looking for someone who can make the most of this—" And he gestured to the bed in the window display which, he told me, was on special promotion. As he described the job requirements, I couldn't believe what I was hearing. The model needed to arrive at the shop just before nine at night, change into their nightwear – in the staff toilet, not the window, he added hastily, as it wasn't that kind of establishment – potter around for an hour and then go to bed. The idea was to convince passers-by the bed was so comfortable that if you could get a decent eight hours' sleep in such an artificial environment, nodding off at home would be a cinch. The money he was offering wasn't great, but it was enough. And I didn't need to be able to speak a single word of Dutch. It was perfect, and I told him so. I was hired. We shook hands on the agreement, and I went off to buy a new nightdress for my first public appearance.

I settled into the routine very quickly. Wim, the shop manager, would be waiting for me every night at about ten to nine. We would exchange a few pleasantries, he would let me into the shop and then go on his way. I would change into my nightdress and get into position on the bed. I had my iPod, on to which I had downloaded a "Teach Yourself Dutch" course, books and magazines to read and an eye mask to block out the glare of the shop's fluorescent lighting.

It soon became obvious, however, that wasn't enough. I was managing to get a surprisingly good night's sleep, once the rumble of the trams on the road outside died down just after midnight, but the reading matter I had brought wasn't enough to keep me stimulated. And if there was one thing I needed since I'd split up from Jamie it was stimulation – mental and physical.

Not only that, I didn't feel as though I was doing enough to attract the attention of passers-by. Oh, they would slow down a little as they walked past, take a quick look at the strange girl sitting in a shop window, reading, but they very rarely stopped and they almost never paid attention to the sign in the window highlighting the low cost and exceptional comfort of this king-sized bed. I needed to put on a performance.

The following night, I arrived with all the equipment needed to give myself a pedicure, and spent a long time massaging my feet with body lotion before meticulously applying a coat of red varnish to my toenails. This time, people did stop, did take notice and did, once they had tired of looking at my bare legs and the tops of my breasts where they peeped out above the lacy edging of my nightdress, look at the bed and wonder how it might fit in their own bedroom. There were a couple of men who did nothing but stare at the arch of my instep and my delicate toes, but each to their own – and after all, I was the one in charge of this little display, they the ones who stood on the outside, gazing hungrily in at their fetish made flesh.

The realisation that I could tease and tempt, safe and inviolate behind glass, awakened in me an exhibitionistic streak I had never realised I possessed. Now, instead of huddling under the covers, ignoring my potential audience as I completed a sudoku puzzle, I perched on the end of the bed, showing off. Making them come to me. Making them want me.

I would wait till a likely looking man approached and then I would casually, carelessly bend forward, giving him a view right down my nightdress to my breasts. Or I would cross my legs, flashing him a pair of knickers pulled up snugly against the contours of my pussy. After a couple of nights, I no longer bothered putting on the knickers. I wantonly let strangers see my pink lips, the little tuft of soft brown hair, and sent them away with a bulge in their pants that ached for relief.

It wasn't just the men who watched me, either. You'd be surprised how many of the women who passed seemed to be hoping for a glimpse of my tits. Perhaps it was just to compare them to their own, but I suspected that some of them looked because it turned them on.

Enjoying myself now, I began to fetch the vibrator I had bought to share with Jamie into work. I will never forget the expression on the face of the first man who watched me run the buzzing toy first along the length of my arm, then slowly down my neck. His eyes bugged in disbelief as I played it over my breasts, causing my nipples to pucker into hardness. He hoped, as every man who followed him did, that I would take the vibrator down between my legs and let it press against my clit. I wanted to, desperately, but something always held me back from going all the way.

Only once I was back in my apartment did I give in to the need for release. I would lie back on my own bed, smaller and with a lumpier mattress than the one I had become used to in the shop, and masturbate, always with the same fantasy in my mind. I would imagine myself in the shop window, legs widely parted, thrusting the vibrator up into myself, and outside, some anonymous voyeur would be watching and wanking his hard cock till his spunk spattered against the glass. And at that point I would always come, screaming out my pleasure in the quiet little apartment and already eager for the coming night.

I had no idea whether Wim was aware what I actually got up to when he left me in his shop for the night, but he couldn't fail to notice the increased custom I had brought in. He told me that every day people would come and lie on the bed in the window. I imagined most of them were hoping for a sniff of my scent, trapped in the sheets, but more than a few of those who sampled the mattress went on to order a bed of their own.

One morning, as he paid me my wages, he told me he had some important news. He needed to take a few days' leave of absence to look after his sick mother and his nephew, Jaap, would be letting me into the shop in his absence. Apparently, Wim had no sons of his own, and so was training the lad to take over the business when he retired. I merely nodded, having been worried he was about to tell me the special promotion was over and he was terminating my employment.

When I saw Jaap, a small part of me found myself hoping that Wim's mother's illness would be of the lingering variety.

The man was gorgeous; in his early twenties, with a long, lean body, short, spiky blond hair and an open smile. I caught him giving me an appreciative glance or two as he let me into the shop, but I told myself not to make anything of it. It was just my hormones responding to the first man in a long time who'd admired my body without there being a pane of glass between us. Still, that night, as I knelt up on the bed and caressed my body, I imagined it was Jaap who was staring at me through the shop window, Jaap who was silently encouraging me to spread my legs and touch myself for him . . .

And as I sat on the end of the bed, looking out into the rainy Amsterdam night, I heard a noise behind me, and turned. Someone was in the shop! The figure stepped out from the shadows of the curtaining display and I realised it was Jaap. But surely he'd locked up and left hours ago? I shook my head, trying to dismiss him as a figment of my overheated imagination, but as he walked over to the bed, I knew he was real.

"I know what you do," he said, coming to stand beside me. "My friend, Peter, saw you a couple of nights ago. He said you gave him a flash of that cute little pussy of yours. And I wanted to see for myself. That's why I volunteered to look after the shop for my uncle. That's why I came back tonight."

"But if you wanted to watch me through the window . . ." I began.

He shook his head. "No, I wanted the real thing. I want to touch it. Taste it."

His words set a pulse beating fiercely between my legs. I watched as he stripped out of his jeans and teeshirt and came to sit beside me on the bed, wearing only a pair of black briefs that held his cock coiled within them. He looked huge, and though I knew we shouldn't be doing this, I couldn't stop myself.

I flopped back, pushed my nightdress up around my hips and slowly, deliberately opened my legs. His gaze was drawn like a magnet to the folds of my sex, already wet from all the teasing and stroking I'd given myself earlier. I couldn't see if there was anyone staring through the window, but if they were, I knew their view would have been obscured by the bulk of Jaap's body. They could only imagine what might be happening, and envy the fact that what I had shown them only in glimpses, he was seeing in all its blossoming glory.

"Beautiful," he murmured, and traced a big finger along my lips. Desire had made me submissive, and I lay there, letting him explore everywhere from the tip of my clit to the pucker of my arsehole. I barely knew the man, and yet already I was letting him touch all my most intimate places. And when he replaced his finger with the firm point of his tongue, I almost squealed in delight.

I forgot I was in such a public place, forgot all about our potential audience as Jaap proceeded to lick me deliciously, thoroughly. Much as I had enjoyed fucking Jamie, he had always felt that oral sex was just a minor detour on the way to the final destination. For Jaap, however, this was clearly a most important part of the journey. My hips arched up towards his face and my hands grabbed fistfuls of the bedsheets as his tongue probed and dallied, taking me all the way to the summit of my orgasm.

But just before he got there, he pulled his mouth away. I wanted to grab him by the hair and force him back into place, but he shook his head. He pressed his lips to mine, letting me taste myself. "Patience," he said. "It'll be all the sweeter when it happens."

As I waited, wondering where he had learned his incredible technique, he fished a condom from his jeans pocket. He casually discarded his briefs, and his cock emerged, big and beautifully in proportion to his six foot frame. I definitely needed to be wet to take that, I thought, as he slid the condom down over its substantial length, but I was ready for him.

It was his turn to lie down now, as he urged me to get on top of him. I thought for a moment I saw a curious, moustached face peering in, but the rain was falling harder than ever and it was hard to imagine that anyone might stand for long in that weather, even with a live sex show unveiling before their eyes.

A wicked thought struck me and I grabbed my eye mask, slipping it down over Jaap's head to blindfold him. He smiled, clearly turned on by such a simple but kinky trick, and let me take charge. I began to feed his cock into me, gradually lowering myself down. I felt myself stretching wide, and the sensation was glorious. I rose and fell on him, controlling the pace, controlling the pleasure. The springs creaked gently beneath us as a bed which had only ever been intended for display purposes was finally christened in the most erotic fashion.

His hands were on my breasts, pressing them together, and he was muttering something I didn't understand, though the meaning was clear enough. He was loving this moment, and so was I. I rode him harder, gripping his thick thighs with my knees, and when I reached a finger down to play with my own clit, my pleasure peaked unstoppably. I was still feeling the spasms gripping me when Jaap groaned and let out what I assumed to be some choice Dutch swear words as he came.

We slumped together for a moment, and when we pulled apart I almost expected to see someone standing on the pavement outside, applauding. But the street was empty, and if we'd had an audience, it had already disappeared.

That was my last night in the window. Crossing the line is fun, but you can only do it once. I asked Jaap to tell his uncle when he returned that I had been offered a job elsewhere. It was a lie, obviously, but a week later an opportunity arose to become a tour guide for English-speaking parties in one of the museums, and I took it. I went past the bed shop on my way back from work – or Jaap's apartment, because even if we couldn't have sex in public, that didn't mean we couldn't keep doing it in private – but I never saw another girl doing Wim's special promotion work. And I always wondered whether anyone bought the display bed, and whether they ever had as much fun on it as I did.

The Intimate Diary of Martha Rae

Mark Farley

The following are extracts from the recently unearthed journal that was kept by one Martha Rae Carnero (1844–96), an Arizona-born girl of Mexican descent, sent by her family to the city of San Francisco at the age of eighteen, at the height of the Gold Rush. The text was kindly donated to us by the San Francisco Arts Library and Museum.

14 June 1862, San Francisco

"That's a fine piece of ass you got yrself there, Mamma . . ."

"She's one of the best girls in the city, Sir. She'll treat you mighty fine too."

"Uh-huh . ."

"Why, yes Sir. You wanna see the goods first? Ahm sure Miss Martha Rae would oblige the kind Sir a peek for thirty cents and a share of three fingers of liquor and some tobacco with her . . ."

"Come and lie with me, Miss Martha Rae."

19 June 1862, San Francisco

I have taken upon writing a journal. If nothing else, but to document what has happened to me in the last few weeks and what will evidently lie ahead of me to those who survive me.

I arrived in San Francisco six months previous. Three weeks it took on the wagon trains from States afar. Word came to us of my grandmother's ailing nature and an obliging sense of family duty fell upon me to tend to her needs and head to

California. Funds were short as my grandfather hadn't left her much so I went out to find work.

I write home on occasion and speak of my long hours at a bakery. I do not tell her of where I actually spend all of my time. I do not tell her of the Dew Drop Inn, where I twist and shimmy for all the local men folk and often do on a more private basis too.

But hey, it aint no deadfall. It's a proper dance hall, upmarket an' all and I certainly wouldn't frequent what would be considered as a deadfall either. At least not like those places what you see on Pike Street or down by Pacific and Kearny. Bagnios haunted by ruffians and skanks and the abandoned that offer no entertainment. Just the sad relief for the desperate. And we sure aint as abandoned as those whores down at the Bull Run either, who happily come and shout their mouths and flash their handsomer wages at us on their nights off.

Despite the odd quarrel though, I do think the Dew Drop is one of the more agreeable venues. It is not one of those places that house the sort that would give themselves away for a mere fifty cents. We serve very much the well-heeled gent along with a healthy mixture of Negroes and Mexicans too, mixing in amongst the thick cloud of cigar smoke. There are gamblers, pimps, sailors and miners. All rowdy and foul mouthed a bunch they are and sure, it can be a bawdy old place too. The upstairs bears no room for discretion or is ideal for a gent with a nervous disposition, as the area is an unkempt array of beds and strewn mattresses, arranged in quite the disorganised way and often there are up to ten of us entertaining at any one time. The girls that live here have their own rooms mind, higher up in the house they use but for us visitin' girls, we use whatever facilities are at hand.

But one thing you can guarantee with the Dew Drop is that we will look after ya and make sure ya leave happy now, not like other places what slip Spanish Fly into your whiskey and lift your wallet. Places like the Bull Run!

22 June 1862, San Francisco

The house is run by Mamma Carter. At any one time, there are thirty of us girls hanging around on a busy Friday night. We all take turns to do dances and make up skits, jokes like, between the two of us. Mamma Carter is like another mother to me and I know she loves to hear it when I tell her. I love watching her get up and do a turn with Old Wayne on the upright. She once fancied herself as a touring singer and had desires on going all the way to New York, so she did. So, I often think it's a damn shame that she aint gotta tune inside o' her. Not that I would ever tell her that. Hell no. She is not a woman to be crossed. She's a no-nonsense Mississippian lady, black as the dark night and as wide as the many schooners arriving in the bay. She takes absolutely no crap from nobody. She once punched a fellow straight in the face, just for questioning whether one of us was worth the dollar fifty she was asking of him to lie with us for a time.

"Aint no motherfucker gonna cheapen my girls . . ." she'd always say.

Then there is Lydia, who is kinda responsible for all of this in the first place, looking back. I was in the General Store on Main Street, almost pleading like, with the manager to offer me some work. She struck up conversation with me while I was feeling up the cantaloupes and wondering whether I could be affordin' one. She is a few years more older than me, is Lydia.

Firstly, I was overwhelmed at how she was dressed. She looked so elegant in her long ruffled skirt and her fancy hat. She looked like she was on her way to the President's inauguration or something. She smiled and pouted at me as I told her of my sick granny and that I was looking for work to get by. I immediately felt an urge to stroke her fabulous corset and she saw me looking at it,

"It's nice, isn't it?"

"It's beautiful. I'd love one just like it . . . You must live in a big house and be married to a Lord or sumthin' . . ."

"Not exactly . . ."

She then proceeded to tell me about the Dew Drop and that I should come over and watch her dance some. I wasn't sure immediately. I'd heard that these places were dens of iniquity, full of sinners and ne'er do wells but she did assure me that it was a respectable place, the men behaved themselves and perhaps I could meet the house Mamma and talk about work.

"Well, I'd be happy to show you now. I'm about to perform onstage . . ."

So right on we went and right there, next to the display of fresh produce, my whole world changed.

23 June 1862, San Francisco

I visited the Dew Drop a couple of times over the next few days. That first trip over the street, with Lydia leading me by the hand, was as unforgettable as they come. She sat me by the bar and disappeared behind the curtain as the patrons all looked my way, curious like. I was kinda uncomfortable at first, but I needn't have been as their attentions were soon drawn to the stage, where my new acquaintance re-appeared to a hearty din and hollering. She'd lost the long frock coat and the fancy hat and had hitched and tied the front of her skirt up to her belly and also the back to the top of her cheeks to reveal her garters and pants. I caught a gasp in my throat and put a hand to my mouth as I caught sight of that pale flesh pillowing out the tops of her stockings for the first time. I had no idea right then how soon I would get so much closer to it.

The out of tune piano played in the corner at her requested nod and she skipped around the stage, with elegant turns and bends to the jazzy beat. She shimmied and shook the lacy ruffles on her bum and ran a finger lightly up her outstretched leg, to the side of her. Desire poured from that girl as she turned once and looked longingly out to the crowd and then another pirouette and a quiver of her blisters. She tossed her hair back and turned towards me, giving me the sorta look I'd never seen from anyone, let alone another woman. She took her breasts into her hands and squeezed them as she crouched down before everyone, grinding her hips and swinging them round.

I know not what I was feeling inside but it had to be released. I slowly ran my hands up and down my thighs through ma dress as I was still perched on that stool, right as a large black woman appeared (Mamma, I guessed) and caught me looking upon Lydia, with what I can only rationally describe as a filth-ridden craving for her body.

She disappeared once more as another girl stumbled from the exit, all dishevelled and with a gent doin' up his breeches. The woman behind the bar raised an eyebrow at me. I shook my composure, corrected myself and headed for the door, panting inside with shame. As I lay in my bedroom that night, I could not stop thinking about the heady display of sensuality onstage and how much I wanted her for myself. Before dropping asleep, I ached upon myself furiously as I replayed in my head how Lydia licked her lips and pointed my way and how I sat there entranced, deeply in love.

The next day, I had to return to see Lydia. It was a lot quieter a time and Mamma Carter nodded my way and tapped a forlorn body slumped at the bar, who turned and beamed my way in surprise. She skipped over to me and gave me a tight hug.

"Child, I was so worried about you . . . You didn't even bid me a farewell . . ."

I apologised profusely, made my polite excuse and fell at her insistence that I visit her room at once and let her dress me. Looking back, I never thought to question the intimacy we had almost immediately between one another, and how we quickly became in the habit of lying like lovers do. Boy, that girl touched me like no other man does or had at that point either and quenches a need I have, deep-rooted in my bones an' all. I told her of this and she gasped at my inexperience. I blushed as she looked at me right in the eyes, deadly serious.

"I aint ever been with no man before, Lydia. Help me."

I was intrigued about her world because of this and soon realised that I wanted to be with her and embody her world alongside her. I took her hands in both of mine as our fulsome, naked forms perched on the end of her bed. I pleaded entirely with conviction to my new friend, "Teach me how to dance, Lydia ... and show me how to make love ..."

That night, Lydia granted my wish and made a woman out of me. She penetrated me with her fingers and broke my insides. I lay on my back and bucked wildly in pleasure on her flowery eiderdown. We lay after and I told her about the pain. She explained that I was like a bottle of wine that needed to be uncorked, in order to be savoured and then drunk.

The next day, I started in the bar alongside Lydia, waiting ... eager to be drank.

25 June 1862, San Francisco

I guess it helped at how pleasant my first gentleman was. We were dancing close with patrons and receiving gropes and intrusions in return for an evening's access to liquor and tobacco as normal. Mamma Carter gave me a light shirt to wear with fancy garters and black stockings. She always insisted we showed class and covered ourselves onstage and in the bar, but as far as anywhere else went, it was anything goes.

I peeled for two gents, subtly mind, and earned myself fifty cents. I had asked the second if he desired to retire behind one of the partitions with me to go further into the matter, but he declined. Not before he took liberties, mind. Him snatching himself a taste of me from down below, regardless. We both knew he shouldn't, but I was new and eager and didn't know any better. He flicked his digit on my button for a few seconds as we both stood there and he dipped it into my bowl, before bringing it up to his moustached lips for a smell. What made me do it, I don't know but I felt the need to sink to my knees. I took him in my mouth for the first time ever. I remembered the way that Lydia had shown me the night before as she suckled on one of my fingers and I wouldn't let him go until he was done, just like she had.

An hour later, during an interval between dances, this fancy gent strides up. He had a high plug hat, curled hair and a crimson frock coat. He looked quite the felonious dandy, if I do say so. His white, ruffled shirt peeked from a fancy waistcoat, which I unbuttoned, as I lay him down on one of the beds upstairs. I crawled on top and giggled as I took my time in revealing what he had to offer me underneath. Lydia was two beds across being done over from behind by this Mexican fella. She winked at me and I felt re-assured my friend was close by. I stroked his waxed moustache and ran my fingers through the hair on his bare chest as I sank down on his hardness.

After that, there was no stopping me. Even Mamma commented on my confidence. She thought I was gonna "run a mile, as soon as any fella revealed it to me", which kinda made me laugh. Lydia and I were like partners in crime and were soon becoming popular as we could offer something that most girls could not. Each other. We'd perform together as often as we could, if nothing for the fun of it. We'd just goof around like we do in private half the time, cavortin' together onstage in nuthin' but our basques and slippers, playing up to the coarse suggesting from the patrons in attendance. We'd tease them by unhooking one another's lacing upon our backs before digging a knee into our partner's back and pulling tightly on the laces. They'd go mad, thinking we were gonna strip all the way for 'em.

We are such teases.

26 June 1862, San Francisco

Mamma Carter is sending me to the naval stores at the Presidio to dance for the officers this week. It will be the first time I have contributed to her long standing arrangement with the soldiers. An arrangement that keeps the house protected and in favour. That, to me is enough of a sacrifice. I can see the pain in Mamma's eyes when "one of her childs go away" and always try to assure her. Mamma sends a different girl each week and it has finally come down to me. I have tended to avoided this task thus far, on account of my popularity on the dance floor. But secretly, I think it has to do with her favouring of me. Normally, just the one lass is taken over on the wagon, but when they have a fancy occasion two go over. Thankfully, it is such this night and I get to go with my Lydia.

"Tell me more about what happens at the garrison?" I ask her, as we both soaked in the tin bath at 4am, our heads soaked in whiskey and our ears ringing from the night's rowdy din.

"Well, I went that one time with Daisy. We rubbed each other on the chest as they whoop away in the background, while abusing themselves and sipping gin."

She tossed her dark curls over her shoulder and continued to suck on her own thumb. The gleeful look in her eyes was very intriguing indeed.

30 June 1862, San Francisco
As we waited in Mamma Carter's room and twittered between one another about the sudden departure another girl took upon, she waddled in and tossed at us each a new herring bone corset each.

"That's for youse girls to keep a hold of. Look after them, mind." We both cooed excited at her and effused gratitudes upon her mountainous frame.

"Now, don't let those fellas maul you much, ya hear? Look after, yo'selves a little . . ." she continued.

"Yes, Ma!" we both trilled.

"The cart's here . . . Go and change, be gone with ya . . . Look respectful now. I gotta reputation to uphold here . . ."

A few hours later, the cart arrived at the Presidio. I took in the warm smell of the recently planted eucalyptus, along with the pine and cypress trees as we rode by the cemetery. I commented to Lydia on the former's soothing nature to one's nose. She feigned boredom and replied that journey was so arduous, wishing for a different mode of transport altogether. I humoured her and longed to hold her, as our ride rocked from side to side.

Despite the lurid descriptions I'd received about happenings at the garrison from the other girls, we were treated as respected ladies as we were escorted down from our mode of journey by the armed hand on offer. We pulled up our long skirts and the heels that we were not used to wearing, which made a clacking sound on the much harder ground of the parade square. In that instant, a more highlighted sense of opulence came over me and inside the building was no different. From the lush fabrics to the antiquities and glorious furniture, me and Lydia were transported to a whole different world entirely. We were ushered into a smoky room and a number of gentlemen in uniform, who all turned and bowed in our direction. They were a lot different to the soldiers we saw out on Main Street and Broadway. They wore fancy tabards and cut trousers and exuded a sense of seniority, for sure. Many were ordained with a number of medals, sashes and other signs of achievement. Some wore hats, some hadn't.

Lydia took my hand and led me into the throng and towards the bar they had in the corner of the room. She instantly greeted and introduced me to a Lieutenant, who nodded respectfully again in my vicinity, to which I replied in curtsey. I tried to waft away the amount of smoke in my face as Lydia took my hand and put a healthy glass of whiskey into it. It was easily four or five fingers and soon I found myself swaying on the spot, not long after I had been handed another. By this time, there were two hands behind me groping at my bits and folds. A number of times, I remember Lydia smacking hands away from my behind, only to replace them with her own.

"She's mine!" she hollered at the men around her. She pulled up the back of my skirt and kneaded ma cheek. I swayed still, but I was more than content with the attentions. She continued to rub my ass before we clasped our faces together, to the obvious glee and erroneous din of the many men folk around us.

Before long, we felt a number of hands at our backs, pointing us towards a door to another room. In there was the large, polished table I had heard of. We were both instantly pushed against its side and the hands and mouths instantly became upon us both.

Gosh, this be a frisky bunch, I thought. Lydia pulled herself up backwards onto the table and grabbed at my shoulders pulling me away from my suitor. She dragged my load onto the sheen of the table top and asked for a quietened hush whilst we performed. She grandstanded with a bravado I hadn't seen in her before.

"I can safely say that tonight will be all of your nights, gentlemen. So if you would all grant us the courtesy of doing our turn, then you can all have your wicked way with us . . . in time. Just be patient." Lydia took my hand once more and raised me to my stockinged feet. "And for those who are extra patient, you will get to see myself interact with my friend here in the act of physical lovemaking. So do, gentlemen . . . be ever patient . . ."

I tried to compose myself through the dance as the whiskey flowed through my bloodstream and filled my head. We continued with our lewd posturin' and Lydia brought me off with her fingers as we stood side by side and leered at the soldiers below us. I'm sure I peeled too quickly, as something sent the throng of men in our vicinity into a lustful rage and they all came upon us. Lydia pleaded and insisted that we finished our turn, to which she turned her attentions upon myself. She lay me on my back and straddled herself over me, covering my face with her desire and playing to the baying crowd, requestin' what she should do to me. Jackets adorned with badges and signs of bravery and daring escapades of which I had little knowledge of were tossed to one side, leaving tunics and ties askew. She rubbed her crotch over my face as she called for a nearby stud to join us on the table.

"Fuck her right here!" she ordered.

"Yes, Ma'am . . ." I heard him over the din.

Before long, myself and Lydia took on the throng of flesh before us. Soon, I found a searching hand which first kneaded my breast but settled on clasping my hand tight. It was my Lydia, in a similar overwhelmed state to me. I squeezed her hand in response as my below was filled with soldier and the weapons of other men hung before me, invitingly. I took each of them into my mouth one by one as each of the men pounded my crotch until they were completely spent and were happy to put their swords back into their sheaths, drained of their ejaculate.

The garrison took us to count on all charges, giving us a thorough search before leaving us on the battlefield, spent, torn and defeated. They chuckled amongst one another, returning to their flowing supply of pillaged Scotch from the smugglers, captured in the bay waters every week. They laughed and bellowed inconsiderately in the background about how they had duly conquered us.

The wagon was called and we headed back to the Dew Drop. We chose to lay with one another on the straw-covered floor, by the baskets of salt and the hung, cured meat. We held each other in our arms, our toes buried in the folds of one another's skirts to keep warm in the Summer night's chill. We yearned for nothing but sanctuary and a nice long soak together, even the hard mattress in Lydia's room to finally collapse on.

4 July 1862, San Francisco
The sky crackles and lights up in multi-coloured sparkles. We are celebrating our independence from the British. I stand outside the Dew Drop with Mamma Carter. The hustle and bustle of life goes on around us. Some celebrate, some need not care. Some are looking for their next taste of opium and some just the next taste of someone like me. They look in wonder and curiosity, these figures who have lain with me in the more recent past. I can see them wondering about the etiquette of approaching me outside the safe confines of the Inn. Mamma Carter puts a big fat arm around me and hollers the first few bars of an out of tune blues number,

"You aint got no hold over me, ma sugar . . ."

Icelys

Michèle Larue
Translated by Noël Burch

Warm ocean air wafted over Icelys' round shoulders and broke in wavelets down her bare back. In her yellow, thigh-hugging bicycle-racer's tights, the beautiful mulata was walking downwind on Avenida Zanja, in the direction of Havana's Chinatown. Two women hobbled past her in the opposite direction, laboring under the weight of their embonpoint. As Icelys squeezed between the two mountains of flesh, she just missed stepping into a pot-hole in the sidewalk, likely to be fatal to wearers of platform soles like hers. She remembered a line from a funny old film she'd seen at school. *Memories of Underdevelopment*: "Cuban women's thighs have been ruined by kidney beans!" If she stayed in Cuba, she'd get fat for sure. The fear of not having enough to eat, the latent anguish, the stress that made her turn up the stereo and get high on decibels, the dread of becoming a shadow, a shadow of herself, on this island where the women were offered up to foreigners like fish in a bowl, the sudden flash of lucidity gave her a shot of adrenaline.

"Pss-pss!"

A line of workers against a wall were lusting after her plump buttocks. Further along, more young men, their arms under the hood of a car in front of a makeshift garage, stared wide-eyed as she passed.

One bare-chested mechanic wiped his hands on a grease-stained rag, snatched a blood-red T-shirt from the handlebars of a bicycle and shouted after her: "*Que calor, eh, mi vida!*"

Breasts held high, Icelys sashayed along in the white light of noon. What was the matter with those hard-up guys, always bugging her like that, trying to get a rise out of her!

"Too hot to walk," the boy observed, giving his pals a wink as he fell in step behind her.

A dialogue ensued, like ping-pong with blindfolds.

"A can of beer under a palm-tree, beautiful!"

"I got a date, man! Think I've been waiting for you to get my kicks?" she answered without turning around.

The boy in the red T-shirt offered to take her to the beach, Santa Maria del Mar, on the other side of the tunnel at the end of the bay. But Icelys wasn't interested in Cuban men. She had just one thing in mind: living in Bologna. It had been an obsession with her ever since she'd started seeing the Italian. Just an ordinary tourist who'd chatted her up one hot night in a bar in old Havana. He wasn't much to look at, but he was going to be the one who would save her. No spring chicken either, fifty, maybe sixty. But an attentive companion, understanding, ideal.

She continued proudly on her way, the mechanic still tagging behind. He was ready to take her anywhere she wanted, he said, and it wouldn't cost her a penny. She shot back: "Riding on a bicycle carrier isn't my style!"

"What? You don't believe me? You just passed my Lada, the green one there, half up on the sidewalk!"

"That heap doesn't have any tires!" Icelys retorted, getting into the spirit of the game.

She crossed an untended garden, stepped over a fat tree-root protruding from the soil. The ground breeze swept a leaf with a purplish gloss ahead of her. Icelys thought she recognized an image of her lips fluttering over the asphalt. Fate was giving her a sign. Skittering across the sidewalk, the leaf flitted about the platform soles of the boy following her. His foot crushed the violet ribs just as Icelys turned into the small, dilapidated courtyard. She wiped the sweat from her forehead and rang the bell on Oreste's building. Her pursuer stood undecided on the sidewalk, then retraced his steps, gnawing his fingernails.

What the garage mechanic could not know was that this young woman had plucked, powdered and generally curried her body merely to receive a phone call, that she worked at the cardiovascular hospital where the whole surgery clinic throbbed to the beat of her love affair, and where all her fellow-nurses admired her stubborn battle for a travel permit.

Seated under the ceiling fan in Oreste's living-room, Icelys thought she could see the end of privations, the day when she would fly away. She dreamt of supple fabrics, fluffy woolens, snowflakes blanketing the Dolomites in winter, while Oreste moved about the room, feet dragging in flip-flops. She began to wonder what he was up to, laying a pair of socks on a chest of drawers, opening a wardrobe, coming back empty-handed. Oreste was well past forty but el Viejo, as he was called in Chinatown, was a wonder. His reputation in bed was unrivaled. This was due to a lethargic temperament according to Mercedes, Icelys' mother, purveyor of neighborhood gossip in the solar where they lived. That Oreste! A bachelor father who pampered his three little daughters, Three Graces by different mothers, all easy enough to marry off with their silken hair and slender bodies.

On the father, not a wrinkle, not a single white hair. Face as smooth as a coffee bean. And a sister who sent him regular sums from Florida. Icelys remembered the benefactress, her bristling hairdo, and everything that came out of those huge suitcases of hers when she showed up in Havana: kitchen robots, blonde wigs, Italian moccasins for her brother. When it was time for her to go home to America, she took a dozen religious statues in her luggage, sacred stones hidden in a flowered tureen or rolled inside an African dress. Was it by virtue of their supernatural powers that the effigies of her saints had gotten through customs? Fifty pounds of ritual objects. Was her brother so busy with his womanizing he couldn't dust off his sister's altar from time to time?

Watching el Viejo busy himself about the room, she remembered some gossip she'd heard: there was supposed to be something special about Oreste's sex, a thing which could really satisfy a woman. Icelys was intrigued by the effects this gimmick evidently produced on the women she glimpsed as they emerged from the bed, faces swollen from love-making whenever she arrived too early on Saturday mornings; women Oreste had taken dancing the night before. She nibbled the inside of her cheeks, lowered her eyes and there, in the crotch of her cycling tights, saw a dark spot on the yellow Lycra. A golden butterfly was gathering nectar on her bulging pubis. She felt embarrassed and swiveled her chair to one side. The faint throbbing of her thighs must have produced a draft, for the shadow was fading. Whistling under his breath, Oreste was hanging up his shirt to dry on the gas-pipe behind the refrigerator. He flattened the sleeves and patted down the starched collar. Graceful in his immaculate tank-top, he poured rum into a porcelain thimble and held it out.

"The call will come soon, *mamita*, I can feel it."

At length the phone rang, and the master of the house nodded his condescending permission: she could pick it up. Armed with her Italian lessons, the young woman leapt in with a heartfelt *Come vai*? But her fiancé would hardly let her get a word in edgewise. She was so churned up just to hear his voice that she wept for joy when he said he would invite her to Bologna the following summer, and only pulled herself together long enough before he hung up to tell him how much she missed him, *Caro mio, amore mio*!

No sooner had she put the phone down than Oreste took a seat on a chair facing her. He put his hand on her knee and warned her about the cold weather in Italy: one would have thought she was planning to emigrate to Siberia.

"It's not just the temperature that's wrong, *muchacha*. Over there, people live shut away in their houses. They pass you in the street, walking fast and looking worried. They don't share anything with their neighbors, can you imagine that? No way to borrow anything from someone who lives across the hall . . . And what's this Italian got that's so special, *mi vida*?"

She told him how kind her fiancé was to her, what fine European manners he had. Then she began running over the list of presents he'd given her.

"A backless dress with yellow stripes . . . You've seen it, I wore it to your last wedding . . . My silver bracelet, here, look: with my name engraved on it. A color TV for Mamma . . ." Oreste's hand crawled slowly on the yellow Lycra while Icelys enumerated her presents on her fingers.

She lost count . . . Her cheeks were suddenly flushed with heat and her voice distorted by lust as she came straight out and asked to see his specialty, his "girl-trap", the mysterious something that gave the women who went with him that languorous gaze. Oreste blew his nose in a little white handkerchief and gazed at her as he folded it carefully: "If I show it to you, you have to try it out."

Icelys' laugh was a bit too loud. Ever since she'd first sat thinking on that chair, watching her host move slowly around the room, she'd had a hard time controlling herself. She dropped to her knees. Her hands were to Oreste's fly, but she hesitated to tackle the buttons, looked up at him, imploring him with her eyes. Oreste was sucking his upper lip with an abstracted air, then finally conceded in a haughty tone: "OK, you can touch it, but after that, you try it out."

At the bottom of the shaft, perfectly visible on either side of the central nervure were embedded five or six tiny balls that rolled under Icelys' fingers.

"Seashells which possess certain special qualities," he revealed to her in prophetic tones. "I was a teenager when the Chinese urged me to have these implants. I must have been about seventeen or eighteen. Most of the younger fishermen have had it done just like me. This way, a man can give a woman extraordinary pleasure!"

"Did it hurt?"

"I couldn't have sex for three days, but it was the result that mattered! Come on, *angelito mio*, get undressed . . ."

Quickly Icelys peeled off the yellow Lycra. Straddling Oreste's knees, one hand around his neck, she pulled away his white underpants, impaled herself and began moving up and down.

"Hey, *viejo*, this gimmick of yours is a lazy man's gadget!" she complained after she'd pumped about thirty times. "You're not making much of an effort, are you? Getting off on your shells is a lot of work!"

Still as a snake basking in the sun, eyes half-closed, Oreste stroked the young woman's voluptuous thighs. When she tried to stick her tongue into his mouth and give his lips a greedy bite, he merely took her chin in two fingers. She came like a fury, waggling her hips. El Viejo had his eyes shut and sucked air between his teeth with a whistling sound.

Icelys ran home to her mother and washed her yellow Lycra. She hated herself for this act of adultery vis-à-vis the Italian. She reproached herself for betraying the trust her cardiovascular colleagues had placed in her, not to mention her mother, who'd throw her out of the house if she knew.

The next day, returning home from night-duty, she bumped into Oreste's old mother, leaning on the arm of a man in white she'd never seen before. The two old people were saying good-bye to her mother, who had a weird expression on her face.

Mercedes had just received a visit from a *babalao*, a holy man of the Santeria. She'd wanted to know if the relationship between her daughter and this Italian from Bologna would ever end in marriage. The *babalao* had laid a raffia mat on the tile floor and spread out his fortune-telling gear. Pebbles, seeds, and shells that he threw into the air several times, like jacks.

Not knowing the results of the lottery that had just been held on the floor of her house, Icelys was on tenterhooks. She guessed her mother's nervousness had to do with the visit from the two cronies, and feared a catastrophe since the woman who had just left was the person in the world who knew most about the little secrets of Oreste's life and body.

And now her mother was pronouncing her Italian fiancé's name. She was convinced the whole affair was ill-fated, advised her daughter not to put all her eggs in one basket, to look for another foreigner who could get her out of the country while she was still young and appetizing. Icelys remembered the two women she'd seen the day before, behinds blown up like balloon tires. She said to herself if this marriage fell through, she'd take it out on food. When some tourist took her to a fancy restaurant, she'd gobble up all the goodies reserved for foreigners, filet mignon, lobster and pargo, the tastiest fish in the world according to her grandmother who'd eaten some in 1955 in honor of the birth of her daughter, Mercedes. Choking back her tears, she asked her mother: "You don't think the Italian's going to send me the plane ticket he promised?"

"*Hija mia*, the shells have spoken!"

Pre-Party

Thomas S. Roche

It's just a little meet and greet before the event; you know, get relaxed, get acquainted, get a cab – nothing big.

Everyone's already dressed when they arrive, but of course as always Jessa's the last one to suit up. She's spent the whole day slicing crudités and assembling complicated hors d'oeuvres and other comestibles she's studied in the pages of esoteric European magazines, which is essentially what she rushes into the bedroom to do when everyone starts to show up. The main exception is that in this case the comestible to be assembled is her.

Justin's left on the couch in his tight leather pants, high boots and wifebeater, making kinky conversation with Tara from the kinky headshop and her girlfriend (or girl friend? He's not sure) named Raven or Blackbird or something, Sherry from the local leather group and her boyfriend what's-his-name (whom Justin isn't entirely sure he likes), Mike from the gay bar and his new boyfriend from Denmark or Holland or Sweden or something, Jens or Jurgen or Jan. They're all strapped to the nines, Mike in the leatherboy uniform, Sven in slick rubber, Tara in a PVC WAC uniform, Sherry in a corset and miniskirt, Boyfriend, kinda lamely, in a black leather duster, short-haired, butch-of-center Raven in PVC pants and halter and thigh-high boots – she's got an overcoat in the hall closet. They're all sipping cocktails and nibbling canapés; nibbling, for most of them, because with clothes this tight there's not really anywhere for most of it to go.

The cocktails, however, they manage to find plenty of room for. For the first ten minutes of Jessa's "quick" shower – she's notorious – Justin freshens the cocktails, but pretty soon the bottles have found their way over and everyone's freshening their own; the conversation gets raunchier and before too much longer Sherry's been dragged over Mike and Sven's laps and the two of them are trading off giving her hard spanks while she giggles and then softly begins to moan.

This seems kind of weird to Justin – like the things you hear are supposed to happen at San Francisco parties before fetish balls, but never do. Well, it's happening, and Sherry's odd boyfriend doesn't seem to have a strong opinion one way or another, but from the slowly rising moans and softly dwindling giggles, Sherry certainly does. Justin shifts uncomfortably; Mike has pulled up Sherry's tight latex skirt and from where he's sitting, Justin can see quite clearly that she is not wearing much at all underneath.

In fact, as the spanking continues, Mike takes an entirely uncalled-for liberty, playfully plucking the crotch of Sherry's G-string out of the way, giving Justin a crotch shot that reveals smooth lips flushed with excitement. Boyfriend gets a funky look on his face, staring daggers or giving a mental high-five, Justin isn't sure. What he *is* sure about is that he has to shift quite nervously and attempt a little hippy-shake to pop his cock out of its awkward down-pointing position, because it's getting harder by the moment, no less when Mike invites him to fondle Sherry a little.

"Oh, I don't think so," says Justin meekly "But thanks." *How do gay guys get away with this?* he's thinking, but he already knows the answer, or perhaps knows that there is no meaningful answer, and besides, he's less concerned about the sociopolitical ramifications of Sherry getting fingered than he is about whether his cock is going to snap in half if he doesn't shuffle it.

"Finger her butt!" guffaws Boyfriend bizarrely, out of the blue, and Justin makes his decision: he doesn't like the guy. What a freak.

"That is a naughty boyfriend you've got," says Jens, the exchange vaguely comical in his Dutch/Danish/Icelandic accent, and Justin manages to sneak a hand along his crotch to readjust the damn thing, but he gets it all wrong and now his cock's jammed in to the waistband of his leather pants. He softly says "Motherfuck," asking himself for the dozenth time why he's self conscious about adjusting his dong when a girl he only vaguely knows is being fingered a few feet away and oh, incidentally, the lesbians are going at it pretty hot and heavy, making out, with Raven's hand between Tara's thighs, pretty far up under the hem of that WAC skirt – things are getting interesting, but all Justin can feel is awkward. Even though he's wearing leather-butch drag, he's not much of a public top, even in his own home. Besides, he and Jessa didn't have that conversation yet – there were too many hors d'oeuvres to make – limits? Boundaries? Who the fuck knows?

"Hey, baby?" came Jessa's voice from the top of the stairs. Justin has never been so relieved in all his life; it gives him the perfect excuse to get up and leave the scene. His relief only lasts a moment, though, because as he walks his mostly hard dick goes wrenching down into the elastic of his boxer-briefs' left leg, and he's right back in discomfort-ville.

"Need something?" he calls up the stairs, his voice as pleasant as he can make it – and fairly pleasant, really, all things considered.

"I need help getting into my dress. Can you send one of the girls up?"

Justin shoots a look at the couch area; Tara and Blackbird are definitely déshabillé; Sherry is most definitely occupied as Boyfriend periodically yelps "Spank her!" and "Smack 'er butt!"

Justin races up the stairs, pausing halfway to stick his hands down his leather pants and adjust his cock; he breathes a sigh of relief. He runs the rest of the way up to the bedroom door, opens it. Jessa is stark naked; she whirls, gasps, covers herself with her hands, tits only, freshly shaved pussy still visible. Justin's eyes go wide, then he gives her a wicked smile.

"I said send one of the girls!"

"They're all busy," says Justin, eyeing Jessa up and down lasciviously. "All of a sudden you're afraid to let me see you naked?"

She glances at the bed, where an immaculate black rubber minidress with a tomato-red stripe down the side sits alongside a pair of rubber panties and a bottle of cornstarch baby-powder.

"I didn't want you to see my dress until I'm ready," she says with a flirty smile. "It's a surprise."

"I'm surprised." Justin smiles, and moves closer to Jessa. For an instant it seems like she's going to move away, but then she melts into him and as his arms go around her he feels the smoothness of her well-dried flesh; four damp towels form a trail from the bathroom, terminating in a limp pair of thigh-high black latex boots, a stripe on the outside of each the exact tomato-red of the stripe on the dress.

"Amazing," he whispers.

She feels the bulge in his leathers just as his finger finds she's not dry all over. She wriggles deeper into him and he fingers her until she whimpers, then pushes away.

"Everybody's waiting," she says. "I need to get dressed."

"They've got crudités," says Justin. "And drinks." He smiles evilly. "And I'm sure they can entertain themselves."

She comes close, kisses him, rubs his cock through his pants. "You can fuck me at the party," she whispers. "They've got that great back alley behind the standing cage." She pulls away; he gropes after her; she dances out of reach. "Help me get my dress on?"

"If you insist," he says, eyeing her naked body.

"I have to put the boots on first," she says, sitting on the edge of the very high four-poster bed – his thoughts going evil places: how many times has he had her tied to that bed? How desperately does he want to tie her to it *right now?* – and lifting one sockless foot into the air as she pulls on one high boot. *She's not going to be able to walk much without socks*, thinks Justin; then again, he's not sure he wants her to.

Jessa wiggles her foot at him. "Zip?"

Justin gets close enough to smell her, his fingers caressing the zipper as he draws it over her ankle, up her calf, past her scrumptious knee, and up her thigh. On the inside. His hand keeps moving. Two fingers go into her, easy as pie, before she can close her legs. She slips back onto the bed, arches her back, moans.

"Stop," she gasps, wriggling her way off of him. She's smiling, but flushed, breathing hard. She kicks him away playfully with her high-heeled latex domme boot; she squirms her shapely foot into the other boot, then shoots him a wicked look, knowing what's coming; with this one he takes his time zipping, letting his hands travel more slowly, and she lets him fuck her a little, two fingers inside her and a thumb on her clit, legs spread, her body looking magnificent, naked except for those boots. He goes to lunge onto her. She pulls and rolls away, seizing the cornstarch.

"Powder me," she orders, handing him the bottle and putting up her arms. He frowns, scowls, dusts cornstarch onto his palms and begins rubbing them all over her. He starts with her breasts, because how can he not? She moans softly as his dusted palms work her nipples. He rubs down lower, turns her around, does her back, dusts her ass, spends more time on her breasts, her nipples now even harder, more sensitive, more responsive to the gentle pinches he gives her.

"You were going to let Sherry do this?"

"Maybe," she sighs softly. "With a few minor variations."

Bending over so that her naked, cornstarch-dusted ass rubs against the swell of his leather-clad cock, she reaches out and gets the dress. She stands, and he takes it from her, stretches it, holds it for her to slide her arms into, then pulls it over her head, then gently pulls it down over her body: shoulders, breasts – going very slowly, caressing as he does – belly – ditto – then hips, and as he snugs the dress down over her thighs to the point where it's just barely decent, she wriggles to help him settle it, and he decides the last thing he wants is this fucking dress *settled*.

She doesn't even realize what's happening; he's bent her over the edge of the bed and has one hand on his belt, the other circling her wrist. She gasps, squirms a little, struggles, pushes back, starts to fight, weakly. When he kicks her booted feet apart, she does not pull them back together; she does not wriggle out of his grasp, and when the zipper goes down and his cock comes free, her hand gropes after it – but no, that's not how she's going to have him. He grabs her free wrist and pins it with the other up high in the small of her back, bending her over harder, shoving her against the bed as he surges onto her. She's played the tease, now she'll play the victim.

He holds her wrists tight and pins her to the bed. He wants to enter her without preliminary, taking her violently, savagely – but he stops at the last minute, holding his pinned captive and biting the back of her neck so hard she surges and writhes against him, crying out. His cockhead teases and rubs her lips, smooth with razor and lotion and cornstarch, in that order, slick with pussy juice and pre-come, in *that* order. Then as he pins her wrists behind her, holding them tighter than ever, he uses his other hand to open up the swollen lips of her sex and his cockhead finds her center.

He's in her with a single smooth thrust, and she tries to stifle it, the scream, but she can't. With the second thrust, deep into her, it's midway between a cry and a yelp; then it's all moan, slow and soft, as he begins to fuck her rapidly, not giving her a chance to acclimate, just taking her, using her, giving her stroke after stroke and not caring that he's going to come well before she can.

But then he remembers his own wicked plan for the evening – a surreptitious, forbidden fuck, in that dark corner behind the standing cage, and Jessa climaxing desperately on his cock because ever the Boy Scout, he's thought ahead.

He no longer needs both hands; the one pinning her wrists is a nice touch, but his cock's doing a fine job of holding her lips open wide as he slides in and out of her. He reaches into his tight leather pants, the belt buckle rattling and making her gasp a little as its coldness grazes her skin. He comes out with a tiny pushbutton vibrator, the size of a robin's egg.

She never sees it coming. He's into her all the way again, so deep that when he pushes the vibe up against her clit he can feel her muscles contracting around his cock. But she holds him too tight; he wants her too bad; as he fucks wildly into her he realizes they're not going to hit it together. Holding the vibrator in place, he stops, all the way inside her; he breathes hard, he shudders, he freezes; every muscle in his body goes tense. He pulls out and his head swells her entrance. She arches her back and shoves herself back onto him.

Fuck it, he figures, and starts thrusting smoothly into her; it's maybe three strokes before it happens. He lets out a long, savage groan. He heaves his body onto her and his hips piston as he pins her against the bed. She shoves back against his pressure, and he floods her with his come.

Jessa lets out a low sigh of satisfaction, obviously thinking she's finished, but nothing could be further from the truth. When he pulls out of her easily, a thick string of his come glistens between his cock and her sex. She goes to get up from under him, but he still pins her wrists. She seems puzzled for a moment.

"What about the guests?"

"By now I think Mike's probably bisexual," I said, "and I wouldn't be surprised if Sherry's boyfriend's gone gay."

She looks at him over her shoulder, her makeup a little messy, one eye open wider than the other.

"Huh?"

Without answering, he clicks off the vibe, holds her wrists tighter, leans over her, grabs the rubber panties, not caring a bit that they're both dribbling his come onto the floor. He has to let go of her wrists to do it, which is a disappointment since that's his biggest turn-on, pinning her wrists while he fucks her; he also has to nudge her legs closed, which is a disappointment since that's his second biggest turn-on. But it's all worth it, as he guides first one booted foot, then the other, up and through the legs of the rubber panties.

"What are you doing?" she whines meekly. "We've got to get to the party."

The cornstarch on her thighs is lost to sweat and friction, so the stroke of the rubber up her legs is not quite smooth, but it's worth it when he snuggles the form-fitting panties over her sex, then tucks the vibe into it and squeezes.

"Oh Jesus fucking Christ," she says, and a few other things, considerably louder, as he climbs onto the bed and drags her bodily over his lap, smearing the remnants of his come over her latex dress and not caring, pinning her wrists with his left hand while with his right he does something he knows she's wanted since the first time he playfully smacked her ass in the kitchen, around three, when she protested weakly that she had crudités to slice.

He pulls up her skirt and exposes her ass for a spanking.

"The guests," she says, her voice all bleating desperation as he rubs the crotch of the rubber panties, forcing the vibe against her clit so that she gasps. Then he draws back and his cupped hand comes down hard on one firm cheek of her ass. She utters a yelp, grinds her hips against him. The vibe goes visibly jiggling around; even in the tight rubber panties it can't stay absolutely still. He brings his hand down again, feeling the taut clench and the give of her ass cheek. This time she doesn't yelp; she moans.

He adjusts the vibe and lifts his hand. This blow makes her whimper, softly, as she fucks herself slowly and rhythmically against his lap, rubbing the vibe between her clit and his thigh while she presents herself, ass high, for his next blow.

He gives it to her, right on the sweet spot, knowing from experience that the burst of sensation is going right into her clit, or her cunt, or her asshole, or something, some magic part of her that's going to get her off, especially with the vibe buzzing crazily.

He starts spanking her faster, a blow every other second, one cheek to the other, then both, then her pussy, careful not to smack the vibe – that would hurt, and worse yet, it might break the damn thing. She's moaning and bucking, and he's let go of her wrists because she needs them to claw at the bed. His hand's in her mouth, now, her biting his palm, hard, as he spanks her rapidly, adjusting the vibe every dozen strokes or so to make sure it's right where it's supposed to be – on her clit, making her come.

But it's the spanking that pushes her over the edge, when he blows off the vibe and just lets it bounce and jiggle in there, and smacks her hard on one sweet spot and then the other, over and over again, faster while she bites his palm until he's afraid she'll draw blood and is surprised he doesn't care – then she moans so loud he knows the guests downstairs are hearing it, and since he's sure they don't care, he doesn't care – but he probably wouldn't anyway.

She writhes until her face is pointing up a little and her back is straight, leaving her rigid across his lap; her eyes go wide, and he catches them – open, lost, empty, focused on nothing but the explosion of pleasure that's about to go through her. Then it happens, and her eyes go tightly shut, and she melts into him again, dissolving into the rapid blows of his open hand on her ass, bucking and humping and shuddering all over as she comes.

When she finally goes slack, she desperately gropes after the vibe to turn it off, but can't manage it, her hands are shaking so bad. He slips his hands into her rubber panties and turns off the tiny machine. Good thing the vibrator's waterproof. Inside, the panties are molten, juices leaking out onto his leather pants and dribbling onto the bed.

She takes a deep breath, goes sliding out of his lap, lands on the floor with her head on his thigh.

"The guests," says Jessa. "We should get downstairs. How rude of us."

Justin smiles, caressing her face as another little set of spasms goes through her body.

"I'm pretty sure they're entertaining each other," he says. "But yes. We should get downstairs."

He helps her up, dries her off a little, and even adds some cornstarch. The vibe goes back in his pocket, and he doesn't even bother to rinse it off first. They've got a fetish ball to get to.

Green Mars

Savannah Lee

"Would you please not masturbate while you're driving."

"I'm not masturbating!"

"You've got your cock out."

"I'm just holding it! It gets lonely on long drives."

"I'll show it 'lonely'."

"You're one to talk. Whenever Janet calls, you get so bored you start playing with the twins."

"The difference being," she points out, "that I am on the *phone* during those times, as opposed to hurtling down the interstate at seventy-five miles an hour."

"In North Dakota," he counters. "Do you see any other cars around? Do you see *anything* around? It's like Mars, only green. We're driving through Mars. Green Mars."

"Ryan loved Mars. Did you know that, Dave? I guess you must have. Speaking of which, I have this memory of him from back before I met you. Naked, actually."

"You naked? Or him?"

"Him."

"Um, I really don't need to think about my naked . . ." (there is another word underneath, maybe one like "dead") ". . . brother. Can we go back to thinking about you taking your shirt off when Janet calls?"

"Actually, no. I want to talk about Ryan. We're halfway to his funeral and we haven't said a word! This isn't just your loss, Dave. It's mine too. I only dated Ryan for three months before I met you, and I know that's not the same as being his brother, but it's still something."

"I'll tell you what's something – when Janet calls and you take your shirt off."

"I have this memory," she insists, "of Ryan sitting naked in his beanbag and staring up at the ceiling."

"By this time it's like Pavlov's dog. The minute you hear her voice, off goes the shirt."

"I forget why we were talking about this, but he smiled up at the ceiling and he said 'Ray Bradbury is the true historian of Mars.' "

"And then you start palming a breast. Usually the right one. I guess that's because you're right-handed."

"He said, 'Someday we're going to go there and we're going to find Ray Bradbury's cities. The tall cities built by the tall Martians. Where rivers ran through the streets'."

"You start out with gentle squeezes, and then you start rubbing it up and down with the flat of your palm. Very lightly. I made a note of that, you know. Have you noticed my tit-rubbing technique improving?"

"Then he said, 'I wonder what fucking was like in those cities. Did they fuck at night? Did they fuck in the early morning? Did they fuck in their strange Martian beds? Did they fuck on the floor? Did they face each other, or were they like almost every other species we know of, and fucked from behind?' "

"After you're done rubbing your tit, you pull back and kind of dig your fingers into it like the legs of a spider, but leaving the nipple untouched. Me, I'd go straight for the nipple. But you, you save it for last."

"He held out his arms to me and said, 'But one thing I know, my darling. However they fucked . . . they did it to the sound of the rivers. The rivers rushing by.' "

"I've always thought that was funny – how you sneak up on your nipples."

"He started singing 'Gather at the River.' 'Yes, we shall gather at the ri-ver, the beau-ti-ful, the beau-ti-ful, the ri-ver; yes, we shall gather at the ri-ver, that flows by the throne of God.' "

"You get the whole rest of your breast tight and humming first, and then you plot the assault on the citadel."

"Only he sang a different version. He sang, 'Yes, we shall gather at the river that flows by the cities of Mars.'"

"Like a ninja you sneak up on that nipple."

"'We'll gather there, Laura,' he told me. 'Someday.' Then he pulled me onto his cock."

"A nipple-ninja, that's what you are. I wonder if that was a specialty. I wonder if the Shinobi had special Nipple Ninjas. I . . ."

"I can feel it, Dave. Like it was yesterday. Like he couldn't possibly be . . ."

"Stop! Just stop. Okay?"

"Why?"

"Because! Rather than my naked . . ." (there's still that other word underneath) ". . . brother, Laura, I'd prefer to think about your fingers creeping across your bra towards your nipple while Janet goes on about her adventures with aphids."

"Okay. Fine. For now. Janet, by the way, does not talk about aphids. She talks about going to the co-op to buy tomato soup."

"Your fingers crawl closer and into position."

"Generally, it's like, she can't find her favorite brand of soup, so she compares the labels on the two other brands, but they both have fennel, and she's allergic to fennel, so . . ."

"I always expect you to pounce like a tiger."

"Uh, Dave? You're no longer just 'holding' your cock. And it's most certainly not lonely anymore."

"But no. Your index and fuck-you fingers rise slowly into the air, stretch out, and then come together like chopsticks on your nipple . . ."

"Dave. You're starting to weave."

"You always give it one or two grinds and then you've got to get that bra out of the way."

"Dave? I don't think it's working for you to drive and wank at the same time."

"And I mean out of the way right now. You dig your tit out like it's on fire."

"Dave . . ."

"And then, oh God, you squeeze your nipple in those human chopsticks again and it pops out like a pomegranate aril – a little red jewel –"

"DAVE!"

"And all the while," is the next thing he says, "you're sitting there going 'uh-huh, uh-huh' to Janet like nothing was happening. As if you weren't even remotely stimulating yourself to orgasm by twisting your jewels. How do you do it?"

"Maybe the same way you're managing to ignore that we just *wrecked* the car. Crashed it."

"I don't really think we wrecked it, not in so many words. The car just needs to rest."

"On its side? In the grass? With a window knocked out?"

"Yeah, right here in this pretty garden."

"In this *what*?"

"Do you hear the river? The river breeze stirring the leaves?"

"Yeah. Yeah, I sure do, Dave. You bet. For Chrissakes, have you still got your cock in your hand?"

"Wanna dip it in the river?"

"By which you mean exactly what?"

"I don't know . . . love?"

"If you define 'love' as 'cock-and-ball-torture on a level that even the folks at Bound Gods couldn't imagine,' then yes. But if you're talking about one of Lady Laura's soft-mouth specials, then you can pretty much take that cock and shove it up your ass. Dry. Now help me get to my phone."

"I love . . . I've always loved it when you talk rough."

"Phone!"

"Okay, okay, I'll play along. Are you going to call Janet?"

"*Janet*? Dave! We're lying on our side in a freaking field!"

"Call Janet."

"But the funeral! We've got to call your mother. We've got to tell her we'll be late for Ryan's funeral! My God, we might even miss it!"

"Call Janet."

"What?"

"Janet. Call Janet. I want to watch you talk to Janet."

"Dave, what are you . . .?"

"Don't worry, I'm just opening your shirt."

"You cannot . . . oh . . ."

"Show me those jewels. Those little red jewels. Oh, they're trembling."

"That's because we just . . ."

"And cold. Here . . . let me"

". . . Oh."

"Yeah. Let me warm them. Just like you warm them with your own hands, when Janet's been going on about tomato soup until you're so bored you can't stand it anymore. So bored you're going crazy. So filled with nothingness that you see the abyss."

"Dave . . . I've never heard you like this before . . ."

"Your fingers crawl across your breasts towards your nipples like pieces of your soul crawling away from fear."

"Yes, something's come over you. What happened to the spider legs? To the citadel? What happened to . . . heh . . . what happened to the Nipple Ninjas?"

"Stop that. Do you see me smiling? I don't have time for that anymore, Laura, and neither do you. That's from another world. I see it all differently now. Your fingers in my mind. Nails painted red. Each red fingernail opens like an eye. Not that Janet knows. Or cares. She keeps on droning. Petty droning that drowns out the river, or maybe it *is* the river, the dark side of the river, the dangerous side, not unruly but shallow. The sound of it is poison. The eyes in your fingers open wide and see the abyss."

"Dave? Is this really you?"

"The abyss is real – but so is this. So is this, Laura. So is this flesh. So are these jewels. These rubies, I've never seen them so red. Your blood's been racing."

"Ryan! Ryan's in the abyss. He saw it and he couldn't get away from it. It came for him."

"Let's give him this."

"What . . ."

"Open the red river, Laura. The Martian river, endlessly flowing. It's not out there. It's in here, it's the heat-river from your jewels to your hole. Didn't you tell me that once? That when I sucked your tit, you felt it all the way down to your hole?"

"Yes."

"When I press my head to you, like this, I can hear it. That river inside. It never goes away. Open your legs. Open your legs for my hand. Let me feel where the river meets the world. Yes. Let me get my finger in the channel. Oh, it's hot."

"Yes."

"Let me stick another finger in you. Let me get my thumb against your trigger. You like that? Yeah. See, you can't even answer me. Where's my tough talker now? Hah. You're riding down the river. I'll tweak you up top here . . . see, I can get both your nipples in one hand, look, look at my wingspan, I've got 'em both, and I won't let go. You can't escape now. You can only go deeper into the river."

"Where does it . . . where does it . . . where does it end? You with your new thoughts – tell me."

"Unbuckle. Come down on me. That's it, I've got you. Come on. There. Yes. Now what did you say back there? You said Ryan pulled you onto his cock?"

"He pulled me on and fucked me."

"Do you want me to pull you on and fuck you?"

". . . Yes."

"Like this?"

". . . Oh."

"Like *this*?"

"The river! I can hear the river . . ."

"You are the river."

"Ryan's river. It's always been around us, hasn't it. I can't remember a time when it wasn't . . ."

"Do you feel me, baby?"

"Oh yes."

"Do you really feel me?"

"Oh, I . . ."

"Is it hitting just the right spot? Is it gonna kick you over? Is it gonna spill you? Are you gonna flow? Drown me, Laura. Drown me. Drown me and I'll meet you at the . . ."

"*Oh,* here it goes *Ah* . . . Oh, I can't even see, that was so hard . . . and I don't even care. After one like that, all I need is just to lie here and listen to the river. Isn't it funny I never noticed it before? Maybe there was just too much else going on. Maybe it took coming out here, where it's so empty, the plains? The primeval riverbed? Green Mars? The strangest country there's ever been. Where you can get off on tales of the co-op and come in a car wreck. Where the river rustles the leaves . . . do you hear it? That river air troubling the leaves? Yes, the leaves. Running its fingers through them . . . it sounds so sweet I just might forgive you for all of this. Now help me find my . . . help me find my phone. We really need to call . . . someone . . . someone . . . they have to hear the river . . . the beautiful river . . .

" . . . *the beau-ti-ful, the beau-ti-ful, the ri-ver; yes, we shall gather at the river, that flows by the* . . .

"Dave?

"Dave, why don't you answer me?

"Dave? Dave . . . are we dreaming?

"Are we . . .

Baby, It's Cold Outside

Marilyn Jaye Lewis

The Philadelphia Flyers had come into the new hockey season ranked down at the very bottom of the Eastern Conference, but Connor Moore, a die-hard Flyers fan, knew there was still plenty of time left in the season for them to get back on top. He was determined to get to the arena in plenty of time for today's face-off – the Flyers were playing the NY Rangers at five o'clock. Another snowfall was heading toward Hellertown, but Connor was undeterred. They would make it to Philadelphia come hell or high water – or even more snow.

Kaylie Moore, Connor's wife, was less than a die-hard hockey fan. She didn't hate it; she simply didn't love it. But she did love Connor and after three years of marriage and two years of steady dating, she'd gotten used to his devotion to the Flyers, to his love of the sport. She saw the home games as a way to spend time with her husband, if nothing else. Still, sometimes his fanaticism drove Kaylie a little nuts. Here they were, already getting into the car.

"Don't you think that two o'clock is a little early to be leaving, Connor? The game doesn't start until five. We're only about an hour away."

Connor slid into the driver's seat and pulled closed the car door. "I'm leaving plenty of time for bad weather and – I thought I'd surprise you."

This perked Kaylie's interest. "Really? Surprise me how?" She fastened her seatbelt.

"We're taking the scenic route. I thought I'd go 611 the whole way instead of the freeway. How does that sound? And we can stop at that old barn thing you like – that farmer's market."

It was a very nice surprise. Kaylie was amazed that he'd even thought of it – on a hockey day, no less. "I'll bet 611 will be beautiful in this snow, but I don't think the market is open in the winter time, Connor."

"Sure they are." Connor put the car in reverse and backed down the long graveled driveway to the semi-rural street they lived on, Fullerton Way. "There must be something farmers can sell in the winter. You know, stuff they ship in from California that we could buy cheaper just about anywhere else. It's the ambiance we're after here and I'm sure they're well aware of it, even in winter. Farmers can be pretty shrewd."

Kaylie smiled in spite of herself. "Pretty shrewd" was her husband's pat way of describing anyone whose crafts, food, folk art, or furniture were packaged in just the right way to get Kaylie to part with her hard-earned money. The Amish, the Quakers, and now, apparently, the farmers were all "pretty shrewd."

"You're sweet," she said. "Thank you for thinking of it."

"I just wanted to make sure you knew that I wasn't *totally* self-centered. I know I've seemed like it lately."

"It's not that, Connor. I don't think of you as self-centered."

"As what, then – afraid? Is that how you think of me?"

"Yes, maybe a little afraid." She was quick to add, "But that's okay."

"It's okay because I'm a man, you mean? We're all afraid of having children?"

"No, I didn't say that."

"Then it's not the children we're afraid of, per se –" Connor drove east on Fullerton Way, past the old filling station that was now called Rosie's Bar & Grille. "It's the *cost* of children, the permanence, the un-ending responsibility of them; that's what we men are afraid of, right?"

Kaylie looked away from him and made sure not to sigh. Sighing usually made Connor feel guilty and then this never-changing discussion they seemed to have almost daily now would morph into an argument and Kaylie didn't want that, least of all today when he was trying so hard to be a good egg about everything.

"You're allowed to respond, you know, Kaylie; you don't have to sit there and just stare out the window. We can talk about this, can't we, without getting into a fight?"

It was such a loaded topic that Kaylie couldn't help herself now, she sighed.

"What?" he said, sounding exasperated already. "I know you want to have a baby."

She looked at him. "*We* want to have one."

"Right. *We* want to have one. Just not –" Connor caught himself before he said it but it was too late.

"Just not now." Kaylie finished his thought for him.

"I didn't say that."

"What are you saying then, Connor? Just tell me."

"I'm thinking about it. That's all."

Kaylie thought this was either very promising news; that he was seriously thinking about it, about being agreeable, finally, and trying to make a baby with her. Or it was merely another stall tactic. She decided to think positive and leave well enough alone for now. No reason to push him if he was indeed trying to be agreeable. "Thanks, Connor," she said. And she thought it would be best to change the subject for a while. "So how are the NY Rangers ranked right now?"

"Third."

"Wow. This should be a good game."

"It sure will," Connor agreed. "I'm excited." At the flashing yellow traffic light, he veered left, toward 611 and the Delaware River; it would be the river and trees and then pastoral foothills from here on out, and all of it, except the madly rushing river, was frosted with a light layer of still-white, two-day-old snow.

Kaylie loved snow, and she loved taking the scenic route anywhere. She hated freeways. She especially loved taking 611, following the bends in the river. In the early days of their marriage, she and Connor used to take a lot of drives along the Delaware, stopping for picnics or to take hikes along the old canal. They hadn't done anything like that in a long while. Now, seeing it all dusted with snow made Kaylie's heart happy; her perspective freshened on everything. And it brought back memories, to boot.

"Remember that time—" she began.

Connor cut her off. "Yes," he said, smiling. "I do."

She smiled back at him. She was feeling her hormones stirring but she didn't want to say anything about it. She was ovulating; it would be sure to lead to a huge argument as soon as he found out. Better to change the subject again, but she didn't feel like talking about hockey. She wanted to have a baby. In all honesty, it was all she thought about anymore.

Not privy to his wife's thought processes Connor was still on the topic of memories. "We were pretty bold that day, weren't we? I mean, even for us."

"I guess so," Kaylie replied distractedly.

"You *guess* so? Jesus, Kay, that's understating it. You know, I think about that day from time to time and I still get off on it."

This took her aback; she thought she'd been alone in that secret pleasure. "You do?"

"Yeah, I do. That was so hot, don't you think? I get a lot of mileage out of that memory. You were such a wild little girl that day. Not that you aren't all the time," he added playfully. "You just outdid yourself that time – and in public, no less."

"It was hardly 'in public'," she said, suddenly feeling shy about it. "We were simply outside."

Connor reached over and squeezed her hand. "Hey, you're blushing."

"I am not."

"Yes, you are."

The simple touch of his hand on hers gave Kaylie that spark; it ignited somewhere between her heart and her belly, and the sudden clarity of the memory overwhelmed her in its intimate detail. They'd been walking along the tow path of the old canal that day; it was late spring, warm enough to be walking without jackets for the first time that season. The sky had been that perfect shade of blue; the clouds, puffy and bright white. The air was filled with the scent of the first May blossoms and the river itself had smelled of spring; a thing alive and fresh and full of new promises. It had made Kaylie feel hungry for life – insatiable for it, in fact. One minute, she'd been kissing Connor; the next, she'd felt ravenous for his tongue. They were *really* kissing then – passionately, right there on the old tow path, out in the open. She was clinging to Connor's neck and his hand was up under her T-shirt. The feel of his fingertips grazing her nipple, even through the lace of her bra, had set her on fire. She'd practically dragged him to the ranger station – a very small, very old clapboard house just off the main path – and thrown him down onto the grass behind the building.

For a mere moment, she'd confined herself to lying on top of him in the grass and kissing him like crazy. But it wasn't long before he had her shirt pushed up, her bra tugged up over her tits and her tits exposed in the air – her tender nipple suddenly in his mouth and swelling from the intense pressure of how fiercely he was sucking on her.

She couldn't stand it then. She'd reached behind her and unclasped the bra but even that had felt too constricting. She managed to pull the tee shirt and then the bra off completely. It had felt so liberating, she remembered; that was the exact feeling, to be suddenly topless in the warm spring air, with Connor so eager to devour her nipples. It had become quickly obvious that they were going to have to fuck – there was no doubt about it. She was too worked up.

Her hands were at his belt, unbuckling it. Abruptly, his mouth was off her. "Kaylie," he said. "What are you doing?"

"You know what I'm doing," she insisted – hurriedly, as she fumbled with his buckle.

"Not really." He was mildly alarmed when he felt his zipper coming down. "It could be a couple things," he stammered, feeling his cock spring out into the warm air. "Oh, Christ, Kay." He gasped quietly; his head fell back into the grass as he surrendered to his wife's mouth in utter delight. Her mouth felt so hot and so wet, and she was so greedy about it. She was really sucking on it, creating too much pressure, letting the head of his cock nudge way back in her throat.

"Shit, Kaylie, I'm going to come."

It was happening too fast. Kaylie stopped. "No way," she said breathlessly. "Don't you do that to me, I'm too excited."

"Kay, what you are doing?" Connor watched his wife with mixed feelings of shock and absolute arousal as she stood up and unzipped her own jeans and then pulled them, and her panties, all the way down. She kicked off her sneakers almost angrily, as if she couldn't get them off her feet quick enough, and in a heartbeat, she was completely naked. Right out there in the open.

She looked so beautiful, so swept up in her own desire. Connor pulled her down next to him in the grass, then rolled on top of her and mounted her. Her pussy was soaking, completely ready for him. The slick hole opened around his cock and her heat enveloped him. "This is not exactly going to keep me from coming," he'd warned her; her lips kissing his cheek, his chin, and then even his mouth as he spoke to her. "I hope you know that."

"I know that," she insisted quietly. "Just fuck me, honey. Be quiet and fuck me. Come whenever you need to."

"You mean, *in* you?" he said in her ear; his voice sounding just as insistent – and just as breathless as hers. "You want me to come in you? It's okay? It's not your time or anything?"

"It's okay," she'd half-answered, half-cried that day as he'd suddenly gone at her with vigor. "You can come in me," she'd said, "– *oh god*." He was so hard and going in deep. She spread her thighs wider, hiked her legs higher; feeling him going *really* deep. "Connor, *shit* – oh god."

She gripped him tight in her arms and then hugged her knees close to him, letting him go at her very hard and very fast, while she whimpered and cried in his ear in rhythm to every repeated thrust.

Miraculously, he had kept himself from coming right away. Once he'd found his rhythm in her, he'd kept it going, entranced by the sounds of her pleasure. He'd gone at her harder than he usually did; he'd felt that caught up in the rhythm of her cries. He'd never known her to sound so full of lust before. It had finally overwhelmed him.

He came in her, and even though she hadn't come yet, she'd suddenly felt very exposed out there by the canal bank, on the grass behind some old ranger station – and she hadn't thought to check if it was occupied or not. She'd hurried to get back into her clothes. It was not a moment too soon.

Connor seemed to be keeping pace with her reveries. "Do you think that the park ranger had been watching us the whole time?"

When Connor spoke, he startled Kaylie back to the present, back to the reality of the car, its heater on high as they drove along 611. It wasn't spring, it was winter. There was snow out there along the canal now.

Kaylie laughed uneasily. "I don't know," she said.

"He sure timed it right, didn't he? Coming around the back of that house the minute you'd finished putting your clothes on?"

"I'd wondered about that, too – his impeccable timing."

"And you'd been making an awful lot of noise. He had to have heard you."

She'd been making a lot of noise; for some reason, hearing Connor say that made Kaylie feel excited again. "Well, he was polite about it, either way," she said.

"I suppose he was." Connor gave the idea some thought: a stranger, a man in a uniform, secretly watching him fucking his wife. For a fleeting moment, Connor found the idea curiously appealing but then he let it go.

Kaylie pulled her coat more tightly around her and then snuggled down into the seat. She couldn't help it; she was horny. Remembering that whole episode had gotten to her. She'd been in a light swoon all day anyway. She tried to distract herself by looking out the window at all the snow-covered scenery: the dusted trees, the hills in the distance, the occasional swath of snowy farmland that would suddenly burst into view. But nothing helped take her mind off it: she wanted to fuck and she wanted to make a baby. In that order. Right now.

"What are you thinking about?" Connor asked her. "You're so quiet over there."

"Nothing," she said. "I'm just looking at stuff."

"The farmer's market is just here up the road, you know."

"Have we already gotten that far?"

"Yep. We've gotten that far."

Why is he looking at me so oddly, she wondered; is he reading my mind? No, she convinced herself. I have a guilty conscience, that's all. But why should I feel guilty? He's my husband. I'm allowed to want to have sex with him.

It was the baby stuff she felt guilty about. She'd been pressuring him a lot lately. She found herself unwilling to let him make his own decision about it anymore. For the first time since they'd gotten married, she was ovulating and hadn't told him. Why was that? Was she hoping to trap him, to assert her will over his constant stalling?

I can't do that, she told herself. That would be so unfair. He would never forgive me. Well, she realized, he would forgive me, most likely. But maybe he would never really trust me again.

"Kay?" he said. "Did you hear me?"

"No, I'm sorry. What did you say?"

"I said it's closed; you were right – look."

They had pulled into the farmer's market and sure enough, it was boarded up for the winter. Not just the outside stalls, which would have been expected, but the inside market was closed for the season, as well. The whole property seemed deserted. The dirt roads that led through the fruit orchards were still dusted in snow; they showed no tire tracks, no footprints.

Connor pulled the car up one of the roads and then stopped the car, putting it in park.

"What are we doing?" Kaylie asked. "Did you want to take a walk in the snow?"

Connor looked at her for a moment. "Not really," he finally

said.

"Connor, what is it?"

"Well, we have plenty of time now. And no one's here."

Oh no, she thought, feeling unnerved by that look in his eye. It was highly unlikely that this had been part of his plans for the day; he probably hadn't brought a condom.

"What do you mean?" she asked naively, stalling a little herself now.

He turned off the car. "You know what I mean."

"I do?"

He smiled at her sudden reluctance. He liked it when she pretended to be shy. "You do. Come on, should we take a little walk?"

"It's cold out there."

"So? It'll be a new adventure. Come on, Kay. Let's go." He unlocked the car doors. The sudden springing sound of it gave her a jolt. "What's with you?" he asked, opening his door. "Don't you want to?"

"I want to," she said. "It's just—"

"What? Are you afraid of a little snow?"

"No," she said.

"Then what is it? Are you afraid I'm going to fuck you so hard you'll come all over yourself – and me, I hope?"

Oh no, now he was going to start talking dirty to her. She was doomed. Just *say* it, she tried to convince herself. Tell him it's not a good time; that he's going to have to be careful because she could get pregnant . . . But then he'll lose the mood – and fast.

"Come on," he said again, getting out of the car. "Let's go. If it's too cold, we can always come back to the car instead and fuck like crazy teenagers in the back seat. Come on." He slammed closed his door. Kaylie didn't move. She watched him come around the front of the car to the passenger side; she watched him open her door. His crotch was at eye level; he had a hard-on inside his jeans.

She looked up at his face. "Surprise," he said, knowing she'd seen it, his erection nearly bursting open his zipper.

This time she knew she was blushing. "Christ, Connor."

"Come on, honey." He reached down and unbuckled her seat belt. "Let's go take a walk in the snow."

"But what about the game – don't you want to be there in time for the face-off?"

"We will. Don't worry about it." He took Kaylie's arm and helped her get out of the car.

The cold air felt sobering but it wasn't an icy blast; it was bearable. Kaylie took Connor's hand and they began walking – up the dirt road into the orchards. The trees were breathtaking in the light dusting of snow. And the sky was heavy with another imminent snowfall. It created a feeling of isolation, of being cushioned against the outside world

Connor broke the silence. "No one's here," he said. "We are completely and utterly alone – look at this."

Kaylie looked, they were indeed alone. Quietly, in keeping with the solemnness of their surroundings, she said, "You're not really expecting me to take my pants off out here, are you?"

"I kind of was," he said.

"Connor, you're crazy."

"Kaylie, come here." Connor pulled her into his arms and they kissed, their down-filled jackets serving as a soft barrier between them. "This won't do," Connor insisted. "Here, let me undo that." He unzipped Kaylie's jacket and then unzipped his own. "This is better, isn't it?" He pulled her to him again and kissed her, this time the warmth of their bodies connected them.

Kaylie felt Connor's erection pressing up against her and it made her push back against him; she couldn't help herself. She was getting too worked up for him and it just wouldn't do, she had to hide it, to keep it locked up tight. It was going to be a lost battle, though, if he kept pushing up against her like this.

"Connor," she said quietly.

"What?"

She didn't say anything more; she returned his kisses, finding his tongue with hers; engaging him fully, and moaning in urgency when she felt his hand going up under her sweater. It was ice cold, his hand, but she didn't care. She wanted to feel him touching her skin.

He didn't go up under her bra, not at first. He seemed content to feel the fullness of her breast while he kissed her. It was Kaylie who wanted her bra undone. She had her coat on, she figured; her sweater was covering most of her; no one would see – if there were anyone watching them, that is. And there wasn't. She pulled up her own sweater, then, and tugged her bra up over her tits.

"*Kaylie,*" Connor said eagerly. Kaylie's nipples were stiff points; her breasts looked too inviting as they rose to attention in the cold air. His mouth was on her in a heartbeat.

Feeling the warmth of his mouth, the pressure of his lips, his flicking wet tongue tormenting her swollen nipple, Kaylie groaned in reluctant defeat. She was too aroused for words now. And words were exactly what she needed to tell Connor to stop, that it was leading them into murky waters; that they, would soon be out of control.

"No," she whispered quietly, too quietly to be taken seriously. "Connor, don't." His mouth had left her nipple and he was kissing his way down her rib cage, down her belly. He was on his knees in the snow and his hands were impatiently pulling the waistband of her pants, her panties, down over her hips. "Don't," she insisted again.

Her mound was exposed, and the light swirl of brown hair. Connor caught her scent immediately. "Why not?" he asked, looking up at her – his eyes on fire with lust already.

Kaylie couldn't resist that look. "I'm going to fall down," she said.

"Okay," he said, quickly rising to his feet. Leaving her exposed, he pulled her to an apple tree. "Lean against it," he said. He went back down to his knees again, only now he pulled her pants and her panties all the way down to her ankles.

"*Oh god,*" Kaylie squealed. It was really cold out. Before she could protest further, though, two of his fingers went up her hole. She groaned deliriously, in spite of herself and the freezing cold.

"Jesus, Kaylie," he said. "You are soaking."

"I know I am," she whimpered in defeat, succumbing quickly to the sheer pleasure of his steady fingers probing up inside her. And once again, words became too much to manage; she was nothing but moans and little whimpers of delirium as she leaned her weight against the apple tree. Connor's mouth was on her down there, all over the swelling, sopping lips, his tongue pushing against her aching clitoris, stroking it; his fingers continuing their steady probe.

"Oh god," she cried again. Her fingers clutched at the rough bark of the tree, her hips pushed her mound out, offering it as best she could to Connor's mouth. She was as good as naked out there in the winter air and it felt fantastic; her tits exposed, the full length of her aroused body on display, and Connor ardently pleasuring her between her legs. She didn't know which felt better: the way his fingers pushed up into her, circled inside her and opened her, making her wish she could spread her legs wide for him; or the way his tongue circled her clit, pushed up into its hood, then mashed against it, then circled it again.

She was going to come, but she didn't want to come like this. She wanted to explode into orgasm on his pounding cock. She wanted to feel impaled on him, ravaged by him while she came. "Let's fuck," she blurted.

"Okay," he agreed, out of breath, his mouth a slick mess now. His nose was filled with the thick scent of just how aroused she was and he could hardly contain his own excitement. "Turn around," he said, getting up. "Hold on to the tree. Brace yourself against it."

She did as he asked, turning around awkwardly, her pants still down around her ankles, when the rough bark of the tree suddenly scraped against her exposed tits. "*Shit*," she cried, pushing herself away from the tree, steadying herself against the trunk as best she could while keeping her breasts clear of it. Her ass arched up, as if on instinct, readying her to be mounted from behind. And it didn't take long, a mere moment was all. Connor's cock was thick and warm and solid as it pushed right up into her sopping, eager hole. It felt incredible, the way it filled her. He felt harder than he'd ever felt to her before – was that even possible?

"Oh god," she cried, not sure she could take this kind of pounding without something closer to hold on to. "Oh god, *Connor.*" He had a firm grip on her hips, pulling her ass up higher, getting his cock into her hole incredibly deep; giving it to her with very hard, very quick strokes.

"Can I come in you?" he asked urgently.

"Oh god," she said again, moaning, her head swimming. It all felt too good, it overwhelmed her – and she wanted a baby; she so wanted a baby. Her ass went up higher, trying to get him all the way up her.

"Can I?" he asked again, his brutal rhythm increasing in her.

"Yes," she said deliriously. This, too, was almost too quiet to be heard – this lie, this deception.

He wasn't sure what she'd said. "Yes?" he asked. "It's okay to come in you?"

"Yes," she said. "Come in me." Then she whirled to her senses. She shoved him off of her with all her strength and nearly lost her balance. "No," she cried. "Don't come in me!"

"Christ," he yelled frantically. "I'm coming, damn it."

They uncoupled gracelessly, with Kaylie falling against the tree, scraping herself, and Connor trying to keep himself from falling by keeping his grip on Kaylie's hips. The unstoppable spurts of his orgasm spattered onto the snow.

He tried to catch his breath. "What the fuck was that, Kaylie?"

"I'm ovulating," she blurted out. "I'm sorry." She was too upset to turn around and face him. She felt ridiculous now, bagging the cold rough trunk of the tree, scraped up, with her pants down around her ankles.

Sheepishly, she bent down to pull up her pants. She still refused to meet his gaze. She could feel his anger and could imagine his humiliation. "I'm sorry," she said again. "I lost my head."

"Really?" he said – his voice heavy with sarcasm now.

He tucked himself into his jeans. "Is that what you call it, losing your head? You didn't know it this morning when you consulted your little calendar like you always do every single day of the year?"

"I'm sorry, Connor. I really am." She turned to look at him now and he looked disgusted with her. A moment ago they had been entwined in such connubial bliss. Damn it, she thought. Why had she done it? Or nearly done it – and which idea was worse? They were both pretty lousy ones.

Connor zipped up his coat and turned to walk back to the car – without her; he left her standing there alone to straighten her clothes and feel like a fool.

"Aren't you going to wait for me?" she called out.

He stopped and turned and looked at her. "Come on, then. Hurry up."

She hurried. She pulled herself together and ran to him, searching his face for even the slightest clue that he didn't completely despise her. "That was pretty sucky of me, huh?" she finally said. "I'm just really confused, Connor."

He didn't reply; he started walking again.

Kaylie kept pace with him, afraid to say anything more.

When they reached the car, a light snow had begun to fall. Connor opened Kaylie's car door for her and held it. She slid into the passenger seat and then looked up at him, smiling hopefully. "Thank you," she said.

"You're welcome, Kaylie," he replied. He closed her car door and went around to the driver's side. He got in and closed his own door. He turned the key that was still in the ignition and – nothing. He tried again. "Great," he spat. "This is just great."

"What?"

"The battery's dead."

"Oh no, you're kidding."

"No, I'm not kidding." He tried the ignition again – nothing, just an ineffectual click. "Shit." Connor got out his cell phone. "Give me the number for the auto club; the membership card's in the glove compartment."

Kaylie complied, feeling that somehow this dead battery

was her fault. "I'm so sorry, Connor," she said.

He took the card from her and dialed the number.

"I need someone to come out and jump my battery," he said into the phone. Kaylie stared morosely out the window while Connor gave the auto club their exact location. "You're kidding," he said. "Why so long?" A frustrated pause; Connor tapped his fingers angrily on the steering wheel. "Okay, then. Well, obviously, we'll be waiting."

He closed his phone. "It's going to be at least half an hour," he told Kaylie. "And probably more like forty-five minutes. There's no one closer. In the auto club's opinion, we happen to be out in the middle of nowhere."

Kaylie looked at him apologetically. "I'm sorry, Connor. I really am."

"Why should you be? You don't work for the auto club."

"You know what I mean. I'm sorry about the whole thing, about what just happened out there."

"And what did just happen out there, Kaylie?" He studied her now unflinchingly. "Do you want to explain yourself?"

"If you'll let me."

"I'm letting you. Who's stopping you?"

"You're not being entirely, well, you know—"

"What? I'm not being what – *considerate* of you?"

The way he emphasized the word "considerate" made Kaylie feel three years old. "Point taken," she conceded quietly. "That was inconsiderate of me, to put it mildly."

Connor sighed. "I *don't* want to fight with you, Kaylie. We were having such a great time. Why would you do that to me? Since when is this just your marriage, huh?"

She had no adequate answer for that.

"And not just the way you shoved me away from you so rudely – and never would I do a thing like that to you, Kay. But this baby thing – it's getting out of control with you. What were you trying to do, trick me into creating my own kid? Like I wouldn't want to be there with you if a thing like that could *maybe* be happening, after everything we've been through about this already?"

"I just . . . I don't know. I guess I was just . . . I'm *thirty-two years old* already, Connor," she finally sputtered in defeat. "I am so tired of waiting for you to be ready." *God that came out sounding mean she thought; why am I being so mean?*

Connor fell silent. They said nothing more for a while. They sat and stared out at the falling snow. It had gotten heavier; their footprints into the orchard were already obliterated.

"It's cold in here," Kaylie finally said.

"I know it is. The heater's not on."

"I know that, Connor. I'm just saying that it's cold."

They both heard it and saw it coming through the snow at the same instant.

Connor said, "What the hell is that?"

"It's a tractor," Kaylie declared.

It was a tractor, all right, with a man in a bright orange cap driving it. He was coming toward them, down the dirt road that was now snowed over.

"I wonder if there's some sort of farm house up that way?" Connor said.

"I don't know," Kaylie said, "but maybe he can help us get this car started?"

"I hope so. I'll see." Connor opened his door and got out. He walked toward the tractor that was now coming to a slow stop.

The farmer called down to Connor, "I couldn't help noticing that you seemed stuck down here."

Connor wondered what else the guy hadn't been able to help noticing, but right now, all Connor wanted was to get the car started. "My battery's dead," he called back.

"I figured as much. I've got a charger up at the barn." The farmer got down off his tractor and walked over to Connor. "I can either bring it down here and give you an emergency boost that'll at least get you to a service station, or, if you aren't in too much of a hurry, we can take the battery up to the barn and leave it connected for a little while, it'll totally recharge you. You won't have to pay me anything. It's up to you."

"Where's the nearest service station?" Connor asked,

noticing that the farmer didn't want to look directly at him. Christ, Connor thought to himself, he did see us. And then Connor wondered if the farmer had been alone, or if there had been other people watching Kaylie and him have sex out there in the bone-dead orchard, where there was not so much as a speck of a leaf clinging to any of the trees.

"Oh gosh, I'd say about eight miles," the farmer said. "If it's even open. It's not always open in bad weather. Rick, the owner, lives pretty far out and doesn't like to risk getting stranded down here in bad weather."

"I can understand that," Connor said. The snow was already clinging to Connor's hair, to his eyelashes, even.

The farmer said, "I got tools in the tractor. It's no big deal taking that battery out. Let's just take it on up to the barn and recharge it."

"You're sure it's no problem?"

"No problem at all. I take care of all my own vehicles around this place."

"Thanks," Connor said. "How long will a recharge take?"

"About an hour," the farmer replied. "Maybe a little longer. It's a pretty powerful little box. There's a gauge right on it, tells you when it's done."

Connor could see the Flyers game disappearing in the distance. Even if they made it to the arena on time, this was more than a snow fall, it was a storm. With the battery acting up they'd be crazy to drive all the way to Philadelphia and back. "I guess I'll take you up on that recharge, then. Let me just double-check with my wife."

Connor opened his door, reached down and popped the hood, and said, "Looks like we aren't going to Philly today. This guy's offered to recharge our battery for free, though. If you don't mind hanging out here for about an hour?"

"But *the game* – you already bought the tickets. You were looking so forward to it."

"It's too risky, Kay. We can't drive all the way to Philly and back in this weather. Besides, if I don't get the battery charged here, we'll just have to stop somewhere up the road and do it, if we can even find a place. And then we'll have to pay."

"I don't mind waiting here, that's all right with me. I just feel bad for you – missing the game."

"I'll get over it," Connor said. "Hand me that card from the auto club again, will you?"

Kaylie handed him back the card.

"I'm going to go up to this guy's barn with him, but I'll come back and sit with you while the battery's charging."

"Okay, honey." Connor shut the car door again and was gone from view. The snow had nearly covered the windshield now. Kaylie couldn't see anything anymore, and she could barely hear the men talking outside. Eventually she heard the sound of the tractor heading back up the road.

One more hour in the freezing cold car, she thought. Well, now they'd *have* to talk things out. She wouldn't be able to stand it, being stuck in the car, all snowed over, and the two of them arguing, or worse – not speaking to each other . . .

With the car battery wedged under the tractor's seat, Connor rode shotgun beside the farmer, clinging precariously to the slippery tractor. He didn't have gloves on and his fingers were freezing. As the tractor made its slow, steady way up the road, Connor could see, even through the falling snow that the farther one went up the road, the easier it was to see the damn orchard. It wasn't even that much of a hill, but it was enough of a steady incline to get a perfectly clear view of everything below.

Well, Connor thought, so what if he saw us? At least that clear view helped the guy see that we were stranded, and he was decent enough to come down and help us.

About fifteen minutes later, Connor opened the car door again and this time he reached in and popped the trunk. "I think we have a blanket of some kind in back and a roll of paper towels. Are you all right?"

He said it with such unguarded affection, Kaylie smiled.

"I'm all right," she said. "Just a little cold."

Connor tossed his cell phone onto the front seat. "I cancelled the service call. That farmer is going to call us when the battery's done charging. He offered to let us wait up in his barn, but under the circumstances, I thought we'd feel more comfortable just waiting here in the car."

"Under what circumstances?"

"I'm pretty sure he saw us, Kay. He was just too polite to say anything."

"Wow," Kaylie said uncomfortably. "That's kind of ironic, isn't it? The park ranger in the spring, and now some farmer in a snow storm. We're not too good at this 'sex in the great outdoors' stuff, are we?"

Connor studied her face for a second before answering. "We do all right," he finally said. "Maybe we need more practice, what do you think?" Before she could answer, he'd closed the car door again.

Why had he said *that*, she wondered; and why was she feeling that spark again? Connor didn't seem angry with her at all now.

In a moment, she heard the trunk slamming closed. Then the back door opened this time. Connor tossed in an old blanket and a roll of paper towels, and then he slid into the back seat. Kaylie watched him unroll a wad of the paper towels. He began drying off his snow-covered hair.

"Well?" he said to her. "Aren't you going to get your ass back here? We had a little unfinished business, didn't we?"

"We did?" Kaylie couldn't believe her ears; was he talking about having more sex?

"We did, didn't we? I don't think you came yet, wouldn't you like to?"

Kaylie was delighted. "Yes," she said doubtfully. "But that guy . . ."

"Don't worry about that guy. I think he's already seen more than he cared to. To be honest, I think that's why he's calling me on the phone when the battery's done, instead of coming back down to get me in person: he must think we're a couple of sex addicts."

"Shit," Kaylie said, finding it funny now. "Do you think he really saw us?"

"I think he really saw us. I was up there, Kay, and it's a pretty clear view, even in the snow."

"Oh my god, I was practically naked!"

"I know you were. I saw, remember?"

Connor took off his wet coat and laid it over the back of the driver's seat. "I'm *freezing*," he said. "But I have an idea of how to kill an hour and get warm at the same time. Of course, the idea kind of hinged on you getting your ass back here already."

Kaylie couldn't refuse him when he talked to her like that.

"Besides, I have a little bone to pick with you," he went on, helping her slip over into the back seat.

"I know, honey," she said. "I'm sorry." Kaylie's heart was on fire again. Did he really mean to see this through? Was it going to happen? Of course it didn't mean she was going to get pregnant, but she sure as hell was going to try. "I guess the shared body heat will do us both some good, huh? It's pretty cold in this car."

"I think we'll manage," he said.

They were in an odd twilight. All the windows were snowed over now. It was neither light nor dark, and they seemed cut off from the world. Connor unfolded the blanket and tucked it over the two of them. They sat snuggled close together in the back seat. He said, "I can't decide . . ."

"You can't decide what?"

"If I should take off my pants or not. They're wet and very cold."

"Then take them off," she said. "What's to decide?"

"The thought of putting them back on again in an hour makes me feel even colder."

"I see. Well, if you take off yours, I'll take off mine; does that make you feel less cold? We'll kind of be in it together."

"Yes, together," he said. He looked at her seriously for a moment. "Kaylie, I want you to know I'm sorry."

"My god, for what? What do you have to be sorry for?"

"For letting you get so fed up with me dragging my feet all the time that it made you – I don't know – not trust me anymore. I'd made a vow to myself, you know? Of course not, how could you know? I never said a word about it, I tried to, but it never came out. It always got stuck in my throat. But I'd made a vow to myself that the next time you told me you were ovulating I wasn't going to start a fight about it. I was going to make myself be okay with it and just move ahead with this already. It really killed me – what you said before."

"What do you mean?"

"Before – when you said that you were thirty-two already and tired of waiting for me to be ready. You made me feel like a little kid, like an immature little kid. And I realized I'm thirty-five already; when the heck do I think I'm going to be ready to start a family with you? I love you. I *want* us to have a family. What is my problem? I was thinking about it as I was riding on that guy's tractor, going up to the barn. You are *so* ready and all I ever seem able to do is work and then obsess about hockey."

"That's not true, Connor. That's not all you do."

He tossed aside the blanket and kicked off his wet shoes. "You're right," he said. "That's not all I do." He unzipped his frozen jeans and began tugging them off. "You know, I think I'm actually less cold with them off?"

Kaylie watched as he took off his underwear, too. He wasn't erect anymore; he looked positively freezing. "Get back under the blanket. You'll catch pneumonia like that." She threw the blanket back over him.

"Aren't you forgetting something?" he said, snuggling under the blanket again – it really was cold in the car. "Didn't you offer to make a little deal, pants-wise, or are you chickening out?"

"I'm not chickening out." Kaylie threw off her half of the blanket, kicked off her own shoes and then wiggled out of her pants, then out of her panties. She was already so cold that the leather car seat didn't feel that much colder. "Are we crazy?" she said.

"I don't know. Maybe. *Now* what are you doing?"

"I figure I might as well, right?" Kaylie had taken off her down jacket and now she was pulling her sweater off over her head.

"I think you *are* nuts. Now you really will freeze."

"No, I won't. I'm planning on being under you, and you're usually pretty hot." She unclasped her bra and took it off. Fluffing her down jacket into a loose pile, she used it as a pillow for her head. She lay down on her side of the seat. She didn't mind at all that she was cold. With her knees up, her thighs open, she knew he had a perfect view, one that was likely to get him in the mood quickly. "Too bad we can't turn on the radio," she said. "This is not very romantic, is it?"

"Maybe not romantic," he said, pulling off his own sweater in a hurry; indeed, getting in the mood; he wanted to be completely naked with her. "But it'll be memorable. Besides, we can make up for the lack of romance later."

"Really? You already know you want to do it again later?" It felt like too much to hope for; he really was trying to make a baby with her.

"We'll be snowed in for at least the weekend, Kay." He stretched out between her legs, lying on top of her, trying to pull the old blanket over both of them. "We only have two days, three maybe, to surround that little bugger that's up inside you and nail it, right? Perfect timing, this snow storm."

"Thank you, Connor."

"Please don't say it like that, like I'm doing you some huge favor. I love you, Kay."

She felt his cock coming to life against her belly. She didn't want to waste time with foreplay; she wanted to get down to business – get *life* going. She reached down for his cock and coaxed it to an erection. He leaned close and kissed her, feeling his whole body beginning to stir.

She said quietly, "This time, you won't have to ask me."

He didn't have to say "ask you what," because he knew what, and the thought of coming in her now was intensely appealing to him. This added dimension of new life, of creating life, of melding who he was with who she was, creating something entirely new and unpredictable that could stand alone from them and thrive on its own – it was suddenly too compelling, too unbelievable for words – making babies, how *crazy* and inexplicable it all seemed. But he wasn't afraid. Connor kissed her again, this time roughly, passionately as he worked to get his cock up inside her.

She assisted him in his mission. Still holding on to his cock, she helped him ease it up into her. She was already wet – in fact, had been wet since the moment he'd told her to "get her ass into the back seat." She'd known this was coming, that she'd be lying under him, that he would be on top of her – the old-fashioned way. It suddenly seemed so erotic. Kaylie raised her knees high as his cock pushed in and opened her. She moaned sweetly. He was very hard now. She hugged him closer to her and held on tight. "Really fuck me, Connor," she said right in his ear. "Fuck me hard; I need to feel it hard today."

He didn't answer with words. He braced himself, his arms at either side of her head taking the bulk of his weight. Now it was an adrenaline-fueled strength that compelled him to fuck her – to fuck her very hard. He pushed deeper into her, feeling the wet heat of her hole swelling around his fully erect cock, hugging his shaft at the same time that it made room for him.

How mysterious it all was, this fucking-business, he thought; this baby-making stuff; how mysterious and how entrancing. "*Oh god,*" she was crying repeatedly, rhythmically. Her need for him delighted him, propelled him in his task to fill her – to make his presence in her good enough and hard enough and filling enough.

Oh god, oh god.

She kicked off the annoying blanket, spread her thighs wider. She pushed open her hole for him, so incredibly open. *Oh god.* He was going in deep. She couldn't remember it ever feeling this good, this incredibly enticing. She was so aroused and so insatiable for fucking, for the feel of his cock invading her, going up into her all the way, until it made her cry out – the pain was so deliciously sweet; she kept wanting to feel that tender pain. Her body pushed itself open for just that feeling

– that thrust of his cock way up into the center of her. She was hungry for it, that's what it was; starving for his cock, for him; to be filled with him. She clung to him tight as they both began to sweat.

In a burst of passion, his rhythm suddenly increased. "God, Kay," he said, panting, breathing hard. The thick head of his cock pushed way up into her, into that place deep inside her that normally blocked his path; now it too was swelling open for him, thick and fleshy and soft, it felt too good, that place. His cock drove up into it repeatedly, seemingly with a will of its own. It pounded into her.

Oh shit, yes. I'm going to come.

Her body held itself entirely open now. She'd never felt this impaled, this delirious with lust. *Yes, yes.* She could feel his whole body stiffen, could tell he was going to come. His breath came out in little explosive cries, that thin line of ecstasy and agony, as his body jerked against her, propelling his whole world out and up into hers. The constant hammering against her cervix shot her into orgasm. And for a moment, Connor was entirely rigid, except for those hard, quick, short little thrusts . . .

"Shit," he gasped, panting. "Shit. Oh man, Kay. Wow." In an instant, his full weight collapsed on top of her. "Wow," he said again. "That was good. Did you come? It felt like you were coming."

Kaylie was panting just as hard. "Yes," she said, nodding her head, feeling happy. "I came."

They looked at each other, wondering if that had been it: the spark of life. And whether it was or wasn't, they still had the whole weekend ahead of them. Connor couldn't wait until they could get the car started, get back home and do it again.

"To think I was so excited about seeing the Flyers take on the Rangers," he said.

Kaylie's hips still rocked gently beneath him; her breathing steadier now, returning to normal. She didn't say anything. She just looked up into his face, luxuriating in the sound of his voice, in the feel of him on top of her, as he talked about hockey and about how little it really mattered in the grand scheme of things. *I am ready for this*, she was thinking, as if in some hypnotic daze. *The unimaginable mystery of life, of everything love is; I am so ready for it.*

Connor eased himself out of her and then sat up. "Christ, it's freezing," he said. "We should probably get dressed, don't you think?"

"Probably," she agreed. "We don't want to catch pneumonia."

"No," he said. "We sure don't."

They hurriedly got into their clothes and then snuggled back under the blankets. They did their best to keep themselves warm while they waited for the call to come. They talked about what they might have for dinner later, about what they had in the house, or should they stop at the store first before they got completely snowed in . . . It was just as easy as that, really – without even knowing it, they were making plans for three now.

Through Alice Glass Darkly

Larry Smith

"I've not gone that far before."

She saw the light in his eyes. It was the light of the lover's triumph, the sort she'd come to adore. The moment she said it, the awesome power she angled for passed right through her. It was all around the room. She thrilled at this power in him, which was all for her. It made him so happy, and she knew how to conjure it. She loved it more than anything else in life.

"No one ever came in your mouth before?" When she shook her head, with the studied timidity she knew men found attractive, he smiled intently, all the more intently because he didn't part his lips at all. Because of her, he would walk home the next day in the early morning autumn drizzle alive with the sense of nonpareil conquest. The October light churned inside him. Elated, he'd greet each passer-by with a hello. The world is yours, Mark Fargus.

Alice Glass was demure, diminutive, nearly exquisite. Her eyes really were green. She had lovely thin lips. Naked, when she'd admire her puckered blood-red nipples in the mirror, she imagined the joy of men seeing them for the first time. How sweet to the suck they must be! Alice walked on girlish little chicken legs. Her back tapered smoothly to her bum. Sometimes, she cropped her dark blond hair. Other times, she put it up in a bun like a schoolmarm's. She knew how men exalt to make a schoolmarm moan. Howling was the gift she gave the men she wanted happy. Alice was not an eye catcher in the sense that strangers stared at her on the street. But men who spent time with her, and got to know her, or just spent an extra moment or two to look at her, realized how beautiful she was.

Jack Rutter, aroused with love in the April bloom, thought it extraordinary to have his thing in her mouth. When he finished up, he marveled at the daisy-like loveliness of the face he had dumped in. It was beauty itself, like an abstraction, the very definition of loveliness and beauty that he'd penetrated. Jack was intelligent enough to recognize abstraction when he saw it and he savored it accordingly. But it was when she bowed her head and smiled, and said, "I must tell you, I've not gone that far before," that his very self hovering above her expanded like a bellows.

"You're kidding," he said.

"Well, no. I'm not kidding," said Alice. She pressed his hand to her cheek. "I didn't think I would, but I was enjoying it so." She looked up, grinning. "I just couldn't stop!"

"I can't believe it."

"Honest Injin!" she laughed. "And might I say thank you?"

"Thank you!" He beamed.

She was studying hard for a Masters from NYU. Her specialty, and her passion, was modern fiction. Alice treasured it for the great sensuality in the best stories her favorite writers wrote even when they weren't writing about love. How wonderful she thought it would be, this power to entrance the world like great writers do. Yet she also spotted a raw adolescent sensibility in some of what she studied, and that she did not admire so much. *The Alexandria Quartet* figured into her thesis, for example, along with *The Magus*. Both works were about illusions, or at least different ways of fabricating reality, and in that theme she found their common ground in modernity.

Yet both fell short in ways that left her dissatisfied. Durrell needed Coptic conspiracies and picturesque foreign hosts because he lacked imagination for the fantasias of everyday life, which, for Alice, were as alluring, or probably more alluring, than most such far-flung exotica. But at least *The Alexandria Quartet* was an adventure, to be savored as such, what with all its strange people doing strange things in their sinister silky places. By contrast, *The Magus* was, finally, mired in the everyday.

Its landscapes are banal despite the Greek island locale (how much more banal, ironically, the real Spetsai had gotten by the time Fowles wrote his superfluous revisions). The beloved's transformations are belabored, clinical, predictable. The fantastic inventions that feed the action are contrived to a point where the narrative is practically amateurish. Nor does Nicholas Urfe justify such extravaganzas. Fowles made all the world a stage just to teach harsh lessons to a British boor. Mystification, she gleaned, ought to have bigger goals and better men in tow.

Dennis Gaffney poured over her. He was an angry sort, a social throwback, rebel without a cause. He even wore a 1950s hairstyle. A flourish of sandy hair sculpted in grease stuck upward from his head. She despised him a bit, yet his pomposity would only make the triumph she foresaw all the more prepossessing. She was happy to flatter the callow persona.

"This would kill my husband," said Alice, smiling uncomfortably.

"Where is he tonight?"

"At a conference in California."

"What does he do?" asked Dennis.

"He's an orthopedic surgeon."

"You cheat on him often?"

Alice averted her eyes. "To tell you the truth, this is my first time."

"Yeah?" he asked, glinting. Later that evening, kissing her goodbye – she had to get back home because her husband would be calling from the Coast – he jabbed two fingers up her ass. He probed her like that deeper, finalizing pride of ownership. Walking down the stairs of his apartment building, the strong feel was still up her there. The arrogant empowerment he took care to convey was exhilarating.

Alice lived in a three-room apartment in New Jersey. The part that overlooked the river had the feel of a studio. The light at certain times poured gloriously across the bare floor. There was an alcove off the bedroom big enough for workspace. The place though small was all hers and fit right. Sometimes the light made it look deceptively expansive. Other times the intimacy was uncanny, as if just she and the sunshine were alone on the Hudson. The sunlight took her over every morning. Of course, there was the sight of the great city too, the steely light off the glass Babels and the great murky canyons down where the island tapered off. Spells are cast by a city that can be anything anybody wants it to be.

A year passed. Soft-spoken Geoffrey Baron reached for Alice's hand across the table as they finished dinner. He was a middle-aged black businessman over six-feet tall, imposing in manner as well, what with a certain vague authoritarianism in the way he carried himself. He seemed to speak from large reservoirs of experience. She returned the gentle squeeze, her fingers creamy white in his deep brown grip. Visual charm became physical longing. She saw herself all white and frail against his big body, a fruit of the mind's eye somewhat forbidden still.

She bowed her head and softly said, "I have to admit it's a little unsettling to be close like this with a black man . . . I don't mean to offend you . . ."

"I'm not offended."

"It's a new experience for me. But I've thought about it, you know . . ."

"Yes, I know," he kindly smiled.

"How do you know?" she asked, amiably.

"I can tell."

"Lord, I guess you've just got my number!"

"We'll have a fine time together."

"Honestly, I've thought about doing this for so long, I'm kind of nervous about what might happen."

"What are you afraid of?" he asked, his eyes narrowing slightly, intrigued.

"Exposing myself," she answered.

She thought hard about what she studied. Ambiguity, the soul of art, infused all life and thought. But, as an insidious medium of hidden truths, it was nearly discredited by Empson and his followers who made it seem so trivial a thing. There is enormous inexorable ambiguity in language and in the images we form of the world but these critics reached into such puny little spaces to find it. "Do, with like timorous accent and dire yell/As when, by night and negligence, the fire/Is spied in populous cities," exhorts Iago. Empson looks real hard at that. Personifying the "negligence," he concludes that there were idlers in the street who must have spied the fire in the dark. It is the only instance, he adds, where Shakespeare makes "a flat pun out of a preposition."

Such a busy mischief of the mind! Of course language disintegrates when you read it hard enough, but what an indifferent passage for exploring the effect. It particularly irritated her to find such exegetical contrivance in the grandiose context of this particular drama. Alice admired Othello. Lust and shame rage on there, apocalyptic, without supportable justification on anyone's part. The white devil, fearing himself cuckolded by everyone, makes the noble black man envision unspeakable ecstasies of the beloved. Power is fed and forced by delusion. But Alice didn't really like Othello. The power was ugly. The delusions were unhappy, a torturous contrast to her own delighted machinations. Othello was a fly in her very private ointment.

Lee Johnson was a jazz musician she admired. "I have to admit it's a little unsettling to be close like this with a black man," she told him, bowing her head a little. "Please don't misunderstand. It was just a new experience for me."

"Are you still unsettled?"

"It would be hard enough for my husband if he knew I was with another man, but this would really threaten him," she said, nervously. "Don't be insulted. I'm just being honest."

"I'm not insulted," he said. Just the thought of the small pale grasping hand aroused him.

"I used to think about you sexually," she said. "From your pictures on your albums."

"I'm flattered," he said, sincerely.

"Once I thought of you when I was with my husband," Alice said softly. "Years before you and I met."

"Oh you knockout!" he exclaimed, drawing her close.

"I love your balls," she murmured lewdly. "Your balls make me happy."

The cherub-like beauty burrowed in his brown body. She fondled him between his legs until he was aroused again. She stared at him in admiration and bent down to put the hard dark thing back into her mouth. She peered up at him as she sucked. Her kittenish green eyes bespoke sheer abandonment – she knew this was so wrong in so many ways, she just couldn't help herself – and the look in his eyes her eyes inspired caused Alice to exalt unutterably.

"You make me feel so white," she whispered, after he came in her mouth.

"Oh baby!" he exclaimed.

These days Alice would often tell men she was married. It prolonged the chase and intensified the conquest. Later, she could escape these men leaving the power she had given them intact. Duty and affection forced her return. This couldn't continue. Her husband was a good man. He'd be terribly hurt, threatened. She had to break it off. She left them, studs at twilight alone on doorsteps or park benches. They would miss her. They even loved her. But they had drunk her full. And, they knew she'd always remember. She'd be haunted through all the mundane domestic rounds ahead. Far from bereft, they savored the last of pretty Alice Glass' passion as she ambled sadly off to face the future.

Taylor Jones pursued her on the Path Train many mornings. "I hope I haven't been intruding on you," he said to her one day. Jones was a burly man with a large beard. She imagined a broad hairy chest. He greeted her gaily and self-confidently whenever they met. Walking out of the station, discussing music or their jobs or politics, he'd bow in her direction, almost imperceptibly. It was a slight gesture that lent him the disarming air of a gallant from some other time. It was tangible masculine power tangibly restrained, made additionally gracious by what was, she sensed, an instinctive appreciation of women on his part.

"I enjoy being with you, but you do know I'm married," said Alice.

"How long?"

"Four years."

"I'm sure you must be very happy," he said, quietly.

"Yes," she said. But there was enough tremulous uncertainty in her reply to hold his interest.

In the meantime, she met Billy Aikens at a restaurant in New York. He was a radiant-seeming young man with chiseled blond features except for a pug nose Alice adored for the way it sat incongruously amid all the Greco-Roman perfection. Other women admired him slyly on the street, which made her feel proud when they walked together. They were an enviable couple. When he licked her between her legs for the first time, she confessed, "I've never done oral sex before."

"Really?"

"Honest Injin!" she said. His features filled with delight. Once again, delight was power, his to feel and hers to give. Her face was so soft the pale skin looked the consistency of powder. Alice whimpered as he sucked, and then she sucked too until he was so aroused with the sweet wet mouth, and the thought that this was the first time she'd ever done this, that he fucked her face like a cunt. When he shot, it was part in her mouth and part down her chin. Alice lay there with his jizz on her. "I can't believe I did that," she said. "I'd be so awfully embarrassed if I weren't so awfully happy."

The white teeth of his gleamed like magic in the pale face. There was a dark power she wanted to wrench out of the world. But she wasn't strong. She'd have to sneak it out. She wanted it in all its abstraction. Alice postulated two kinds of abstraction. One is a calculated avenue to power when a Goebbels or Stalin uses concrete imagery, e.g., heroic peasants, to caricature experience until it stands for something they want it to stand for. The other is power itself, a Platonic real, the raw essence of reality which can often be seen in fine abstract paintings.

Yet Plato was also a fascist. She thought hard. Fascists can be very sexual. They dramatize crude power in the abstract, like a Nazi bitch in leather. On the other hand, fascists and communists hate abstract art. Why do they hate abstract art? Is it simply because they don't understand it, and so fear it? At the same time, educated imaginations dote on sexual abstraction because it objectifies the lover in order to make him or her pure concept – like she herself on many occasions. A lovely innocent tasting cock for the first time. The Idea of a lovely innocent tasting cock for the first time is an abstraction for which the fascist and the connoisseur of abstract art alike must yearn.

She found something interesting in Camus. A combatant in fascist Europe, Camus abhorred abstraction. In his *Notebooks*, airplanes are infernal Olympian machines. Your view of the world from an airplane abstracts and dehumanizes it. Pure thought aloft chews up the earth. Gertrude Stein, though, remembered how, when she was first on an airplane, she looked out the window and grasped at that moment the truth of cubism. From up there you see that things really are square. Things really are cylindrical. They do indeed intersect and bend around each other. And Picasso the abstractionist was as impassioned an anti-fascist as Camus. Yet both Picasso and Camus abstracted women to a point where they used them like doormats. Maybe she was a fascist too.

Taylor Jones asked her why she seemed down, and she told him it was nothing in particular.

"How does dinner sound to you?" He extended his hand toward hers in a gesture that seemed all the more gallant from such a tall, hirsute man. Once again he was bending slightly in a charming eighteenth century sort of way.

"What does your husband do?" he asked.

"He's a stockbroker," said Alice.

"So New Jersey's convenient for him."

"We're thinking of moving soon."

"I imagine he does very well."

"Yes, very well . . . You know I never called him to say I'd be late. He's still at the office. If you'll excuse me a minute, I'll ring him there."

It was raining outside and a day-long fog was still settled. Alice was eager for some formless beast to burst out of the fog. Lure it with a lovely web. Catch the beast and give it form. "Everything all right?" he asked when she returned.

"Oh yes," she said.

"You have such a lovely sadness about you," he said.

"Do I?" she asked. She knew how to conjure vague thoughts that put vulnerability in her eyes. Men loved that. Her eyes were special. They truly distinguished her. They made men like Taylor at once lustful and tenderhearted. Alice's face made men like Taylor want to ravish and revere it.

Any man could have been hers had she wanted a man in the conventional way. "I hope your husband appreciates you," he said, lightheartedly.

"Oh he does!" she said, affecting a chipper, self-satisfied tone. Taylor hated Alice's husband for the man he imagined him to be: wealthy, getting wealthier, turning this subtle woman into a trophy. Proving to the world that beauty is a rare commodity but a commodity nonetheless.

Taylor smelt a strange perfume, an exotic odor incongruously brazen. "I don't usually feel so attracted to unattainable women," he said.

She gave a little start as if to show that any such hint of sexual advance was jarring to her in her observant life. "Oh no?" she asked nervously.

"Are you unattainable?"

"This is a very strange situation for me," she said, still tremulous. She felt him growing stronger across the table.

"Are you? Are you?"

"I can't believe this is happening," she said, almost mournfully.

"Spend some time with me. I live on Third and 17th. Forgive me if I . . . It's raining pretty hard. I'll get a cab."

"No, no cab."

"We'll get soaked."

"I don't care," she said, almost angrily. "I need to walk. I don't care."

He bought two umbrellas from a street vendor but the rain was coming down too hard to stay dry. They were sopped when they reached his place. The outline of her nipples was sharp under the pink-red paisley blouse she had on. A smell of city rain mingled powerfully with her perfume. His beard and the hair on his arm were glistening like grass, like jet-black grass.

They kissed passionately. "My God," she said, "I don't believe this is happening."

"It's wonderful," he said.

"Strip me naked," she whispered, and he peeled off the wet blouse and undid her skirt. He caressed Alice's breast and tugged on the band of her panties so he could peek down at the few strands of her colorless pubic hair.

"You're trembling," he said.

"I can't help it," she said. He stripped too. Taylor's raw masculine body was streaked with thick strips of black hair. His penis was very large and hairy. His balls were too. But he didn't look like an ape. He looked like a man. She stared wide-eyed between his legs and whimpered girlishly.

They embraced. He was holding her up in the air with his large flat hands astride her rump. "You smell so good," he said, with a sudden edgy, guttural tone.

"I need it," she said. "I need it bad."

"I'm fucking you, baby."

"I need it. Oh God, poke me!"

"Open, baby," he said. He was losing control.

"I need it! Do you understand?"

"Open! Open!"

"I need it," she said. "You don't know, you don't know . . ."

"I know."

"Ahhh," she went as his cock pierced into her. She started to gasp, almost to convulse, a weird hot sound half lust and half sheer physical torment.

"Baby?" he called. A slight alarm cautioned his instincts. "Are you okay?"

"Oh your fuck, your big fuck," Alice cried aloud.

"Sweet thing," he growled.

Then her eyes widened as if in shock, and she exclaimed, "My husband's teeny-weeny!"

With that, her lover let out a feral growl and went into her as far as a man can go.